SILENCE

OF THE

APOC

Silence of the Apoc

Apoc Series Volume 2

Copyright © 2018 by Tannhauser Press

ISBN: 979-8-89719-049-2

Art and graphic layout by Luca Oleastri and Paola Giari
- Copyright © 2018 by Rotwang Studio
Edited by Donna Royston and Martin Wilsey
Published by Tannhauser Press

Contents

DEDICATION

For Tom Richter, Ray Clark, Keith Plough, Eric Wilsey, Tom Bilodeau, Kevin Peck and Carl Wilsey.

My favorite dead guys.

FOREWORD

Ever since I watched the original *Night of the Living Dead*, I have loved stories about the Zombie Apocalypse. *Dawn of the Dead* ramped it up a notch soon after.

The survival stories by using your brains before you get eaten was the key. Maybe that and the fact that it is a guilt-free way to shoot some assholes in the face that always deserved it.

When I put the call out for submissions, I was buried in them. It took no time to put together *WHISPERS OF THE APOC*. I decided to do a second volume.

SILENCE
OF THE
APOC

I picked stories I liked to share with you. Some are from established authors, some are from people just beginning their work as published authors.

All of them are fun.

A few authors that I know had intended to submit a short story for this anthology, and it got away from them. The stories grew and are now approaching novel length. Keep an eye out, because I think Tannhauser Press may be offering them in the future.

I may even use the seed of my short story for a novel set in that same world. The possibilities are endless. Each of these stories and authors have been great to work with.

I hope you enjoy reading them as much as I did assembling this anthology.

Martin Wilsey
Managing Editor
Tannhauser Press
www.tannhauserpress.com

1 QUARANTINE BY VINCENT L. SCARSELLA

We were taxiing out to the runway when the pilot's soothing, southern drawl came over the intercom telling us that we'd been called back to the terminal. A collective groan went up from the full plane. But we all knew why: Z.

Everyone deplaned and gathered outside Gate 113 where an airline rep, a frumpy lady in a navy-blue uniform, confirmed it. Because of Z, the city had been quarantined. All flights in and out were cancelled. She directed us to ticketing for free room and meal vouchers at one of the hotels near the airport. FEMA was paying for it. Shuttles would take us to our assigned hotel.

I had flown into the city yesterday morning for a two-day law seminar at a hotel conference center downtown. I had taken only a carry-on packed with a change of an extra polo shirt, dress pants, underwear, toiletries, and my laptop. The seminar ended by three that afternoon and I had hustled out of there and grabbed a cab to catch the four-thirty flight for a mere hour and fifteen-minute jump home. Instead, here I was, stuck in the city.

On the way to ticketing, I stopped at a bar near the main concourse and tried to catch the latest news about the quarantine on the small TV above the bar. I couldn't hear much above the chatter of the bar crowd and clinking of glasses and ice. I wondered why everyone was drinking and laughing as if nothing mattered. As if we weren't stuck in the city and Z wasn't happening.

I finally backed out of there and took an escalator ride up to ticketing. There, I joined an already-long line of grumpy stranded passengers waiting to get their hotel and food vouchers. In line, I called my office. Jenna answered, said she was sorry I hadn't gotten out.

"What're they saying?" I asked. "How long?"

"Nobody's sure," she said. "Few days, I guess."

I gave her instructions for the next couple of days, what to adjourn, reschedule. Then, I had her patch me into my partner, Chris Brewer.

"It's like being stuck in a third-world country during a revolution or something," I told him.

"Well, at least you won't be on the street," he said and assured me he'd take care of things back at the office.

After the call, it took another half hour to get to the harried ticketing agent. She was a fortyish, attractive blonde wearing the airline's navy-blue uniform that was long past crisp. After taking my boarding pass, she furiously clicked on her keyboard, and a moment later, her printer was churning out my vouchers. Without comment or smile, she handed them to me, and I went outside the terminal to stand in another line for the hotel shuttle.

Twenty minutes later, I entered the lobby of my assigned hotel along the main highway straddling the airport just as the mayor's news conference was being broadcast on a large flat-screen TV just beyond the reception counter. People were sitting on couches and chairs or standing shoulder to shoulder, anxious to get the latest news.

The mayor started off by assuring everyone that there was no cause for panic. The quarantine had been imposed only due to an abundance of caution. He then denied that Z had spread outside the districts where it had previously been reported and chastised the media for saying otherwise. "Let's be responsible, people," he scolded.

The mayor announced that the governor couldn't get into town before the quarantine was imposed but thanked him for his complete support in this crisis. He then took questions from the reporters in the crowded conference room.

"How long do you expect the quarantine to last?" was the first.

"Two days," he said flatly. "Three at the most."

"And it's your position that the stories about Z spreading to the northern districts are false?" the same reporter asked.

"Absolutely false," the mayor snapped, glaring at the questioner.

"Bullshit!" some guy shouted from the other side of the nook.

That was all I could take. I walked over to the registration line that snaked out from the front counter. Ten minutes later, I handed my vouchers to a desk clerk. After checking my name on his computer screen, he nodded and pulled my room key-card and meal ticket from a rectangular, cardboard box. Handing them to me, the clerk told me that there weren't enough rooms to accommodate everyone, so I had a roommate. Skipping the crowded elevators, I took the back stairwell four flights up to Room 413. I used the keycard to open the door and found the room empty. My roommate had not yet arrived, and that was all right with me. I had the bathroom to myself.

After a shower, I stretched out on the queen-sized bed nearest the window and clicked on the TV on top of a dresser. Nothing new was being reported, just the same loops of what appeared to be Zs roaming dark streets exhibiting the horrific symptoms of the disease — the wild, bug-eyed look, the idiotic screeching and, of course, the frightening, clichéd desire for human flesh.

After a time, I got off the bed, went over to the window, spread apart the heavy curtains and looked down at the parking lot. Beyond it was an expanse of high grass and beyond that, the airport terminal and a runway. Silent and dark. No planes in, no planes out.

I fetched the remote and started scrolling through the channels. CNN and Fox News had continuous coverage of the quarantine with names like "No Way Out!" and "Q-Day 1," while the major networks had resumed regular programming. Not much new was being reported, and I soon grew tired of the talking head experts. The human-interest stories, such as a dad trying to get home for his sick daughter's birthday (she was in a cancer ward of a children's hospital somewhere), a bridegroom unable to get to his wedding, and an Army guy returning from Afghanistan whose wife was expecting. Finally, I clicked off the TV and decided to get down to the Lassiter Ballroom for my meal, a turkey sandwich and chips in a white cardboard box.

I took the stairs and walked down a long corridor to the lobby. Toward the back of it was another hallway leading to the hotel bar from which wafted voices and the thump of music. Halleluiah! I thought, and headed in that direction, feeling the need for a drink more than a bland sandwich.

I wasn't surprised to find the Take-Off Lounge wall-to-wall with my fellow stranded guests. I edged through them to the wrap-around bar with two overwhelmed bartenders and one barmaid trying to keep pace with the orders. After a minute or so, the barmaid acknowledged my raised arm, came over and took my order for a double seven and seven. She was back within moments, and when I asked for a bill, she told me it was on the house, courtesy of Uncle Sam. I liked the government more and more.

I left her a five-dollar tip and drifted over to the far corner of the bar where a morose-looking guy was staring into his drink on the last barstool next to the wall. I backed against the wall behind him and scanned the crowd, scouting for a decent looking woman.

"Fuck it," the morose guy blurted, and I turned to him. "Excuse me?"

He swiveled around and lifted his drink as if toasting something. He was in his late fifties, a gangly, long-faced man with short, gray hair and a devious glint in his eyes. "To the end of the world," he said.

I lifted my glass and with a shrug, said, "Sure, to the end of the world. And getting laid."

The guy took a healthy sip of the dark brown liquid in his glass, pure liquor, I suspected. After a wince, he glared at me.

A moment later, a dark-haired woman, about thirty-five, slightly overweight, on the tall side, squeezed in toward the bar between me and him and bumped my arm, spilling my drink on my wrist in the process. "Oh, sorry," she said.

I looked at her and was immediately struck by dark, intense eyes. She had a pretty face, with reddish freckles spread along her nose and forehead. "No problem," I told her. "Can I help you get in there?"

"That would be great," she said.

"What's your poison?" I asked her.

"Gin and tonic," she said.

I moved toward the bar, and after a time, a bartender came over and took my order. Next to me, the morose guy was mumbling to himself. Finally, the bartender brought the gin and tonic. As I squeezed back out and handed her the drink, I leaned into her and said, "Name's Paul. What's yours?"

"Cindi," she said. "With an i."

"Nice to meet you, Cindi, with an i," I said and shook her hand.

"Pleasure's mine," she said and smiled, which got me to thinking that this certainly was starting off well.

From behind us, we heard the morose guy say, "Fuck it." He called the bartender over for another drink. Cindi nodded at the guy and smiled at me as if to say, *what's with him?* I shrugged and asked her what got her stranded in the city. She was a real estate agent, she said, here for a conference.

The morose guy swiveled around. "You wanna know why I'm here?" He shifted on the barstool and looked me straight in the eye. "I'm CIA."

"CIA?" I said and smiled. "Okay."

But now somebody at the bar looking up at the TV was shouting for all of us to shut the fuck up. Then everyone was looking up at the four flat-screen TVs hanging above the bar. The basketball game that had been playing was interrupted by a banner blaring, "Breaking News!" "Turn it up!" someone shouted, and a moment later, the barmaid was aiming a remote at the TV and pressing the volume button. The voice of an anchor boomed through the bar that had quieted suddenly to silence.

"And there you have it," he said. "The head of the CDC has just confirmed that Z has mutated and can be spread by airborne transmission. I repeat, Z can be spread by airborne transmission. That means Z germs can be spread from an infected person through the medium of the air, like the common cold. Previously, it was thought that Z could be spread only by an exchange of bodily fluids— sweat and saliva, for instance, and, of course, through Z bites. Now, it appears that it is a lot easier to catch, and therefore spread."

A collective groan went up from the bar crowd like hearing someone famous had died.

"Well, that's fucking it," whispered the morose, self-proclaimed CIA guy.

"What's it?" I asked.

"It," he said. "The end. The plan."

"What plan?"

He looked at me with heavy eyelids and a smirk. "What do you think, what plan," he said. "Nuke us. That plan. Take care of Z."

"What?" I gave him a dubious frown. "Sure, pal. I think you need a break from that." I nodded to his drink.

"I don't care what you fucking think."

I shrugged and turned away from him. Cindi was looking up at the TV, more reporting on this bad new turn of events. Z could be spread easier. Fucking great. Finally, the bulletin was over, and the station resumed coverage of the basketball game. When I looked back at the purported CIA guy, his barstool was empty.

"Where'd he go?" I asked Cindi.

"No idea," she said. "Good riddance."

I tipped my drink to that and drank down the rest of it. Seeing that she had already finished hers, I said, "I think we should eat. Another one of these, and I'll be CIA."

She smiled and said, "Yeah, me too."

We left the bar and made our way to the Lassiter Ballroom. Naturally, there was a line to the long table where a couple of bored hotel clerks were handing out box dinners. As we inched forward, my cell phone rang. It was Susie, my ex.

"Why didn't you get the girls?"

It was her demanding, snarky voice, the one I had to listen to for eighteen years until I couldn't take it anymore. It was almost a good thing that I was stuck in the city, because, in truth, I had forgotten my promise made a week ago to take Ciara and Morgan off her hands for the night. She had a book club meeting or something. After telling her I was caught up in the quarantine, she softened a bit, said she didn't know. Though still sounding annoyed, she told me to take care of myself and hung up.

"That was pleasant," Cindi remarked.

"My ex," I told her.

"I've got one of those, too," she said, and winked. "Two, in fact."

We laughed and finally reached the front of the line where a tired-looking clerk handed us boxes containing bland turkey sandwiches with a small bag of chips and a bottled water. We took them to the lobby and, as all the chairs were taken, we sat on the floor and watched TV. The throb and general din from far down the hall off the lobby told us that the Take-off Lounge was still hopping.

"After this, I want a nightcap," I said and nodded in the direction of the bar. "Lot more fun than sitting here, watching that."

"Sure," she said. "I could use another."

In the next moment, the anchor was breaking away from her talking head guest to a young, pretty female reporter who was interviewing some guy in the Hanover District, wherever that was. "I'm standing on the corner of Geddes Avenue and Swan Street," the reporter said into her microphone. "With me is Douglas Keane. An hour ago, Mister Keane took some extraordinary video on his cell phone of a Z attack from his third-floor apartment, and we've been able to patch that video into our studios." She looked to the cameraman. "Is it uploaded?" Now, she looked out at us. "I warn you that the images are quite graphic."

After a moment, the screen morphed from a picture of her standing before us to a bouncy series of frames. The guy taking the video, Douglas Keane, added narration from time to time, his voice rushed, panicky.

On the street below was a group of fifteen, twenty Zs, hunched over as they edged forward down the street below Douglas Keane's apartment, with one or more of them emitting that annoying screech like a bird caw every now and then. They were closing in on a small group of civilians who had somehow become cornered by these Z scavengers.

"Run," the Keane guy kept whispering to himself. "Run."

But the people below him seemed confused, rudderless. Or maybe, they had nowhere to run. The Z approach was relentless and deliberate. Some of the people were shouting, taking up defensive stances, waving at them, and finally, pushing them back. A few screamed. Others just stood there mesmerized.

"Get away," Keane whispered. "Break through. Run."

Some of them tried that. It didn't work. The Zs latched onto them and bit into their necks and arms and faces and thighs and feet. The screaming of the bitten was horrific.

Keane aimed his smartphone at the mayhem and slaughter taking place below his apartment for a few seconds longer, enough for us to realize that every single person in that hapless crowd—men, women, and children—were being ripped to pieces, eaten alive.

Everyone in the lobby was quiet after the video stopped.

The TV reporter was back. The "authorities," she told us, estimated that fifteen people were killed in the videoed Z attack and that a National Guard unit had been dispatched to eliminate the pack of Zs responsible.

I threw what was left of my turkey sandwich into the box on my lap and turned to Cindi.

"I lost my appetite," I told her. "I need a drink."

"Me, too," she said.

***

The Take-Off Lounge was still hopping. I led Cindi to that same corner where we'd met and saw that our self-proclaimed CIA acquaintance was back in his seat, sipping another drink. He spotted us and waved us over with a scowl and, with my arm over Cindi's shoulder, we approached him.

"You're back," he said. He held up something and waved it at me. Squinting in the dim light, I saw that it appeared to be an official CIA badge in a leather case. It had a name on it.

"That's me," he said, pointing to the name. "George Reed." He burped and slumped to his left, clearly feeling too many drinks after however many hours he'd been occupying that corner seat. "You can call me George."

"Nice to meet you, George," I said. "I'm Paul. This is Cindi."

"Sorry for being such a crab before," he said. "Let me buy."

He raised an arm and yelled over to one of the bartenders serving the still-overflow crowd in the bar. The Z epidemic was definitely good for business. We gave him our orders, and the bartender was off and back with them in no more than a minute. George Reed turned to us, lifted his drink and made a toast: "To survival."

Cindi and I raised our glasses. We took long sips. George was drinking straight whiskey. He winced.

"I wasn't bullshitting you," he said. "What I said before. They have no choice."

"Nuking us," I said with a hint of incredulity in my voice. "The whole city."

"To save the world, why not?"

"Why are you telling us this? If you're CIA?" I asked him as Cindi leaned into me and whispered, "Let's go."

"I can't be part of it," he said as he held his drink at a precarious angle. "All the killing, the excusing. A lifetime of compromise." He looked at me, then at Cindi standing with a frown against my left shoulder, still wary of him. "Like, look at you two. Why should you go up in flames? And you know, I can help you."

"Help us?" I asked.

"Yeah," he said. "See, there's a way out. A secret passage." He swiveled around and plucked a small, square drink napkin from a holder on the bar, then looked at me. "You got a pen?"

Cindi fished in her purse and handed one to him. He started to draw something on the napkin. After a time, he handed it to me and said, "This is the way out." He'd drawn a series of lines in thick, blue ink with neatly printed names of streets identifying the lines. In the upper right-hand corner, in a clear space, he had drawn an arrow and next to it, "Zone D."

"Zone D?" I asked.

"That's where you have to get out," he said. "Couple days ago, we identified several soft spots in the quarantine. Dark areas. You go through Zone D, you escape. You run fast enough after that, you escape the nukes."

"So why don't you leave?" I asked. "Save yourself?"

"I got no reason to leave," he said with a shrug. "My life has been this, the Company. No family. No wife. No kids. I gave them everything. And anyway, I'd never make it there."

"Why not?"

He pointed to his wrist and said, "The implant." He took a long sip of his drink and swayed a moment. "We all get them now. Let's them keep track of us. They know I'm here. That I quit and settled here, in some hotel bar, drinking myself to oblivion. So, I'm no threat. They'll come and get me when they're ready. Or not at all. Won't matter when the nukes fall."

Cindi leaned into me again. "Let's go," she whispered.

I looked down at the napkin with the scribbled map and stuck it into my jeans pocket.

"I wouldn't wait," he said and nodded up at the TV. "Zs spreading. Pretty soon, it'll reach the tipping point, and they start dropping the nukes."

***

"What a nut," Cindi said after we left the bar with our drinks and strolled the long hallway back toward the lobby. She laughed. "Nukes."

I looked at her as we walked.

"Yeah, I know," I said. "But somehow, it makes crazy sense. And he had that badge."

"Any nut can fake a badge," she said with a laugh. "You really think the CIA gives out badges?"

I shrugged. I truly didn't know. I put my hand inside my jeans pocket and felt for the napkin with a crude map he'd drawn that, crazy as it seemed, promised to save our lives.

As we approached the lobby, I suddenly pressed Cindi to the wall and kissed her, and she kissed me back. Maybe it was the drink, the excitement of becoming lovers in a crisis. Whatever. We let our passions race as the kiss lasted, and I soon found my hands all over her. We were oblivious to other guests walking by until some guy let out the comment, "Get a room."

I backed off at that point and said to her, "You know, that's not a bad idea."

But that wasn't happening. Our assigned rooms had roommates, certainly moved in by now, and every other room in the hotel was taken. Instead, we ended up in the stairwell at the other end of the first-floor hallway. We started necking again, and at some point, I snuck a hand under her blouse. Finally, breathless, she backed away.

"Maybe we can find a janitor's closet or something," she gasped and laughed.

"Or," I said, "a room in a motel outside the city."

"Escape through Zone D?" she said with a sarcastic frown.

"Why not?" I shrugged.

"You serious? You believe that guy?"

"What's to lose?"

"There are Zs out there," she said.

I shrugged. Or nukes dropped on the city, I didn't add.

***

The stairwell began to be a source of considerable traffic after that. Some guy stepping over us told us apologetically that the hotel elevator was out of order.

With a sigh, Cindi and I decided to head back to the Take-Off Lounge. As we approached, we heard what sounded like a scuffle or fight coming from inside with people avoiding whatever was happening by spilling out in the hallway. We edged through them to get a look at what was going on.

At the entrance, we saw that it was George Reed in the middle of the altercation. Three or four guys in dark suits and thin, black ties had latched onto him, trying to escort him out of the place.

"Bastards," George shouted as he struggled to free himself. "They're going to kill you all!"

After that, I saw one of the guys place something across George's mouth. A moment later, George went limp. No more struggling. They simply dragged him out of the bar and down the hall toward the lobby and, presumably, out of the hotel.

I turned to Cindi and said, "See that?"

She swallowed, nodded.

I pulled her out of the bar into the hall, no longer wanting a drink.

"Maybe he isn't crazy," I said to her.

Cindi turned and stared at me, her eyes wide, wondering.

A couple walked out of the bar just then, with the guy telling the girl, "Now there are carriers."

"Hey, what?" I called after them.

The guy stopped, turned. He frowned as if to say, me?

"What'd you say? Carriers?"

"That's the latest," he said. "Just on the news. Zs mutated again or something. Some people just carry the disease, spread it to other people. Like that lady, Typhoid Mary. Could be you, could be me, could be her. Fucking carriers—people who are immune infecting other people."

He made a face, turned to his date, locked arms with her and off they went down the hall toward the lobby.

After that, I led Cindi to the same stairwell, and we sat trying to determine what was what.

Finally, she asked, "So how much time do you think we have? If it's true."

I looked up at her and shrugged. "Not much, I don't think," I said. I stuck my hand in my pocket and felt for the napkin. I took it out and examined it for a time.

"This looks pretty straightforward," I told her. "I mean, he marked the streets. We just follow them to this open area. Zone D."

"How far is it?"

"I have no idea."

Echoes of steps came toward us, and another couple was stepping over us.

"Bad place to sit," the guy, a burly, scowling fellow said.

When he had opened the door to the first-floor hallway, Cindi said, "Everyone's so tense."

"Maybe they can sense the worst," I said.

"So, should we try it, go?" she asked. "Listen to that nut. It still sounds…"

"Crazy," I said. "I know. But, geez…"

We both settled into our thoughts. A few hours ago, I didn't even know her, and she didn't know me. Now we were plotting to evade a federal quarantine, no doubt a serious felony. Then, I came to a decision. "I think it's real," I said. "Those guys who took out George Reed didn't look like hotel security to me."

Cindi nodded. "Me neither."

I waved the map at her and said, "This is our ticket. Let's use it."

***

She had a small carry-on bag where we would store some bottles of water for the walk. I decided to leave my belongings behind, not wanting to carry anything we didn't have to. It was Cindi who thought of a weapon—steak knives from the restaurant or something.

She'd get the carry-on while I got the knives. Twenty minutes later, she was standing by the stairwell door waiting for me. Her face filled with relief as I approached from the other end of the first-floor hallway. "I thought you'd left without me," she whispered, as she grabbed hold of me.

"It was tougher getting the knives than I thought," I told her, keeping my voice down. I held up a white cloth napkin holding the two. "But I got them."

As I placed them in her carry-on, Cindi said, "Well, let's hope we won't need them."

"Ready?" I asked.

"Yes," she said and held onto my hand. "Ready as I'll ever be."

We burst through the exit door by the stairwell into the chilly night.

***

The CDC had only theories as to why and how Z had started in the city. It had been established that the first Z patient was fifteen-year-old Sarah Ambrose who, about a month ago, inexplicably lapsed into a coma. Her parents took her to the emergency room at St. Barnard's Hospital in the Gross Pointe District, and she was given antibiotics and intravenous meds. A couple days later, she was declared dead but then, within the span of minutes, she woke up, or seemed to.

She was described by the attending nurse as having a wild, ravenous look after her gaunt, dark eyes opened. When the overjoyed girl's mother went to hug her, the girl bit her, tearing a deep gash out of her shoulder and neck. Blood splattered everywhere. Somehow, the nurse and the woman's husband pulled the mother away and restrained the savage girl.

The mother was hospitalized, and within hours, she lapsed into a coma. Like her daughter, she was given a regimen of meds but soon appeared to have died. And, like her daughter, minutes later, she woke up in a savage state and bit her husband, a nurse and an orderly. Her daughter, in another room, had bitten a doctor. Within hours, anyone bitten by the mother and daughter had contracted what one CDC doctor had termed a "zombie-like" disease. The spread of Z was textbook after that.

Some news reporter picked up on that and started calling the strange new disease "Z." And shortly after that, anyone who contracted it became known as a Z.

There were unconfirmed reports of Z epidemics having occurred at various times in the dark corners of Africa, or in under-developed areas of South America. It was noted that Sarah Ambrose and her parents had recently returned from a safari in central Africa. How those Z outbreaks had been contained, or if they had been, was not explained. Perhaps the disease simply ran its course and fizzled out. But Z had never gained a foothold anywhere else.

Until now.

What was especially disturbing, of course, was that, as recently confirmed, Z could now be spread by airborne transmission. And even worse, though unconfirmed, it had been reported that some humans were carriers—that is, they could spread the disease but not develop its horrible symptoms. Though scientists were working furiously on a vaccine, to date there was no known cure or antidote. The only way to stop a Z was to kill its brain—shoot or stab it in the head. All the zombie movies ever made had gotten that part right.

Thankfully, by all accounts to date, Z had been confined to the city. And the quarantine was meant to ensure that.

***

Once outside, it felt as if we had left our space capsule untethered and had entered a dark, remote void. Fortunately, Cindi was wearing a leather jacket, and I had on my sport coat to fend off the damp, chilly night.

"This way," I told her, pointing right. And off we went.

We followed the napkin map as best we could, stopping every few blocks under a street lamp to figure out where we were. The streets were deserted, dark and silent, adding to our dread. Then, we headed onward in the same direction. After another few blocks, we feared that we were hopelessly lost.

"This map is worthless," Cindi said waiting for me to figure something out. "That guy was crazy, and we're crazy for listening to him. Let's go back."

"No," I said. "That's not an option."

In the next moment, I heard the skittering of steps or something along the asphalt from out of the darkness beyond the glare of the streetlamp.

"What's that?"

"Shhh!"

I took Cindi's arm and moved us out of the light into the shadows of a storefront. After a few moments, there was no more skittering, and I pulled her back onto the sidewalk.

"This way," I said.

We hustled up the street hugging the storefronts in a direction I hoped was the right way according to the napkin map. Then, after a few blocks, we ran into a National

Guard platoon. As we approached them out the darkness, the skittish soldiers turned and pointed their M-16s at us.

"Don't shoot!" I shouted and raised my arms. My voice bounced off the dark, silent buildings around us along the entire street. "Don't shoot!"

The platoon trotted up to us, and its captain stepped forward. He was a nervous looking guy around thirty-five who'd gotten way more than he had bargained for on this assignment after signing up for duty some years ago.

"What the hell you doing out here?" he whispered. "Almost got yourself killed. This sector's infested with Zs."

"We got lost," I told him. "We're at one of the hotels. We were going stir crazy. Went out to get some fresh air."

"Fresh air?" he laughed. "The airport hotels are five clicks that way. That's three miles that way." He gestured behind us. "You really got lost."

I shrugged.

"Look, man," the captain went on. "It's not safe out here. There's Zs everywhere just north of here. Where you're heading, where we're going. You really need to turn around and head back the way you came. Now."

"Yes, sir," I told him. I turned and nodded toward the airport hotels, three miles east of us.

He gave me one last nod then waved to his platoon to head out. Off they went, double-timing it, their boots echoing over the asphalt road, leaving us alone on the dark street corner.

"We going back?" Cindi asked.

"No," I told her. "Let them get ahead of us. That's the way we need to go."

"But he said there's Zs that way," Cindi said. "We'll be heading right into them."

I sighed. There was no answering that. It was either death by Zs or death by A-bomb. "We've got no choice," I said and waved the napkin map at her. "C'mon."

We started walking in the same direction as the National Guard platoon had just marched. A couple blocks up, the map indicated a right turn, and just as we turned that way, there was a flash followed by an explosion. We stopped a moment, getting down on our haunches.

"What's that?" Cindi asked.

At first, I thought it was too late. They were already dropping the nukes. But then another flash and explosion came from where the National Guard unit had gone.

"Artillery," I guessed. "Rocket launchers, maybe. Let's go."

We got up and quickened our pace down the dark, narrow road for about half a mile until it intersected with another. After squinting at the map, I pointed right, and we followed yet another narrow, deserted road for a while longer until turning right onto Jergen Street. There was a yellow "Dead-end" sign posted just after the street sign. Jergen Street ended after about a quarter-mile, becoming, as the map indicated, a nameless gravel road leading through a short grassy strip into thick woods.

"There it is," I told Cindi and pointed to the map. "Zone D."

We ran down the gravel path to the trees and, after stopping a moment, went for it. We kept walking, scattering the brush with our arms, ducking to avoid branches. After an indeterminable time, we came out of the woods into a wide field. To the east and west of us, we saw helicopters lighting the ground below them. For some reason, none of them patrolled the open field that we just had stepped into.

"I have to rest," Cindi said, panting, bent over with her hands on her haunches.

"No," I said. "We have to keep going. We're still too close."

She nodded, and we started moving again. After a hundred yards or so, we entered another space of trees and brush. We edged through it like before, brushing away or ducking under low branches. My legs ached, and my feet burned, and I was thirsty and winded, and I knew Cindi must be as well as she trailed maybe ten yards behind me. Finally, we stumbled into another clearing with the interstate running through it. The helicopter patrolling the quarantine perimeter was no longer visible.

"Thank God," Cindi whispered, as she stepped forward even with me.

We had to climb a high fence and somehow made it over without breaking an arm or leg. We drank some water and stood there a moment as I tried to figure our next move. I vetoed hitchhiking along the interstate as we might draw attention to ourselves as escapees from the quarantine. Instead, we kept in the shadows far off the shoulder heading north away from the city.

The hours passed. As I checked my watch, Cindi asked, "How far away do you think we've come?"

I checked my watch. It was close to two in the morning, and we'd found Zone D around eleven. "I don't know," I told her. "Fifteen, twenty miles."

"I'm so tired," she said. "I can't feel my legs anymore."

"Me too," I said. "Next exit, we'll get off, find a hotel. I think we're far enough."

It took us another hour to get to the next exit. We trudged along the shoulder of the winding ramp onto a state road that had some gas stations, a McDonald's,

Burger King, and an inexpensive chain motel near the interchange.

"Thank God," Cindi said, as we limped to the motel office.

"Hope they have a room," I said. "I could use a bed."

We entered the office and found the clerk munching a candy bar behind the counter while several guests were glued to a small TV in the corner of the cramped lobby. The clerk turned to us as we walked in, but quickly turned back to the TV.

"What's going on?" I asked.

The clerk nodded at the TV. I looked up and saw the President seated behind his desk in the Oval Office.

"…and so, my fellow Americans," he said, "after considering all options, we have no choice but to take this drastic action to avoid a larger tragedy. With great sadness, I have ordered that five nuclear weapons be dropped at various strategic points of the city." He hesitated a moment, swallowed, then, still staring straight into the camera at us all, continued, "The astronomical loss of life is unfortunate, of course, but cannot be avoided. For the greater good, indeed to save mankind, we must do this. I beg God's forgiveness." He sighed and added, "God bless all of you, and God bless America."

The screen went blank until an anchorman with a stunned expression popped up and tried to clarify what the President had just told us. In the next few minutes, Air Force bombers would drop five 500-megaton nuclear bombs on various strategic locations in the city. Three million people would die in the initial blasts with another million severely injured. In the resulting fires that would follow and blasts by more conventional bombs, those million and more would die. No rescue missions would be sent. In short, every last living person in the city would die.

And with them, it was hoped, so would all the Zs and the disease with them.

"Holy mother of Jesus," the clerk said, as he turned to me. "Those poor saps."

Cindi gave me a dumbfounded look as the guests with numb expressions ambled out of the small office. I held her then turned to the clerk.

"We're safe here?" I asked him. "I mean, far enough away?"

"Think so," he said, as he took a bite of his candy bar. He was a tall, lean guy in his forties. After another bite of his candy bar, he added, "At least, that's what they said. The blast zone is forty miles or something. We gotta be at least seventy miles out. And these are clean bombs or something. Minimal radiation but with lots of blast and heat to kill people and Z germs."

"Jesus," I said and looked at Cindi.

The clerk put down the candy bar, stretched back and asked, "So, you want a room?"

"Yes," I said. "Our car broke down on the interstate, few miles back."

"Okay," said the clerk.

He slid a registration card over the counter, and I filled in my name, address, cell number. When I got to the car information, I told him, "Car's on the side of the interstate."

He shrugged.

"I'll need a credit card," he said. I took one out of my wallet and slid it over to him. He typed the numbers into the hotel registration site and booked us the room. It cost $69.

"You're all set," he said, handing me a key on a blue plastic holder.

In the next moment, there was a flash over the hills miles from us. A few moments later, we heard the blasts. Each of us ducked down below the counter and stayed there while several more blasts came. Then, the ground shook.

"Holy shit!" I heard the clerk say.

Cindi nudged close to me on the floor, and I held her. And then it was over, and we stood and stumbled out of the office. Birds were chirping, and there was the rumble of aftershocks. The sky was lit like daylight had bloomed over the hills in the direction of the city. I noticed that dozens of guests were outside staring that way, lost in the enormity of the tragedy, the simultaneous death of four million people. For some reason, I wondered what the stock market was going to do today and wished I had pulled all my money out my 401k.

***

Room 211 was cramped and musty. The bed was narrow and lumpy and musty as well. I nodded to the small TV on the dresser. "Wanna watch?"

Cindi shook her head and replied, "I wanna sleep."

We'd been on the run five hours. Sleep sounded good.

Cindi slipped out of her jeans and shirt and got under the covers, wearing only a bra and panties. I stripped to my boxers and climbed in next to her. I thought of turning to her, taking her into my arms, and finally making love.

"We can't go home," she said out of the darkness.

I thought about that. She was right. Everyone knew we'd been in the city. To our family and friends and co-workers at this moment, we were dead. If we went home tomorrow, they'd know we'd escaped, had violated the quarantine. And that Z might have escaped with us. Once the authorities found out, we'd be arrested.

"I know," I said. "Not right away." Then, an idea came to me. A resolution of sorts. "Maybe after a few days, weeks. When the dust has settled, and there's no more Z. Then, we surface." In the next moment, I asked, "Do you want to make love?"

But by then Cindi was asleep.

***

I woke up on my back and turned to look at a small, digital alarm clock on the night table on my side of the bed. But the clock wasn't plugged in, so I sat up and reached for my watch on the table and saw that it was five minutes after eleven. I slipped out of bed and spread open the musty, tan drapes of the small window looking out to a parking lot on a gray, misty day.

I got back onto the bed and turned to Cindi who was lying on her right side, still asleep. I wanted to celebrate our freedom, our very lives. I thought that I was in love with her, and I wanted to make love to her. I crawled back onto the bed and licked her right earlobe. When that did nothing, didn't even make her flinch, I moved down to lick her neck, with the same result. Then, I got to my haunches and leaned over the top of her head.

"Cindi?" I shook her. But still she didn't move. Then, louder, "Cindi?" I pushed harder on her shoulders for a time, then turned her onto her back. "Cindi!" I called to her.

Finally, her eyes opened. They were blank, lifeless. After a time, they widened. And then, she began to snarl. She licked her lips and started to lift herself while I moved away and jumped off the bed.

32

"No," I whispered. "This can't…"

She sat up, and her snarling became a growl. Her face was tense and twisted as she moved forward and got off the bed. I looked at my carry-on bag on the small loveseat in the corner of the room. She was off the bed and stalking me as I went for the bag and searched for the steak knife I had taken from the hotel restaurant. By the time I found it and was lifting it out of the bag, she had grabbed my shoulders, about to bite.

There was no doubt. Cindi had turned Z.

In the next moment, I whirled around with the knife tightly gripped in my hand and without another thought, thrust it into her forehead. Part of it broke off, but enough of it had sliced into her brain that she fell backward, then down to her knees. I went to the night table and lifted it. The lamp and alarm clock fell off as I brought it over and smashed it down onto her skull. She fell forward onto the carpet, her head a bloody mess.

I staggered back and sat on the edge of the bed, all the while staring at Cindi's corpse. I still held what was left of the knife in my right hand and started sobbing.

A few moments later, I heard the bird-like screeching of Zs on the hunt. Then, it occurred to me. All of this was my fault. I must be a Z carrier. How else could Cindi have contracted it?

After an indeterminable time sitting in the dark room, listening to the screeching of Zs roaming outside, I heard sirens. Cars screeched to a halt in the parking lot of the motel. Then shots rang out, and cops were shouting.

I looked down at the knife. I knew what I must do, but could not do it.

On a hot southern day, off a two-lane county road, a walker snarled outside an abandoned drug store.

Vines grew through its body, pushing leaves through its face and ribcage. The walker had been still so long it was rooted in place. Caked dirt fell as it struggled forward with rotten, outstretched fingers.

Tommy, a red-haired ex-salesman, lay underneath it. His foot had gotten caught on the other side of a busted storefront window, and now the walker was just a few feet above him, the vines snapping one by one.

Pike, a former athlete with a shaved head, rushed in to kill it but two more walkers emerged from inside the store. She shifted her balance and stabbed the first one in the head as she sprang backward. Then Hemingway, a huge ex-Marine, used his farming gloves to reach inside the second one's mouth and rip the top of its head off.

They all stood catching their breath, except for Tommy, who was still on the ground with a walker hanging over him.

"Next time, when we've got a plan, you follow it," said Keats, their skinny, ragged leader.

"I'm just trying to save some time," said Tommy.

"There's a reason we don't just barge into places," said Hemingway. "How the hell have you survived this long?"

Twigs snapped in the woods behind the parking lot. A ponytailed man with a golden retriever emerged from the trees.

"He's right, you know," he said. "You gotta learn to speak up if something feels wrong."

Keats and the rest readied their weapons.

"What'd you do with the others?" said Keats.

"Your friends?" said the man. "They're right here. They're a little timid." He stepped to the side. Duck, Jamie, and Katie, the other members of Keats' party, walked out at gunpoint.

"By the way," the man said to Hemingway, "where did you learn that technique? Ripping the head off? I haven't seen that one in a while."

"I was going to say the same thing about your rifles," he said. "You make the bullets yourself? Get lucky on a run?"

"I can hear those thoughts!" the man said with a laugh. "Thinking about taking us on? Trust me, friend, the guns are loaded. Now, tell me, what the hell are you doing breaking into one of our buildings?"

"Didn't see a sign," said Keats.

"You think the apocalypse means no property law? Anyway, what are you looking for? Maybe we can help."

"Bug spray," said Keats.

"Bug spray! Lemme guess—you've got food and water, but you forgot about the damn mosquitoes. Is that why you're all covered in dirt?"

"We heard mosquito bites spread the plague," said Tommy. This brought a chuckle from the man's gang.

"That's not what spreads the plague," said the man. "We figured that out, as you will soon see."

The dog began to whine and bark softly. "Looks like we got company. Let's hit the road. Hang on to your weapons for now. We might need you to cover our flanks if we meet some walkers."

As the group gathered on the road, Keats said from the side of his mouth: "They could have killed us already."

"They might be waiting till they're ready to eat us," said Pike.

"True. But I think they've got supplies. Who knows.... maybe they just want to check us out, make sure we're good people."

Before Pike could respond, the man called out: "Let's move! Ol' Lady here's reliable, but it's tough to account for the wind. A swarm could be a mile away, or it might be 50 yards. By the way, my name's Flak." He marched ahead like a guide on a nature walk.

Everyone moved forward. After walking what felt like a couple of miles, Keats saw something on the road ahead: The gate for a tall, barbed wire fence next to sign welcoming them to Davis.

***

Keats' group had come together over the past five years.

At first, it was just him and Hemingway. They met each other at a shelter that had held strong for eight years after the outbreak. The place was self-sustaining and well-guarded, but eventually, someone inside got infected, and the relative lack of security within the compound itself meant that it spread quickly. Neither Keats nor Hemingway had a family, which is probably how they survived, as most people there got trapped after spending precious time rounding up loved ones.

They met Pike on the road a week later. She saved their lives by sharing her food with them, and they paid her back by ambushing the group of bandits that had been stalking her.

Pike was a good hunter, but the days on the road were hell. They'd meet occasional relief when they'd stumble across a camp, and when those camps collapsed (as they always did), they'd have a new member or two. Sometimes they were assets, sometimes they were burdens, and unfortunately, how valuable they were to the group rarely seemed to matter to fate. Just last week, for instance, they'd lost a nurse. The fighters usually survived, but survival needs more than fighters.

Keats relayed all of this to a man named Marco as they sat in a living room. He was short and thin and had an actor's broad, expressive face. He wore black slacks, a long-sleeved dress shirt, and a revolver in a holster.

"And your last camp was overrun?"

Keats nodded. "They had lookouts but underestimated how fast some of the hordes can be."

Marco laughed and nodded like a parent hearing a familiar comedy about someone else's child. "Oh yes, there are still some fast ones out there!"

"New ones keep getting made, I guess."

"We're doing what we can. We've currently got about one square mile of this neighborhood fenced off. Working on more. But eventually, we don't want the fences anymore. We want to take our planet back."

"Now that's a new one," said Keats. "Most people are day-to-day. Scavengers or predators. Nobody holding the big ideals anymore."

"We're different," said Marco, who spread his hands and smiled. "I'm different."

On the coffee table in front of them sat two cups full of homegrown tea. Marco picked one up and sipped it. "You ever wonder what drives them?" he said.

"Hunger, I guess."

"You think a severed head gets hungry? No, it's about more than that. It's hatred. They hate us."

Keats paused. "How do you know this?"

"I've witnessed it. And soon you will, too. But for now, it suffices to say I'm convinced. And what can beat hatred?"

"Hell. More hatred?"

"Cynicism has kept you alive a long time," Marco said. "I don't blame you for relying on it. But you're wrong. It's love."

***

They emerged from the house and walked down the steps onto a quiet neighborhood street, Lady trotting behind them. The grass in all the yards was overgrown, but the sidewalks had been cleared of weeds by hand. Birds chirped in the late afternoon sunset and squirrels chased each other around trees. Flak and another man walked behind them with rifles, keeping guard.

There were hardly any mosquitoes. Keats mentioned this to Marco.

"We've got a team, goes out once a week and collects any standing water," said Marco. "Plus, we have a stash of the all-important repellent."

They passed a house with a chicken coop. Hens clucked and pecked in the yard. The yard next to it had been converted into a small garden with beans and tomatoes growing.

"Looks like you've got quite a few of those little plots around," said Keats. "About how many folks you got to feed here?"

"Enough to feel safe."

"Then what do you need us for? Why keep us prisoner?"

Marco grimaced. "Those aren't the words I'd use, but you're forgiven for seeing things from that perspective. We just want to make sure your stories check out, and you're not going to do us any harm."

"So if we check out," said Keats, "we can go?"

"Of course. You have my word." Then Marco stopped and turned towards Keats. He grabbed him by the shoulders. "But if you want to stay, you can do that, too. We need all the help we can in this fight."

Keats didn't say anything. There was nothing he could say. Like it or not, using whatever vocabulary you want, they were prisoners. And when it came to bats and spears versus rifles, the rifles always won.

Marco smiled as they made their way to the house where Keats' group would be staying. It was a two-story brick townhome with a makeshift wooden fence and an ancient, rusted Chevrolet in the driveway.

"This used to be what they called 'affordable housing'," said Marco as they entered the yard. "But believe it or not, they make the best castles. Bars on the windows. Fireproof. The door's made of solid steel."

Keats smiled for the first time and said: "Could be a lot worse. It's been—God, months since I've slept inside."

"Tonight won't be easy. You'll still wake up in the middle of the night. Force of habit. But who knows? Maybe you'll get used to it."

He turned to the men who'd been following them. "You've met Flak. This gentleman here is Cochise. They'll be taking care of your immediate needs. Get some rest, and we'll see you tomorrow." He walked away quickly as if he still had lots of business to attend to in whatever daylight remained.

The rest of Keats' group joined him in the yard. Flak walked up and put his hands on his hips. He looked to be about 25 years old and had slate blue eyes. Like all survivors, he was rail thin, but his frame suggested an athletic past.

"Howdy," he said. "You want to know why we let you keep your weapons?" He looked at Jamie, who smiled at him. Jamie was a teenager who'd grown up in a post-outbreak shelter. She had long brown hair and was very pretty, but slouched forward a bit with the awkwardness that came with being her age.

No one in the group answered Flak. Besides Jamie, they either eyed him suspiciously or looked at the ground.

"Well, if there's one thing I've learned since the world ended," he said, "it's that you should never rely on a fence. So just in case you guys get a knock in the middle of the night from Mr. Walker, we know you can at least hold your own. Because when it comes to the undead, we're all on the same team, right?"

"Sure we're not just a front line?" said Hemingway. "Keep us out on the periphery, close to the fence, while you guys stay in the middle?"

"Now that doesn't sound like gratitude," said Flak. "You know we're feeding you, too, right? I'm coming back this evening with dinner. Now, why don't you all go inside, get yourselves settled in."

"Maybe we like it out here. Fresh air."

Flak stared at him, still with his sparkling smile. "You ask yourself how you'd treat a bunch of folks you'd never met before, with things the way they are nowadays."

Hemingway flexed his arms, straining the brown leather armor on his forearms. Keats stepped in. "We had a good talk," he said to Hemingway. Then to Flak: "We'll go in."

"Good," said Flak. "Be sure to clear the rooms first. You can never be too careful. And don't spoil dinner! It's a stew tonight."

***

The house was full of empty cans, and other refuse from whoever had last used it as a shelter. To Keats, it

40

seemed like a waste to throw away anything that had any potential for reuse. Then again, perhaps that's what long-term shelter did to people: It brought back wastefulness, one aspect of humanity he'd been glad to assume extinct.

A steward had delivered half a barrel of water, and now Keats used some to clean off the river mud on his skin. He soaked a cloth and ran it along his arms, which were thin and veiny.

He looked into the hazy bathroom mirror and cleaned his face. It was a long, bony, and not particularly handsome face, especially with the wild beard he now sported. But he did have kind eyes, and a pang of sadness hit him as he thought about everything he'd lost, most especially the fiancée who fell in love with those eyes and had been gleefully waiting for him to finish school when the world ended.

She was in North Carolina; he was in Florida. The last message he got about her was from her father, who texted that she'd been bitten by some "drug addict" and had to be hospitalized as a precaution.

He tried to call his own parents and couldn't get through. He tried texting, but it failed. He remembered a gigantic line outside the one pay phone still operating in town. He recalled the sound of helicopters, which were unnerving at first but then reassuring as the news brought reports of growing civil unrest.

Then the power went out. That's when he decided to leave for North Carolina. That was 13 years ago—or was it? Every group they ran into had a different take on how many years it had been.

A knock on the bathroom door startled Keats. He opened it and saw Hemingway.

"They're here," he said. "Think you should come down."

***

In the kitchen were Flak, Cochise and one other man, laughing and chatting with some of the same people they'd held at gunpoint only a couple of hours prior. They had just set up the stew pot, and Katie and Duck were scooping small bowls of it for everyone.

Flak was talking to Jamie, leaning against the wall like he was at a frat party. The only thing missing was a red plastic cup in his hand.

Keats and Hemingway stood at the staircase like disapproving parents, but eventually, Keats went to get some stew. He brought a bowl for Hemingway, who didn't want it, but Keats insisted.

After everyone had been served, Keats announced: "Thanks very much for this. I think we need to keep the house closed for tonight, though. We've got a lot we need to talk about."

"We're just trying to be friendly," said Cochise.

"I know that, and that's nice of you. But we've been on the road a long time. Half of us still got mud all over us. So socializing will have to wait until tomorrow when we see Marco—"

"You think he's some kind of dictator?" said Cochise. "If we decide to mingle a little bit with you guys, he's OK with it." He tilted his head in mock sweetness. "As long as we don't hurt you."

Hemingway strode forward, the floorboards creaking as he did so. He stopped two inches from Cochise and stood eye-to-eye with him. "You got a boss, we got ours. And he wants you to go."

Cochise pressed against him like a boxer at a weigh-in. "When's the last time you fought someone who wasn't already dead?"

"You think we've lived this long playing pushover?"

"Enough," said Flak, and Cochise relaxed a little. At the same time, Keats put his hand on Hemingway's shoulder and pulled him back.

"You want us to go, we'll go," said Flak. "Y'all have a good night."

The third man with them, whose name was Joseph, said, "Eat the rest of the stew. You need it, and there's no way to refrigerate it, anyway."

He turned to leave. Katie looked disappointed.

"Wait a minute," said Jamie. "Flak's going to stay a while." Her voice had the same lilt of constant sarcasm that was so popular among teenagers before the outbreak. Keats marveled at how such an accent could survive the apocalypse, especially since she'd come of age in a shelter.

"You gotta be joking," said Hemingway. "No way. We don't know this guy from Adam—"

"We? Who's we? Me and him were in the middle of a conversation. If you don't want him around, we'll go in one of the rooms and continue there."

"Hell no. We are not allowing you—"

"Allow? You're not going to 'allow' me to talk to someone? My parents got eaten a long time ago, mister. I can do whatever the hell I want."

"She's right," said Keats.

Hemingway turned and looked at him with a confused expression.

"She's right," Keats said again. "Let her visit with him. They can take the side bedroom while the rest of us talk about our plans."

Hemingway started to say something else but stayed quiet. Cochise smirked and left. Joseph followed him after saying goodbye.

Jamie and Flak walked towards one of the bedrooms. Stuffed inside it were dishes, clothes, electronics, and other various crap that gets left behind after a quick exit. Jamie went to shut the door, but Keats grabbed it.

"Leave it cracked," he said. Jamie rolled her eyes but relented.

Everyone else gathered in the living room and went over the day's whirlwind of events. They spoke quietly, mindful of Marco's man being in the other room.

"I trust them," said Tommy. "You see what they're doing in this camp. Gardens, trying to clean things up. They wouldn't do that if they were bad people."

"What the hell makes you think that?" said Duck. He was a short, stocky man who was a mechanic in his former life. "Maybe they'll make us do the shit jobs, and they'll be the kings."

"That's called earning your keep," said Tommy. "I'll work for stew and shelter. Better than running around the woods sleeping in trees."

"Agreed," said Katie. "What's the harm in staying a while?"

A white-light scream shook everyone from their seats. It had come from the bedroom.

Keats was the first one there. He gripped his bat halfway up as he rushed in through the door.

Flak stood there holding his nose. "Fucking bitch," he said.

"I told you to stop, asshole," said Jamie.

Hemingway and Pike entered the room and looked ready to rip Flak in half.

Suddenly the front door flew open, and Cochise stormed in with a rifle at his side. Some of Keats' group screamed or shouted "No!"

"What the hell is this?" said Cochise.

"She was leading me on," said Flak, "but hey. It's OK. Just a little roughhousing." He glanced at his hand and the small amount of blood that had come from his nose.

"I thought all you guys wanted to do was socialize," said Hemingway.

"Oh, please," said Katie. "She dragged him in there. And you can see what kind of mouth she has on her."

"I think the best thing to do," said Keats, "is for everyone to just go home."

"We gotta teach him a lesson," said Hemingway.

"No, it's OK, please," said Jamie. She sniffled. "Just leave, OK? Just get out."

Flak began to leave. "Believe what you want," he said. "But I'm not a rapist. She's the one who freaked out." He paused like he was going to say more but walked away instead. Cochise followed him, walking backward.

Pike tried to talk to Jamie, but she refused. She ran into the bedroom and slammed the door.

"That settles it for me," said Pike. "I think we need to leave—now. No telling what they're getting ready for."

"That's just what they expect," said Hemingway. "I think we should lure someone in here for hostage."

"Are you crazy?" said Tommy. "What happened there—Marco will handle that. He respects us. Why else would he feed us? We'll let Jamie say what happened when she's ready."

"It's only fair to Flak, too," said Katie. Pike glared at her, but she stayed firm. "It's not like we know her that well, either."

There was a knock on the back door. Everyone hushed nervously.

"Who is it?" yelled Keats.

"Bart."

"Who?"

"Bart! You asked my name, and I told you!" The voice sounded like it belonged to a 12-year-old boy.

Two of them moved to the door, everyone else prepared to fight. They opened it and saw not a boy but a woman, in her early 20s, who stood about five feet tall and looked like an elf in her faded black hoodie. She had a smooth wooden plank piercing her nose and a homemade tattoo of a hammer and sickle on her upper cheek. She held a pillowcase full of something in her hands.

"I heard there were some females here," she said. She placed the bag inside. "That's some, uh, hygiene stuff. Also, some toilet paper. That one's for the girls AND guys."

Pike chuckled. "Thanks. You had us worked up, though, banging on the back door like that."

"Sorry. There's sort of a curfew. Why'd the big man rush inside?"

"He forgot his chew toy," said Keats. "You wanna come inside?"

"No thanks. Gotta run!" She darted away like a cartoon.

"Wait," said Pike, who ran outside. "Can we trust these guys—?"

But she'd already disappeared into the night.

***

The square mile of town that Marco had fenced off had a building in the center: A church.

This was not an accident, Joseph explained as he escorted Keats' group from their shelter. It was mid-morning, and the heat was starting to make itself known.

The church, he said, was one of the few buildings with a basement. It also had lots of square footage for gatherings and, if need be, a final stand against invaders.

"What about God?" said Duck. "Or did people give up on him a long time ago?"

"People can worship here, sure," said Joseph. "One of our residents is a pastor, and I believe there are a couple of Jewish folks among us. In the end, it all comes back to love, right?"

"That's the second time I've heard something like that," said Keats. "I don't think everyone here follows that 'love' doctrine."

"I heard about that," said Joseph. "We'll get to the bottom of it, I promise you."

"So, is this a regularly scheduled service?" said Keats.

"Not exactly. This was something Marco called together at the last minute, once you all showed up. He figured it would be a good time to 'gather the flock,' as it were."

They rounded a corner, and the church came fully into view. It was a majestic building, with a giant spire on top of a belfry. Marco's men had done a good job of keeping it all clean, considering what they likely had to work with.

The inside was even more impressive. The crucifix behind the altar looked newly painted. The pews had all been polished and the sunlight beamed in like a colorful flood. The only thing that looked out of place was a large wooden octagon. Keats guessed that it was the base of a soon-to-be-constructed statue.

Duck crossed himself and prayed. "It might be a Baptist church," he said, "but it's close enough."

People began to walk inside and fill the pews. Unlike yesterday, when almost everyone Keats saw was armed and male, this was a more diverse group, young and old, men and women.

Before long, nearly every seat was full. Except for the rifles some people had propped up on the benches, it felt like a normal Sunday service, pre-apocalypse.

Jamie walked down the aisle and sat next to Keats without saying anything. She stared at the ground until Keats asked if she was OK.

"Fine," she said. "Just embarrassed."

"For defending yourself?"

"Look," said Jamie, "for the record? I don't think we should write this whole shelter off just because of that one prick. At least he stopped when I punched him. Walkers don't."

Keats was about to tell Jamie that he didn't want to give up on this place, either, when someone turned around and shushed him. Everyone else fell silent as a beautiful woman walked in from a vestibule. She had Lady on a leash and sat down in a reserved seat in a front pew.

Soon after, Marco walked in to loud applause. He wore a dress shirt like the one he had on yesterday except now he also wore a tie. His gun was still there, sitting in its holster.

He walked to the pulpit, waving and smiling at the crowd, who were still clapping. Eventually, he had to gesture for them to settle down, but he waited a while to do it.

"Thank you," he said, booming his voice like an old theater actor. "So how are we today? Are we hungry?"

"NO SIR!" said nearly the whole crowd in unison. They said the words quickly, like taps on a snare drum. The only people silent were in Keats' group.

"Are we weary?"

"NO SIR!"

"Are we pushing back against the hatred that's trying to overcome this earth?"

"YES SIR!"

"And how are we doing this?"

"LOVE!"

"Absolutely right! We've got love here that keeps us safe, but we're going to turn it into a love that conquers. A love that destroys, with holy blessings, the corruptible evil outside those fences."

There were a few random shots of "Amen!" and "Yes sir!" throughout Marco's speech. Keats looked at Jamie, who rolled her eyes.

"And lest you think we have to do it ourselves," said Marco, "we received a most holy blessing yesterday. We received, with open arms, a group of pilgrims who traveled here because they know this is where the battle begins to take back the earth!"

"What the hell?" Hemingway muttered under his breath. "We were looking for bug repellant, not on some fucking pilgrimage."

"Let's just see where this goes," said Keats.

"As if we have a choice."

"Yesterday, I talked to their leader," said Marco. "A fine man who I trust quite a bit. Sure, they're road-weary and haggard. We should all remember how fortunate we are to be protected here.

"But this man—Keats is his name—I could sense it in him. I could sense the love. The grand love that destroys evil!"

Katie sat in the row ahead of Keats. She turned back to him and smiled.

"LOVE is what the undead hate. LOVE is what can cure the sickness. LOVE is what keeps them away from our fence. LOVE—"

"Bullshit," yelled a voice. The church hushed like a hermetic door sealing an airlock.

It was Hemingway. He stood up. Several of Marco's men reached for their weapons, but their leader raised his hand to still them.

"You can hug and kiss your way out of one of those swarms? I lost my whole family, who I loved. I lost my whole platoon, which I loved. They got ripped apart and eaten. Love didn't do a thing for them."

Marco locked eyes with him. His gaze was soft, not challenging. "You're right," he said. "For a long time, hate was stronger than love. How could now be different?

"It's because the love here flows as one. All our love comes together like strands of a rope. And who is threading it together? Who unifies the love?

"Let me be frank: I did not ask to be chosen. I never sought out enlightenment. Never wanted to be special. I was just a corporate stooge when the world ended. Woke up for work one day and the Army was going door-to-door, evacuating people.

"But not long ago—just after I arrived here, back when it was just a few boarded-up homes and some guys with a stash of guns—something happened. I had an epiphany, not just of the mind but of the soul."

Marco started unbuttoning his shirt. The crowd seemed to know where this was headed, and they stopped glowering at Hemingway and cheered and hooted for Marco instead.

"I was lost!" said Marco, undoing each button with stage musical flourishes. "I was loveless! I was weak! And when a walker got into the camp, I wanted to cower and hide. One walker, can you believe it? But then a flame entered my heart and grew into a fire. I charged that evil beast and fought it hand to hand—"

The front of his shirt was now completely unbuttoned. He reached back and whipped it off in one furious movement.

"—and it did this!"

Everyone in Keats' group gasped, while everyone in the crowd frowned and shook their heads as if reliving a great tragedy. From Marco's left shoulder down to his wrist was a deep groove of brownish pink scar tissue. It looked like half his arm was missing.

"Lord, what pain. And I had no idea they were so strong! I struggled, kicked it with my legs, but it just tore into my arm like a drumstick. When they finally got it off of me, its face was so red with my blood that I couldn't help but faint. My last thought was to hope they'd put a bullet in my brain so I wouldn't come back as one of those things.

"But then, many hours later, I woke up. The doctor who stitched me up, may she rest in peace, said she did it out of instinctual obligation. No way I would survive. But I did. They tied me up and kept me under guard for a whole month, and I never turned.

"It was the flame that kept me alive. The flame of love."

There was a commotion as the doors to the church opened and two huge men, Cochise among them, escorted a struggling figure down the center aisle. The captive's hands had been bound, and a black hood covered his head.

"And my love protects you, too," said Marco as his men brought the captive before him. "That is, if you're willing to accept it."

He yanked the hood off the prisoner. It was Flak. Gone was his sexy demeanor. He looked panicked.

"What the fuck is this all about?" he said.

"There may come a time when our love needs to be tested," said Marco. "John 'Flak' Watt, you've been a good soldier. You work hard. But last night, something happened that tested your commitment. Your love."

"Goddammit, it was a stupid, little thing! Nothing happened!"

Lady jumped up and began to whine and scratch at the floor.

Flak's eyes widened. "Tell him!" he yelled towards the crowd. "Tell him I didn't hurt you!"

The door to the church basement opened. A man walked backward out of it while holding a pole at waist-level. At the other end of it was a walker.

The walker was not one of the years-old rotters that could barely crawl through the weeds; it had turned recently and looked to have been a pretty good-sized man before death arrived.

Jamie stood up. "He's right!" she said. "He doesn't—he doesn't deserve that! I punched him, and he stopped!"

"Dear girl, you've got a heart of gold," said Marco. "But Flak here will be perfectly fine since I'm confident that his love is pure."

Marco stepped down and sat in one of the first pews. Like a well-directed stage play, several groups of people came out from side doors and positioned the wooden structure that Keats thought was a statue base. In fact, it was a fighting ring.

Flak now stood ten feet from an undead beast that was missing half the skin on its face. He could see its teeth grinding to dust as it snarled at him.

"Since you've been a fine lieutenant," said Marco, "there won't be any handicaps. Just one on one, you and the former Mr. Lane here. Remember, you love, and you are loved. A bite means nothing to one whose love is pure! I'm proof of that."

Before anyone else could protest, Marco stepped aside and nodded to the guard. He twisted the pole, unlatching it and setting the creature free.

Flak was a good fighter. His favorite weapon was a billy club he used with deadly precision.

But now he was bare-handed. He had no room to maneuver, to duck and dodge. He expected the walker to charge straight at him, which it did, but he wasn't expecting the quickness with which it seized his hair and chomped down on his shoulder.

His scream pierced the silence of the church. Many of the onlookers covered their eyes. Marco, however, yelled, "You can still get him! Pop your leg back!"

Amazingly, Flak heard him and swung his leg back like a mule. He knocked the walker off balance and threw him to the ground. Then, while grasping his wound, he stomped on its head until it collapsed into mush.

Blood streamed from between Flak's fingers as he pressed down on the bite and looked out into the crowd with a look of fear. "Help," he said.

"I have helped you," said Marco, ducking into the ring. He clasped Flak by the shoulder. His lieutenant winced and screamed. "The love I've shown you will heal that wound." Then, to his soldiers: "Take him to rest."

An older woman in one of the pews stood up and began clapping rhythmically. She sang a hymn, one that Keats, never much of a churchgoer, didn't recognize. But apparently, it was a popular one, as nearly everyone in the church joined her in song:

God's got a great big love
We got a great big God
Gotta love God cause we gotta stay good

So, we gotta open up our arms

Duck and Katie clapped as well. Keats nudged Hemingway and started clapping. The rest of the group followed his lead.

***

There were probably lots of cults in the world nowadays, thought Keats as he sat in his shelter's living room. Seeing the dead rise and eat the living reinforced a belief in the supernatural, and who knows how many people were just going through the motions of prayer and devotion in order to stay alive?

But Marco's people wore expressions of genuine love. Maybe they were right. Keats had never seen anyone survive a walker bite, not without amputation.

He went out the front door. Sitting in an old car was their minder/guard/spy. He nodded to him and walked out into the street.

It was twilight. The air was not much cooler than the day's, and the mosquitoes were beginning their shift. He saw a person on a bicycle and two people working in a garden, but most of the population seemed to live closer to the center, near the church.

After cutting through a couple of yards, he came to the fence that encircled the compound. It was about ten feet tall and topped with barbed wire. A hundred yards down the line was a guard tower made out of an old bucket truck. Someone inside it stood with a rifle on his hip.

From far in the woods came a scream. It was high-pitched and forced, like a song off key. It was not the scream of someone caught by a walker, but it was unsettling nonetheless.

A Rottweiler ran up from the brush beyond the fence and bashed against it. He growled and snarled at Keats but didn't bark.

Keats squatted to get eye level with him. Before Lady, he hadn't seen a dog since before the outbreak. If there were any stray packs, they stayed far away from people.

This wasn't a stray. His coat was clean and black, his body stout and healthy.

"How do you survive out here, buddy?" said Keats.

The dog bashed the fence and gave a low, quick bark.

Keats wished he had a treat for him. He stood up and was about to leave when something seized his arm.

***

Convincing Bart to come in the house and repeat what she'd said to Keats in the woods wasn't easy.

"You think I want the love test?" she said. "Or sent to Siberia?"

The information, Keats told her, needed to come from a long-time resident. He wasn't sure everyone would believe it if it were just him.

Eventually, she agreed to do it. Nervously, she stood in front of the group and said, "It wasn't a walker that bit Marco. I was here when it happened. There was this guy, William. He was always strange. One day he just lost it. Chomped down on Marco's arm like it was a turkey leg."

"I've seen people alive one second and turn the next," said Tommy. "Maybe he had a stroke and died right there, standing up, then turned."

"When they yanked him off, he was still babbling and talking about the end of days. He wasn't dead."

"You said 'they'," said Pike. "Why hasn't anyone else told the truth about what happened?"

"They've all gone away, one by one. They went out on runs and didn't return. Or a walker surprised them in their sleep."

"No witnesses," said Hemingway. "Except for you."

"I was upstairs in one of the houses," said Bart. "I saw it from the window."

"You've never told anyone else?" said Pike. "Why us?"

"Because I want to get the fuck out of here. The people here are as mindless as the things out there. You saw them, how they break into fucking song when someone gets their neck ripped into."

"You could play along if that's all it was," said Pike. "We all could. It's not like Flak was completely innocent."

"You think that was about her?" said Bart, pointing to Jamie. "Flak didn't get the love test because he tried to rape you. He got it because he violated one of the biggest rules here. Marco gets first dibs on all the females."

Jamie's face curled like the news made her sick.

"Well, fuck that, then," said Pike. "We're busting out of here."

"They're not going to let you leave like that," said Bart. "But there's another way. You know what Siberia is? How they keep walkers away from the fence? It's a shack out in the woods. If you mess up, but not bad enough for the love test, you get sent there to make noise all day and draw walkers."

"Jesus," said Keats. "How do they keep them from busting down the door?"

"It's reinforced with concrete slabs. The only way in is through a storm drain access. Goes to a hatch 100 feet away. The people there get a supply run every month."

"You think he'd trust us to make the run?"

"If you earn it," said Bart.

"So," said Pike, "we stick around for a couple months until he gets to know us and trust us. No big deal, except for the women get raped."

"There's another way," said Bart. "The love test."

***

Early one morning, about a year after the outbreak, Hemingway was sleeping in a small cave on the side of a cliff when something hit him in the face. Startled, he sat straight up and nearly fell out of his hole.

Twenty feet below him stood a scar-faced man holding a handful of stones. He had two other people with him, and they all looked the same: Filthy flannel shirts, holey jeans cinched with rope, and gaunt faces.

"Sorry," said the scar-faced man. "A rude way to wake up, I know. My name's Teddy. This here's Curtis and Bobby."

"Why shouldn't I take my rifle and make a new entrance on the top of your head?" said Hemingway.

"Sorry again, but we got it already." Curtis held up Hemingway's assault rifle by the barrel.

Christ, thought Hemingway. They must have scaled the cliff and gotten it while he was asleep. That's what he got for going too long without rest—he slept so hard he didn't hear the danger, and now it was too late. But then why—

"Why not just kill me, then?"

"We're not like that," said Teddy. "But we do need to survive. So, we figured, you look pretty healthy. Maybe you can show us where your food stash is?"

"Well," said Hemingway. "I'd rather share what I got. Lemme see, I think it's over there—"

The edge gave way as Hemingway shifted his weight. He tumbled down the side of the cliff in a whirl of rock and dust and slammed into the ground face first.

"Oh, shit," said Teddy, as he walked over. "I think he's dead."

He was not. Hemingway slowly pushed himself up, hung there like a drunk, then suddenly vise-gripped Teddy's windpipe, crushing it. Then he limped over to Curtis, who was trying desperately to figure out the AR-15. Hemingway yanked the gun from his hand and clobbered him with it. In his peripheral vision, he saw Bobby running at him with a knife, so he spun his leg around, tripped him, and stomped his face in.

The fall hurt Hemingway more than the fight afterward. He had to camp out at that cave for a week before he could fully move again, and in the meantime, his former robbers turned into walkers and nearly spotted him.

Hemingway told all this to Keats, Pike, and Tommy the morning after Bart's revelations. He said it matter-of-factly as if relaying directions to a store, and he either didn't care about or notice the looks of disquiet on his friends' faces when he told them how brutally he had killed those people.

"And since then," said Hemingway, "I've killed others, and I couldn't even count all the walkers I've put down. So, this love test? No problem. But it's afterward that worries me. What if he won't let us make the supply run?"

"Bart says it's a shit job," said Keats. "Marco needs volunteers for it."

"What about Katie and Duck?"

"We need to talk to them," said Tommy. "See what they think about what Bart said."

"I think Katie's love is pure," said Hemingway.

"We owe it to her to find out for sure," said Keats, "but I think you're right. She'll probably be staying."

"The best way," said Hemingway," would be to do some counter surveillance, cut a guard's throat, and rip through the fence. But we'll try your way first."

***

Behind the townhome, Jamie sat in a swing set. It squeaked lightly as she slumped forward and wrote in a notebook on her lap.

Keats took the swing next to her. "What are you writing?"

She didn't respond right away, which made Keats feel more like an annoying parent than a rebel leader in a post-apocalyptic zombie stronghold. He regretted invading her privacy, but he needed to let her know about their plans.

"Diary?" he guessed.

"God, no," she said. "Like it or not, I won't ever need help remembering this place. It's fiction. I've had ideas in my head for as long as I can remember."

"And now you've finally got time to write them down."

She shrugged. "We could get eaten tomorrow. I wanted to leave something in case things ever get back to normal."

Keats realized that she'd grown a few inches taller since he rescued her a month ago. Her jeans now stopped above her ankle, so he made a note to rummage through the upstairs rooms for some clothes.

"Can I read some?" he said.

He expected her to decline, but she was eager to share it. The opening scene featured a police officer driving his car underwater.

"It's good," he said, "but you know they couldn't do that, right?"

"Really?"

"But it's a story, so you can make it do what you want."

"I want it to be realistic, though," she said, suddenly angry. "There was this idiot at the shelter where I was raised. I knew he was full of shit."

Keats watched her scribble some angry notes about her story. "You know we have to leave here," he said.

"No kidding. I don't want to get passed around like a toy, and I don't want to worship that freak."

"Can you pretend to, though?"

She looked down and kicked the dirt as she swung over it. "Are you going to make me hang out with him?"

Keats hesitated. "Not by yourself," he said. "But if you can manage to hide your disgust a little bit..."

She jumped off the swing and held her hand out impatiently. Keats realized she wanted her notebook, so he gave it to her, then she stormed off.

Great, thought Keats. I'm just like a parent, only with less authority.

***

It was going to be Pike's job to talk to Katie and Duck and see if they could be saved from the savior.

She had her doubts about Katie, who looked eager to peel her jeans off for Marco already. But Duck's case was tougher. He was intelligent, but he didn't turn away from the horror inflicted upon Flak in the church. Should she write them both off as lost causes, or did she have a moral obligation to tell them what Bart had revealed about the town's leader?

For now, she was going to train. She stood in the yard, no birds in the trees as the cool wind portended a change in weather. The clouds looked sick and congested as she snapped her spearhead from her sleeve into her palm while at the same time slipping a wooden pole from a sling on her back.

In less than a second, she'd attached the spearhead to the pole. She swung, jabbed, and slashed her spear at invisible enemies around her. She backflipped onto a low-slung tree branch. Improvising her routine, she believed, was key to staying sharp.

But sharp she wasn't. She slipped and fell to the ground. She was lying on top of her spear when she heard the crunching of leaves as something moved through the brush. She tried to spring to her feet, but it was too late. A large silhouette appeared above her.

It was Cochise, his bald head slick with early rain, his smile a showcase of ruinous teeth. "Those are some moves you got," he said. "You do more than just fight?"

***

When he saw the walker, Hemingway got scared.

Of course, he'd seen and killed plenty of them, but he took his body armor for granted. Now, dressed only in jeans and tee shirt, he thought about how it only took a small scratch to become infected.

The walker itself unsettled him as well. It was Flak.

Dried blood matted his golden hair to one side of his head. His ravenous eyes glimmered with what looked like tears. If there were such a thing as a soul, it still clung to him, mournful and furious.

"You can see his sadness, can't you?" said Marco. "I tried hard to love this man." He gestured for Flak's handlers to position him into the fighting ring.

"He refused my love. But you, Hemingway, have not. I can see it."

Hemingway thought about mimicking the starry gaze Marco's followers had. He decided he'd be more believable if he maintained his stoic expression and simply nodded.

"And I have no doubt you could pass the love test," said Marco. "You're a big, powerful man, and I heard about your exploits outside of town."

There was a commotion in the crowd. Guards hustled Keats from the pews to the front of the pulpit. They stripped his shirt off. Underneath it was a boney chest and a nearly concave stomach.

"What the hell is this?" said Hemingway.

"A love test should be just that," said Marco, "a test. You'd mince the former Mr. Flak here in a split second. But your leader here, why, he's not much more than a bag of bones. Skinny before the outbreak and positively skeletal since then, right? But love can provide all the strength he will need."

There was more shouting from the crowd. Marco's tone turned brittle as he continued speaking.

"For others among us, however, there need not be a test, but a penance. It saddens and enrages me to report that we have a piece of filth traitor in our flock."

Two guards brought Bart forward and held her right outside the fighting pen. Flak was practically running in place against his constraints.

"She didn't do anything," said Keats.

A new voice from the crowd rose up. "You don't have to lie." It was Tommy.

"She planted that seed of doubt," he said. "Lied to us about Marco. Tried to use us so she could escape. To what? She's so blind with hatred that she doesn't even have a plan. Just keep running and running—"

"You rat piece of shit," said Hemingway as he lunged at Tommy. A guard hit him with a rifle butt and pointed it at him until he stood down.

"You're a good man but too weak to lead," Tommy said to Keats. "But Marco understands. He likes you. Loves you. You'll pass this love test, and everything will be OK."

"And before the test," said Marco, "comes the penance. Bart's last moments shall be spent being devoured by Flak here. We'll tie her up just in case she has more fight in her than it looks. After that, you should be able to pass the test with no problem. Walkers don't have the same, ah, bite to them when they've had a meal. Excuse the pun."

He signaled to the guards, who tried to tie Bart's hands together but were having problems. She headbutted one of them in the nose, sending a stream of blood shooting across the floor. Flak reached towards it in hunger.

Two more of Marco's men jumped in and grabbed Bart's legs. As she kicked and screamed, Pike maneuvered from the pews to the aisle. Others in the church looked at her in curiosity. She stretched up like she was about to exercise, then grabbed something from under her seat. It was her spear. She hurled it into the neck of one of the guards.

Someone raised a rifle at her. "You're fucking dead!" he said, but he stood dumbfounded as Pike unveiled a dagger and flung it into his eye. Everyone else froze. Even Marco had no words.

Several other people raised their rifles and looked at their leader for answers. People in the back of the church ran towards the exits. Someone with a machete swung it at Hemingway, who grabbed his wrist and flung him into the fighting ring.

Flak's handlers couldn't hold him any longer. He broke free from his constraints and fell upon the machete-wielder, who shrieked in agony.

Chaos broke out. Keats grabbed Pike by the arm as she moved about the scrum, bashing Marco's men in their heads and dodging their counterattacks. "What the hell is this?" he said.

"No bullets," she said. "Their guns don't work."

Someone slashed Hemingway's arm with a bayonet. Hemingway lunged at him but missed. When he turned around, Cochise had shoved his finger so far up the man's nasal cavity that he pierced his brain.

"You gotta work on your quickness," said Cochise, smiling.

"What the fuck," said Hemingway.

Pike yelled out, "He's with us."

There were more screams from the back of the church as people surged back inside. They began to barricade the doors, even as more townspeople beat on them desperately to be let back in.

"Walkers!" said an older man with blood streaming down his face. "About twenty of them right outside the church!"

Marco's men stopped fighting and circled around their leader, who had retreated to the pulpit. Some of the townspeople ran towards the basement door for safety, but when they opened it, two walkers, both former residents who had failed the love test, burst out and attacked them.

Keats, Pike, Cochise, Hemingway, and Jamie hastily gathered by a wall. "Who else is with us?" said Hemingway.

"Duck's outside," said Pike. "He's the one who cut the fence, but he was supposed to warn us if walkers came through."

Keats stuttered in anger. "This wasn't how it was supposed to happen."

"Will you look at these people?" said Hemingway. Although many of the townspeople panicked, there were several, Katie among them, who kept a cool demeanor as they piled chairs on the doors and gathered weapons. Others, their faces glowing with religious ecstasy, put down the walkers inside the church.

Keats looked towards the pulpit and caught Tommy's eye. Tommy raised a shaking finger at him and shouted, "You! You infected this church with hate!"

Marco emerged from behind him and lifted his revolver. The information Cochise gave to Pike wasn't entirely correct; there was still one gun left in the compound that was loaded.

Marco fired at Keats. Jamie pushed him out of the way and grunted as the bullet pierced the flesh between her neck and shoulder.

"Jesus!" said Pike as she grabbed the girl and pressed her hand on the wound. Marco aimed for a second shot but was pushed by his own men towards the basement, which had finally been cleared of walkers.

Hemingway gathered the unconscious Jamie in his arms. Pike climbed a pew and smashed a window. Jagged plates of stained glass crashed to the floor around them.

Cochise was the first over the wall. He helped everyone else down just as a group of five walkers noticed them.

Hemingway charged and clotheslined them into a pile, allowing Pike to guide everyone down the street towards their escape. Before they could turn the corner, she heard a bullet rush by her head.

Marco had escaped through the outside basement door. "God's vengeance is firm and cruel!" he yelled as he fired again.

Keats and the others ran, crouching, down another street and through several yards to the place where Pike had arranged for Duck to cut a hole in the fence. Next to it was a pile of red bones and torn clothes. Keats recognized the shirt; it was Duck's.

"Goddammit," said Pike. "They surprised him. How did they know to enter here?"

"We'll have to worry about it later," said Hemingway.

He was right. A newly dead walker burst from the trees and nearly clawed into Keats. Pike went to grab a weapon from a bag stashed nearby, but the walker was on the attack again.

As it struck towards Hemingway, who still had Jamie in his arms, the same Rottweiler Keats encountered earlier sprung out and pulled the walker to the ground. Pike then drove a hammer into its brain.

Bart whistled, and her dog bounded towards her, tongue wagging. "My ace in the hole," she said. "Don't worry, he's a sweetie."

On the other side of the fence, Pike bound the hole closed with wire.

"We don't have time for that," Hemingway said.

"There are innocent people here," she said.

"It's not a matter of—" Cochise cut him off by grabbing his shoulder. Hemingway almost headbutted him before he saw that he wanted him to lower Jamie to the ground.

Marco's former top lieutenant looked at Jamie's neck. "There's an exit wound," he said. "We'll need a way to disinfect it, but she's ok for now."

"So, you're a doctor now?" said Hemingway.

"Nurse, actually. Thanks for asking."

The group moved further from the fence. People shouted, and walkers snarled, but no one ever appeared.

"What now?" Keats said, covered in a sheen of sweat, still shirtless from the battle at the church.

"We're headed east from here," said Pike. "There's a county road about half an hour away. We can start a fire there and cauterize Jamie's wound."

Keats stared at the ground and said, "Thanks."

Jamie groaned. Hemingway relaxed some of the pressure he'd applied to her neck.

"We better get moving," said Cochise.

Bart's dog pointed his ears back and growled. Pike grabbed her hammer and looked towards the fence, but the Rottweiler faced the other direction.

"Cute dog," said a voice.

Before anyone in the group could do anything, three men with handguns were upon them. They didn't look like anyone Keats had seen in the compound.

The man in the middle lowered his weapon. He was handsome, like a soap opera villain, with dark curly hair and a long scar on his cheek.

"What do you think, Roth?" said one of the others.

"I think we flushed out some folks who doubt their faith," said Roth. "Apostates."

"Wait," said Pike. "You sent walkers in there?"

"Amazing what a few sharks can do in a pool full of minnows."

"You got our friend killed."

"You're one to talk. Ask that sicko leader of yours what he's done with our people."

"He's not our leader," said Keats. "I am. We're trying to get the hell out of here. Please, do you have a camp? Do you have alcohol, anything for wounds? She's not bit."

Roth looked at Jamie for a moment. "Let's go," he said. "And shut that dog up."

Within the compound, the sounds of chaos began to silence.

69

3 THE SKELETON PEOPLE BY MATTHIEU CARTRON

It doesn't rain much in New Mexico, but for the first time in a long while, I feel cold, heavy droplets against my arms, and then on top of my head, trickling down my long tangled hair and onto my face. As thunder echoes across the desert sky, I can feel the rain wash away the dirt, blood, and sweat that has clung to my battered body. From the back of a pickup in front of the Walmart, I have a clear view of I-40, but there are no cars that pass by, and no people on foot either.

I hop off the back of the pickup and turn around, facing the highway. My nose bleeds from the dryness, and my hands crack like the parched earth around me. The store is like any superstore, huge, but I can't stay in it for too long before feeling like I might be trapped in there forever. I think about heading out west to California. But if I make it that far, what will I find? I'll run into more of them—that goes without saying. But what about those unaffected like me? By then maybe we'll all be gone—maybe we already are. If only there were a safe zone somewhere. . . .

"Safe zone," I scoff, shaking my head. I haven't been able to pick up any kind of signal from anywhere. Just static on the TVs and radios inside. In the movies, there's always some safe haven to get to when the world ends, a safe place with people who aren't too far away from finding a solution or something close to one. But that's in the movies. I spit on the ground, letting the droplets of rain dissolve and tear away at the sizzling white bubbles.

I hear a gentle whooshing sound. I look up to where it's coming from, squinting. At this point, I can hardly trust my senses anymore, and I wonder if the events of the last few days have maybe sharpened them, or have instead made me go numb. No. I see it. A small speck at first and then quickly something I can recognize.

A navy-blue car, approaching fast, and behind the wheel, a man with little time left.

***

The paper-thin walls and the restlessness of my roommates made it always far more difficult to study than it should have been. Instead, I'd go to Dane Smith Hall, a three-story building on the northwest side of Main Campus, sometimes between classes and sometimes at night. People would ask me why I'd go all the way over there to study when there were so many better, closer options like the Zimmerman Library. And that's the thing. The "better" options were the ones with people, the very thing I was trying to avoid.

In the first few seconds of waking up, it's hard to make sense of anything—it's like your brain has to warm up, and if it doesn't, it might just unravel into stringy, purplish brown threads. I feel the coldness of the syrupy floor first, peeling away my tanned face as I draw my head up to look around, my eyes still groggy from what must have been a long nap. I sit up on my knees and rub my eyes. I can see that the hallways and stairs are empty, which is strange. It doesn't matter if students are in class or not; there are always some people around, maybe studying or waiting for their next class. I pull my phone out of my pocket and check the time: 9:20 a.m. I must have come here to study last night and fallen asleep instead. "Typical," I mutter. And to add to that, my phone is only minutes away from dying.

I drag myself onto my feet and bumble to the nearest classroom. If the halls are empty then there have to be people in the classrooms—maybe there's been a lockdown? But when I peer through the small, rectangular window in the door, I see nothing. Just empty chairs and an erased chalkboard.

"Shit," I mutter.

I check the next classroom. Same result. Then the next one, and the one after that. Every classroom on the second floor empty. It's Wednesday, I remember. I check my phone again just to be sure, hoping I'm wrong and that I've just lost my bearings, but no—the little white letters on the home screen agree.

I head down the steps to the first floor and check those classrooms as well. Nothing again, and my heart is now beating a little faster.

There are several entry points into Dane Smith, some of which I probably don't even know about. Most people use the doors on the south side, which open up to a concrete sitting area with several gum-ridden benches and cigarette-stained tables. I'm nearly at one of the two entrances on the south side when I realize that I forgot my light jacket—the blue one I always carry with me—on the second floor. I race back up the stairs and return to the place where I'd fallen asleep.

My jacket is on the floor a few feet from the window. I pick it up and flap it against my knee to shake it out, and out of the corner of one eye, I see it, through the smudged window, just on the other side of campus.

A wide column of smoke. I can see the chemical gray and black rising into the somber sky, but I can't see what's burning, except that I know my dorm is in that direction, and maybe just about that far away. I pull out my phone again—god, it needs to be replaced, the screen is cracked in so many places, and the volume buttons haven't worked for who knows how long. It's my fault too. Every time you drop something like that, you care a little less about the next time it hits the ground.

I'm not connected to the internet, and when I try to connect, my phone says it can't find the UNM Wi-Fi address—or any address, for that matter. And no service, not even the one bar you get sometimes in the middle of nowhere.

I turn my gaze back down to the window. It seems that the more I look around, the more questions I have, and nothing is making any sort of sense. Just over the grassy hill that separates the dull, concrete patio from the street, I see the figure of a man, contorted and prostrate in the grass, his head concealed beneath one of the bushes. There are homeless people around campus, but they don't sleep like that. No one does.

"What the hell?" I whisper.

I run down the stairs, this time with my things, to the south entrance. I open the front door and prop it open with my bag; I don't know if I might need to go back inside, and I'm not sure if I'm locked from the outside. Carefully, I walk across the patio toward the stricken figure in the grass. He's well concealed from the front doors—invisible, even—which is probably why I missed him when I first came down.

He can't be much older than I am, and he's short, and his ankles are turned unnaturally inward. He's shaking, ever so slightly. As I approach the man, I can hear him whimpering, or maybe panting, soft but harsh at the same time. I can't see much of his face, but the skin on his neck and arms is wet from the sweat pumping from his bubbling pores. Once I'm standing over him, I crouch to the ground and ever so delicately place a hand on the back of his head. I want to recoil when I feel the warm, clammy moisture, but I force myself to hold still, hoping to stir a reaction so that I might be able to help him.

A few seconds go by. And when I grab his shoulder to try and turn him onto his back, his head swivels around, cracking like a snapped branch, and the soft whimper turns into a vicious, inhuman snarl. I jump back, horrified by the sight of the ghastly creature. The man's face is discolored, and his eyes are bloodshot, the skin on his sickening face half-peeled away and his teeth sharp and rotting. Desperate, I take off back in the direction of the door, not daring to look back at the crazed, grotesque human. I grab my things and quickly shut the door inside Dane Smith, and as I do, I feel the impact of the man slam again the steel frame. The creature is astonishingly quick, and his limbs move with the frenzy of a flailing insect. He's looking at me, through the glass, and although his pupils seem to twitch in a panicked fear, I know right away what his intentions are.

I sprint back up the stairs to the window on the second floor. I know that from there I can watch the creature, and if need be dart into the classroom that lies only a few feet away. The creature continues to pant by the door, looking at the place where I stared back. I begin to collect my thoughts, but I don't dare leave the window—what if I were to lose sight of that thing? Then what? I think of my family and our home in El Paso. But then I close my eyes. No, I say to myself, I can't let my thoughts wander in that direction. It would be foolish of me to think that what I've just seen might be more widespread.

I stay in front of the window for what seems like hours. The creature is now ambling around the patio, although I know he's just waiting for me to come back out. When I look at the creature now, I can't help but think of vampires or zombies or those fake monsters you'll see at the costume stores with the cheap masks and unsightly fake teeth. Monsters you're supposed to be afraid of when you're small and laugh at when you're grown up. Funny how things are scarier when they're right in front of you.

I can still smell the plastic smoke from the fire in the not-so-far-off distance, but the dark fumes have cleared some, and I'm almost positive now it's the dorms that are burning. And still no sign of a firetruck, or a police car for that matter.

As I look back down at the concrete patio, a cottontail scampers out from the grassy area where the creature had been lying down and then pauses to sniff around, and for a moment the creature takes no notice. Then, as the rabbit begins to saunter east of the building, the creature throws its head to the side and utters a gurgled, choking sound, and launches itself in the direction of the rabbit. Before the cottontail can reach the cover of an overstuffed trash can, the creature has it in its jaws. As I watch in horror, I can see through the gaping holes in the creature's cheeks the rabbit get torn apart, crushed, and swallowed. I shudder and turn away, remembering how close the creature came to catching me.

When I summon up enough courage to look back again at the creature, I hear more echoed chokes and gurgles, and see that two more of them—also wearing tattered clothes—are stumbling down the hill to the south side of the building. When they reach the creature at the bottom, they begin to shuffle around, their heads rolling back like their eyes.

They must be able to see, I say to myself, but what about hearing? Did the other two hear the rabbit get caught and eaten? I cock my head to the side and purse my lips together. I can't stay here. And I might die if I leave. I decide to move to a window on the opposite side of the second floor, one with a view of Las Lomas Road, a street that cuts across the northwestern part of campus.

The street has several cars parked alongside it, and I see no movement—at least, not yet, and I can't quite see Buena Vista Drive from here.

My Papá showed me a while back how to hotwire a car. He had never stolen one in his life, but he grew up with plenty of people who had. I'd asked him jokingly if he was trying to nudge me on a certain career path, and after he'd laughed, he quickly became serious, and then with that Chicano accent told me that if I found myself in trouble one day, it might save my life. I doubted it. Fuck, I thought he might've been crazy.

"Might come in handy for the apocalypse, right, Papá?" I mutter to myself. Then, in the butchered voice of my Papá, I come back with "Sí mijo, and you wi' remember me when it happens."

I was beginning to doubt I would hear from them again, my family. I felt as though I should've been more upset. You're never really sad, though, unless you witness pain in some way yourself. Maybe you see it, or somebody you trust tells you, but unless you've seen it first hand, the heart will always cling on to hope, even if the brain doesn't.

There's a gray Subaru parked in the parking lot of Sigma Chi—one of those school fraternities, and in my opinion the place you go to sell your health for "friends"—and although I'm not certain of the year, I figure it's my best bet. Trouble is getting there without causing too much attention.

With my things, I hurry down the stairs to the exit on the north side of Dane Smith. I know that once it's been shut behind me, I'll be locked out of the building—and that I'll be no different from the cottontail.

My right arm quivers as I inch the door open, and I'm ready to close it at a moment's notice. The horrid gurgling noises never come, though, and instead I hear the gentle coo of a white-wing dove come from an aspen only a few feet away.

When I was growing up, we had an enormous tree in the front yard, a mulberry, and the doves—mourning doves usually—would use it to build nests and raise their young. The doves might've been good parents, but they were lousy builders; their fragile and crudely constructed nests meant that their offspring would often fall to the ground before they could fly. Papá and Mamá would let me hold the birds, and then Papá would lift me up and let me place them back safely on one of the low branches of the tree. No, they wouldn't be back in the nest, but maybe that was better. The parents would still feed them, and even on a lower branch, they were usually safe from the neighborhood cats.

I step through the door and guide it as it closes, careful to make little noise. The street is still empty, and the brutal rays of the afternoon sun beat down on the pavement. My stomach growls and scratches against my insides, and I feel that each hollow roar might bring the creatures to the street, and this time maybe a horde of them. That couldn't be impossible, could it? If that's what has happened to everyone. I still couldn't bring myself to believe something like that.

As I'm edging my way to the Subaru, I'm hoping that it might be unlocked, or that one of the windows might be rolled down enough for me to fit my hand through and unlock it. In the Sigma Chi lot I don't see any other old cars, and to start the engine on those, I'd have to do a whole lot more than strike a couple of wires together. With all the additional security in place—most of which is digital—I doubt most car thieves even know how to hotwire anymore anyway.

I test the doors—locked, all of them, and the windows are rolled up. I crouch alongside the car and glance around, assessing my options. I could break into it, which would make a lot of noise, or I could go look for another one— along the side streets near Central or University, or maybe somewhere else around campus. I could also try and get into another building, but who knows what might be lurking inside, and Dane Smith is probably the best option in the immediate area anyway, considering the lookout points on the second and third floors.

The Sigma Chi lot is unpaved, full of ordinary rocks about the size of my palms. I pick up the nearest rock and weigh it in my hand, sizing it up, and then look inside the car underneath the steering wheel. I know I can get this one started in maybe ninety seconds, a minute if I'm lucky. Smashing the car window, though? That would wake up the whole fucking neighborhood.

I don't have much of a choice. And once I'm in the front seat with the door closed they can't get me—at least, that's what I'm hoping.

I stretch my arm back, ready to slam the rock into the window, and just as I'm about to throw my arm forward, I hear the grinding lurch of tires against the pavement. A black truck nearly flips over as it swings onto Las Lomas, and it's speeding in my direction, picking up as much momentum as it can.

And following the truck, only a few yards behind, is a flurry of limbs flailing around, propelling a mob of people. But those aren't people. I recognize the way they are moving, and then in my mind, I see the face of the diseased man, the creature, our noses a few inches apart and separated by the thick glass of the doors.

My arm comes crashing down onto the window, and the thump of the impact is followed by hundreds of shrill, delicate clinks of glass hitting the sandy concrete. The glass has only cut me slightly in a few places on my right arm, but I ignore the bright red lines and immediately search for the lock on the door. When I find it and slide the locking bolt up, I jump back, and my entire body coils and constricts. The car alarm has gone off.

And in the seconds that follow, the neighborhood comes alive.

Amid the deafening, honking of the alarm, I hear the wails and uncouth moans of the creatures, and there are many of them, coming from all directions. I look back at the pickup that's barreling my way. It's only a few seconds from me now, but I still can't see the driver through the tinted windows. As the truck is about to pass me, it screeches to a halt, and with the side window already rolled down, the man in the front seat gestures frantically for me to get in. I glance behind the truck and see that the creatures are close behind, but from the corners of Dane Smith, I see more coming, some crawling, other leaping and wobbling in our direction. I sprint to the truck, and before I reach it, the driver shoves the door open.

"Now!" he yells, glancing back through the rear windshield.

I land on my knees in the front seat, and as I'm attempting to slam the car door shut, a sinewy, blistered hand wedges itself between the car and the door. The force of the door nearly takes the hand off, but the driver hardly waits for that to happen before flooring the gas pedal. He takes one look at the hand and yells at me.

"Fucking close it!"

I open the door again, and as I do, I trace the maimed hand to a long, female creature. Her head is strained backward, and a nasal, sibilant scream echoes from her bright red throat, and she's desperately hanging onto the side of the truck. I see other creatures wriggling alongside her, ignoring her cries of agony and instead focusing on finding a way to us.

Avoiding the savage and desperate glare of the female creature, I slam the door again, this time taking her hand clean off. The blood sprays onto my arm, and I see her body, along with her severed hand, fall back into the flurry of arms and legs, tripping a few of the creatures as it flies behind the truck. Panting, I turn around and look through the rear windshield. Some of the creatures have managed to pile onto the bed of the truck, and with their long, ingrown fingernails are now scraping at the rear windshield, knocking each other off the truck as they struggle to find a way inside.

At the end of Las Lomas, we take a sharp turn onto University Boulevard, throwing most of the creatures still on the truck onto the curb. The driver allows a brief look in his rearview mirror and curses under his breath, but he is calm, as if this weren't the first time something like this has happened. The street is mostly empty, with only the occasional car parked alongside the curb. I see a Nissan Ultima lodged a few feet off the ground into a stucco wall that separates two home properties adjacent to the street, and then I look into the distance, searching for signs of normalcy. Has the whole city been affected by this?

"There are only a couple of them behind us now."

"What?" I answer. The sound of the man's voice slaps me in the face as if I hadn't heard a human voice in some time.

"The zombies," he says. "Only a few of those fuckers on our trail now. More will come after us as we get to I-40, but more of 'em will also fall behind."

"I-40?" I ask.

"Getting out of the city," he says. "Going west."

I want to ask him what's going on, but I don't. I've never been in shock before, and maybe I'm not right now, but it doesn't matter. I feel frozen all over, overwhelmed. I fold my arms across my lap and take deep breaths, swaying back and forth, and I feel lightheaded—as if I were tight-roping across the edge of consciousness.

***

"Mijo, what did he do to you?" Papá says with both of his hands on my shoulders. He's squatting so that he's eye level with me, and with his gentle, calloused thumbs is wiping away the tears from my cheeks.

"He kicked me," I say. "Hard."

"Mamá is already on the phone with the school," he says. "But I ha' no heard the story."

"I told you, he kicked me!" I cry, a fresh set of sobs echoing across the small kitchen.

"I'm sorry, mijo," he says as he draws me into his arms. "Do you know why he kicked you? The boy. Why would he do that?"

I snivel. "He calls me know-it-all. And says that no one likes me."

"In school, when you're youn', you're with all kinds of kids. As you ge' older, the bullies start to go away. They don' make it. You wi' meet people you like, people like you, and you wi' be successful. Mijo, the popular bullies who are liked when you're youn' age are no' liked when they're grown up."

"But I can't wait that long!" I cry.

"We will look to see if we can fin' you another class," he says.

I nod and try my best to smile.

"Papá?" I ask.

"Yes, mijo."

"Were you bullied?"

My papá gets up and sighs, smiling down at me.

"I was. And look now. America and two sons. I am thankful to those kids for telling me who I wasn't."

***

"You're fine," the driver says to me, pulling me back to reality. "There's some water on the back seat if you're thirsty."

I expect more from him, a reaction similar to mine maybe. But he seems more impatient and angry than shocked, as if this were just an inconvenience.

I look at him, forgetting to blink. I don't really register what he says, but my body does, and I feel myself turn to the back seat. There, I see boxes of water bottles and food—mostly granola bars and trail mix—and sprawled across the back is a large black bag. As I reach for one of the water bottles in the plastic casing, the bag moves.

I jump back in my seat and withdraw my right arm like I just touched boiling water. From the bag comes a soft groan, and the movement of the bag sends some of the food tumbling onto the floor.

"Hold the wheel for a sec," the man says, looking over at me. I stare back dumbly, then place both hands across the top of the steering wheel. My arms are shaking, and I grit my teeth together as I try to follow the road. I can't see what the man is doing, but at the sound of another groan— this time one of pain—my grip loosens, and I look back at the man—and my eyes widen when I see the empty syringe and the long needle extending down from it. The car nearly veers onto the curb before the man catches the wheel and pulls us back onto the road.

"You have to calm the fuck down, okay?" he snaps.

"I'm sorry," I say, turning away. After a few seconds of silence, I turn back to the man.

"What is it for, the needle?" I say.

"Sedative," he says.

"She's a woman, isn't she?" I ask him.

"Yeah, picked her up like you," he says. "She wasn't crazed like the others."

"Then why did she need the sedative?" I ask.

"She handed me a couple," the man shrugs. "Said she needed them for shock or something like that. Said she would die otherwise."

I nod and face the road again. I'm not sure whether to believe the man. Or even trust him. But my thoughts continue to return to the creatures, their squalid, foul faces etched in my mind. I shudder convulsively in my seat, trying to think of something else.

We go another mile or so before turning onto the freeway. Again, few cars and none of them are moving. I see the occasional creature sprint after us, but the truck is too fast.

As we merge onto the freeway, I speak again.

"You called them zombies earlier," I say.

The man continues to stare forward. The polarized glasses hide his eyes and his red beard makes him look older than he probably is. Mid-twenties, I'd guess. Maybe he's also at UNM.

"What do they look like to you?" he asks.

"I don't know," I say. "Guess that'd be one way to call them. Makes it seem unreal, though, don't you think?"

The man shrugs and adjusts the mirror a little. I notice for the first time that he has a Glock pistol holstered along his waist.

"The creatures, they're humans, right?" I ask. "I mean, they were and then … I didn't see it happen, whatever it was."

"Good," he says.

"Did you?" I ask.

"Look I'm not … " He pauses for a moment and then bites his lip.

"What's your name?" he asks. For a moment I want to ask him to answer my question first, but I know he must not want to talk about it. I know that feeling. Better than most.

"Lorenzo," I say.

"Rolling your r's I see," he chuckles. "Speak Spanish?"

"I understand it," I say. I knew a little, but not all that much. My parents didn't speak it with me when I was small—only here and there—although they would to each other. They figured it would make me like them, foreign. Some immigrant parents are like that.

"I see. Got a last name, Lorenzo?" He rolls the "r" in my name the best he can, but it comes out sounding more like a squashed W.

I chuckle. "Medina. You?"

"You can just call me Jay. Started telling people to call me that a while back."

I nod and look back out the window. A few minutes later we drive over the Rio Grande River, passing onto the West Side. Looking down at the city from the "Foothills" or even farther up the Sandia Mountains, it isn't hard to spot where the river meanders through the city. The green belt of cottonwoods cuts through like a throbbing vein, and in the distance, you can see the exhausted corpses of the Three Sisters—a group of ancient, dormant volcanos out past Volcano Vista High School. The city is the strangest combination of poverty and southwestern beauty, and I can never decide whether I like it or hate it.

My eyes eventually tire from staring out the window, and after an hour or so, a sudden jolt wakes me up.

"We hit one this time, take a look," Jay says, pointing at the windshield.

I rub my eyes. The windshield wipers are on, and on them are bits of torn flesh mixed with rotten tissue and pus. The dark blood covers the windshield like a film, and through the lens, the desert appears a crimson red. My head starts to spin again, and the muscles in my body constrict and twist like a gnarled, ingrown tree. I faint in my seat, and the darkness takes me again.

***

"You finish your plate, mijo," Papá says from the wooden chair next to me. "There would be days before I was born, that tío Ernesto would no' even ge' the chance to eat. You are lucky. People would see him and call him "el niño esqueleto." Do you wan' to have a name like that?

"Esqueleto, what does that mean?" I ask.

"I wi' tell you after you are finished."

I take a few more uncomfortable bites and then point at my empty plate.

"Skeleton," he says. "The little skeleton boy. Skinny arms an' skinny legs. You then ge' afraid of what people think when you look like that, and then your eyes, they fall back into your eye-holes to try an' hide. The dead must stay dead, and we should no' confuse the living and the dead. Do you wan' me to call the people at the graveyard to com' an' ge' you?

I shake my head furiously. My papá is a strong man who works hard. He is a living man.

"Tomorrow, you make this easier for me an' Mamá," he says. "You eat? Okay?"

The eight-year-old me nods.

****

I awaken to Jay's hand on my shoulder, pushing my body back and forth. It's still dark, and the insides of the creature are mostly gone from the windshield, but some of the grumous blood has dried.

"What time is it?" I ask. I hear a faint whimper from the back seat.

"Evening, sixish," he says. "But you should probably get out of the truck at the next stop. Maybe in like a couple of minutes or so."

"How far are we from Gallup?" I ask. "Should be easy to find something there."

Jay doesn't answer. The cords in his neck are rigid, and I can see that his arms are shaking as he holds the steering wheel.

"Jay? I ask.

He remains mute for another moment, and then, through the coagulated, crimson windshield, I can see several lights off to the side of the road. The whimpering in the back grows louder. Like a panting. A soft, harsh panting.

"Here's good," he says, sounding more stressed than before.

Jay pulls off the road to the lights, which belong to a Seven-Eleven. The sign is flickering, and there are only a couple of cars parked out front.

"There will be more cars in Gallup, Jay. It really isn't that much—"

Jay pulls the Glock from his belt and points it right at my face.

"Get the fuck out of my car. You keep riding with me, you're dead."

The woman in the back seat begins to lurch wildly in the bag, and my eyes widen when I hear the tortured screech coming from it.

"Thought I could get that far, but I'm out of the sedatives. Just go!"

"You've got the gun, Jay, use it!" I yell as I walk backward in the direction of the gas station.

Jay shakes his head, then suddenly hops out of the truck and runs toward me. When he reaches me, he puts his fist in my hand and drops two small objects in it, then cups his hand around mine, closing it.

"Bury these for me if you get the chance …" His voice trails off. He glances up at me, and I can see the strain in his eyes, the blood vessels crisscrossing like lightning, wishing me luck, even if he knows that I won't find it. He then races back to the truck. I hear the sharp jangle of keys as he starts the engine, and the rumble of the motor soothes the fragile silence. And then, he's gone, up the road and fading into the dry, juniper-scented night.

Jay gave me no choice, and now, unless I can find a way to start one of the cars at the Seven-Eleven, I'll have to walk. A little voice pipes up in my mind. *Or you could just cozy up inside this gas station and eat all the shit inside to comfort you. You would like that, wouldn't you? Nobody to bug you. A wide-open desert around. You didn't like people and look what you have now. A fucking miracle of a way to die, don't you think?*

"FUCK!" I scream. I don't care about the noise I make. A part of me wants them to come crawling and charging through the weeds and elms around the station. I expect them to come, but then I realize that unless they're in the station, there's no place to come from.

And they don't.

***

I almost forget what Jay gave me, and it explains everything and makes it that much worse at the same time.

He gave me a pair of rings.

He'd known, the whole time, that she was turned. Maybe he knows how it happened, the beginning of it. He'd held onto her, his wife, maybe hoping it'd get better. And maybe it would eventually pass, like the flu or a cold—except that now—now he wouldn't be alive to have that chance.

One of the cars parked in front of the Seven-Eleven is dead, and the other is too new for me to start. And no keys. It's after midnight now. The clock inside the gas station is still working, and from outside the building, I can hear the ticking. Tick. Tick. Tick. Just like the classroom clocks in middle school and high school. The things were so hard to change that sometimes they were more than a few hours off and changing them wasn't exactly in the State's budget.

I grimace—I know what my only option is.

Jay's truck would be far by now—only if he'd brought himself to use the Glock.

Otherwise, I'd probably find him up the road somewhere.

Before I decide to hike through the darkness, I grab some water and devour whatever seems easiest to open. I haven't eaten all day, and when I remind myself of the food inside the store, my stomach nearly rears itself up and out my throat. The inside of the station is empty of creatures, but I already knew that walking in. If anything had been inside it would have heard me yelling outside. I check behind the counter just in case, but I see nothing except a fallen mop and a few starburst wrappers. I bring my hands together into the shape of a gun and point it at the invisible man behind the counter.

"Manos arriba," I whispered, remembering the costume of the bandido I had when I was seven. Papá had told me to say that to the people at the doors on Halloween. The ones who knew what I was saying got a kick out of it. Some even gave me extra candy.

I walk a mile down the road, and still no sign of Jay. The desert moon lets me see some, but if the truck had gone off the road, I doubt I would be able to see it, even if the bushes and junipers are small.

And what if I don't find the truck? Then what?

Maybe it's best that I don't. I'd forgotten that if I did find the truck, I'd also probably find Jay's wife, and I have nothing on me to defend myself with. I can't believe I didn't realize what was really going on with the sedatives and the large, black bag. And Jay. He knew what was going to happen, and he didn't tell me. I want to be angry with him, want to tell him that he'd be alive if he'd just shot her. But his wife. I shudder at the thought.

I walk by an abandoned car after going another mile, but the front and inside of it are burned. I wonder if some of the people driving out there on the open highway were untouched by what happened and if they too have gone west. There is no logical reason for it, but without a goal, even one that doesn't make much sense, then what's the point of continuing, of trying to escape this nightmare?

After walking another mile, and rounding a small plateau, I stumble upon a pair of headlights, dim and red. I'm exhausted, on the verge of sitting down off to the side of the road and calling it a night, but the lights inject my body with a fresh boost of energy. By now I'd given up on Jay still being around, but when I get closer to the lights, thinking that they might belong to a different vehicle, my heart nearly bursts out of my chest, and I duck to the ground.

It's Jay's truck. And the engine is on, humming in tune with the even breeze and the rustle of desert grass. And there's no sign of Jay or his wife—and if she's there, I would have heard her. But where's Jay?

I cross the road and tiptoe over the dirt, stepping only onto the bare patches of ground to drown the sound of my steps. Even in the cool air, I'm sweating, each muscle in my neck rigid and my shoulders taut. And then, when I'm only a few feet from the side door of the truck, I hear it—a gentle, heaving whimper coming from the other side.

My first thought is to run. Maybe back to the gas station or farther down the road. But something about the noise isn't quite the same. Less harsh. More human. I decide to continue, and when I reach the truck, I open the driver's side door and clamber into the front seat.

I see nothing. Maybe the creatures are less active once they've eaten after they've satiated their urge to hunt—to kill. A cold shiver undulates through my body, and as I sit up straight against the seat, I picture Jay, ripped apart and devoured by the very person who cared the most for him. Or maybe he put a bullet in his brain before she could reach him.

The truck is in park, my hand clasped around the clutch and my foot hovering over the accelerator, waiting, waiting for the right moment—whatever that means. Didn't make a difference what I did. Maybe Jay's wife breaks the window and finds her way to me now, or maybe someone else's wife somewhere down the road. Maybe a child. A fucking kid? I close my eyes.

And then there's a tap at the window.

I jump in my seat. In the window, I see the back of a bloodied hand rasping lethargically, like the pendulum swing of a brown leaf falling from a tree. At first, I think it's the hand of one of the creatures, but it isn't. Their hands are shriveled, discolored and sickly. This is the hand of a man.

I get out of the car and loop around to the other side. Sitting against the opposite door is Jay, his head hanging to one side and his mouth just barely open. His chest is moving up and down, and as I take a few steps toward him, he opens his mouth and whispers to me.

"Medina."

His eyes close again after the words trickle out of his mouth. His blood-stained white shirt is plastered to his chest, and with another grunt, he looks back up at me, his blue eyes pleading.

"Go," he coughs. "Go!"

Then I hear it—the spine-tingling, gurgled scream— and when I turn around, I see her, lumbering over from only fifty or so feet away. She's moving slowly, though, limping and falling over, and, realizing that I have a few seconds, I run over to Jay and pick him up in my arms. I've never been able to lift much weight, but with the adrenaline pumping through my veins, I swing the limp man into the back of the truck, all the while failing to hear the slithering, wounded woman come sliding through the desert brush.

When I turn back around, I stop in my tracks.

Where has she gone?

The air is still, and when I begin to move back to the other side of the truck, a hand grabs my ankles, pulling me under, and my head hits the ground. Hard.

✳✳✳

"Por favor, manténgase sentado, con los brazos, manos, pies y piernas dentro del vehículo, y cuiden—"

"Please, Papá," my sister interrupts. "It's not that funny, even if you can imitate the recording."

"Di' you at least like the rides?" my papá asks, looking at us both.

"Yes, Papá, thank you," we both answer at the same time.

Papá grins and puts his arms around us, giving us each a warm pat on the back.

"And Disneyworld is even bigger?" I ask.

"So I've heard," Papá smiles. "But you wi' ha' to do that when you're grown up. It's too har' to drive to Florida. Maybe you ca' bring me in your suitcase when you fly one day."

"Maybe we can all go," I chuckle. "Maybe you'll be an old abuelo by then, maybe—

Papá suddenly lets go of us and places his hands on his stomach, wincing in pain.

"Luís!" mamá says, almost shouting. "Again? Are you okay?"

Papá stands back up straight and grins through the pain, grunting as he leans over to give Mamá a kiss.

"It's nothing," he says. "I'm okay. I am okay."

***

I hardly feel myself sliding under the truck. My head is spinning, sloshing against the inner walls of my skull, and I can't think—as if I were in the tight embrace of a giant snake. The sharp, dry rocks of the ground scrape my ribs, and I can do nothing. Nothing but kick as hard as I fucking can.

And when I do, the sole of my shoe comes crashing onto something hard, and as I make contact I hear a crunch and a cry of agony. And then silence.

I dare not look at my legs, afraid that if I do she will come back at me. But then I remember Jay in the back of the truck, and my legs twitch to life, pushing me slowly out from the metal underbelly. I moan as I stand, and my scraped hip shines a bright red through the rip in my now-filthy jeans. After I check that Jay is in the back, I crawl into the truck, ease onto the accelerator, and slam the back of my head against the headrest.

"Gallup," I mutter. We'd be there soon. But soon didn't mean shit. Every hour that passes is just another step toward the morgue. I picture myself lying on an icy table, waiting for an autopsy, and instead of a pathologist standing over me, there's a creature. A corpse examining one of its own kind.

***

I make it to Gallup, barely. I nearly nodded off a dozen or so times on the way there, with only the pain in my hip to keep me awake. I had been to Gallup once before, with some of my roommates. I hadn't wanted to, but living in New Mexico—I figured I had to visit some other cities besides Albuquerque. It isn't all that different—dry, brown—but it feels older and certainly smaller.

I decided to drive almost past it. On the western edge of town, there's a Walmart that one of my friends had insisted on stopping at, and I figure if I stop there I'll at least have supplies, and maybe a way to heal Jay. I haven't checked on him since I threw him in the back—I haven't even had time to look at myself after what happened last night.

I park out front, directly in front, so that I can see somewhat into the store. Given the number of creatures I saw through the town, I figure that there are at least a couple inside the Walmart. Maybe more.

Once I've parked the truck there, I fall asleep almost immediately, but the pain from the night before comes back in my dreams, my nightmares. No matter what else I'm dreaming of, they're there, the creatures, infesting every fold in my brain. When I wake up early the following morning, anything but rested, I try to get out of the truck and move, but then I remember Jay, probably dead in the back of the truck, and my limbs freeze. I feel like sitting in the front seat and rotting, cooking under the unforgiving sun until I look like one of those damned creatures.

And then, only a few minutes after waking up, I hear a hollow echo of movement from the back of the truck. And a sliding, dragging sort of noise. It takes my tired brain a second to realize what I'm hearing.

"Lorenzo. Get up. Get the fuck up," I tell myself.

My weary limbs fumble for the door handle, and when I push open the door, the weight of my body sends me tumbling onto the pavement. I groan as I lift my head off the ground.

And then I hear a moan, followed by a hair-raising, inhuman screech. My blood turns to ice and my face contracts and twists when I hear it, but not because of the wretched, painful ring of the sound. But because I know who it's coming from.

Using the last drop of energy I have remaining, I climb back into the truck, turn on the engine, and without thinking, floor the accelerator and then slam on the brakes, crashing the vehicle through the entrance. I take a part of the wall with me, and the force of the truck sends some of the concrete overhead tumbling down. And through the rising dust and the hiss of a tire losing air, I see Jay limp out in front of the truck, a metal shard lodged into his shoulder and through his heart—but he's still alive. A chunk of flesh is missing from his calf as if it's been bitten and torn off.

And then I know why he's turned. And how most of the others turned, too. The creatures aren't interested in feeding on us. Not on the beings that could host whatever this terrible disease is, if that's even what it is.

Several other creatures from inside the store, after hearing the crashing noise at the entrance, come toward Jay, just in front of the truck. I think about Jay's wife, probably lying back in the middle of the desert, blistered body turned pale under the sun. She likely died before Jay even found me, and as I look at Jay now, I realize that he too is dead. I feel the tears collect around my eyelids as I feel the rings in my pocket.

I send the truck lurching forward.

***

I sealed off the doors to the Walmart without much trouble, using furniture and whatever else is heavy but not too heavy to move or slide. At the front, I put up metal tables as a barrier, and all the barricades are working so far. Or maybe there just aren't any more creatures close enough to know I'm inside.

There is food and water to keep me alive for months, maybe even a few years. But after several days inside I only feel worse. I can keep the creatures out, at least for a while, but I can't take the agony of waiting. I'm going to leave. I have to. There are many cars to choose from out front, or in an adjacent parking lot, but I need more rest before I head back out. My hip is feeling better, but I can't clear out the images frozen in my mind from the first day. At UNM, then with Jay and his wife, and then finally here at the Walmart. Did that all really happen in one day?

I've been at the Walmart for three days now, which has allowed me to plan ahead and create a plan of some sort to head out west. There's no real reason for it, no guarantee that I'll be any better off over there. But it's a goal, something to keep me going.

I buried Jay on the other side of the parking lot with a brand new shovel from the garden center, and put the rings there with him, nestled tightly between his lifeless hands. I hardly got to know him, barely even spoke to him, really, but somehow I feel like we've known each other for some time. I have to remind myself that we were never friends. Maybe I thought so because we had something in common, the fact that we weren't infected. Didn't last long though, did it? my mind interjects. I gulp down the pollen and dried saliva collecting in my throat. I'm now a prisoner of my good fortune, and Jay is now free. Maybe even with his wife, too. I can find some comfort in that.

***

The approaching navy-blue car is a small Honda, and the driver pulls into the Walmart without braking, and when I see his face through the windshield, wide-eyed and panicked, I know something is wrong.

When he parks, he slams the door closed and looks around. Seeing me at the front, he races to the back of the pickup and begins to ramble.

"Psychos, all of them—and they're after me," he groans, looking over his shoulder.

I cower back and look at the road.

"Sir," I mumble, "I don't know what you're talkin—"

"Some people bandin' up, gettin' together with guns and then they, they—"

He grabs my wrists and squeezes them hard, his eyes threatening to pop out of his skull.

"They're catchin' people, puttin' 'em up in a facility and studyin' 'em—" the man continues. "Please, fucking help me!"

The desperation of the last few words sends my skin crawling.

"Who, who's catching people?" I ask.

"I don't know," he says, glancing around. "Crazy ass researchers—I don't know. Fuck. But I know I saw them."

"You know this for sure, that they're catching people?" I ask.

The man continues to look around, and the tears are beginning to well in his eyes.

"Not just anybody," he moans. "Oh, fuck. Oh, god. Please! They want the ones who haven't turned. The ones who haven't, not just yet. The ones who haven't but are gonna soon."

And with that, the man slumps onto the ground, and as he does his jeans slide up along his legs, revealing a yellow, bubbling wound. A bite. And before I have time to get back inside the store, the gunfire comes, and at the same time the sound of a convoy of trucks, maybe four or so, moving slowly down the road. I lie on the other side of the truck and clutch the back of my head with my hands, wincing at the sound of each glancing bullet clipping metal and plastic plating.

I hear the trucks pull into the lot, and the gunfire intensifies, but I still hear the moans of the man on the other side. And then the moaning stops, along with the gunfire. But they haven't killed the man. The zombie. They only lost sight of it.

I look underneath the truck to see if I can find the body of the creature, and as I do, I notice that I can no longer feel rain beating down on my back. The faint shadow behind me looms and staggers onto its feet, and I feel the plop, the saliva, the drool pooling onto my nape. But I don't turn around, and instead, my eyes shut. This is it.

And then I feel pain in my shoulder blade, like hot iron, and the sharp, piercing snap of bullets flying at us both. The shadow staggers back, and I lose consciousness.

***

"Papá. Papá, do you hear me?"

Lying on a hospital bed, my tired and bone-thin father struggles to move his neck in my direction. His head is the only part of his body that isn't covered, and the machines pumping fluids into him click and beep.

He blinks his eyes a few times and looks at me.

"Mijo," he whispers.

The tears are streaming from my eyes. I know this is it. Mamá and Bianca know too.

"Papá, why you?" I sob. "Why us? I can't—"

"Shhh," Papá whispers, stroking a strand of my long hair. "We all go. Some of us just ge' checked in early."

I try and smile. Even at the end, he was like this.

"I can't, Papá," I say. "I can't."

"You will," he whispers back. "We fight until the end, but accept that there is an end. Your time, everyone's time—it wi' come. Death is no' evil, it jus' waits for the right moment, even if we can no' understand. Be good to your family, mijo. I will be waiting. Con paciencia."

***

"Get up," says a soft, commanding voice.

I groan, only hearing the sounds but not the words.

"Get up." This time I know it's a woman, and before I can move my legs she has me by the shoulders, and with incredible strength helps me off the floor and onto my feet.

"Let's get you cleaned up," she says, her nose nearly pressed against mine. "The bathroom is this way."

She leads me down a white corridor and points me to a small room with a sink. She gives me clean clothes but leaves the door ajar, as if she doesn't trust me.

I turn the knob above the sink and scoop up the cool water, splashing it against my muddy, bloodied face. Then I do the same with my legs, my arms, not knowing if I'll get a chance to shower. I take off my tattered shirt and peer at my reflection in the mirror, turning around slowly, as if it were the first time I saw my body. I stop when I see the gauze pressed against my right shoulder blade.

"Shotgun shrapnel," the middle-aged woman says, from the door. "You'll be okay. Just don't touch it, or take off the gauze."

I look over at her. I feel numb as if I'm only half-attached to the world around me. I don't know where I am, just that the building is clean, and that the static air is an artificial cool. The woman has a coat on. White, too.

"This way," she says. "Your room is around the corner."

She leads me down the rest of the corridor and from there we take a right down another. At the end, there is a glass chamber, the bulletproof kind—thick, sleek, and almost invisible.

"Where am I?" I ask her. The question should have come sooner, but I couldn't think. Not about Jay or UNM or Bianca or Mamá or Papá. Not about anything.

"A safe place," she says as if that was the response she had to give.

"The men of the convoy, they took me … are we in California?" I ask.

"Those people in the trucks, my team, they saved you; they work for me," she says. "And, sure."

My body drips with sweat, and a tear falls from my eye. I just want it to be over, for things to be back to the way they used to be. Maybe I'll see Mamá and Bianca again someday. I want to ask the woman in the white coat if it's over, if I'm safe, but my voice only cracks when I open my mouth.

The woman leads me into the room and then closes the door. On the other side of the glass, I see her look back at me with a curled, wicked smile. She doesn't care that I reach behind and feel underneath the gauze on my back. Or that I feel grooves that no gun or shrapnel could have made.

"Everything will be okay," she lies.

I glare back. Then smile. Then laugh.

And then I gurgle.

Silence of the Apoc

4 THE JILTED LOSER BY A. P. SESSLER

Carrie stepped into the garage-floor elevator, car keys in one hand and her habitual morning latte in the other. She was instantly greeted by conservative talk show host Doug Heder in disembodied person as his assertive voice chimed through hidden speakers.

When she pulled the top of her purse open and dropped her keys in, her glasses slid down her nose, stopping just at its delicately curved tip. She traded hands with her latte and pushed her glasses back to the bridge of her nose.

While Heder prognosticated, time seemed to come to a crawl, as well as the elevator's ascent. "Zombies. There, I said it. Everyone knows that's what it is, so let's call an ace an ace, a spade a spade, and a zombie a zombie," Heder said. "It's not some psychological phenomena or viral outbreak; it's the end of the world, people."

Carrie's stomach sank as the words came out of his mouth and the elevator halted.

"Just because they call it Romero Syndrome doesn't make it a syndrome. It's not some mental illness that can be fixed by further drugging society into increasing subjugation."

When the doors opened, a caterer with several plastic bags wrapped the length of his arms quickly stepped in. Whatever was in the bags (labeled U-Boats) smelled great.

"Which floor?" Carrie asked aware the caterer's arms were too full to press the button.

"Fifth floor. I hope," he said. "Our coordinator didn't give me the right floor."

After she pressed the appropriate button, he thanked her. She noticed his bare arms from the plastic bag handles down had turned blue. She couldn't help but remember the blue-skinned people she'd seen on the nightly news.

The doors closed, and the elevator resumed its ascent.

"Hope you have the right floor this time," she said.

"Yeah, me too, before my arms fall off."

Heder's program continued to gnaw at her stomach. She forced a smile to hide her unease.

"The idea that somehow zombie pop culture has so infiltrated the collective consciousness of society that normal people like you and I have been hypnotized into thinking we're the living dead is preposterous," said Heder.

"Isn't this horrible?" she asked. "I hope Jesus comes back and takes us all away real soon."

"Me too, sister," said the caterer. "It's the end of the freaking world, and I'm still working for less than minimum wage and tips."

"I admit," said Heder, "I'm as much against this kind of garbage they call entertainment as anyone, but the whole 'devil made me do it' mantra has to stop, that is, if your devils are music, films, books or video games."

The elevator stopped.

"Keep looking up," said the caterer, before lugging his bags of food out of the elevator.

"I will," she said and pressed the CLOSE DOORS button.

She ran her fingers through her frazzled hair and took a deep breath to calm her nerves.

"Speaking of devils, the conspiracy nuts are promulgating the lie that the American government that I love has experimented on its citizens with mind-altering drugs and some cannibalistic virus," said Heder. "That is as equally preposterous and to be honest, it's downright offensive.

"Just a moment, fellow Heders, I see we have our first caller. Go ahead, Logic89 from Burbank, you're on the air."

Another voice spoke. "Why is it that whenever it fits your narrative you claim entertainment is responsible for all the evils in the world, but when it doesn't, it has to be the Apocalypse? Isn't your version of the devil supposed to be in charge of both?"

"Well, Logic89, I suppose your moniker indicates you were born in 1989, but as far as logic I think your moniker has earned you today's first Epic Fail."

An analog synthesizer played a triad chord, ascending from bass to alto, followed by deep male voices in offset stereo declaring "Epic fail!"

The elevator bell rang, and its doors parted.

Heder's voice followed Carrie out of the elevator through the foyer's sound system.

"Thanks for being a first-time caller and first-rate loser," Heder said and hung up the phone. "You see, America, Loser89 didn't get my analogy. I have long stated I hold the entertainment industry responsible for the moral decay of our society. As far as the epidemic that is ravaging the Left Coast to the point of extinction, God willing, I believe that to be a divine judgment from a very angry God, who does in fact, vote Republican."

"Good morning, Carrie," said the gray-haired receptionist seated at the desk to Carrie's right. On her desk was a coffee mug with a yellow "smiley" with quite the opposite expression. Beneath the angry round face, text in bold comic sans proclaimed "I'M A HEDER"—a play on words for fans of the conservative host.

"Good morning, Deloris. How are you?" Carrie said.

"Blessed and highly favored."

"Wish I could say the same," said Carrie with a self-deprecating smile.

Deloris searched through piles of paper atop her desk. "Oh, but you are. Somebody left you something."

Carrie approached the desk. "Left what? Who?"

Deloris found the folded letter and handed it to Carrie. "A young man. He was in scrubs. Are you dating a doctor-in-training?"

"I don't date," Carrie said matter-of-factly and took the letter. Without looking, she crammed it into her purse.

"Courting—whatever you kids call it."

"No, at the moment I'm not courting anyone, either."

"Well, don't be too picky or you'll end up an old maid."

"I have to be picky, but it's all right. I know God has someone set aside just for me," Carrie said and resumed her course to the office.

Deloris rolled her eyes and shook her head.

Carrie passed the break room down the narrow, unlit hallway and was immediately greeted with the buzz of busy drones flitting around the bright hive of cubicles. The fluorescent lighting lining the ceiling was outdone by the baking sunlight shining through the office's wall-to-wall windows.

To combat the heat, an artificially-induced Arctic wind pumped through the ceiling vents, leaving the cold-natured clinging to sweaters and jackets, and the hot-natured in shorts or knee-length skirts and short-sleeve shirts.

The office's horrible acoustics amplified everything that happened, whether it was typing, sharpening a pencil, a screaming fax machine or the numerous laser printers. It was a constant stream of noise that employees had to reacclimate to daily.

She made her way through the cubicle matrix to her personal block on the grid, placed her purse and caramel latte on the desk and sat down in the swivel chair. With a sigh, she retrieved the letter from her purse.

The neatly-folded letter sat by her coffee. It called out incessantly, demanding her attention. She placed her hands around the pleasantly hot cup and was about to take a sip when the nagging letter accused her of neglect.

She stooped beneath her desk and pushed the power button on the computer tower, and tried halfheartedly to unfold the letter with one hand while turning on the monitor.

The letter was practically a work of origami, a reminder of the writer's anal-retentive nature. In the process of opening it, she tore one of the letter's complex folds, then gradually arrived at its proper solution.

Again she looked at the still-hot latte but refrained from indulgence. She reluctantly took the letter and read:

Dear Carrie,

It's been so long since I've heard from you. Did I do something to offend you? If so I wholeheartedly apologize. You know I would never do anything to hurt you, so I just don't understand what went wrong. We were so good for each other. We had great, long talks and laughed, and you said yourself we have so much in common. I just don't see why it's so difficult to pick up the phone and call or text me or just drop me an email sometime. You know I would do anything for you, so why are you giving me the silent treatment? Please, if you care for me or have any feelings for me at all, call me. I need to hear your voice just once more.

Forever yours,
Alex.

She took a deep breath and tried to fold the letter back as neatly as she found it, but the longer she tried, the more frustrated she became. Finally, she ignored the telltale creases and folded it in half twice, still managing to leave Alex's signature on the top fold, and she wished it wasn't.

Her eyes returned to the monitor, where a LOGIN prompt awaited her password. She carefully typed it in with one hand and pressed the ENTER key. While the operating system finished loading, she sank into the chair, its squeaky back flexing to cushion her weight. She took hold of the warm thermal cup and got lost in the first comforting sips of her latte.

Ben interrupted the moment. "Hey, Carr. How's it going?"

The chair squeaked again as she straightened her back. "Hi, Ben. Okay," she said, brushing the letter aside to her left.

Ben's eyes followed the motion of her hand and focused on the writing. His eyes darted back to her face.

"I'd be better if I didn't have to listen to Doug Heder every morning on the way up," she said. "He scares the heck out of me."

"I'm not a fan myself," said Ben. "I wish people would stop equating him and the Republican party with Jesus. The guy's theology is crap, too."

"You mean junk, don't you?"

He sighed. "If it offends you, then yes."

"What do you think about what's happening?" she asked.

"I could get into it, but it's a bit lengthy. Definitely not a one-paragraph answer."

"You're so smart," she said, half-smiling.

"Just well read. You finished with your cookbook yet?"

"No, but I finally made it to the Desserts section, so not too much further." She perked up. "I wish Gramma Collins could spell as good as she can cook. If I see one more p-e-e-can or a-l-l-mond, I'm going to s-c-r-e-a-m. That or q-u-i-t."

"You think Gramma would have learned how to use spell check by now."

Carrie groaned. "You mean a word processor? She still sends us Notepad files."

"I don't see how that makes it past Submissions."

"Because Submissions doesn't have to sit here for hours replacing ASCII characters with tabs and returns. And because she's Gramma Collins. They'd rather die than let another publisher get hold of her."

Ben laughed. "I hear you."

"In any case, her oatmeal cookies alone are worth the hassle. I made some last night. I probably gained two pounds from the butter alone."

"If so, it doesn't show," he said with a glance from head to toe and smiled.

She returned the smile. In the mutual silence, the letter that previously demanded her attention caught his.

"Is he still bothering you?" he asked.

"He left it with Deloris," she answered, her eyes trailing back to the letter.

"He was in the building?"

"Yes."

"You need to report him to the police."

"He doesn't mean anything by it."

"Hey," he said, placing his hand firmly around her elbow. "I'm serious."

She turned quickly to face him, half-startled, awoken from her fixation. "But he's a really sweet guy. He just—"

"He's just an obsessed loser who won't take no for an answer. You need to put a restraining order on him."

"He's been rejected enough as it is. Something like that would destroy him."

"He needs to man up. He'll get over it."

She rubbed the palms of her clasped hands together between her closed legs. She gazed at the smooth flesh of her forearms, and the red WWJD bracelet around one wrist, which to her seemed suddenly agleam like wet blood. "He's tried to commit suicide twice."

"He told you that?"

"Yeah."

"Since you stopped talking to him?"

"Before I met him. He's had his heart broken a million times, but twice he tried to kill himself."

She was fixated again. He moved to shake her out of her apparent trance but refrained.

"Better him than you," he insisted.

"Don't be so cold-hearted," she said, her eyes full of pity.

"Cold-hearted would be ignoring your safety. Carrie, this guy is bad news. If you don't protect yourself now, you'll regret it later, I promise you."

"Now you're scaring me."

"Good. You should be scared. How many girls have ended up dead because some loser can't handle rejection?"

With a deep sigh, she placed her hand on the mouse and opened the word processor, then the file named Grannys_Cookbook.

"You want me to look up the statistics and prove it to you?" he asked.

"But if I'm wrong I could push him over the edge," she said, scrolling down the file to the next dessert recipe.

"If he can be pushed over the edge, that's still his fault, not yours. You're not responsible for his actions or how he handles yours. Don't worry about his emotional well-being; worry about your physical safety. Either he'll be fine and get over it, or he'll learn the hard way when he gets locked up."

Her eyes trailed away again, this time to the boss. Mr. Anderson traversed the maze of cubicles on his morning rounds. She cleared her throat in case Ben didn't get the clue.

"I'll let you be," he said. "Think about what I said. I'll talk to you later."

***

It was 12:15 when Ben made good on his promise. Carrie was oblivious to his first attempt to get her attention.

She jumped back in her seat when she saw the open hand wave between her face and the computer screen. His fingers left strobing trails, thanks to the outdated monitor's slow refresh rate.

"Earth to Carrie," she heard him say, as if for the hundredth time.

"Sorry," she said and swiveled around to see him towering above her with his leather jacket draped over one shoulder. "You caught me in my zone."

"No kidding."

"How's your book?"

"Awesome."

"No, silly. I mean where are you at?"

"Oh. Making progress."

"Awesome," she mocked him then smacked his gut softly. "Wish I could say the same. You get fiction and theology, and I get stuck with self-help and cookbooks. What's the name of your book again?"

"*The Fifth Angel*—you know, from the Book of Revelation."

"Is it like *Left Behind?*"

"No, it's non-fiction. Still, some whiz in marketing wanted to put the tagline *It IS Your Grandmother's Zombie Story* on it."

"Sounds like a cheesy movie."

"I'd pay to see it."

"Considering the epidemic that's happening right now, it's a pretty serious topic to be taken so lightly. Not that anyone takes Father Jerome's writing seriously."

"There are a few of us who do."

"And my division gets called the Ichabod section," she said, rolling her eyes.

"His stuff is scripturally sound."

"Says you."

"His stuff is more sound than half the nut job charismaniacs we publish."

She huffed, blowing a long lock of brown hair away from her green eyes. "Did you need something?"

"What?" he asked, then shook his head when he noticed her offense. "Lunch. I'm heading to U-Boats to grab a sub. You wanna come?"

"Thanks, but I brought leftovers."

"Would leftovers include Gramma Collins' oatmeal cookies?"

She smacked his belly again. "Don't you dream of it!"

"I'm just saying, if I come back from lunch and see them in the fridge I'm all over it."

"You better not!" she said playfully.

"Okay, I'll leave your cookies alone if you have lunch with me tomorrow."

She frowned. "Can't tomorrow. It's women's lunch day. What about Friday?"

"Cool," he said, smiling as he donned his jacket. "I'm off. See you in a little while."

"'Kay. Bye."

She watched him from behind as he walked away. She liked how his tan khaki pants clung to the contours of his strong legs, and though she wouldn't dare admit it to a living soul, she really liked his butt.

She was admiring him all the more when the round yellow sticker on her monitor caught her eye with its purple flowery font: "Whatsoever things are true, honest, just, pure, lovely, of good report, virtuous or praiseworthy, think on these things. Phil. 4:8."

She mouthed a silent "Sorry, Lord," and straightened her glasses to continue typing, but half a minute later her stomach growled. It was definitely lunch time. She took the folded letter and balled it in her hand, and dropped it in the wastebasket on top of the empty coffee cup. She saved her work, grabbed her purse and headed for the break room.

***

The clock on the break room wall read 1:20 when Ben returned from lunch. He was pleased to find Carrie quietly nibbling one of her oatmeal cookies and reading something. He returned to his cubicle, and not much later saw her return to hers.

He smiled at the sight of her and focused more intently on his work, until he, too, was lost in the theology of a somewhat higher caliber.

***

The LED clock above the elevator read 5:15 in large, red numbers when Ben emerged into the cavernous underground garage. A dense cacophony of echoing footsteps, voices, slamming car doors, starting engines and rubber tires on concrete welcomed all who entered its architectural abyss.

Ben jogged nearly 10 yards before he was within earshot of Carrie.

"Hey," he called from behind. When he witnessed a dozen turning heads, he lowered his voice to that just above the noise. "You shouldn't be walking by yourself."

"Keep it down," she said, her face turning red. "I don't want the whole office to know."

"Fine, but at least be smart enough to let me walk you to your car."

"Okay, but if you make a scene like that everyone's going to start talking."

He smiled and kept his thoughts to himself. When they reached her car, she took her keys from her purse and unlocked the car door.

"You want me to follow you home?" he asked.

"Then I'd have two stalkers," she joked and sat inside.

"Be careful, please."

"If anything happens I promise I'll call you, cross my heart," she said, making a large imaginary X over her chest with a finger. Though she wore a modest sweater, it didn't conceal she was especially endowed.

Ben's throat tightened as he followed the movement of her finger, but he quickly regained his thoughts. "Don't call me. Call the police. I mean that."

She smiled and glanced at his hand resting on the door. Her eyes traced the thick veins running along his forearm. She cleared her throat to distract from her blushing face.

"Oh, sorry," he said and checked to ensure nothing was in the way before closing the door for her.

He returned to his own car and soon pulled out of the garage behind her, catching up with her at the traffic light. When it changed, the two went in opposite directions.

***

Alex sat straight in his car and turned the key in his ignition. He pulled out of the garage and followed her from a distance. When she exited her car, he casually drove past and parked on the curb half a block away.

He adjusted his rear-view mirror to get a glimpse of her walking in burgundy slacks that revealed she was pleasantly endowed from behind as well. The short concrete drive and grass lawn ended at her modest one-story home's high brick foundation. Carrie ascended the stair to the front door and disappeared inside.

Alex was still staring at the closed door in the rearview mirror when he heard two voices. He lowered his eyes to see a pair of young men coming down the sidewalk. His hand fumbled on the gear shift and put it into drive, only to pull out in front of an approaching car, whose driver blared the horn and blasted him with expletives. He sped ahead of the angry driver into the setting city sun.

***

Carrie's dinner performed an endless pirouette inside the microwave. An aroma of brown rice pilaf and black beans escaped through the crack of the microwave door, making her habitually wonder if more dangerous waves were escaping from the maximum security prison through the same convenient chink.

With her hands under the running faucet, her mind wandered. Maybe microwave food and radiation were responsible for the zombie mutation. She should ask Ben again. He was smart and would probably know.

When she thought of handsome Ben, her eyes were drawn to the framed stained glass that hung over the window above her sink. Dusk sunlight shone through colored glass, casting orange shapes across Carrie's tired face.

The monarch butterfly design lent itself naturally to the medium. The solder line framework spread through the butterfly's wings in the form of metal veins, separating orange and black polygons from one another.

She was momentarily lost in the glass's dancing light when the microwave chimed. She smirked when she realized the water was still running and she was no longer lathering her hands. She returned the now soft bar of soap to its dish then dried her hands off.

The same warm sunlight that cast butterflies on her face flooded the other west-facing windows of her house. Gilt-edged drops of perspiration made locks of her thick hair cling to her forehead. Through the sink window, she saw an inviting breeze blowing the trees beside her home.

She gave the windowsill a push only to discover the thick layer of paint around the frame had swollen it shut. She pounded the bottom of the sill with the butt of her palm to loosen it. With a spirited shove, she launched the window into the top of the frame, which shook the stained glass free from the nail it hung on.

Refracted flashes of broken light passed before her as the stained glass fell into the sink, shattering into fragments of orange and black. After her initial jump, Carrie's shoulders drooped in disappointment.

***

Outside she emptied the broken contents of the dustpan into the trash bag and pulled the drawstrings tight, then made sure to snap the lid on the trashcan shut—she had learned the hard way the neighborhood dogs were far too curious.

***

She finished her meal when the phone vibrated. Though she saw ALEX on the caller ID, she reluctantly answered. "Hi, Alex."

"Carrie, I've been trying to reach you," said the throaty voice. "Did you get my letter?"

"Yes," she said, already exhausted. "I wish you wouldn't have come to the office."

"Why? You don't want people to know we're friends?"

Already. Couldn't he just once go five minutes without making every comment part of his persecution complex?

She sighed. "I don't want people to think I'm dating someone."

"Why?"

"We've talked about this before."

"Oh yeah, it's against your religion."

When she didn't comment, he continued. "I was on my way to the stained glass class and was wondering if you needed a ride."

"My car works fine."

"I know. I just figured we could carpool; save you some gas money."

"Thanks, but I decided to quit the class. It just wasn't in my budget. I can't justify being late on rent or car payment because of a hobby."

"I thought you liked making stained glass."

"It's fun, but it's not something I can invest all my time and energy into. Certainly not my money."

"If you need help, I can spot you."

"That's generous, but I couldn't make you do that. You have bills to pay, too."

"It's no big deal. Just a small sacrifice to make for someone you enjoy spending time with."

"You enjoy, or I enjoy?"

"What?"

"Never mind."

"It won't be the same without you."

"It's something you enjoy doing, and there are plenty of friendly people there."

"I don't know. It just won't be the same."

"Just go. You'll have a good time."

"It won't be the same."

"Look, I hate to cut it short, but I have to run."

"Yeah? What are you doing?"

"Dishes, then a little cleaning, and if I have time, a little TV before bed."

"I could come over and help."

"No, thank you."

"Aw, come on. I'm not afraid of getting my hands dirty, and I do dishes all the time."

"No, really. I can do it by myself just fine."

"If I helped, you would have more time to watch TV. I could even watch with you."

"I don't think you'd like the kind of TV I watch."

"What is it? Some chick flick stuff? I can handle that. I've seen *Fried Green Tomatoes*. Best chick flick ever. It even has cannibalism. How many chick flicks do you know that have someone eating the flesh of another human being?"

He face twisted in revulsion. "I wouldn't watch something that disturbing."

"You've never seen *Fried Green Tomatoes*? It's great! Kathy Bates, the fat chick from *Misery* is in it."

"No. Don't think I've seen that one, either."

"Sure you have. Where she kidnaps the writer and breaks his legs with a hammer?"

"I'm sure I haven't seen it."

"Aw, man, it's great. It's based on a real-life stalker Stephen King dealt with, only she didn't break his legs like Kathy Bates does in *Misery*."

"It sounds disgusting."

"It's horror—it has to be a little disgusting. But they're not bad films."

"I don't watch R-rated films."

"*Fried Green Tomatoes* isn't rated R."

"There's cannibalism in it, and it's not rated R?"

"Nah. It's only PG-13."

"It should be rated R."

"No way. There's nothing in it that would make it rated R. There's no nudity—well unless you count the scene where Kathy Bates wraps herself in Saran Wrap."

"She what?"

"Yeah. It's hilarious. She wraps—"

"Alex."

"What?"

"You know I don't like that kind of stuff."

"Oh. I'm sorry. What kind of stuff do you like?"

"I work at a Christian book publisher. I read Christian books. I watch Christian TV. I listen to Christian music. I rent Christian movies. None of that worldly stuff. That's just a door for the demonic to enter into your life."

"Well, okay. I'd be willing to watch some Christian TV with you."

"Alex."

"What?"

"I have to go."

"Don't you want me to come over and help?"

"No, Alex. I want to do it by myself."

"Why?"

"I just got off work. I'm tired, and my hair is a mess."

"I don't care how you look."

"But I do."

"Well, I could give you a little time to clean yourself up if you want. How long do you need? Fifteen, 20 minutes, half-hour tops?"

"I'm going now, Alex."

"Wait, wait, wait—Carrie—wait just a second."

"What is it, Alex?"

"I love you."

"Goodbye, Alex," she said and pressed END-CALL.

***

"Wait, wait, wait!" Alex yelled at the silent phone. "Damn it, you slut! Just let me finish talking, will ya?"

125

He threw the cell phone against the wall, cracking the screen and knocking the battery cover off. "Why in such a hurry?" he shouted at the top of his lungs.

He paced the floor like a ping-pong ball bouncing back and forth. "Not like you have anywhere to go or anything to do! Certainly not the stained glass class we've attended together for a month straight, stupid whore!"

In all his shouting he didn't hear the banging door.

"Who are you yelling at?" the voice shouted and the door swung open. Mrs. Owen stood on the threshold with the key ring in hand.

"You have no right to come in here!" he yelled at her in mid-argument with himself.

"The hell I don't. Why do you think I carry these?" she said and jangled the key ring.

Alex' face was red. A bulging, throbbing vein ran up the center of his forehead, pulsing with hot, angry blood. He wanted to smash her head in, but the .45 strapped to her hip was a good excuse not to try it.

She surveyed the scene. His cell phone sat on the floor by the wall. Across the room was the battery cover. The orange prescription bottle on his computer desk appeared nearly full.

Glancing up from the floor she saw the dented drywall, and all around the room, the dizzying array of shapes and colors from his myriad stained glass pieces: butterflies (his recent obsession and ode to Carrie), tigers, zebras, pandas—everything dual-toned, positive and negative, light and dark. She often wondered if the hypnotic colors were the source of his manic madness or peace.

He marched back and forth a few times while swatting himself in the head. She turned away while he finished his argument as she had several times before. She sighed and waited until her own anger subsided, overcome by a recurrent flood of compassion, mingled in a muddy, rushing river of guilt.

"Are you taking your medicine?" she asked calmly.

"Of course," he pouted. "I'm not stupid."

"Good. Now why don't you cut on the news and relax," she suggested.

He sat down in the swivel chair and reached for the remote. "Cut on the news and relax," he echoed her advice. "Cut on the news and relax."

Mrs. Owen pushed the lock on the door and quietly pulled it shut, then backed out of the room. "Thank you, Lord," she whispered with raised eyes.

Alex flipped through channels until he found the local news, which featured an excerpt from a syndicated news channel.

"As Romero Syndrome continues to spread on the West Coast, a new discovery has been made concerning the virus' method of transmission," said the female journalist. "Believed until now to be transmitted by bite alone, a recent incident reveals the disease is far more contagious."

Her soothing voice calmed Alex' nerves. He leaned back in the chair and found himself grinding his teeth, eyes closed, focusing on the woman's voice.

"Los Angeles resident Thomas Hardaway was defending himself against undead resident John Hugo when both fell from a second-story crosswalk onto a concrete walk beneath. Upon impact, Hugo suffered a compound fracture. When Hardaway fell upon Hugo, the exposed bone pierced Hardaway and infected him within minutes, as seen in this footage captured by a bystander."

Alex ceased grinding his teeth and opened his eyes.

"Teeth," he said and gave them another grind. "Bones." He smiled. "Teeth are bones."

The malignant machine's gears turned inside his poisoned brain, oiled by a viscous flow of imbalanced chemicals. He leaned forward and open the web browser's search engine on his computer. He typed:

Zombie teeth.

Nearly 900,000 results came back.

"Now that you've had a chance to calm down, you can fix that ding you made in the wall," said Mrs. Owen.

He spun around to find her standing at the threshold with a gray plastic bucket and putty knife.

"I didn't do anything to the wall," he said and spun back around to use the computer.

"You threw your phone at it. Don't you remember doing that, Alex?"

"Yeah, but I didn't throw it that hard."

"Alex, look at the wall."

He stopped scrolling through the search results with an annoyed sigh and glanced at the wall. "What? I don't see it," he said and continued scrolling.

She returned an equally annoyed sigh and walked to the wall and pointed at it with the putty knife. "There, Alex.

Right there," she said, poking the spot with the knife three times.

"Hey! Don't do that, you're making it worse!"

"What? Now you can see it?"

"Yeah, but why should I have to fix it? That's why I pay rent."

"You pay rent to live here, not for me to fix everything you break. But if you don't want to fix it, I can just raise your rent $25 a month to help pay for all your damage."

"You can't do that!"

"I can and I will," she said, holding out the bucket and putty knife for him to take.

He stood there, breathing heavy, then snatched the tools from her.

"I'll be back in a while to see how it looks," she said and exited the room.

He looked at the small bucket and read the label aloud with clenched jaws. "Spack-O-Line. Pre-mixed putty for dents and dings. No water necessary," he finished, his jaws relaxing into a smile. "Sounds like a jingle."

He removed the lid and dug the putty knife into the bucket while singing his improvised melody. Within a few minutes of scraping and spreading he had the spot repaired.

The door opened again. Mrs. Owen approached and peered over his shoulder.

"So, dummy, did you do a good job or do I have to raise your rent?" she said, her hands on her hips.

He turned around and smiled. "I did a great job, Mrs. Owen. Do you know what else I can do, really good?" he asked.

She shook her head and scowled at him. "No, wise guy. What's that?"

"This!" he yelled and jabbed the putty knife between her collarbone and neck.

"No, Alex!" she pleaded.

A stream of blood shot onto the wall when he pulled the knife out. He stabbed her again in the throat. Another stream of red sprayed the wall.

"Please," she gurgled. "Stop!"

"What do you think of that, you old bitch? Is that good enough for you?"

He looked over his shoulder at the blood-spattered wall. "Oh, look. I messed up the wall again. That's all right, nothing a fresh coat of paint won't fix."

He stabbed her again and again until he and the entire wall, minus his masked shape, were red with her blood. Trickles fell from the masked head and shoulders and proceeded to fill the blank void.

He gazed at her body, covered front and back with three-inch puncture wounds. Her eyes and mouth were frozen open. He stared into her eyes, nearly rolled behind her eyelids. He exhaled and laughed.

Her eyes rolled forward, fixated on him.

He gasped and dropped the putty knife.

"Alex?" Mrs. Owen called.

He saw her reflected in the putty knife on the floor. He turned around and found her standing in the doorway.

He swallowed the lump in his throat. "Is that good enough?"

She approached the spot and rubbed a finger over it. "It will do," she said.

He placed the lid back on the bucket of Spack-O-Line and handed it and the putty knife to her.

"Thank you. And next time, don't let your anger get the better of you," she said and left.

He stared at the empty doorway with a twisted smile. "But anger is the best part of me," he murmured.

***

Alex killed the headlights on his car. The two lit windows and a parked car in Carrie's driveway declared she was indeed home, so he parked on the curb two houses away, turned off the engine and exited his car dressed entirely in black.

He made his way to her driveway, careful not to make a sound. The streetlamp provided just enough light to see inside the trashcan and sift through its contents.

"I knew it!" he said, loud enough to garner another light turned on.

He ran around the dark corner of the house to avoid being seen. He waited a moment before peeking around the corner. The light was off. He wasn't sure if he had imagined it or not. He returned to the trashcan, and after collecting two pocketfuls of refuse, he scampered off.

***

Carrie sat up in her bed reading a book by lamplight.

Her cell phone rang.

Instinctively she reached over and answered, immediately regretting she had not read the number.

"Hi, Carrie. Alex," he said, his crackling voice reverberating in a wide, walled space, accompanied by a cacophony of sounds.

"Hi, Alex. Where are you? It's really noisy," she said.

"Oh yeah. I'm at the bowling alley."

"The alley's open this late at night?"

"Sure. It's where all the worldly people hang out."

She rolled her eyes. "Look, it's late. I need to sleep."

"I know. I'm sorry. I just wanted to ask you a question before you hang up."

She sighed. "What, Alex?"

There was a long pause. Disturbingly so. "Do you still have it?"

"Have what, Alex?"

He refrained from mocking her. "It."

She huffed. "It, what? Just say it."

"My gift to you. You know. The butterfly."

Her heart skipped. Why would he ask that? "Of course."

"Are you sure?"

Did he know? She swung her legs out of bed and stood. "Yes, I'm sure. Why wouldn't I be?"

Over the phone, she heard a crashing, clashing sound. It was distorted by the cell phone's varying signal.

"What was that?" she asked, her legs carrying her step by step, inevitably toward the bedroom window overlooking her driveway.

Another disturbing pause. "That was the third strike. Gobble gobble gobble."

She was unsure what to say. "Congratulations?"

His nasal breathing silenced the noise of the room. "Yeah. You have a nice life," he said and hung up.

She put her face to the window and looked down. The trashcan sat uncovered, the lid leaned against it, and the plastic bag open. Her heart raced. Panic seized her.

She glanced up and down the street for any sign of him or his car. Finding neither, she ran downstairs and made sure the doors and windows were intact and locked.

She made her way to the kitchen and looked out the dark window where the glass butterfly had so innocently flitted over her sink. She glanced at the counter on her left, where the knife rack sat.

She reached for the handle of the largest knife and slid it from the rack.

***

She sat up in bed, clutching the knife, staring at the bedroom door, listening for any disturbance outside the fragile cocoon she called safety. Privacy. Nothing was sacred to the venomous black spider she had let into her life.

She prayed for forgiveness for not trusting God. For wanting to drive the knife through the fat abdomen of the sick, confused spider. For wishing Ben lay beside her, ready to protect her, to hold her.

She cried herself to sleep.

***

"Here's your double-shot espresso," said the teenage cashier.

She held the coffee and change out the drive-through window. Carrie reached beneath the swiveled visor to take the cup and signaled with a raised palm for the cashier to keep the change.

"Long night?" the cashier asked, only seeing Carrie from the nose down.

Carrie flashed half a smile and put the car in gear. When she pulled out from the covered drive-through, the harsh morning sun poured into her car. She swiveled the visor right to parry the sun's blinding assault.

After a few turns, she pulled into the underground garage, gathered her things and exited her car. She pressed the UP button on the elevator and waited. When she glanced down at her feet, she froze.

There at the elevator doors sat fragments of orange and black glass, the remnants of the butterfly Alex had given her. She couldn't help but continue imagining him as a spider, his red hair an hourglass against his black soul, and she, the broken butterfly pulled into his mad web.

She felt his intimidating venom seep inside. It flowed from the back of her mouth, down her throat, into her glands. She wrapped her first two fingers around the head of the largest key on her ring and gripped it tight.

Her eyes shot left and right and back, ready to defend—no—attack if provoked. She jumped when the elevator doors open. She looked inside, even up at the car's metal ceiling before entering. The doors closed behind her.

***

"Keep it down in there!" Mrs. Owen yelled in front of the door then pounded it with her fat hand.

The blaring noise Alex called music rattled the framed family portrait mounted on the wall. The wilting plant on a nearby end table vibrated helplessly in its pot like a condemned prisoner in the electric chair. Mrs. Owen frowned when she saw a single brown leaf shake loose from the plant.

It dropped, lifelessly for a single moment until it landed on the table, where it returned to life, reanimated by the music's heavy vibrations. A diet lacking Vitamin Mozart and a steady stream of poisonous heavy metal pumping through its veins was surely the cause of its demise.

When the volume didn't decrease, she pounded on the door again. "If you don't turn it down I'm calling the cops!"

A moment later the volume lowered by a half.

"Gets him every time," she said with a smile as she put one swollen leg in front of the other. She gently scooped up the dead leaf in her palm and walked slowly and laboriously down the hall, her face clammy with perspiration.

***

Alex sat in the swivel chair, still in his green scrubs, reciting a poem by literary genius Tyrone Greene.

"C-I-L-L my landlord," he said, holding Carrie's photo in front of a styrofoam wig head on his desk. He applied enough downward pressure on the head to keep it from moving and fastened Carrie's photo to it with the strained squeeze of his staple gun's trigger.

He retired the staple gun to a wall-mounted shelf to the right of his desk, where several books on medicine and anatomy sat.

"C-I-L-L," he repeated with a laugh, then swiveled to face his monitor.

On his web browser were several open tabs. He bounced back and forth from page to page to page. The first featured a news article on the current epidemic, plainly referred to as the "Zombie Holocaust."

The zombie genre, having long been ingrained in popular culture internationally, had made such terminology commonplace. Whether it was someone under the influence of Haitian voodoo, a man high on bath salts, a biological experiment, genetic disease, or the evicted residents of hell itself, a zombie by any other name was still a zombie.

He skimmed the text, reading under his breath. "Subjects initially experience confusion and eventually turn rabid to the point of attacking and feeding on uninfected subjects. The infection spreads from Subject A to Subject B through any bite or scratch strong enough to break the skin. Less common infections occur whenever contaminated body fluids come in contact with the exposed mucus membrane or orifices of Subject B."

"Life imitating art," he mused, then moved on to the second tab of his browser.

The site, usbiohazard.com, boasted "HIGH-GRADE MATERIAL HARVESTED FROM ZOMBIES FOR YOUR MEDICAL RESEARCH." He scrolled down the page and entered the number 2 in an empty box next to the product label HUMAN TEETH x1 lb, then clicked ADD TO CART. Having met the minimum purchase requirement, he was presented with a new screen that read:

"TO PURCHASE MEDICAL WASTE SUPPLIES FROM THIS SITE YOU MUST POSSESS A VALID MEDICAL LICENSE OR CURRENT STUDENT ID FROM AN ACCREDITED MEDICAL UNIVERSITY. PLEASE ENTER YOUR INFORMATION BELOW."

After he provided his student ID and the site verified its authenticity, he was given a 25 percent discount and allowed to check out. He pressed the PROCEED WITH ORDER button and soon his purchase was processed.

He closed the tab and opened his email provider, finding the Order Confirmation in his inbox. He closed that tab and returned to the final page, the Anarchist Cookbook. He saved the web page to his hard drive as a text file, closed the proxy server he used to mask his IP address, then as an added precaution deleted all his browser's data.

"Only one more thing to X out of," he said, and he retrieved a red Sharpie from a coffee cup full of pens. He held the styrofoam wig head in his lap and drew a large X over Carrie's photo.

He reached behind him to the open pizza box on his bed and grabbed a cold slice of Supreme pizza. He took a large bite and wiped his oily fingers on his trousers. A small piece of green pepper stuck to his short, unkempt beard.

"How's that for closure, bitch?" he said, speaking with his mouth full, to Carrie's image.

***

The metal oven door creaked open, ready for the next pizza. The fit, young man in tee-shirt slid the large, stone pan carrying the pie into the oven, then pulled the one above it out and placed it on the countertop. He slid the pizza off the stone pan onto a silver metal pan and placed it in the order window.

With a tap of his hand, the order bell rang. He bit the large oven mitt off one hand and wiped the sweat off his forehead with his other arm before removing its glove with his free hand.

"Pizza's up," his voice boomed as he turned around and grabbed a ball of dough to make another crust.

The aromas of tomato sauce, oregano, grated Parmesan, crushed red pepper, bubbling cheese and crust baking brown were all swirled together by the spinning blades of the ceiling fans and carried throughout the dining room of Pizzacato's.

Beside each booth were framed black and white poster-sized photos of early Hollywood celebrities like Marilyn Monroe, Elvis Presley, the Brat Pack, and the obligatory homage to the mafia films of Coppola and Scorsese. Above the booths were stained glass lamps casting soft light perfect for any mood.

The equally soft music piping through the sound system alternated between Italian folk songs and opera, providing the perfect ambiance.

Ben and Carrie laughed, making small talk across from each other in a red, leather-cushioned booth. Though the wide booths easily seated six, the pizza joint was only half full, giving diners their choice of tables. The bar, on the other hand, had few vacant stools.

Eli, a bald-headed mountain of muscle, laughed it up with the regulars while doling out drinks. If the full tip glass was any indicator, he did a good job of it.

Televisions on either corner of the bar displayed separate sporting events, eliciting periodic boos and cheers from tipsy fans. The two remaining televisions featured weather and national news in the dining area.

Carrie watched the broadcast of a recent attack. The zombie, its ethnicity hidden by the pale hue of infection, had its face digitally blurred to protect its former identity.

"Family members of infected individuals have already brought several lawsuits against news agencies worldwide for showing their relatives without a formal conviction or authorized consent," the news anchor reported.

"That's civil rights for you," said Ben, not even turning to watch the screen.

The zombie, male by gender but occasionally dubbed "it," by the female news anchor, approached two Hispanic men standing their ground. The men took turns retreating backward to confuse the zombie, but eventually, the six-foot thing grew tired of their tactic and rushed the shorter, stouter man.

A black square covered the victim's head as the broadcast continued to censor the graphic content. The taller man circled around the zombie and eventually pulled him off his companion long enough for a state trooper in beige hat and uniform to come into frame brandishing a firearm. He motioned for the unscathed man to step back and then fired several rounds into the head of the zombie, dropping it to the street completely dead.

"Think that will ever reach us?" Carrie asked.

Ben sipped his Dr. Pepper through a straw. "Not if they quarantine it," he answered. "Unfortunately, the bleeding hearts will keep crying foul, and Congress will drag its feet until it's too late."

"But the Book of Revelation doesn't talk about zombies."

"It does, and it doesn't."

"Is that what your book is about? I know you've been dying to tell me."

"Oh man, it's brilliant. Then again, everything Father Jerome writes is."

"When it's not about demons."

"He doesn't write about demons. He writes about amoral multi-dimensional creatures—things, monsters, whatever you want to call them—that have free-will just like a man."

"Most people would say demons and monsters are the same things."

"Those would be the people who don't know squat about Father Jerome."

"Let's not get into an argument. Just tell me if it's fiction or not."

"Strictly theology, none of the monster stuff."

"So what does he say about all the zombies? Is this the Tribulation?"

"No. He makes a clear distinction between the zombies of the natural order and the zombies of the supernatural."

"And this kind is?"

"The natural order. They're either a genetic defect exploited by a virus, something engineered in a lab, or even Romero Syndrome."

"That's it?"

"Pretty much."

"Does he believe they're dead? And where do their souls go?"

"He puts two ideas out there. If they're dead, their spirits have gone on to their reward, leaving their bodies running on purely motor and primeval instincts, or they're still alive in a sort of sleepwalking coma, again operating on the most basic level possible. In either case, that's why they only cease functioning when their brains are destroyed. They're not possessed by evil spirits, in other words, if that answers your question."

"So he basically says he doesn't know?"

"No, he's pretty emphatic that they're of the natural order. His reasoning is that though the zombies of Revelation can't die, either, they consciously seek death. They don't go mad and start eating people. Besides, they're infected by locust stings—the giant, demonic kind."

"You mean your grandmother's kind?"

He laughed. "Yeah, my grandmother's kind. You remembered that?"

She laughed, too. "Who could forget a tagline that bad?"

"Your grandmother?"

She frowned. "Hey."

"Pizza is served," said the waitress, placing the large pan on the metal stand center of the table.

Carrie's eyes widened. "Look at the steam coming off it."

Ben smiled. "Man, that looks good."

Using a silver server, the waitress placed a slice on a plate for Carrie, another for Ben. She twirled the hanging foot-long strands of mozzarella around the server and plopped them over each slice.

"Can I get you anything else?" she asked.

Ben looked at Carrie, who shook her head. "No, thanks," answered Ben.

Carrie smiled at Ben as the waitress walked off.

"You want me to say the blessing?" he asked.

"Yes, please," she answered.

The two bowed their heads and closed their eyes.

"Heavenly Father—" Ben began.

"That is one good-looking pizza," a voice interrupted.

The couple looked up. Ben unclasped his hands and placed them palms down on the table.

"What are you doing here?" Carrie asked.

"About to have lunch. Yourself?" Alex asked with a cocky smile, his hands in his pockets. He rocked back and forth from the tip of his toes to the ball of his heels.

"Would you mind leaving?" Ben asked.

"Oh, don't worry. I wouldn't want to bother such a good-looking couple," said Alex, still rocking on the ends of his feet.

He looked at Carrie with one brow raised, waiting for her to contradict him, to declare his assessment of her and Ben's relationship status as friends or co-workers or acquaintances—any answer other than a couple would do.

He sighed when no amendment was made. "Your pizza looks pretty good," his voice cracked. "Only one thing would make it better."

Ben's right hand balled into a fist. He took a deep breath and asked, "What's that, sport?"

Alex smirked. He removed a gloved hand from his pocket and extended his closed fist in front of Ben.

Ben looked at the latex glove then into Alex's eyes. He reached his balled fist toward Alex's to knock knuckles, only out of feigned respect, when Alex opened his fist, releasing a handful of glistening, yellowed teeth onto the pizza in a small pile.

Carrie's stomach convulsed. She swallowed to keep from vomiting.

Ben jumped to his feet. "You son of a bitch!" He shot a hand out to take Alex by the shirt.

Alex stepped back, just out of Ben's grasp. He raised both hands palms forward. "Watch the language, sport. There's a Christian lady present."

Ben stepped out of the booth to take hold of Alex, who took another cautious step back to dodge him. Before Ben could even take a swing, Alex left the floor and flew sideways several feet.

The hulking Eli stood in profile before Ben.

Alex looked up from the floor, shaking his head, unsure what had happened. He looked up in time to see Eli stooping down to take hold of him. He scurried in a backward crabwalk until he ran into the front door.

He quickly stood up and backed through the door to avoid the approaching Eli. Having watched the event unfold through the glass storefront, a group of onlookers standing on the street corner stepped away from Alex.

He turned to his right, expecting to find sympathy in their expressions, but saw revulsion; to his left, he only found more. Voices rose through closed lips from all around, mumbling, condemning. The verbal assault of the crowd terrified him.

He tucked his hands into his pockets and walked down the sidewalk with his head low and his face red with embarrassment.

"Hey, Jackass!" a voice came from behind. "You forgot your pizza!"

Alex turned his head just in time to see the pizza he had defiled leaving the giant hand of the bald bartender-turned-bouncer.

The large pizza folded around his back, clinging long enough to leave half its toppings stuck to his shirt before it slid down to his waist and fell off, landing face-up on the sidewalk.

The crowd who had previously shown utter contempt burst into laughter, the imagined voices of condemnation now echoing the insult "Jackass" one after another, until eventually the multiple voices caught up with each other and declared in unison "Jackass! Jackass! Jackass!"

The crowd continued to laugh as he walked off, one young man even recording the event with his cell phone camera.

***

Carrie opened the break room fridge and placed half a tin-foil-wrapped submarine sandwich inside.

"Here you go," said Ben, handing her his half-sub to place beside hers.

She closed the fridge.

"I'm sorry," she said, glancing into Ben's eyes then looking down.

"It's not your fault," he said gazing at her until she faced him.

"No. You were right all along. I should have known nothing good would come of being nice to him."

"I don't know," he said, cradling her right elbow with his left hand. "We got two free sandwiches out of the deal."

She laughed. "Thanks."

"For what?"

"For what you were willing to do for me."

"You mean pounding the living hell out of him?"

She nodded, then placed her left hand on his right bicep. Even through his long-sleeve dress shirt, she could tell the muscle was large and firm.

He smiled. "I don't know that I deserve credit for that. I would have done that purely out of self-gratification."

"Don't sell yourself so short. I think you deserve a lot more than that."

His eyes sparkled with curiosity. "Yeah? Like—"

She stood on her toes and leaned into his arms, kissing him for the first time.

He pulled her closer, tighter, her breasts pressing against his broad chest.

"Hey Carr—Ohhh..." someone said, drawing a single open eye from the lovers.

Neither Ben or Carrie knew who it was. They heard hurried footsteps and rustling papers. When they pulled away to see who it was the doorway was empty.

"Sorry," she said, placing her hand over her mouth. "I have salami breath."

"So do I," he said, then pulled her close for one more kiss.

A moment later she pulled away again. "We better get back to work before—"

"Before people start talking?" he asked with a sheepish smile.

"Yeah," she smiled and lowered her head bashfully.

She found herself holding his hand. She looked at their clasped hands and swung them back and forth several times before pulling her hand gently from his.

"Get back to work?" she repeated.

He playfully rolled his eyes. "Sure."

She walked ahead of him slowly, smiling like a school girl.

He put his hands on her shoulders to make her walk faster through the narrow hall, but she only stopped in her tracks until she felt his chest against her back.

She turned and gave him a quick kiss.

"Back to work, remember?" he teased her.

She turned and headed back toward the office.

Before they parted ways to their cubicles, he asked, "Does this mean I'm allowed to walk you to your car now?"

She glanced back and nodded three times.

They sat at their desks to finish the day's work, completely invigorated yet thoroughly distracted by their incessant need to peek or wink or smile or just plain stare at one another over the cubicle walls.

***

Alex dropped a handful of green and yellow teeth inside a gray PVC pipe. Sealed on its bottom, the plastic pipe was 18 inches long, three inches in diameter. He squeezed it between his knees, allowing its bottom to rest on his bedroom floor.

He took a second, slightly smaller pipe, also sealed on its end, and dropped it in the first. Inside the second he placed a lead rod. He raised the second pipe (and its rod) and thrust it toward the floor. There was a satisfying crack.

He removed the second pipe and glanced inside the first—a tiny mound of green and yellow pebbles lined the bottom. He gave the pipe a twirl and watched the contents tumble about, its sound like a forgotten pocketful of just-cleaned coins in a spinning dryer.

He replaced the second pipe in the first and repeated the mashing process until the teeth were pulverized into a fine frit.

***

Alex pulled the hot metal pan out of the oven and placed it on the range. He shoved the door shut and looked at his steaming creation. It wasn't a bad pie for a doctor-in-training. He was tempted to inhale its buttery, sweet aroma when he recalled its contagious contents.

In fact, he wasn't quite sure just how contagious Alex's famous apple pie would be. Would the baked-in frit seep into her bloodstream while in her mouth? Would a tiny chunk be embedded in the lining of her digestive tract? Or would it wait until her stomach did its job and disperse the necrotic nutrients throughout her entire being? Then again, there was always the chance she'd just crap it out and be none the wiser.

But that was the science of medicine: hypothesize, experiment, results.

"Mrs. Owen," he called.

"Alex, what are you cooking?" her voice came from down the hall. "It smells delicious."

"Oh, I'm sure it will be."

"I'll be there in a minute," she said from her canvas-covered chair. She leaned forward and reached for her cane when he called back.

"No, no. Mrs. Owen. You stay right there. I'll bring you a slice."

"That's very considerate of you," she said, leaning back into her chair.

He came down the hall, a sickeningly sweet smile on his cherubic face and a tray in both hands bearing fine china plate, saucer, and cup.

She smiled when he entered the living room. "You shouldn't have."

He shrugged and thought, "You're probably right."

She noticed the cluttered end table beside her and swiftly removed a book and magnifying glass to make room for the tray, placing the reading materials between her hip and arm of the chair.

He lowered the tray to the end table and placed the plate and pie in her anxious hands. She raised the plate just beneath her nose and inhaled the pie's aroma. She smiled ear to ear, her gray teeth peeking through dry lips.

The muscles in his throat involuntarily constricted to keep the rising bile from coming into his mouth, his smile considerably weakened, until he noticed her glancing about for something.

"What do you need, Mrs. Owen?" he asked.

She looked at the tray to her side. "Silverware," she said, satisfied she had located it.

"Oh. I'm sorry," he said and handed the fork to her.

"Thank you."

He smiled.

She pressed the fork into the tender crust, breaking its surface and pressing down till metal prongs scraped against china. Alex winced at the shrill sound. His hands clenched into fists, and he fought the desire to punch or strangle her on the spot.

A second scrape sounded as she scooped the bite off the plate into her mouth. Alex winced again, twitched even.

While he watched her chew with her mouth open, the muscles in his throat gave way to the rising bile. He squeezed his eyes shut when the foul acid filled his mouth. He swallowed and hurried from the room.

"This is good, Alex," she called from the living room.

He turned off the kitchen tap and quickly gulped the lukewarm water from a glass and gasped. "I'm glad you like it," he hollered back.

She took another bite when he returned to the living room. "This is really good," she said, sure he hadn't heard her.

His jaws clenched to keep the words "I heard you the first time, bitch," from coming out. "I'm glad you like it," he repeated.

"What'd you put in this?"

His smile flashed wide for just a second. "Something special," he said, the muscles of his throat tightening again, this time voluntarily keep his maniacal laughter from bursting forth.

She placed the plate in her lap and lowered her fork, then faced him with a concerned look. "What did you put in this, Alex?"

He took a deep breath. "Love, Mrs. Owen."

Her concern melted into tearful gratitude. "I don't know what I would do without you, Alex."

"What do you mean?"

"I couldn't survive here on my own. You renting that room is what keeps my head above water. I'd be sunk on the bottom if not for you."

He pulled a wooden chair from the dinner table behind him and sat beside her. "Well, that's sort of like the lamprey and the minke whale."

Her pitiful smile turned into a playful scowl. "Are you calling me fat?"

"No, not at all."

"Good," she said and raised her cane. "'Cause I'd give you a knot on your head if you were."

His eyes fixated on his distorted reflection in the cane until she set it back down, then turned back to her. "The lamprey and minke whale are friends. They help each other survive."

She took another bite and spoke while chewing. "You're so smart, Alex. You're going to make a great doctor."

"Thank you. I sure hope so."

"You will. And I think it's really nice of you to say you need me, too, like the ... lamp— What did you call it?"

"The lamprey."

She yawned.

"Are you tired, Mrs. Owen?"

She blinked slowly. "I am. I don't know what's come over me."

"Well, you just close your eyes and take a nap."

"But I haven't finished my pie or touched my tea."

"Don't worry," said Alex, as he carefully took the china and placed it on the tray. "I'll put it in the microwave. You can heat it up later if you want it."

"That's real thoughtful of you, Alex."

"You're welcome, Mrs. Owen. Now, get you some rest."

"Thank you, I think I will." She closed her eyes, and her neck went limp.

Alex held the tray, perfectly still as he waited for the desired sign. At first, it was a quick, choking sound. The china rattled atop the tray in Alex' startled hands. He regained his composure and waited again until he heard the sound of soft snoring.

He made his way to the kitchen while Mrs. Owen rested, in something not quite peace.

He emptied the cup of tea and scraped chunks of pie off the plate into the sink. He turned the faucet to hot and let the scalding water wash the meal down the drain. With the water still running he flicked on the garbage disposal and listened to the metal mouth gargle and grind its meal to mush.

His callous and unblinking reflection stared back at him from the kitchen window until it disappeared beneath a thick layer of mist.

***

Alex exited the open door, a hand momentarily shielding his eyes from the bright sky as he bounced down the concrete porch stair, car keys in hand and duffle bag over his shoulder. He got in his car and quickly drove away.

The front door remained open; the hall beyond, dark. A wide shape lumbered forth out of the darkness onto the short grass lawn. Across the street, two boys worked on an overturned bicycle. One fiddled with the loose chain while the other helped, more or less.

Mrs. Owen crossed the street without looking either way, but it wasn't an exceptionally busy street for the small neighborhood. Her eyes were a lifeless silver, the same color eyes one might find in a baked fish. Her mouth hung open, drool running over gray teeth and gums onto her crumb-covered muumuu.

She approached the careless boys, made aware of her presence only when the sun cast her looming shadow over them.

"Hi," said the mechanic.

"Are you okay?" the supervisor asked.

The mechanic screamed when the fat, clammy hands reached for him. The wrench in his hand fell to the sidewalk with a clank, and the supervisor went running off, shouting "Mom!"

Mrs. Owen bit the boy's shoulder and pulled a juicy, red chunk of meat away. He screamed. She chewed.

"Let go of my son!" a thin woman shouted, running at Mrs. Owen.

Mrs. Owen glanced at the noisy thing running for her, then took another bite of her squirming prey. Soon fingernails dug into her arm, fists pounded her flabby side and head, but it didn't hurt much—just a dull ache of deadening nerves that would soon be silenced.

Mrs. Owen dropped the motionless meal and turned her attention to the tall, skinny one trying to hurt her. She grabbed the bottom of its noisy hole with one hand and its top with her other and pulled in two directions.

After the loud crack, the noise didn't so much stop as it changed tone: instead of a high, shrill sound now it was a low, gurgling, warbling sound, and now delicious red juice shot up and poured out of the broken hole.

The tall thing was still pounding and clawing at her, but she didn't mind. Mrs. Owen put her face inside the hole and bit the flapping red thing with the purple line on one side.

After a moment the meal stopped moving like the other one had and lay down beside it. Mrs. Owen wasn't sure what this new food was, but she was sure she wanted more of it. More and more and more. However much more, she knew only one thing: it would never, ever be enough to satisfy the growing hunger inside her—that was the only pain she would know from that point on.

In a moment, other meals burst forth from the trays up and down either side of the street. They pointed at her and made noises, and soon a tray came rolling up the street. It had lights that flashed and made high, whining noises like the skinny, second meal had made.

The tray stopped and out stepped two more meals. Then behind that tray came yet another tray with flashing lights, and out stepped two more meals. It was like a buffet. A heavenly buffet that would never end.

Mrs. Owen smiled as more and more meals came right to her.

***

Deloris was on the phone when the elevator bell rang. The doors parted, and she glanced to see who it was. After recognizing the face from a previous encounter, her attention returned to the phone call.

She waited until the man approached the desk. She motioned for him to wait with a single finger.

"Just a moment," she said to the person on the other end of the phone, then looked at the man in front of her. "Yes? May I help you?"

Carrie was busy typing when she heard the bang.

"What was that?" someone called out from behind a cubicle.

Then came Deloris' cry for mercy.

Heads peeked up from behind cubicle walls.

There was another gunshot, and Deloris' crying stopped.

"Somebody call 911!" a coworker yelled.

Carrie didn't doubt who the shooter was.

Like terrified rats in a maze, employees scurried from cubicle to cubicle, climbed under their desks, and prayed—some out loud for fear of going unheard (by God), others silently for fear of being heard (by the shooter).

Several employees ran down the narrow hall toward the elevators. As each tried to pass the other, their bodies jammed the hall, preventing those behind them from proceeding. A man pushed someone in front of him to dislodge the clogged lifeline, long enough to move past the blockage and create another.

"Single file!" a woman yelled from behind.

"Keep moving!" yelled a man.

The crowd managed to break into a line at least two people wide. Those to the rear of the line saw a bright flash. There was a floor-shaking boom. Those in the front of the line were hidden behind a cloud of smoke. The rest of the line either turned aside into the kitchen or retreated to the office.

Those in the office looked to the sprinkler system on the ceiling, which remained inactive. There was no fire nor enough smoke from the explosion to set the sprinklers off. The only thing coming from the ceiling were bits of tile and dust, that and at least one fluorescent lighting fixture cover, which came loose and hit a woman in the head, leaving her dazed and bloody.

Her expression froze in a grimace. She reached for the rectangular plastic cover which was still hanging from the ceiling by one corner. She raised the end jabbing into her crown and slid it away from her head. When the cover had nothing to balance itself on it fell from the ceiling and landed on her desk, half of it suspended over the floor.

She ran both hands through her thick, orange curly hair until she found the gash. She looked at her bloodied palms with the same unchanging expression.

Ben stood within his cubicle and took a panoramic view of the office. He saw the back of Carrie's head just over her cubicle doing the same, her hands gripping one of its partitioned walls. When their eyes met, he motioned for her to stay low.

He stooped down and scoured his desk for anything resembling a weapon. The stapler? Not quite. In the ceramic Baylham & Zast coffee mug there was a pencil and pen—sure, they could do damage at close range, but to a shooter, they were far from threatening.

Behind the writing utensils, a pair of bright orange-handled scissors stuck out. He gripped the handle and stuck his head out the cubicle's entrance.

The gunshots and screams were getting louder, closer.

Carrie dialed 911 on her cell phone.

"What city, please?" the operator asked.

"Carrie," said Alex.

She looked up at the sneering man—his red, kinky hair spiked like a crazy clown wig.

"Put the phone down," he said, waving the pistol at her.

"Just one moment, please," the operator said.

In a moment another operator answered. "What's your emergency?" she asked.

"Or don't," said Alex. "Not that they'll get here in time. Go ahead, tell her."

"Why are you doing this?" Carrie asked.

Alex was about to humor her with an answer when he noticed Carrie's eyes focus to one side. He turned around to find Ben charging him with the pair of orange-handled scissors.

"Not so fast, sport," he said and lobbed the plastic pipe bomb in his other hand toward Ben and took cover in a cubicle.

Carrie dropped to her knees and stuck her head under the desk when the explosion shook the floor. She heard things whizzing through the air and cracks and squeaks and grunts of pain from men and women in the room.

Her cell phone sat atop her desk, the 911 call still active. "Stay on the line," the operator said. "Don't hang up. We'll trace the call."

"It's safe now," said Alex. "At least for the next minute or so. Come out and see for yourself."

Carrie slowly rose to her feet. There was Ben, and the others, their bodies pierced with gray PVC and yellow bits of shrapnel. Ben sat slack-jawed, his eyes lost in some incomprehensible thought. He brushed limply at the pieces of shrapnel stuck in his chest as if they were crumbs from something he ate.

He managed to remove one of the yellow pieces from his torn, bloodied shirt and held it up in front of his face, gazing at it as he tried to decipher the object and its name.

"Human teeth," said Alex proudly. "Infected human teeth. Purchased them off the Web. You know that plague everyone's worried about coming here? Well, it's here. I guess they can really start worrying."

The others, like Ben, stood still with the same lost look in their eyes. They, too, pawed at the dental shrapnel stuck in their faces, arms, torsos, legs. The color drained from their skin and changed slowly to an undead hue.

Carrie took a step back. She bumped into the desk behind her and lost her footing, landing on her bottom right beside the monitor.

"How could you do this?" she cried.

Alex glanced at the edited copy of Gramma Collin's dessert on Carrie's monitor.

"I just followed the recipe," he said.

"What recipe?" she asked.

"You have your cookbook, I have mine."

"You're a monster."

"No. I'm not a monster. Your boyfriend is a monster. And so is he, and she, him, her," he said, pointing at her infected co-workers. "But to show you how much I love you I'm going to give you a way out."

He replaced the pistol's near-empty magazine with a full one and handed it to her, then looked intently at his wristwatch, calculating.

"In about one minute their transformation will be complete. The virus will have hijacked all of their organs and rewired their brains, turning them into nearly unstoppable killing machines. Unstoppable, that is, save for a single clean shot to the brain—or several messy ones—to them, it doesn't really matter. But aim carefully— you only have fifteen shots. And while you're busy fighting them off, I'm going to make my way to the elevator."

Carrie looked at the semi-automatic pistol in her hand. She turned it side to side repeatedly.

Alex slowly walked backward through the aisle toward the narrow hall, past Ben and the other infected co-workers. "If you manage to escape, you have my number. Call me sometime," he said, holding his thumb and pinkie to his ear like a phone. "We'll do lunch."

When he made it to the hall, he looked at his watch again. "Time's up," he said then turned around.

The lost look in Ben's eyes was replaced with one of absolute hunger—a ravenous, maddening hunger, unending and insatiable. And he only had eyes for Carrie.

The others had the same look, and only for Carrie as well.

She screamed.

Alex stepped over a body and into the narrow hall when he heard the trigger click. He smiled at her helplessness, the kind of vulnerability that made her so attractive. He turned to tell her, "You have to turn the safety—"

The gun fired.

Smoke rose from the pistol's barrel. Alex gazed down to find the source of a sudden stinging sensation. He found a bleeding hole in his abdomen. "The safety—" he repeated, then stumbled into the corner wall of the hallway.

All the zombies, save the one formerly known as Ben, turned to see what the commotion was. They saw Alex slump down to the floor, his legs spread out and his back to the wall. They saw the irresistibly appetizing blood pour from his side, their official invitation to dine.

"Why me, Carrie?" he asked sincerely. "I'm the only one who ever loved you."

As the crowd of undead onlookers approached, he heard a multitude of voices, all laughing, all calling out "Jackass! Jackass! Jackass!" all at once, just as he heard on the street corner earlier that day.

"Stop it!" he yelled. "I'm not a jackass! I'm not! I'm not! I'm not!"

The undead things slowly descended upon Alex until he was covered in a mass of bodies riddled with the infected teeth from his bombs. While they feasted on the screaming schizophrenic, Ben stepped closer and closer toward Carrie.

With both hands on the grip, she adjusted the path of the gun for Ben's head. She raised and lowered the gun repeatedly until she was certain it was dead-center his forehead.

She cried as he grew closer.

"You're the only man who ever stood up for me," she said. "The only man I've ever kissed, and that for the first time today."

Ben didn't comprehend her words, or whatever the sounds were that the animal before him made.

"You're the man I want to live and die with," she said and forced a quivering smile through her sobs.

She lowered the gun to her side, then opening her hand, let it fall to the floor.

Ben's arms reached forward, as did hers.

As they had embraced for a moment in life, they embraced in death.

Three passionate kisses then.

Three ravenous bites now.

The two were joined in an unbreakable union. Unbreakable, save for a single clean shot to the brain—or several messy ones—to the undead lovers it wouldn't really matter.

5 SWORDS AND CUPS BY EDWARD J. CHARLONIS

He awoke inside a small country house. The sun was shining through the wood-covered windows. He could feel the heat of the day already creeping into the wooden floors. It was July 24th, and it was going to be a very hot day. He had slept with his back up to the front door. To his right was the living room. A comfortable cream-colored sectional couch sat before the sixty-inch flat screen television over the mantle. To his left was a dining room. Its furniture, a cherry-colored china cabinet and matching eight-person table and chairs were the room's only occupants.

He had secured the windows and back door the night before. There were none of "them" for at least a two-mile radius. He had seen to that last night. He stretched his arms over his head and groaned. If he were ten years younger, this would not have bothered him as much. His tailbone was numb yet ached at the same time. An empty glass sat next to him where he had left it the night before. Its contents (water) had been drunk hours ago.

He stood on stiff legs, making sure to grab the object to his left. He gripped the black leather-covered scabbard, making sure not to drag it on the floor as he picked it up. He turned and cracked his back. He sighed as he rolled his neck to release the night's tension. He walked over to the dining room window and peered between the boards, looking for any sign of his enemy. As he scanned the area, he took note of the sun's position. Must be seven or eight in the morning. The only thing he saw outside was the beat-up taxi he had come here in, and the brand new Ford Escape parked next to it.

The house sat on an open lawn. He had been there since the morning before. At least a thousand feet separated the structure from the wood line. It was perfect if you were trying to keep surprises from sneaking up on you. He had made sure to cover the windows and secure the house. The light was not a problem, as there had been no electricity for a week. He had scrounged some food that was left in the pantry for himself and his guest.

A small smile passed across his hard features, and a chuckle escaped his throat. To think of where he was just over a week ago and where he presently was made him think, *God has a sense of humor sometimes.*

He walked back out into the main hallway. The stairs were to his right, and a hallway ran to its side down to the kitchen in the back of the house. He could see the light stealing into the large room. He thought for a moment to go upstairs and wake his guest, then thought better to let her sleep a while longer. Rest was in short supply these days. Not everyone had to be as disciplined as he was. He walked down the hall to the kitchen to see what he could prepare for breakfast.

The kitchen's walls were red. Its black marble countertops made the room seem even darker than it was. In one corner was a breakfast nook with a light-colored table and chairs. The kitchen smelled faintly of rotten meat, since the refrigerator had stopped working days ago. He had made sure to take the spoiled food out far away from the house so as not to attract any unwanted company. It became an unintended trap for his enemy. He had made many kills around the browned food.

He had tried to avoid the personal effects of the home he had taken up residence in. It pained him to think of the fate that may have befallen the owners of the home. He could not help looking at the picture hanging on the opposite wall of the kitchen counter. It showed a family, a father and mother with three children, a girl and two boys, throwing leaves into the air. The smiles on their faces saddened him. How had it all come crashing down? Where would they all go from here? Was there any going back to life the way it was before?

He laid his weapon on the counter and turned to see what was left in the cabinets. He found a box of Cheerios. No milk was available. He moved aside a can of chili to find a box of complete pancake mix. All that was required was water. He checked the stove. The electricity was out, but this was a gas stove. He only hoped it still had fuel. He rooted through the drawers until he found a box of matches. He turned the dial on the stove and struck the match. He held the flame to the burner, and with a short whoosh the burner came to life. He quickly turned the dial, shutting the stove back off. His guest would appreciate this.

He took his weapon up once more and went upstairs. The upstairs was arranged in a ring so that all the bedroom and bathroom doors faced the center of the second floor. He went upstairs and made a left. He opened the door into a pink room filled with everything that was cute and fluffy. Sheer purple curtains covered the windows and lace adorned the top of the window. Trolls with big wild hair and yellow pill-shaped creatures in blue overalls were everywhere; an enormous teddy bear took up on the whole corner of the room. In the bed, the covers tossed off of her small frame, was a little girl no older than nine.

She wore a dirty dress that was once a bright white, blue, and red flower print. Her light brown hair was all over the bed and gave her the appearance of someone who had stuck their finger into an electrical outlet. She tossed over to face the wall with the window and let out a small groan. He felt bad waking her, but she had to eat, and he did not want to stay in this house much longer. The man crossed the room to the bed.

"Sarah," the man said, gently shaking her shoulder. "Wake up, Teacup. There is breakfast downstairs."

Sarah turned over once more, her hazel eyes half open. She rubbed the slumber from her eyelids and looked at the man before her.

"Good morning, Teacup," he said smiling.

"Good morning, Mr. Wak," Sarah said.

Shintaro Wakayama looked back at his young charge, still smiling. His 45-year-old frame was draped in a filthy white dress shirt, his cufflinks were long gone, and his black pants were ripped in too many places to count. His hair was cut short and was once styled to give him a gentlemanly look. A week-old stubble beard finished off his hardened frame. He held the katana in his left hand.

Sarah Lowe had a grand appetite for a nine-year-old. At first, Shintaro made half the box of pancake mix. Then he had to make the remaining half to sate the girl's hunger and his own. He found butter in the fridge. After sniffing and tasting it, he put it out on the table next to a quarter of a bottle of maple syrup. Sarah declined water when she spotted a familiar red label and gulped down a glass of warm Coke. He allowed her to overindulge. Who knew when they would have a banquet like this again? Sitting here with her, in this kitchen, at this table, it almost felt normal. He thought of his own daughter, now a young woman, and wondered what she was doing at this moment.

"These are very good Mr. Wak," Sarah said between mouthfuls of pancake. "Thank you for a yummy breakfast."

"You are welcome, Teacup," Shintaro said. Having eaten his fill, he left the remainder of the batch for Sarah.

"Mr. Wak," Sarah said, before shoveling in the last bite of pancakes, "are we staying here much longer?"

"No, little one," Shintaro said. "We must be on our way soon if we are to get to our destination."

At that moment he heard something. It was faint, but he caught it, nonetheless. It was the sound of something being dragged across the grass. He stood up slowly, grabbing the sword as his feet came under him. He put his finger up to his lips to tell Sarah to stay quiet. He turned and walked to the small window over the kitchen window. He saw nothing.

"Stay here, Teacup. If I am not back in ten minutes, get the keys to the blue car in the driveway and leave. Understood?"

"Yes, Mr. Wak," Sarah said, without question.

Shintaro had taught the girl how to drive on the trip up here. He had taught her the basics but never let her take the wheel by herself. Their flight from the city had been too important to jeopardize on lessons she was too young to learn but had to.

He crept through the door bridging the dining room and kitchen. The boards made no sound under his worn dress loafers. He held the sword in his left grip firmly. He made his way to the front window and spied through the boards. It was then he saw it. One of "them."

Its leg was broken at the ankle. The bone protruded, and it walked on the side of its foot which was encased in a brown work boot. It wore a flannel shirt and worn blue jeans. Shintaro concluded it must have been a local farmer. He spied the large chunk of flesh that was missing from his lower jaw. Its eyes were a milky blue color riddled with red veins and its flesh was variegated like marble. Blue veins ran throughout its face, and a kitchen knife stuck out from its chest. The wound would have killed it if it were human. The creature moaned sorrowfully as if it were lost.

Shintaro moved into the living room and then into the laundry room which connected the study to the living room. The door to his right led to the garage. He pushed the door open and stepped into the garage. Tools and boxes lined the far wall. To the left was a door that led out into the yard. He had to keep the creature from the front door. He could not risk any more of its kind following its lead. He moved like a calm breeze, his shoes making not one sound on the concrete floor.

He reached the door and unlocked it, making sure to keep the clicks muffled. He flowed out of the door and pulled it closed behind him. He took his first step on the blacktop driveway and headed right, holding the sword in his left hand and thumbing the tsuba (hand guard), releasing the blade just a fraction to make for an easier draw. With his right hand, he gripped the sword high on its tsuka (handle) and continued towards the corner of the house, but widened his arc to bring him out and away from the structure. He wanted the room to fight.

Shintaro came out from the cover of the house and spotted the creature still coming in his direction. It sniffed and turned its head jerkily, as if it sensed something. It brought its face forward and looked directly at him. It snarled and doubled its pace There were sixty feet between the creature and its prey, and it was impatient. Shintaro, however, was not.

He waited for the creature to hobble to him. At the last moment, he sidestepped the monstrosity and brought the blade from its scabbard in a fluid motion. A thump sounded on the ground, and the shambler walked past him, leaving its head behind it. A second later the body dropped lifelessly to the blacktop a few feet from its severed head. Its mouth was frozen open, and its face stopped in a moment of hatred. Shintaro swung the blade to remove the dripping ichor. The creature smelled rancid. He thanked the powers above that this was one of the slower of its kind. It also meant this one had died its real death a few days ago.

Shintaro heard a scuff behind him and turned just in time as another shambler lunged at him. She was a black woman dressed in blood-drenched hospital scrubs. Her flesh was a grey color, and a large part of her neck had been torn out. Shintaro's left arm shot up, planting the scabbard into the creature's neck. With his attacker at bay, he brought his sword sweeping out and took the top of the thing's head off. Diseased blood squirted out of the wound, and he could see the gray matter of its brain exposed.

Shintaro swung the blade to his side once more to remove the fluids from its razor sheen. The body dropped backwards to the ground. In the back of his mind, he could hear the words of his master, Mifune. "Do you expect the wind to guard your rear?"

Shintaro scanned the grounds, making sure no more of the creatures were lurking about. Satisfied, he went back inside. He found Sarah still sitting at the table where he had left her. "Everything is fine, Teacup," he said to her, trying to smile comfortingly.

He went to the sink and grabbed the dish rag from behind the faucet. He lovingly wiped down the blade, making sure not to leave a single drop of the blood on its surface. He put the rag in the garbage, not wanting any other passersby to mistakenly use it with the diseased fluids on it. He resheathed the blade. A good swordsmen knew when a weapon was needed.

"Come, child," Shintaro said, grabbing the keys for the Ford Escape off of the key rack on the wall next to the fridge. "We have overstayed our welcome here."

Sarah stood up and pushed her chair in. Even in a grave situation like this, the little girl still had manners. She picked up a bag that had been sitting next to her. Shintaro knew it had not been there when he left. Sarah came over and grabbed Shintaro's hand. He had hooked the key ring to his middle finger where it draped off the back of his hand. This allowed him to hold the girl's hand simultaneously. He looked at Sarah, who nodded her readiness. "Did you pack snacks for the road?" Shintaro asked, smiling. Sarah nodded again as her cheeks flushed with proud timidity.

"When we get out there," he said, "I want your eyes to the sky. You don't want to see what occurred out there." Sarah nodded once more, knowing Mr. Wak was trying to protect her.

Shintaro opened the door from the garage to the driveway. He closed it behind them. Far be it from him to allow those things inside and deny anyone else a viable shelter. He made sure Sarah was looking up, and away from the two bodies that littered the blacktop. He hit the button on the car remote, and he heard the door locks click open. He placed Sarah in the passenger seat and closed the door as she was buckling her seat belt.

Shintaro went around them to the driver's side and entered the vehicle. He placed his sword in the back seat with the handle of the weapon facing into the front seat for easy access. He started the car and backed up. He swung the vehicle out onto the lawn of the home and shifted the car into drive. He accelerated slightly and made a left once he came to the end of the driveway. He looked reassuringly at Sarah, who smiled back.

"Mr. Wak," she said, "how long until we get home?"

Shintaro almost laughed. He was glad, even in a calamity such as this, that a child could still be a child. "Let's turn on the GPS and find out, child." Shintaro activated the dashboard GPS and asked Sarah her home address. He typed it in slowly, keeping his eyes on the road. They passed an abandoned car halfway into the road. The passenger side doors were open, and blood was smeared onto all of the windows.

Shintaro did not drive fast. There were too many obstacles on the roads. He drove no more than thirty miles an hour. They were traveling on the road called Route 17M through a town called Wawayanda. The route they were on seemed like a minor thoroughfare, but, as Shintaro could tell from the GPS, it was leading them to a major state route and a small city called Middletown. Shintaro wanted to avoid any center mass of the population. Those areas seemed to have been hit the hardest. People clustered together seemed to make whatever this was spread faster.

***

Shintaro had been in New York City when the event started. He was to be a guest of honor at the World Martial Arts Expo. The event this year was held in the Jacob Javits Center in the heart of Manhattan. Shintaro was a throwback in the martial arts world. He lived his life by the Code of the Samurai. His job was his shogunate, and his boss the shogun. He was not a complete samurai, as he valued his family above all else. His wife Kaori and his ten-year-old daughter Yuki were the center of his world. They were expecting a fourth member of their family. His son, Toshiro, was due in two months' time. It was the only reason he agreed to travel so far for this event.

He brought along his assistant, Emiko, and promised her a working vacation. Emiko was a beautiful 25-year-old woman. She was the talk of the company. Shintaro's colleagues would joke that he should work late with her some nights. Shintaro laughed at their childish chiding, knowing there was only one woman he spent late nights with. Emiko wore a black skirt with a cream-colored tight jacket. Her blue silk blouse and black high heels completed her look. Shintaro had worked with her for over two years now. She would make any man very happy, and he would be lucky to have her.

His job paid him to travel for martial arts conventions. It was only good business, and Shintaro plugged his company any chance he got. The company had become both his employer and sponsor. Everyone, after all, needed to drive a car. He had become known as the Samurai Salesman. In the areas where he appeared, automobile sales for his company rose five to seven percent. What they spent to ferry him around the world was a drop in the pond compared to the money he made for them.

He strode through the event center like a king, Emiko in tow. He was the undisputed Kendo champion and master of the katana. There were few who could come close to matching his skill with the sword, and even fewer who had the potential to surpass him. Some joked he was Musashi Miyamoto reborn. Others joked he was born five hundred years too late. None of the praise ever went to Shintaro's head. For him, the sword was a pastime. His life was his work which provided for his family.

He and Emiko rushed along to his next demonstration. He was growing tired of cutting watermelons or apples that were thrown in the air. The sword he carried in his left hand was not the sword he simply cut fruit with. That would insult the weapon. This was his battle sword. It was the finest blade he had in his collection. He never let anyone else hold the sword, as he believed a katana was a part of a warrior's soul. It even had its own special place in his home, placed where no one else could or would touch it, in a locked display case above the mantle of the fireplace in his study.

The main gallery of the event center served as the arena. Martial arts tournaments and demonstrations rotated as the attraction of the hour. Various panels and speakers occupied the smaller conference rooms. Shintaro ascended the stairs to a full crowd. They cheered as he entered. To receive such an ovation for an outdated skill warmed his heart. He smiled and raised his hand in a wave to the crowd.

Fruits of all sizes lined the outer ring of the mats that were set up. In the center, on a small folding table, was the sword he would use to slice the fruits. It was a far inferior sword than the one he carried, fit only to cut objects that could never fight back. A man in a tuxedo stood next to the table with a wireless microphone. "Ladies and gentleman, Master Shintaro Wakayama!" the announcer loudly proclaimed, and the crowd grew more raucous. It almost hurt Shintaro's ears. In a way, he did love their adulation.

He stopped at the edge of the mat to remove his shoes and his jacket. He left them with Emiko and strode out to the center of the mat. Three helpers came out, each one stationed at a different point on the mats. He placed his good sword on the table and took up the demonstration sword. It was lighter and off balanced. All the weight was on the blade as the handle was of cheaper quality than his other katana.

One of the helpers brought out a watermelon and placed it into a display that was two U-shaped holders on top of a wishbone-shaped base. Shintaro drew a breath. He centered himself as he did whenever he was about to draw live steel. He glared at the watermelon as if it were an enemy combatant. Shintaro drew the sword in Iaido style and sliced the melon in half with a quick stroke. He swung the sword, removing any juice that might remain and sheathed the blade once more. The crowd cheered. Flashes from cameras and phones created a thunderstorm effect in the room. A hint of a smile crossed Shintaro's features.

Before he could rest, two apples came toward him from either side of the mat. He drew his blade quickly and sliced both apples as they passed each other in the air. The fruit fell in four even pieces. He swung the sword again, removing the juices, and replaced the katana in its sheath.

The crowd cheered louder. His demonstration lasted another ten minutes with Shintaro cutting various fruits in different positions and angles. When he was done, the crowd roared as he placed his temporary blade on the table and took up his finer sword once more. He slipped his shoes back on at the edge of the mats, and Emiko handed him his jacket. He put it on, switching his sword from one hand to the other to slip his arms through the sleeves.

"Excellent, Wakayama san," Emiko said in Japanese.

"Thank you, Emiko," Shintaro said, straightening his jacket. "I knew I paid you for something."

Sharing a smile, the two were off once more. He was now on a panel discussion in one of the smaller conference rooms. Behind him, the mats were being cleaned and wiped down for a tournament that was about to begin. In his mind, he wished the participants luck and would have loved to stay and watch the combat. He himself had retired from the tournament scene years ago when he had nothing left to prove and thought of his family's well-being if he had ever been seriously hurt. These factors allowed him to retire unbeaten as a master of aikido and judo. He had even fought a few matches in the Mixed Martial Arts of America and had won his bouts.

On his way to the panel, an old acquaintance stopped him. "Still swing a mean blade, I see, Wakayama san," the bearded man said.

"Ah, Norris san!" Shintaro said, clasping the bearded man's hand and shaking it vigorously. "I had not heard you would be here."

"It was on again, off again," Mr. Norris said patting Shintaro on the side of his arm. "My schedule cleared at the last minute. Glad it did, too. I was getting tired of hopping on a plane to come see your skills."

"You honor me with your words," Shintaro said. "And it is nice to see you with the words matching your mouth movements."

The two laughed and exchanged a further brief conversation before going their separate ways to different conference rooms. It had been years since Shintaro had seen the rugged American. Perhaps he would invite him for a drink later if time permitted. He would love to pick the man's brain about what the American's master had been like. Shintaro was due at his conference, and he was already going to be a minute late. Shintaro prided himself on punctuality and abhorred being late.

As Shintaro reached the doors, he heard a commotion on the other side. Screaming and crashing sounded from behind the doors. Before he could open them, the doors burst open. A man in his late thirties slammed into Shintaro and almost took both of them to the ground. Shintaro recovered quickly and put his feet firmly back under him as the other man crawled and frantically got back to his feet. He was wearing a blue button-down shirt with a pair of stylish jeans. His glasses had a crack in the left lens. He stared at Shintaro in abject horror and ran away as fast as he could. Shintaro noticed he had dropped an ID badge. He could not make it out, but it had the seal of some sort of armed forces branch. Turning his attention back to the door, Shintaro saw pure horror inside.

In the center of the room were two individuals going wild. They were covered in blood, as was the floor around them. Bodies lay about them in the sea of blood. Each had suffered a fatal wound to the neck. As Shintaro watched the scene unfold, one of the people he took for dead shot up and attacked the nearest person. The woman he attacked attempted to fend him off by putting her hands around its neck. The attacker was not to be stopped and sank his teeth into the woman's jugular. He ripped the flesh off as a lion would from a zebra or antelope.

"Get behind me!" Shintaro shouted in Japanese at Emiko.

Emiko put Shintaro between herself and the carnage of the room. Another person Shintaro thought dead opened his eyes and quickly got to his feet. His blue t-shirt was soaked in blood which ran down to his jeans. His bloodshot milky eyes locked on Shintaro, and he charged through the room at him. Shintaro planted his feet. He had not been in a fight since his school days. He knew he could take this man down with one well-placed blow. However, something inside him wanted him to draw his blade and cut the man down. He fought that urge, knowing that was a door that could never be closed.

When the man was within reach Shintaro's left arm snapped out, and the sheathed blade caught the man perfectly in the temple. The man stumbled and turned but spun back around and came right back at Shintaro. The two went to the ground. The man tried biting Shintaro, but Shintaro got the scabbard under the man's chin and pushed up. His jaws were snapping like a crazed animal. His hands clawed at Shintaro incessantly. Blood and saliva splashed all over as they struggled. As he looked, he could see the wound now clearly. The jugular was severed. Veins under the skin turned black. The most frightening thing was that the man did not seem to tire.

In desperation, Shintaro lowered himself to knee the man in the genitals. His knee rose and fell three times in rapid succession. The man did not seem to notice it. Shintaro was shocked. There was no conceivable reason this man could not feel that pain. Every man knew the pain of that brutal blow. Three such blows would put any man, any size, down on the ground writhing in agony. Something was very wrong.

Emiko appeared behind the struggling men and swung a fire extinguisher. The heavy red metal canister connected with the back of the man's skull. It seemed to stun him for a moment. Shintaro pushed the man off him and managed to get to his feet. Just as quickly, the man recovered and attacked Emiko. She swung the fire extinguisher once more, scoring a glancing blow on his shoulder before he was upon her. She tried backing away, fending the man off with her makeshift weapon. He was relentless. He found a handhold on her suit jacket and tried tugging her closer.

Shintaro's blade flashed out behind Emiko and her attacker. The swing caught the man on the back of the neck where it cut clean through. Emiko's attacker left his head behind as the body still surged forward. After a few seconds, the movement stopped, and it fell lifeless to the floor.

"Come on!" Shintaro said in Japanese, offering his hand to Emiko. She took the offered hand, and the two ran, leaving the body and discarded fire extinguisher behind. It was at that moment the carnage of the room swept over the entire convention center.

Shintaro discarded his suit jacket. Everyone was now running. Some people panicked and stood screaming. Those were the first to fall to the wave of crazed people overtaking the Javits Center. A mob of at least forty people attacked and they took down individuals like a pack of hyenas. They tore into their victims, feasting on their internal organs. They consumed intestines, livers, and hearts before moving on to the next victim. The group seemed to grow minute by minute, as if other people were being infected by the madness. Seemingly dead people were rising from the floor to attack others.

Shintaro and Emiko made it to the main entrance of the convention center. Shintaro found his phone in his pocket and dialed 911 as the pair ran. He was met with a message informing him all circuits were busy. "Of course they are," Shintaro said, cursing the criminals of America.

He tried several times to connect to the emergency line, to no avail. He tried to hail a cab but found traffic was at a standstill. It appeared an accident had happened down the block. Shintaro could see multiple sirens through the sea of cars. He saw a separate incident of two medics attending to a man lying prone on the sidewalk. "We'll have to run," Shintaro said, as the two continued down the sidewalk.

As they ran, Shintaro punched in the address to the Japanese consulate on his cellphone GPS. Two miles.

Shintaro could run that in twenty minutes. He could not, however, do that with Emiko and certainly not while she wore high heels. "Emiko," Shintaro said, stopping abruptly, "lose your shoes. We can run faster without them. I will stop at the first shoe store and get you sneakers."

Emiko complied and kicked her shoes off, and the two began running once more. Behind them, he could see the crazed mob pouring from the convention center and out into the streets. If his eyes were not deceiving him, the size of the group had more than doubled since they had escaped the building. They fell upon people passing by in the streets. Shintaro kept running with Emiko in tow. There was no going back. He had killed. He had witnessed death. He knew the world was about to change, and not for the better.

As they neared the end of the first mile, Shintaro saw a sporting goods store. They went in and noticed everyone was standing at the glass windows watching something across the street. "Find your size, and we must go," Shintaro said as Emiko hurried into the back of the store.

He turned his attention to what the other store patrons had been watching. Two NYPD officers were struggling with an uncooperative man across the street. The man was lying on top of one of the officers as they fought on the ground, a discarded taser nearby. The other officer was hitting the man repeatedly with his baton. Nothing seemed to affect the man. The man sank his teeth in the officer's neck and ripped free a section of the man's throat. Blood spouted like a geyser. The other officer wrapped the baton around the man's neck and hauled him from his partner. It was then that Shintaro saw the milky bloodshot eyes.

Shintaro whipped the door open and made his way through the stopped cars as he crossed the street. He could hear the animalistic snarls of the man as he struggled with the police. The officers never noticed as Shintaro drew his sword and slammed the point of it through the man's ear. The katana came cleanly out through the other side of the man's head. His struggles stopped immediately, and his body went limp. The policeman was stunned by what they had just seen. They looked at Shintaro with a look of shock and appreciation. "Kill them," Shintaro said to the officer. "They are not human anymore."

"Hold it," the standing officer said to Shintaro as he drew his gun. "You're under arrest! Officer down—I repeat, officer down!"

Shintaro knew they would not yet understand what was happening. They had not seen what he had at the convention center. He kept walking across the street. He heard the officer's radios come to life telling them to report to the Javits Center to assist in controlling a riot. "You should go," Shintaro shouted, as he crossed the street. "Aim for their heads. It seems to stop them."

"Stop right there!" The officer shouted again, now crossing the street to come arrest Shintaro. He stopped and started talking on his radio, telling his dispatcher he would be making an arrest, required backup, and cursed about where the ambulance was.

Before he could finish his sentence, his partner attacked him from behind. Shintaro heard the man scream as the other officer tore into his neck. The two struggled as the officer pleaded with his partner, asking why he was attacking him. With a heavy heart, Shintaro went back and killed the infected policeman. He put the katana into the officer's eye and forced it through the back of his skull. The man dropped instantly. Only then did Shintaro see the gaping bite wound on the officer's forearm.

The other officer was still standing clutching his wound. Shintaro felt sorry for the man. He felt sorry for anyone who had no idea what was descending on this city. He leaned down and picked up the officer's discarded Glock. He put the gun firmly in the man's hand and said, "What happened to him will happen to you. If you value the lives of others, use this weapon on yourself." Shintaro turned to go. "I am sorry."

The officer was too winded and stunned to answer or try to arrest Shintaro again. Time was precious now. Shintaro went back into the store to fetch Emiko. The other people in the store all backed away from Shintaro. Fear and amazement played across all their faces. Emiko was coming from the back of the store wearing a brand new pair of cross trainers. Shintaro pulled a few bills from his pocket and threw them onto the counter. He and Emiko exited the store and continued on their way to the consulate.

Two blocks later they came across another accident. Shintaro knew this was no coincidence. Firemen were cutting one car open. Medics performed CPR on the driver of the other car. Blood poured from a deep wound in the woman's head. Shintaro quickened his pace. As the firefighters pulled the door off of the other car, a child leaped out and sunk his teeth into his rescuer's face. The man had not been wearing his helmet. The face shield may have saved his life. The crazed child ripped the man's cheek clean off and began chewing on it. Two other firemen came over to help, pulling the child off their friend. The child bit into their coats but could not penetrate the tough material.

***

Shintaro and Emiko continued on. They were only a few blocks from the consulate. He had to make it. Hopefully, the consulate would have security and a means of air travel to get out of this crazed city. No one seemed to be going anywhere on the roads. He passed by a cafe and saw horror. Inside, three infected people were clawing at a restroom door. Shintaro thought he heard screaming from inside. Screams of a child. He stopped.

"Emiko," he said, as he handed her his phone with the directions to the consulate still on the screen. He rolled up his sleeves, switching his sword from hand to hand so he could do each arm. "Do not come in. If I fall, run. Do not look back. Just run. "

Shintaro entered the cafe. Soft jazz played over the speakers in the ceiling. He gripped the hilt of his weapon. He thumbed the blade out half an inch for an easier draw. He silently walked up and beheaded the man on the left. The woman in the center turned just in time for Shintaro to shove the blade through the roof of her mouth and out of the top of her skull. The third turned and charged Shintaro. He had no time or room to make a killing swing. He dropped his blade and scabbard and used the man's momentum to hurl him over a nearby table with an expert aikido throw. He retrieved the blade quickly and made ready to combat his foe. The infected man recovered quickly. A fork had pierced his cheek and flopped on his face. Shattered shards of a broken coffee mug and water glass embedded themselves in the side of his head. The man did not notice as he charged once more. Shintaro took the man's head clean off.

Shintaro could no longer hear the screams from behind the door. Swinging the sword to clean any blood off the blade he sheathed his weapon, then opened the door. It had not been locked. These people had simply had to pull the door open. Clearly, they had lost the capacity to think. Inside was a young girl, no older than nine. She was sitting with her knees to her chest. A half-broken teacup was still on her finger. Blood stained her jacket and dress. She had a shallow cut under her left eye. She stared at Shintaro. He could tell she was terrified. Perhaps she thought he was one of them. The little girl stared at him, not moving. "What is your name, little one?" Shintaro asked softly.

The little girl continued to stare. Shintaro did not want to scare the girl any more than she had been. He had to be gentle and patient—something that was difficult at this point in time.

"Shintaro san," Emiko said in Japanese from the doorway.

Shintaro turned. "One moment, Emiko," he replied in Japanese. "I only need a moment."

He turned back to the girl in the bathroom. "Where are your parents?" Shintaro asked.

He heard screaming and panic from outside.

"You can't stay here, dear," Shintaro said, with a hint of pleading in his voice. "There is danger."

But she did not speak.

Shintaro sighed. "Please, little girl," he said, "we have to be going."

Her only answer was her vacant stare. Shintaro looked at her for signs that she had been bitten. He saw nothing that would suggest the three attackers had wounded her in any way. Perhaps one or two of them had been her parents. He had to understand what had happened to her and try to handle the situation without using force to take her with them. He tried once more to get the girl to her feet.

"Come, Teacup," he said to her, extending his hand and smiled warmly, "you can come with us. We will keep you safe."

Slowly the girl got to her feet and walked to the door. She took Shintaro's hand tightly. She inhaled sharply and began to cry. "Aunt Cindy!" she screamed, as Shintaro looked in the direction the girl was facing.

She had spotted the infected woman's body. Shintaro felt a sliver of shame. He had killed someone's family. Although the woman who was this girl's aunt had tried to kill her, the girl still felt remorse upon seeing the body of the woman she had loved. "I'm sorry," Shintaro said genuinely, as if they were at a funeral.

"She started acting funny," the little girl said, between sobs. "After the man bit her. She thought he was trying to rob her. But he just bit her. Two policemen came and helped. They took the man away."

Shintaro found himself bending down to hug the girl. He thought of his own daughter and what he would want a stranger to do in a situation such as this. The girl hugged him back. He heard a faint "tink" sound behind him and realized the girl had just dropped the cup that was hanging from her finger. The two parted, and Shintaro looked her in the eyes. "Let's go, Teacup," he said motioning towards the front door with a nod of his head. "Let's get you to safety."

They left the cafe behind. Shintaro and the girl stepped out into a world of chaos. Sirens sounded from every street corner. People ran, some cursing as they could not get a signal on their phones. Shintaro looked at Emiko. She was looking around like a frightened bird, her head darting in every direction as she tried to take in all the activity.

"Emiko," he said to her sternly, to get her attention. When she turned to look at him, he continued in Japanese. "Take this girl's other hand. Hold her in between us. She is to be our charge until we can get her to safety." Emiko nodded in understanding.

"What is your name, Teacup?" Shintaro said, looking down at the girl.

"I'm Sarah Lowe. I'm from Elmira New York. I live with my mom and dad and my brother," she said in the rehearsed style of every lost child.

"Hello, Sarah," Shintaro said, aware that he was spending precious time to make this child feel comfortable. "That is Emiko. I am Shintaro Wakayama."

Sarah looked confused and tilted her head slightly to the right and said, "Can I just call you Mr. Wak?"

"That you may, Teacup," he replied. "Come. We have to hurry."

The trio continued in the direction of the Japanese consulate. Car accidents and people convulsing on the sidewalk surrounded their every step. Time was short. This city was only going to sink further into an abyss of disorder. He pulled his phone from his pocket. Only two blocks until they reached their destination. He knew Sarah would be an issue. She was obviously not Japanese. He only hoped they had some way of helping her get back to her family. They rounded the final corner onto Park Avenue. Shintaro could see things were as bad as he thought they were.

In front of the glass doors to the consulate stood a wall of eight armed men. Japanese agents. Each one carried a rifle and wore tactical vests over their pressed black suits. Shintaro only hoped those men standing there did not mean what feared. He had to get back to his family. He had to help Sarah and Emiko escape the madness of the city. He would not be denied. He held the lives of two people in his hands.

He walked swiftly up the stairs, and the two men in the middle held the hands out in a gesture to stop.

Before either could speak, Shintaro boldly cut them off. "I am Shintaro Wakayama, and I demand to enter the consulate of my country. I have two ladies who need help and a way out of this city. Let us in."

"Wakayama san," the guard to his left spoke, bowing slightly, "we know who you are."

"We can let you in," the right guard said, "but we cannot promise there will be help for any of you. The consulate has been ordered shut down and evacuated. We are here merely here to deter any trouble before the last helicopter leaves."

"From the roof?" Shintaro said, nodding up.

"Yes," the right guard said. "The ambassador and his staff are gone already. We will be the last to take off."

"Is there no one you can call that we can speak with?" Emiko said, almost panicked.

"The phone network has stopped operating properly," the guard said pulling his cell phone from a pocket on his vest. "I will attempt to reach someone and see what we can do."

Shintaro allowed the man a moment. He scanned his surroundings. People ran to and fro. The city had become a hive of frantic activity. "Wakayama san," the guard said, and Shintaro turned his head quickly to acknowledge the man. "The network is down. Most likely too many people on their phones. I cannot get a connection."

Shintaro nodded. "How many can fit on one of your helicopters?" he asked.

"Ten comfortably," the guard began, knowing where Shintaro was going with his question, "but I cannot get authorization to let you on."

"Damn your authorization!" Shintaro roared. The guard took a noticeable step backward, and a few others tightened the grip on their rifles. "There are two people in need of help."

Emiko turned to him at this last line. "But Shintaro san," she said, "there are three of us."

"If I can get you and Sarah out of here, it will be a victory," he said, looking down at the girl. "I can find my own way if necessary. You have a lucky man to find. This little one has a life she has not yet begun to live."

Emiko started to cry. Sarah looked between them, confused. They were talking funny, and she wished she could understand what they were saying. Why was the other lady crying? What had Mr. Wak said to upset her? Sarah felt tears in her eyes. What was happening? Were they not getting into the building? Were these men going to shoot them? Was that why Emiko was crying?

"Don't you hurt us!" Sarah screamed at the guards.

The men looked confused. It was obvious none of them spoke English. Shintaro smiled. Emiko put her hand to her mouth in shock. "What is your name?" Shintaro asked the guard.

"Itto," the guard answered.

"Itto, do you have children?" Shintaro continued.

"Two girls," Itto said. A hint of a smile played across his face as he mentioned his children.

"If these were your daughters," Shintaro said, "and you were in my place, what would you want the man in your place to say?"

The man stared for a moment. Shintaro had caught him off guard. It would catch anyone off guard. To reverse roles and force someone to make a decision on the opposite side was not an easy scenario. Shintaro had used it many times when he could see a negotiation was not going to be won. It was his calling card as a negotiator. He had used it on many union officials on his visits to the plants his company had in America.

Itto exhaled and stepped backward. He pulled open the door to the consulate building. "We will take all of you," he said. "I will deal with my superiors and face whatever consequences."

Shintaro hurried the girls inside. "Thank you, Itto san," he said, bowing quickly before entering the building.

The lobby was beautiful. There were multiple businesses and firms besides the consulate in the building. Emiko sat down with Sarah on a small couch by the main desk. Shintaro paced. They had made it. Now it was only a matter of time before the helicopter came to take them out of this city. He would get Sarah back to her family and Emiko home. He would return to Japan a changed man. He had killed. No matter if they were infected, he had killed people. He would live that the rest of his days. His children would never know their father had used his sword to take a life.

A few more minutes passed. Shintaro grew impatient. They had to get out of here before the situation went even more out of hand. His thought was interrupted by a slam against the glass windows. He turned quickly to see a mob of people attacking the guards. Weapons fire rang out as the guards shot. The guard on the far right went down under a dozen people. Blood spattered against the clear glass, his weapon firing until its magazine emptied. The other guards backed in through the door being held by Itto. Once the seven remaining men were inside, they secured the door with one of their belts.

"There is no need for that, Itto san," Shintaro said from behind them.

"They can just pull the door open otherwise and get in here," Itto said, sweating, his face red with exertion. "They have already killed Takeshi."

The people were now banging on the windows and doors. Some smeared blood from previous victims or wounds. "They do not understand that," Shintaro said, counting twenty-three of the infected people outside the building. "They seem to have an animal's intellect. They are unable to solve a problem as simple as pulling a door."

As they stood watching, Shintaro's point was proven correct. The infected simply bashed at the windows and doors. Some tried biting, only to have their lips smear down the glass. In a way, they looked comical. "The glass is bulletproof, six inches thick," Itto said from Shintaro's side. "They will not be getting through there."

"I think to keep their excitement down we should go upstairs or into another room," Shintaro said. "If they can't see us, they may move on."

"We can go up to the consulate floor on eighteen," Itto said, issuing orders to his men to fall back to the eighteenth floor.

They all piled into the elevator except one of the armed guards, who was ordered to stay downstairs. It was cramped, but they all fit. Shintaro had Sarah behind him and Emiko to his left. A moment or two passed and the elevators opened onto the consulate floor. A few people were gathering files and papers into boxes. The office had been ransacked. Chairs were turned over. Paper littered every inch of the floor. It had been little more than an hour since the start of this catastrophe. Everyone had left in a very big hurry. Did they know something that Shintaro and the public did not?

He let Sarah and Emiko out first, and he was last to leave the elevator. Itto stopped and jammed the elevator door open by rolling a chair between the doors to fool the sensor into thinking someone was standing there. Workers began bringing boxes and piled them into the elevator. Shintaro grabbed the first officer worker who came near him. "What is happening? How long ago were you told to evacuate?" Shintaro said, gripping the man's arm tightly.

"We were given the order an hour ago," the man said. "The ambassador was the first out. We are awaiting the last two helicopters to take us to the airport. We are all to return to Japan. This is happening with all of our embassies."

Shintaro let the man go. This was a worldwide event. Not just New York. There was more to this than he or the consulate worker knew. What's more, two more helicopters were inbound. Itto had made it sound as if only one more was coming back. He could get Emiko and Sarah out of here and follow on the last transport if necessary.

His hope was renewed. He would fulfill his personal obligation and get the ladies to safety.

"The chopper is coming in," one of the office workers shouted.

The other two men brought the last of the boxes (fifteen in total) and put them into the elevator and stayed. The third conversed with Itto.

"Can the girls go out on this helicopter?" Shintaro said, interrupting the two men.

"A moment, Wakayama san," Itto said, and returned to his conversation.

The two men parted, and the office worker went to the elevator. "He said you can go out with them, but it will be tight," Itto said. "Those documents have to be loaded as well."

"As long as they are on the flight I do not care," Shintaro said. "Just please get them to safety."

"We will. You as well." Itto said, waving them onto the elevator.

Shintaro bowed to Itto. "Thank you," he said, "for everything. I am in your debt. Whatever you need. Please let me know." Shintaro handed Itto a business card out of his pocket.

Itto smiled and accepted it. "Go," Itto said. "We will be on the next one."

Shintaro got into the elevator as the chair was moved out of the way. The doors closed on the seven men, and they were on their way to the roof of the forty-two floor building.

The elevator opened into a small room. The drab grey walls held only a single stairway up to a door that read "Roof Access." A worker went to the door and played with a set of keys trying to find the correct one to open the door. Another worker shoved a screwdriver into the elevator doors to jam them open. The third man grabbed a box and went up the stairs as the first got the door open. The second grabbed a box as well. Shintaro pitched in. Shoving his sword into his belt, he took a box. "Go up," he told Emiko and Sarah. "I will help them to make this quicker."

Sarah and Emiko ran up the stairs, with Shintaro lugging a box behind them. The first worker kicked a block under the door to keep it open. After a few minutes, the boxes were stacked neatly, and the roof door closed, as the helicopter approached and landed. The men blocked the boxes with their bodies to keep the lids from blowing off and the papers from scattering. When the rotors had died down, the side door of the helicopter slid open, and the men began piling the boxes inside. Shintaro helped once more.

"Who are they?" the pilot said to the worker who had spoken with Itto.

"Itto insists we take them as well," he answered. "The man with the sword is Shintaro Wakayama."

A look of shock crossed the pilot's face and he seemed impressed. "All right, then," he said, as he started the engines back up, "get them on board."

Before they could board, Itto burst onto the roof. He was covered in blood, and his clothes were torn. His left leg was a mess of blood and exposed muscle. It looked as if he had stepped in a paper shredder. He left a thick trail of blood behind him. Shintaro's sword was out of his belt as he crossed over to see what had happened. He knelt down next to Itto.

"Ichiro attacked us," he said, as he coughed up blood. "We shot him over fifty times, and he kept attacking. He killed Takeshi in the elevator. The others are dead. I almost didn't get away. He tore at my leg like a wild animal. Takeshi should have been dead outside! How was he able to come back? How did Ichiro survive? His throat was gone."

"Itto," Shintaro said, "did Ichiro bite you?"

"As we struggled in the elevator," Itto said, coughing up more blood, "he may have bitten me."

"Is there ammunition left in your gun?" Shintaro said, looking down at the Glock in Itto's hand.

"Yes," Itto said, looking down as well. "He stopped after I shot him in the head."

"Use one on yourself, Itto san," Shintaro said, sorrow filling his features, "or you will become what Ichiro became. Along with all those people now killing on the streets below."

Itto looked shocked and horrified. The lead worker came over to them. "He is hurt," the man said. "We have to get him on the helicopter."

"If you do, he will kill you all," Shintaro said. "He has been infected. He will not live much longer, and when he dies, he will become an animal."

The man snatched the gun from Itto and pointed it at Shintaro. "You're crazy!" he said. "Get away from him!"

The man called the other two over, and they lifted Itto up and carried him over to the helicopter. "You cannot!" Shintaro roared, and the man with the gun tensed, keeping it pointed at Shintaro.

"We're leaving," he said, backing away. "Stay where you are, or I will shoot you."

"But the women," Shintaro began, " they must be taken to safety."

"No," the man said, beginning to yell to be heard over the rotors. "You are all crazy. Come near this helicopter, and I will kill all of you."

"You cannot leave them here!" Shintaro said, taking a step forward.

The man pulled the trigger from fear and the shot embedded itself into the roof. His eyes were wide as he looked from the bullet hole to Shintaro. "Stay away," he said, as he climbed into the helicopter and closed the door behind him.

The helicopter lifted off from the roof. Shintaro had no doubt those men were canceling the last helicopter to this building. They were on their own. "Goddamn you!" Shintaro screamed at the departing chopper.

He looked back at Emiko and Sarah, who were both crying. He would get them both out of this city alive. This was merely a setback. "All right," he said to them, "back downstairs. There has to another way out of the building where those people at the front can't see us." He repeated what he had said in English for Sarah.

✳✳✳

An emergency exit brought them out onto East 49th street. They turned right and headed for Lexington Avenue. The airport was too far away. He did not want to be stuck in the Lincoln tunnel, which was no doubt gridlocked by now. He wanted out of the city. Going east would only take them into Brooklyn and Queens. More city. He wanted to get out into the country. The George Washington Bridge was their only choice for that. It was a two and a half hour walk under good conditions. He had to try. These ladies were his responsibility. He had to try.

As they approached the intersection of East 49th and Lexington, Shintaro saw smoke. As they got closer, Shintaro made out what used to be the blade of a helicopter. He could make out a mangled burning husk. The chopper had struck the building on the corner and come down in the street. Itto must have died and come back. Those poor, stupid fools. Shintaro led the girls down Lexington. The GPS on his phone was really leading the way. It was a straight shot down Lexington, followed by some twists and turns, and they would be at the bridge. He only hoped they did not run into any more of the infected.

"The chances of that are low," Shintaro said to himself.

As they reached East 59th Street, Shintaro saw his first obstacle. A massive accident had taken place at the intersection. Over a dozen cars had destroyed each other. The street was completely blocked. "This way," he said, as they turned left down East 59th.

"We can cut through the park," Shintaro said to Emiko, looking at his phone, "Hopefully we will run into fewer people that way, too."

"I hope you are right, Wakayama san," Emiko answered. "This city is becoming more dangerous by the minute."

Shintaro knew she was right. Seeking refuge at the consulate was a mistake. He saw that now. However, if he had not gone that way, Sarah would still be locked in that bathroom or dead. The heavens had an odd way of bringing circumstances together. None of that mattered now. What mattered was safety and getting out of this city. The only place to be safe was the country. If they made it into New Jersey, perhaps it would be less dangerous, and he could even get a car to the nearest airport away from Manhattan and the rest of New York. He had to try.

As they entered Central Park, Shintaro noticed fewer people, which confirmed his guess. They stayed in the woods and away from the drives, which would no doubt be clogged with cars and the infected. The woods were empty. It was as if the animals themselves knew what was coming and were all in hiding. Not one squirrel or bird crossed their path as they came to the outskirts of the Central Park Zoo. They were now traveling between East Drive and the zoo. Shintaro could make out cars on the street. They moved slowly, but the cars were moving.

Shintaro thought for a moment to go out and try to flag a taxi. He had second thoughts when he envisioned being trapped in a car in standstill traffic surrounded by crazed killers. They pressed on through the park, avoiding the roadway. "Mr. Wak," Sarah said, "I'm tired."

"I know, Teacup," Shintaro said. "But we have to get out of the city and away from the bad people trying to hurt us." He stopped and knelt on the ground. "Here," he said, motioning to his back. "Climb on, and I will carry you."

Shintaro shoved the sheathed weapon into his belt, and Sarah got onto his back. They started off once more. Sarah's weight barely slowed him. Emiko smiled behind them. As much as Wakayama tried to appear to be a hard man, he was a gentle soul inside and put others before his own needs. It was one of the reasons Emiko enjoyed working for the man. Although he was a butcher in the business world, his demeanor changed outside of the confines of work.

They came to the 65th Street Traverse. Now Shintaro saw strife. The traffic was stopped. Over a dozen of the infected roamed the street pounding on cars, trying to get to the people inside. It was almost humorous, like a person trying to get at the food inside of a can without an opener. One car had its windshield caved in, and the driver was dragged out into the street and torn apart. Another woman rolled her window down to yell at them. One of them jumped through her opened window and began eating her alive. No doubt there were similar scenes all over the city. Perhaps even worse.

Shintaro pressed on with Sarah on his back He could hear Emiko behind him, crying for the poor souls dying right in front of their eyes. They heard the sound of something scraping against the rock behind them. They all turned to see two of the infected pulling themselves up over the side of the bridge. "Down, child," Shintaro said, as he knelt down to let Sarah off of his back. "Emiko, behind me," he said in Japanese, as he thumbed the blade an inch out of its scabbard for easy drawing. The infected fell to the ground as they brought the rest of their bodies over the side, then they stood up and ran at them.

Shintaro planted his feet in preparation for battle. It would be hard to fend both of them off and keep the girls safe. "You must move with me," he told Emiko, without taking his eyes off of their attackers. "Stay behind me. Keep me in between you and them."

The infected never made it to them. There were two sharp cracks of gunshots and they both went down hard in a jumble, blood spraying from the back of their heads. Shintaro turned to see where the shots had come from. Off to the right stood two men. Each wore camouflage pants, sunglasses, and baseball caps. One was a head taller than the other, standing around six foot two. He had a full black beard trimmed neatly and wore a yellow shirt with a coiled snake on it. The other man was around Shintaro's height and wore a black shirt with a white American flag on it. His facial brown hair seemed only a few days old. Each man wore an olive green tactical vest and carried an M-4 rifle.

"You folks OK?" the shorter of the pair said.

"Yes," Shintaro said. "Thank you for the help."

"Where you guys headed?" the taller man said.

"I have to get these ladies out of the city," Shintaro replied, securing his sword in its scabbard once more. "Before this gets even worse."

"And it will," the taller man said.

The shorter man shot the other a quick look before looking back. "We could get you out," the man said. "Might be a bit of a chore, but if you're willing…"

"I will do anything," Shintaro said. "These girls have to get out."

"All right," the shorter man replied as he turned to start walking. "Let's get moving."

"I'm Shepard," the tall man said. "He's Maxwell. C'mon. Times a-wastin'."

"Can we trust them?" Emiko asked in Japanese.

"We have no choice," Shintaro said. "We must get out of the city. These men may be our best chance."

Shintaro took Sarah's hand and Emiko the other. They followed the two men, hoping this was not another grave mistake.

***

Contact was minimal and put down quickly by Maxwell and Shepard. These men were professionals. They were not mere weekend warriors. They had seen real combat. Perhaps even Black Ops. Shintaro saw their movements, one covering the other, each one taking the opposite direction of the other. They killed six of the infected during the rest of their jaunt through the park, each time taking them down with well-placed single head shots. What were men like these doing operating in New York City?

They came out on Central Park West not far from a traffic circle. Parked there was a huge black truck. It was like a hybrid of a pickup and a Hummer. Its chassis was almost three feet off the ground, and the frame was supported by huge, deep-treaded tires. Running boards helped those climbing into the monster vehicle. The front of the vehicle had a V-shaped inverted plow. Shintaro noticed a mounted machine gun on the back of the truck. This was no joyride.

"OK," Maxwell said. "Everyone meet Agatha. Agatha meet everyone. Climb aboard, people."

"Shotgun," Shepard said, covering their entrance into the truck. Shintaro got Emiko and Sarah into the back and climbed in last. Shepard took his place in the front passenger seat and rolled his window down. "This was originally made for a combat zone," Shepard said, as he noticed Emiko's puzzled look. "Windows are all bullet proof. I don't expect to run into much gunfire from these things."

"She doesn't speak very good English," Shintaro said and translated for Emiko, who still looked nervous but understood Shepard's intentions with the window.

"Do you know what is going on?" Shintaro asked, buckling Sarah in. "What is wrong with these people?"

"Not sure, friend," Maxwell said, kicking the truck into gear and starting down the street. "One thing for sure. They're dead."

"What do you mean?" Shintaro asked.

"Well, they die and come back," Maxwell said. "The only way to put them down is the head. So, they're dead already when you kill them."

"How?" Shintaro said, both fascinated and horrified.

"No clue," Shepard said from the passenger seat. He did not even turn as he spoke, "It's viral, that's for sure. People who die from the attacks are getting back up to kill. We've seen it."

"I have, as well," Shintaro said solemnly.

"Well, where can we drop you guys?" Maxwell said breaking the tension.

"We are trying to get to the George Washington Bridge," Shintaro said.

"Guess you know about the tunnel, then, huh?" Shepard said.

"No, what happened?" Shintaro said.

"These things caused a bad accident," Maxwell stated. "A tanker truck flipped and exploded. The Lincoln's become a dead end."

"Why not any of the other bridges?" Shepard asked. "Or do you want out of the city altogether?"

"Yes," Shintaro said. "I do not want to go into the other side of the city. That would be no safer."

"You'd be right," Shepard said. "The other boroughs aren't faring any better."

"All right," Maxwell said. "Riverside drive it is."

He stepped on the gas and pushed anything out of the way with the huge plow and pure muscle of the vehicle. Shepard popped off a few shots at a few infected that got too close to the truck. Maxwell ran a few of them down. The crunching and bumping as their bodies were pulped by the truck were unsettling. Shintaro told Sarah to keep her eyes closed. The child had seen and been through enough. These men had no qualms about taking a life. Living or dead.

Maxwell swung out onto Riverside Drive, taking the turn very sharply. The truck's wheel struck an oncoming car knocking it out of the lane. Shintaro was starting to see the relationship between the two soldiers. Maxwell was the driver; his skills were obvious. He navigated the streets of the city as if it were a video game he had played a hundred times. Shepard was the sharpshooter. He took his targets down with almost mechanical efficiency.

They raced along Riverside, moving in and out of any space no matter how small. Maxwell let out a slight laugh every now and again as he almost crashed or collided with another car. "You have no idea how many times I've driven this road," Maxwell said, smiling, "and wanted to drive it just like this."

Shintaro could see the bridge in the distance. They were close. So close. Maxwell veered sharply to the right onto another road. Which one it was Shintaro could not tell. Around him, the city was awash in violence. Fires burned, cars collided everywhere, and the dead—the dead hunted and killed, adding to their swelling horde. This city's final hour was coming. He could tell that. These two men could tell that. Who were they? This gnawed at Shintaro. Why would they help them? Was the American government activating sleeper agents that had been dormant, awaiting a calamity such as this?

"Almost there, folks," Maxwell said as he passed cars on the shoulder. "We appreciate you driving with 9MM Taxi. Tips are appreciated."

A sudden jolt sent Shintaro's head into the back of the driver's seat. He shot his hand out to secure Sarah between himself and Emiko. As Shintaro looked out of the window, he saw Maxwell had just bulled his way through a two-car accident. The drivers yelled at him and made rude gestures. As Maxwell came to the upper level of the bridge, he had to slow down. Traffic was gridlocked with nowhere to go. Even his plow would do him no good.

"Shit," Maxwell said, slamming his palm into the steering wheel. "Looks like you folks may have to walk from here. Unless you want to sit here with us a little longer."

"We will walk, Mr. Maxwell," Shintaro said, unbuckling himself and Sarah. "Thank you for getting us this far."

Shintaro handed Maxwell his card. "In case you men ever need anything, once this is all over," Shintaro said, "feel free to call on me. I owe you a debt."

"No need, bud," Maxwell said, taking the card. "We get paid for this kind of shit. Hell, Shepard there would do it for free."

All three smiled as Shintaro exchanged nods with the two men and exited the truck. Sarah, Emiko, and he began their long walk across the bridge.

"You suppose that guy knew how to use that sword of his?" Maxwell asked, looking at Shepard.

"Damn," Shepard said. "As good as you are at driving, you're blind to details. The guy was covered in blood and not a scratch on him. 'Course he knew how to use the damn thing."

"Woulda been a handy guy to have in a fight, then," Maxwell said, sighing. "What now, big guy?"

"Throw this big bitch in reverse," Shepard said, checking his weapon. "And let's get back to what we get paid for."

With that, Maxwell threw Agatha into reverse and headed back down the ramp they had just come, once again hitting the two cars involved in the accident.

Shintaro and Emiko held Sarah's hands once more. "Those men turned out OK," Emiko said, as they half ran along the side of the bridge.

"For once, today," Shintaro said, "we caught a break. We'll try to get a taxi once we get to the other side. The Palisades Parkway will take us further into the state. There is not much up there besides one or two smaller cities."

"I hope you are right," Emiko said. "We must get this child home."

"We will," Shintaro said, sparing a glance at Emiko. "Then we will find our own way home."

At mid-span, there was a five-car pileup. It blocked the whole road, with one of the cars resting atop two others. They would have to climb the wrecks. He only hoped no one had died. They moved through the stopped cars and went to the left lane. There was a safe place to traverse the cars. They ran over to the spot and Shintaro scanned the other side for any dangers. He lifted Sarah onto the hood of the now-ruined car. "Emiko," he said, offering his hand to help her up as well, "go to the other side and help Sarah down."

Emiko stepped gingerly across the smashed hood of the car. She jumped down on the other side and motioned for Sarah to come to her. Shintaro hopped up onto the car so as to not leave the ladies alone on the other side for long. He looked around as Emiko held Sarah's hand while she jumped down. Another car had hit the right side of the bridge. A taxi was stopped a few feet away, the driver door open, and the engine was running. Shintaro thumbed his sword from its scabbard.

The traffic on this side of the accident was light, as no one else could get through. Emergency services had not arrived yet; they were spread too thinly as it was. Shintaro was no thief, but the opportunity of a car to get them away from the city was all too tempting to pass up. This was a desperate time unlike any other. Some decorum had to set aside for the sake of survival.

"Hello?" Shintaro called out, trying to track down the driver of the taxi. "Stay behind me. We'll be taking that car one way or the other."

He crept closer to the taxi. He saw the driver of the car beyond slumped over the wheel. Blood streamed from a cut in his head, no doubt caused by the collision with the bridge. When they neared the taxi, Shintaro held his hand out for them to stay where they were. He saw a stream of blood coming from behind the back tire on the other side of the car. Shintaro went around the front of the car and saw what he had feared. Four of the infected had murdered a man. His abdomen was ripped open, and his organs had been consumed. He saw one of them eating his liver and two others fighting over each end of his intestines, as the fourth ate what might have been one of his kidneys.

Shintaro backed away slowly and silently. To draw their attention was to get one of them killed. He would not have that. He went to the other side and spoke to Emiko in hushed, hurried Japanese. "When I tell you," he said, "get Sarah into the car and then yourself. Close the doors behind you if I do not make it in."

He knelt down, careful to keep an eye on the other side of the taxi. "Teacup, listen to me," Shintaro said. "We must be very quiet. You are going to get into the car with Ms. Emiko. I will be right behind you, OK?"

Sarah nodded her head, determined but frightened. Shintaro slid his sword out, slowly and quietly. There was no time for a draw. These people would be on them before he could enter the car and he knew it. He would save Emiko and Sarah even if it cost him his life, which it looked like, this time, it would. "Go," he told Emiko.

Emiko nudged Sarah, and the girl climbed into the open door, trying to make as little noise as possible. As Sarah climbed into the passenger seat, and Emiko the driver's seat, another infected slammed his body into the side of the car, snarling at the two women within. It was the taxi driver. Shintaro cursed himself for not taking him into account. "Close the door!" Shintaro yelled, as Emiko settled into the driver's seat. She slammed the door, tears streaming from her eyes.

"Come at me you, you bastards!" Shintaro roared, as he took his sword in a two-handed grip and set his stance.

The infected that had been eating the liver was the first at him. Shintaro brought the sword down vertically and chopped into the man's skull. He dropped immediately, and the taxi driver was on Shintaro. He put his blade up like a staff and the driver bit into the metal of the blade. Shintaro pushed back against the man, the blade cutting into the cheeks of the infected attacker. The other three were making their way around the car. Two went in front, and one was climbing over the car on its roof.

The car tires screeched as Emiko put it into drive. She rammed into the two in front, running them over and dragging them a few feet before she stopped. The one on the roof was thrown clear and landed awkwardly on its left leg, snapping it clean. The bone was protruding from the skin. Of the two she had run over, one stirred. Its arms were clearly broken, and its left leg was mangled. Despite this massive trauma, it still tried to crawl towards where Shintaro struggled with the last of the infected. The other's head had been caught under the front driver's wheel and crushed like a ripe fruit.

The taxi driver brought Shintaro to the ground. He snarled, bled, and drooled all over. Shintaro's sword had stopped cutting into the man as it hit his spine at the back of his head. Its snapping was awkward but still dangerous. He was so preoccupied with his attacker he failed to notice Emiko walking up behind them. She raised her right arm, and the front of the taxi driver's head exploded onto Shintaro's chest and face.

He threw the twice-lifeless body off of him and sat up. He looked at Emiko, who held a nickel-plated Smith &

Wesson revolver in her hand. The barrel still smoked and the report of the weapon was still ringing in Shintaro's ears. "Where did you find that?" Shintaro asked, surprised and amused.

"In the glove compartment," Emiko said, smiling. "Remember. Every American has a gun." They both laughed.

A woman smashed into Emiko and rode her to the ground. She lost her grip on the gun, and it went sliding under the taxi. The infected woman bit deep into Emiko's neck. She screamed in agony as the woman tore a chunk of flesh free and chewed it.

"NO!" Shintaro screamed and in one fluid motion got to his feet and beheaded the woman in a clean swing.

Emiko lay on the ground clutching her neck. The woman had missed the jugular, but the wound still bled profusely. Shintaro turned as he heard movement around the crashed cars. Seven more of the infected were climbing the wreck and coming straight for them. Shintaro became possessed. He met the attackers, and in a rage slew all seven before they could overwhelm him. His breathing was labored as he heard over a dozen footsteps running from the other side of the cars. "Emiko, we have to go," Shintaro said, as he turned.

Emiko stood looking at him. Blood had ruined her blouse and run down her leg. "Get her to her family, Wakayama san," Emiko said, wiping the blood from her mouth. "Thank you for always being a gentleman and a man of honor."

With that, Emiko ran. Before Shintaro could stop her, she had made her way to the side of the bridge and climbed the railing. With one glance backward, she smiled, and then she was gone. Her jump outward took her clear over the side and head first into the river below. Shock and shame took Shintaro. Tears welled in his eyes. "I was supposed to get both of you out safely," he said to no one.

The noises behind him interrupted his grief as he remembered Sarah was still in the car. The little girl was crying uncontrollably after witnessing Emiko's sacrifice. Emiko had always been smart. She had been too good to just be Shintaro's secretary. Now that potential was gone. He swiped his sword to remove the blood and sheathed it as he ran to the car. He put the sword next to Sarah and closed the door. He put the car in gear and took off as three of the infected reached the back of the taxi. They still ran after them, too far gone to realize they could never catch up.

***

A week later, driving a different car, Shintaro wiped his eye as a tear came out.

"Are you OK, Mr. Wak?" Sarah asked from the passenger seat.

"Fine, Teacup," he replied. "Just something in my eye."

"Ms. Emiko was a nice lady," Sarah said.

The child was very perceptive. Perhaps even too much for her age. Losing Emiko pained him emotionally and as a man who had responsibilities. He would not fail with

213

Sarah. "That she was, little one," Shintaro said, smiling for Sarah's sake. "That she was."

They still had a long way to go before Shintaro returned Sarah to her family. Elmira was a long way from here. How long it would take to get there, he could not say. It all depended on how many obstacles they encountered. Where they just left should have been an hour and a half drive by normal standards. Normal standards, however, had been thrown from the playing board. He would have to find gas eventually. Without power, he might even have to find another vehicle altogether if gas was not readily available.

The world had changed in a week. To think of all the little things people took for granted that were now gone. The world had taken a step back by over a hundred years. Simple things like electricity and phones were taken out of the equation. Perhaps permanently. It was a whole new game of life. Shintaro was making the rules up as he went along. He just hoped that no one was playing the game better than he was.

POW!

Bill sits bolt upright on the small cot in the jail cell he's been stuck in since the dead began to get up and walk and eat the living.

With his ears ringing, he gets quickly to his feet and takes two big steps over to the cell bars and sees Deputy Burke—or rather what's left of Deputy Burke—slumped against the back of his desk chair across the room, with only the lower portion of his head and face left intact. His eyes rove down to the shotgun lying on the floor nearby, and he hangs his head and sighs. He feels sorry for the man, the man who wouldn't let Bill out of his cage for the better part of two weeks because he was convinced that the National Guard was going to show up with guns blazing and set things straight. It hadn't seemed to matter that the news broadcasts had stopped maybe a week after everything started, and the sounds of gunfire, or any other form of resistance, had ceased not long after that. It was a small town, after all, and once the "zombies"—as the news reports had begun calling them—started spreading, it hadn't taken more than a day for it to be overrun.

And they weren't like what you'd think they'd be. They weren't slow, shambling menaces who beat weakly at the windows. You couldn't just walk right past them at arm's length to safety. Bill saw some dumbass with a camera get about ten feet from an old woman who had fallen while fleeing and hit her head on the curb. At first, she just seemed disoriented, but once her eyes locked onto the gawking idiot with some kind of far-off wildness, she moved as fast as anyone Bill had ever seen, practically pouncing on the guy, and tearing at his flesh—tearing it away—and eating it by the handful.

And you didn't have to be bitten or scratched or anything to come back. Bill hadn't known that until one of the news broadcasts had said so. When they'd heard that, Bill had tried to use it to his advantage, to convince Burke to let him out and let him go, but Burke rightly pointed out that he'd still be safer with Bill inside the cell. It was a long shot, Bill had known.

"You're safe from me," Bill says, "but what about from yourself?"

He stares in awe at the grotesqueness of the mostly headless man, and only after moments begins to realize that he may be even more fucked now than he had been.

"Oh, shit…" Bill says quietly. "The keys…

"Where're the fucking keys, Burke!?"

By the dim light of an oil lamp—the power had gone out two days before and never come back on—Bill's eyes search frantically about the Sheriff's office, hoping that Deputy Burke had the goddamn common decency not to take Bill with him when he decided to play his pussy card and cash out.

"Where're the keys, you fucking PRICK?"

Bill kicks the cell door and then staggers back, wincing. With a knot of dread in his stomach, he plops down onto the edge of the cot and tries to think.

"How the hell am I gonna get out of here?"

He ponders the question for several moments and then sighs. "I'm not..." he says quietly.

With a groan, he gets to his feet and steps over to the toilet—which hasn't been flushable in a few days—and unzips. The only sound inside the office is that of piss splashing down on the reeking load he absolutely had to drop the night before. While he tries to ignore the horrid stench, he half-heartedly wonders if that was why Burke did it.

Maybe he just couldn't take the smell...

Bill chuckles in spite of himself, shakes it and zips up. He instinctively steps over to the small sink, and immediately remembers that it will do him no good. But when he glances down amusedly at the dry basin, he realizes that it just might after all.

"Holy shit..." he mutters quietly. He glances back over his shoulder, to mostly-headless Burke, and then turns his eyes back down to the basin—and the ring of keys that lie therein.

***

Bill stands at the back door to Sheriff's office. It's been locked for days, and it's a good heavy door made of steel, but he can hear the zombies just on the other side of it in the alley behind the building. He listens silently to the sounds of dead things moving about just inches away from him and looks down at the twelve-gauge shotgun in his hands. He'd only found a couple of boxes of 00 buckshot shells in the gun locker behind Burke's corpse. He'd topped the shotgun off, filling the magazine and loading the chamber, and then pocketed the rest loosely. He could fully reload once and then he'd be out. The Deputy normally would've had a sidearm as well, but Bill had seen him lose it out in the alley the day it all started. Brief thoughts of maybe trying to retrieve it skirt Bill's mind, but he knows it's a bad idea; they are just too damn fast.

He starts to reach for the door's lock and then stops. If there's any number of them out there, he'll be totally fucked. They'll have no trouble forcing their way inside with only him to hold the door, even with the gun. Instead, he takes a breath, raises the butt of the gun to shoulder level, and taps it against the door.

For just a moment there is nothing but quiet from the other side; then, all at once, a barrage of thuds and bangs begin to actually rattle the door.

"Fuck!" Bill swears, jumping back at the sight of the shuddering door. He backs away and wonders if there's any other way out of the building. Burke had mentioned blocking off the glass front doors that open into the small front office of the building with his truck. But Bill had searched both Burke and the Deputy's desk and found no truck key, so simply hopping into the dead man's ride and hauling ass out of town wasn't really an option either.

If only, Bill thinks as he goes to the double doors that separate the two halves of the building. Each door has a small safety-glass widow that allows him to peer through and into the other room.

He can see the front doors, and the truck just on the other side of them, but he can also see beyond the truck—

to what looks like a small horde of zombies. Once more the idea of simply walking out of the building seems out of the question. So, with a sigh, Bill sets out to do something he'd always wanted to do but never got to: explore the Sheriff's office.

***

There isn't much to it.

There is a small evidence room, though in a small town like Redfield, Missouri, there isn't much crime—and that means there isn't much evidence of a crime. There are male/female restrooms, practically identical except for the urinals. There is a small lounge/break room, which connects to a kitchenette. And, lastly, there is a small supply closet, which mostly holds the standard office supplies: pens, pencils, paper, et cetera. Bill is about to leave said closet when, by a trick of the pocket-flashlight that he found in the evidence room, he notices that up in one corner was a trapdoor marked ROOF ACCESS. He feels a jolt of excitement at the idea of a potential small victory, and lays the shotgun across one of the empty supply shelves while he steps up onto a spare office chair and lifts the ceiling panel out of place. When he shines the light up into the hole, he sees a hatch leading up to the office's roof.

"Hot damn, I'm free at last!" Bill says, as he studies his surroundings. Soon he sees, as he'd suspected he might, a ladder built into the wall, hidden behind one of the shelves and positioned right under the hole. Quickly he hops down from the chair, shoves it aside, and goes to moving the shelf out away from the wall.

At first, it's quite heavy, and Bill wonders if maybe it's bolted in place. Then he realizes the damn thing is simply being weighed down by dozens of reams of paper, as well as other supplies—and the shotgun. So he sets the gun aside, then starts pulling the reams and other supplies down—simply tossing them aside—until the shelf is almost bare. When he thinks he's lightened the load considerably, he gives it another try, and this time the shelf moves. He pivots it on one edge until he's made a space where he can get to the ladder, then holds the button-end of the flashlight between his teeth, picks up the shotgun, and climbs up the ladder.

***

Jim sits next to the covered attic window, clinging to a blood-smeared flashlight—the Sheriff's flashlight, the long, heavy, metal kind—and occasionally lifting the corner of the window's curtain just enough to peek out and make sure the dead are still up and walking around. In the last two weeks, he's seen them nab countless would-be survivors (fewer and fewer as the days go on), probably a dozen dogs, and even a squirrel that ventured out after a fallen acorn from the big tree just outside the Sheriff's house. Maybe worse than that was watching a half-eaten dog come back to "life" and begin dragging itself—entrails and all—around the Sheriff's yard.

Inside the Sheriff's house, the things had managed to pull a Trojan horse of sorts. An elderly man that the Sheriff had taken in—along with numerous others—had suffered a coronary, and just minutes later had come back and attacked the person nearest him; his eleven-year-old granddaughter. Sheriff Patrick—ever the stalwart heroine—had tried to pull him off the girl; tried to subdue him non-lethally, but in the end had had to put a bullet from her .44 revolver right between his eyes. Everyone who wasn't already screaming hysterically had screamed then, and the girl lay sobbing next to her granddad.

Over the day and a half after the incident, the girl, Gloria, had gotten sicker and sicker; she was sweating like crazy, and someone had said to keep her hydrated—which made sense. Sheriff Patrick had assured and reassured the others that help was coming, and just to "hold tight." Then, nearly thirty hours after being attacked by her granddad, someone had tried to give the girl a drink of water, but when they brought the glass to her lips, she recoiled, refusing to drink. One of the others had mentioned some bullshit about rabies; a third person had pointed out that rabies doesn't turn people into flesh-eating freaks. But Jim had watched as even in a weakened state the girl fought like her life depended on it.

Eventually, they'd managed to get a little of the water into her mouth, but not before she bit a few fingers, eliciting more than a few swear words from otherwise seemingly kind and caring folk. And she still ended up vomiting afterward, despite the fact she hadn't eaten anything since she'd been there. In fact, there hadn't been much food to go around, and it was gone after just a few days. Once the Sheriff had taken Jim and the other men aside and suggested that they all—her included—venture out in search of "supplies." Jim hadn't really been keen on the idea, but it was the other men who steadfastly refused to set foot outside the Sheriff's walls—and supposed safety. She'd then turned her eye to Jim—just Jim—and asked if he was willing to try. He'd shrugged and simply asked if she really thought they'd make it past the yard. She didn't.

The morning after the finger-biting incident everyone in the house was awakened by a man's screams.

Harold, a middle-aged man Jim knew from coming into the gas station where Jim worked as a clerk, was supposed to be taking a turn watching Gloria. Whether he had been awake or asleep Jim still doesn't know; all he knows is that Gloria finished the job she'd started the day before, and when the others came running to see what the screaming was about Harold was kneeling next to Gloria's supine body and clutching his hand to his chest. Blood stained the floor at his knees, and it was immediately evident who it belonged to. Gloria's head had been crushed in by a nearby lamp whose base was made of heavy wood, and it was clear that she hadn't done it to herself. Sheriff Patrick didn't hesitate in pulling her revolver once more and aiming dead-center between Harold's eyes.

He'd pleaded with her, swearing that the girl had turned, and when some of the others—not all—voiced their disbelief, he held up a trembling right hand lacking in digits. Luckily for him, that had made the Sheriff holster her weapon. Then she'd wrapped Gloria's body in a sheet and moved it down to the basement—where before she and one of the other men had stored the girl's granddad's body.

After that Harold had begun to act just as the girl had, getting weaker by the hour and sweating like he was in a sauna. And just like with Gloria they tried their best to keep him hydrated until eventually, he cringed away from even the sight of a glass of water. And while most of the people in the Sheriff's house were quite willing to tend to a cute, eleven-year-old girl in pigtails, none seemed overly interested in going very far out of their way to look after a crotchety, forty-something man who seemed to do nothing but whine about every little ache and discomfort.

It was about ten days into their forced lockdown when a much longed-for silence settled over the house. For days Harold had constantly been moaning and groaning, tossing and writhing on the couch in the Sheriff's den and coddling his bandaged hand. Just like the girl, everyone had been taking shifts watching over him, doing their best to get a little bit of liquid into him and more often than not just giving up when he resisted. And on the night that he finally quieted there was almost a collective sigh. Jim can't recall how much time actually passed, but remembers thinking *Not again!* when there was a blood-curdling scream—this time from the woman who was watching Harold—followed by a ruckus from the Sheriff's den. Jim arrived on the scene, followed by the Sheriff and an older woman named Esther. What they saw from the double-wide doorway of the den was Harold—kneeling over the presumably dead body of one of the others—and scooping up handfuls of intestine from a raggedly torn-open abdominal cavity. The woman who had been watching Harold—Rachel something—was laid out on the couch where Harold had been sleeping, a deep, seeping gash torn into her neck with a tattered flap of skin hanging from it.

Jim heard Esther scream from right over his shoulder; or rather he heard part of a scream, quickly cut off by the sound of violent regurgitation. The Sheriff swore hoarsely before pulling her gun and taking dead aim at Harold. She did call his name two or three times, giving him every chance to acknowledge her and to stop eating Charlie Reynolds. But Harold was seemingly oblivious to anyone else in the room, be it Jim, Esther, or Sheriff Patrick.

He watched in awe as the shot rang out and Harold's head popped like a balloon at a carnival dart game, splattering the wall behind him as well as one arm of the couch with blood and brain matter.

***

After the massacre in the Sheriff's den, they hadn't had much time to gather themselves. There were three more dead bodies in all, including Harold, and it was while Jim and the Sheriff were moving body number two—Charlie Reynolds—that the other woman had gotten up, just like the rest, and gone after Esther. When Jim reached the top of the basement steps right behind the Sheriff, he watched as Esther bolted through the foyer and out the front door. The Sheriff had called after her to stop, but the woman was frantic, and well beyond reason. Jim did see that she didn't get far, as she was met at the front gate by a number of zombies that took her down with utmost ease.

Didn't even make it past the yard, Jim had thought.

And when the Sheriff had tried to make for the door after her—to shut it—the Rachel something-zombie that had chased the old woman out had turned on her with catlike reflexes.

"DOWN!" the Sheriff had said, prompting Jim to get back to the basement. But when he started to descend the steps, there was Charlie Reynolds, struggling up toward him. And if it hadn't been for Charlie's lack of core strength, he probably would've managed.

Jim raced back up the steps and slammed the door shut behind him, bracing himself against it just in case. He saw Sheriff Patrick put a bullet into the dead woman's face at point-blank range, leaving mostly just a gaping hole with a hairline. When she turned back to Jim, he just shook his head.

"Upstairs!" the Sheriff had said with a grunt, leading the way with her gun still drawn. Jim had briefly considered closing the front door as he followed the Sheriff up the steps, but a backward glance showed that the dead were on the Sheriff's doorstep.

Now it is just the two of them; trapped in the attic of her house with no end to the plague of the undead in sight.

Jim lifts the corner of the curtain and glances lazily down at the street, quickly skimming over the remains of Esther, and then he briefly searches the starlit line of the small town's horizon. From several blocks away, something catches his eye.

Bill moves along at a crawl, crouching and kneeling as much as he can as he traverses the rooftops of Redfield. Some gaps are bigger than others, and he figures it's only a matter of time before he makes a misstep and falls to asphalt or concrete, likely breaking one if not both legs, and becoming meat for the beasts. But he knows that if he can just make it to his place on the southern edge of town he can get the hell out of Dodge. His truck—just like Deputy Burke's—is a four-wheel-drive, and it has no problem handling the rural landscape that surrounds the town. When he comes to the edge of the roof of the gas station where he works as a mechanic, he quietly maneuvers around to the south side of the building, where a tall maple tree stands, offering at least partial cover and a less disastrous way to the ground than falling. The only real problem is the few dozen zombies that walk the street on that side of the building.

Staying low, he studies them, trying to discern any kind of pattern to their movement. There is none.

While he watches the grotesque, nightmare versions of his former friends and neighbors, noting a number of them that he once knew socially, a slight breeze kicks up, cooling his skin nicely. But the relief only lasts a moment, because it doesn't take long for Bill to realize that he is upwind of the creatures. Momentarily they all seem to turn his way, dead eyes searching the relative darkness until they seem to find the one thing out of place: him.

"Fuck me…" he whispers.

As if in response, one of them lets out a strangled, guttural cry and quickly moves toward him. Bill starts to panic, starts to flee, but there is nowhere left to go. He jogs around the edge of the roof, searching for a clear spot on the ground to drop down, but there seem to be zombies pretty much on all sides. He thinks to himself that it would've been nice if the station had had a roof access hatch, and scoffs. Going back to the south edge he sees that, although the zombies can get around pretty well on relatively flat land, they seem somewhat incapable of climbing the tree up to him.

Small fucking favors, he thinks.

Then he hears something; something even more distressing than a few dozen flesh-hungry maniacs: a few hundred flesh-hungry maniacs.

He sees that even more zombies seem to be pouring onto the scene, and he isn't sure where they're coming from. He'd only seen so many just moments ago, but now they are swarming to the gas station from every street corner and every shadow in sight.

"You have got to be fucking KIDDING me!"

Bill shoulders the butt of the shotgun and takes aim down at the nearest of the zombies—the screamer—and lightly fingers the trigger. He wants to squeeze—if only for the catharsis—but figures it's probably best to save each shot for when it really counts. With a sigh of exasperation, he lowers the gun, searching the surrounding darkness for any means of exodus and only finding a sea of death and ravenous monsters.

"Out of the frying pan…" he says quietly.

Then, by happenstance, he catches a glimpse in the periphery of his vision. At first, he thinks he imagined it, then, as he searches the distance for any telltale vestige of what he thought he saw, it happens again.

"Holy shit…"

From across town—to the south-west—there is a flash of light, signaling him from an attic window. He squints into the darkness and realizes that it is coming from the Sheriff's house. Instinctively he waves his arms through the air, not sure if she—or whoever—can really see him.

***

"He sees me!" Jim says excitedly. "He really sees me. I can't believe he's still alive."

"Don't celebrate too soon, James. He's way over there, and we're stuck in here," says Sheriff Patrick.

Jim looks down at the yard, down at the street, and sees that after the monstrous, animal scream that pierced the night, the herd seems to be thinning.

"Maybe not, Sheriff—look."

She goes over to the window where he sits and peeks out from the opposite corner of the curtain. Indeed the dead do seem to be departing, heading almost excitedly toward the center of town, toward James' friend William. She hasn't the heart to point this out to him.

"Come on," he says. "I think we can get out of here and get to him. Then the three of us can get out of this—"

"Hold on, James. Slow down. I'm not sure that's such a good idea."

He stops and looks at her hand on his arm, then pulls away.

"What are you talking about? We have to go get him."

"James…" She hesitates. "Why do you think they're leaving?"

He doesn't answer, and looks down dejectedly.

"You've seen how fast they are—how dangerous." She places a hand on his arm again, this time for comfort. He looks up at her sorrowfully.

"No," he says, shaking his head. He pulls away from her again. "I came to you and begged you to let him out of jail when this started."

He backs away, and Sheriff Patrick takes a step toward him.

"And even if we hadn't gotten stuck in here you wouldn't have. Would you?"

She sighs. She knows he's right. Then again, it isn't as if she knew that everything would go to utter shit with no end in sight. Who knew the dead would rise with an insatiable appetite for destruction?

"Maybe leaving him locked up was what kept him alive, James."

Jim looks at the older woman warily and thinks, I hate it when she's right.

"I'm going to get my friend," he says. "See you around, Sheriff." With that, he starts toward the attic's hatch, flashlight in hand.

Sheriff Patrick sighs, unholstering her .44 and following after him.

"Hold on," she says, moving past him to the hatch. "I'll go down first."

Jim watches as she lets the small door fall open, and, as quietly as she can, she lowers the ladder. There is no sound coming from the second floor of the house so far as he can tell, and as Patrick cautiously descends the steps, she doesn't seem to react to anything. After a moment, Jim moves up to the opening and peers down. The Sheriff is nowhere in sight, and for just a moment Jim wonders if maybe she hadn't had time to react before being attacked by one of them. Then she pops back into view and motions for him to come down—quietly.

When his feet touch down on the hallway's carpeted floor, Jim sees the Sheriff waiting in a crouch at the top of the stairs. Quietly he creeps over to her, taking a knee just behind her.

"Well?" he whispers.

She motions for him to stay silent then holsters the gun. He assumes that to mean the coast is clear, but then she takes hold of his flashlight and gives it a tug. At first, he resists, not wanting to give up his only weapon, but when she tugs again he relents.

With catlike stealth, she begins to descend the stairs. Jim is impressed, considering the woman is pushing fifty and watches as she rounds the landing. Moving into position where she had been, he sees now that there seems to be a straggler. At first, he thinks the Sheriff will get the drop on the creature, no problem, but when there is the slightest, barely-audible creak of wood under her weight, the thing seems to perk up and listen. Jim thinks of a dog sensing something nearby, even when it can't see it.

The zombie turns, and in an instant lunges for the Sheriff. Again impressing Jim, Sheriff Patrick swings the flashlight—fast and hard—and catches the dead woman at the left temple. There is a sickening crack and a dull, metallic thwack as she—it—goes down at once, collapsing like a sack of bricks. Patrick looks up at Jim and motions for him to follow. He does so quietly.

As Jim and Sheriff Patrick move toward the doorway it looks as though the way will be clear; they can neither hear nor see any sign of the living dead beyond the threshold. But when they get there, they see that not all of the zombies have yet departed. There are still a half-dozen or so lingering, and when two fresh meals step into view, it is only a heartbeat before they lunge into motion, hauling undead ass across the yard and even spilling over the low picket fence.

Sheriff Patrick barely has time to get the front door shut before the zombies are on the porch. Then, as their bodies collide with the portal, it is nearly smashed in off its hinges. Both Jim and the Sheriff throw their own bodies against the thin slab of wood in hopes of keeping it in place. For the most part, it works, though there is no way for them to get away while they're holding up the door; and they won't be able to do that for long. Also, there are the many wildly reaching, clawing hands of unreasonably strong dead flesh that curl around the edges of the door—seeking any and all purchase.

"I don't think we can hold 'em for long!" Jim grunts.

"No," Sheriff Patrick agrees as the door shudders at her back. "We can't."

Jim looks at her as she's looking at him, and starts to shake his head.

"Go, James…" she says, through gritted teeth, "Take the gun—and go."

"I'm not leaving you, Sheriff!"

"Take the gun—"

"No!"

"Take the damn gun, Jim!"

With a growl of annoyance, Jim reaches around and pulls the Sheriff's gun from its holster. He starts to angle it around the edge of the door, intent on firing blindly and hoping to hit something, but Patrick tells him to stop.

"You'll just waste the last few rounds. And you'll draw more of those things back here."

Again Jim lets out with a defeatist growl, banging the back of his head against the door.

"Go, James."

"Sheriff—"

"Go…"

Growing up in Redfield, having known and dealt with Barbara Patrick from the time she was just a fledgling deputy, and he was old enough to break even the pettiest of laws, Jim knows that there's no arguing with her. He lunges away from the door, turning back to her briefly and seeing that it's all she can do to keep it in place as it is.

"Good luck," he says, hating the words and knowing they are utterly meaningless.

"Run like hell…" Sheriff Patrick says, forcing a sorrowfully crooked smirk.

He does as she says—turning and bolting through the house, through the kitchen and out the back door. There seem to be no zombies on this side of the house, maybe due to the high back fence, and Jim stays low as he runs for the back gate. He reaches it, and as he works the bolt that locks it, hears a crash—the sound of the door being forced in—followed immediately by the sound of Sheriff Patrick screaming. For an instant he wants to turn back, to run in with his one gun blazing (and likely missing everything), but knows that it's already too late for her anyway.

And it was her choice, he tells himself. Trying to believe it, he quietly opens the gate and slips from the backyard.

***

Bill stares into the distance, toward the Sheriff's house, waiting—hoping—for another sign that someone is there; that someone sees him. Even if there's no way for them to reach him—or he them—just knowing he isn't the last would make things marginally better. It's been several minutes, though, and there haven't been any more light signals. He even tried flashing his light that way, offering the standard S.O.S., but nothing more happened. He considers that maybe it was just some kind of fluke, maybe a sparking fuse-box or something, but doesn't really believe it. The circle had been too perfectly formed; the on/off sequencing too meticulous. Someone had been signaling, he is sure, but he has no idea if they were even still alive.

And now, trapped on the roof at his (former) place of employment, he is surrounded on all sides by more zombies than ever, probably the entire population of Redfield—minus those who had since been eaten.

Sitting on the south-facing edge of the roof and hanging his feet over the edge, he feels a small measure of pleasure at the thought of being just out of the zombies' reach. They stretch and strain, trying to get to him, but his boots dangle a good many inches above their grasp. Looking down at the slavering, monster faces with their blood-stained teeth—laced with ragged strips of flesh—he snorts a good glob of snot into his throat, hacks it up, and sends it bombing down to the screamer. It takes no notice as the thick, whitish dollop impacts against its forehead, then drips down into one pale-colored, bloodshot eye. It snarls and gnashes its teeth; they all do—hundreds of hungering jaws working almost in unison at the sight of food.

***

Jim sprints from shadow to shadow, taking cover behind any and every hedge, bush, and a tree trunk that he comes to. He probably doesn't need to, considering that all of the zombies seem to have congregated toward the center of town. Still, he decides it is better to be safe than sorry as he makes his way toward the south-most edge of town, toward the home of his best friend, Bill.

Just a little further, he thinks, hunkering down next to a row of rose bushes that run along the edge of the trailer unit nearest the street. From his position, he can just see the gleam of moonlight that reflects off the front fender of Bill's only remaining pride and joy: his truck. But here there do seem to be a couple of the lesser-informed walking dead. One he recognizes as Bill's promiscuous neighbor, Sherry. The other he doesn't know—and doesn't want to—because even though he's a zombie, he looks to be built like a brick wall, easily head and shoulders taller than Jim and as broad as an ox. With a sigh, Jim attempts to sneak as quietly as he can around the row of bushes and around the back-end of the trailer.

There is a beat-up, compact car in the trailer's port, and it, too, offers some cover. Unfortunately, it also serves to obstruct Jim's view of the zombies, and that's why he doesn't notice when Sherry-zombie starts to wander his way—scenting the air like a predator on the trail of wounded prey. As he rounds the far side of the trailer, he lays eyes on brick-wall zombie and sees that the brute seems to be elbow-deep in a gopher hole. From where he hides, Jim can't see the truck anymore but knows that Bill's trailer is all the way at the end and furthest to the east side of the park. He also knows right where Bill keeps the spare key: tucked up in the wheel-well on a magnetic clip.

He watches quietly as the big zombie digs desperately for whatever has gone down the hole, and wonders whether or not he'll be able to sneak past the both of them.

Edging stealthily forward he tries to peer around the front end of the trailer with the rose bushes, trying to pinpoint Sherry-zombie's precise location. He can't seem to find her. Shit, he thinks, fingering the trigger of the .44. Where the hell did she go?

Staying low, he inches toward the front end of the trailer, glancing back toward the giant zombie every other step. It snarls and growls as it struggles at the hole in the ground, and Jim sees that it is actually doing damage to itself—twisting, and ripping the flesh of its lower arm—and doesn't seem to care or even notice. Nearing the corner, Jim gets right next to the trailer and slowly peeks around. There's still no sign of the Sherry-zombie.

Where the hell?

Suddenly there is a yowling, animal-like cry from behind him, and he feels cold hands at the back of his neck.

"SHIT!"

Scurrying away on all fours, Jim turns to see Sherry-zombie just as she lunges. Losing her balance, she falls face-first to the concrete slab that the trailer sits on. Jim hears a thick cracking sound and can't help but cringe. When Sherry-zombie's head snaps back up to glare at him wildly, he sees that she has not only broken her nose, leaving it crooked and blood-soaked, but several of her teeth now lie on the concrete in a thick red puddle. Frozen, Jim watches as she struggles to get to her feet to get after him, in such a hurry that she can't quite get her feet under her and ends up once again lunging face-first to the ground, this time to the hard dirt just beyond the concrete.

Now Jim becomes aware of a ruckus over his shoulder. With a jolt of panic, he turns to see Brick, trying like hell to free his arm from the hole in the ground. Luckily, he seems to have actually gotten it lodged, and is having to throw his whole body-weight into the effort of trying to remove it.

Jim turns once again at the sound of Sherry-zombie screeching deep in her throat, a sound similar to fingernails on a chalkboard, mixed with gargling blood. And this time she manages to get to her feet, immediately racing for Jim. Lying on his back, he raises the gun, pulling the trigger twice without aiming or even looking. When Sherry-zombie falls on him, she is truly dead weight, no longer revenant. With a shriek, Jim pushes her off, seeing that one of the bullets tore a burnt-edged, ragged hole in her pale flesh just above her left breast right at the neckline of her tank top; the other made a perfectly round entry wound just under her left eye—the exit, however, is quite a bit larger, embedded with minute fragments of skull that glisten in the moonlight.

At the guttural howls of Brick behind him, Jim gets shakily to his feet, turning to aim the gun at the undead behemoth. Just then, with a final violent lurch, the zombie pulls free of the gopher hole—minus one arm from the elbow down. Jim has only a moment to gawk at the raggedly dismembered appendage before it breaks toward him in a sprint.

"Oh, shit!" says Jim, backpedaling and firing the gun as the monster rushes him. It takes a bullet to the chest—which barely has an effect—another in the belly, which has just as little, and finally a grazing wound at the right side of the neck. Jim pulls the trigger again, and the gun only clicks; he tries once more and realizes he's out. With another curse he throws the gun; it bounces off Brick's chest and clatters to the dirt. Turning, he runs full-out, doing his best to evade the rapidly approaching zombie. With its one arm, it reaches out, swiping at the back of his shirt and grabbing only air. Jim realizes he's running the wrong way and turns wide, changes direction, and starts back toward Bill's truck. He doesn't look back as he sprints full-speed, and only slows when he reaches the truck, practically sliding across the ground and onto the concrete.

Brick still grunts and snarls, and from the edge of his vision, Jim sees that he is nearing, but already Jim has the key—is standing and working it into the door-lock. He ventures a glance just before yanking the door open—just in time to see Brick tripping over the body of Sherry-zombie. With a hoarse chuckle he hops up into the truck, yanks the door shut and jams the key in the ignition. It takes a couple of tries for the engine to turn over, and by then Brick has gotten to his feet and is right outside the truck. The zombie's face is level with Jim's shoulder and pressed against the window grotesquely. Jim thinks if it were smarter it could just smash the glass with a single blow from its one good, muscular arm.

The engine roars and Jim puts the truck in drive. He jams his foot on the gas pedal and tears out of the carport, sending Brick reeling to the ground and leaving him in a cloud of dust. As he speeds out of the trailer park, he feels

Sherry-zombie beneath the front left wheel, like a soft, squishy speed bump.

***

Bill paces the rooftop of the gas station. The drone of the zombies has begun to fray his nerves. He could hear them before—from inside the jail—though only faintly. And moments ago a number of gunshots rang out from somewhere in the distance, off to the south. It wasn't exactly from the direction of the Sheriff's house, but that doesn't mean it wasn't her. After all, Bill figurs, if there was one woman he knew who would be able to take care of herself with all that was going on, it was Sheriff Patrick.

The shotgun is heavy, and he keeps swapping it from hand to hand; grimly he wonders if he'll end up using it on himself—just like Burke did. He tells himself no because he'd rather die trying than just give up like that. But there are literally zombies on all sides of him, and absolutely no way to get past them.

Can't go over; can't go around; have to go through.

And even if he tried to clear a path, with only a dozen shells he wouldn't make much of a dent in the dead-sea. He groans and it crescendos into a yell, aimed at the zombies, though doing no actual good. Then he hears another sound—something familiar that starts beneath the unintelligible "zombie-talk," then growing louder.

It sounds like a truck.

It sounds like his truck.

Can't be...

Suddenly, from a few blocks east, Bill sees four bright points of light—a light bar—and two more below those—headlights.

"No way…"

He watches as the truck—indeed, his truck—tears up the street in his direction. Many of the zombies take notice, and a good number of them begin to turn and run in that direction. Hopeful, Bill jogs over to the building's edge; but his hopes are dashed at the sight he sees: there are still a good many zombies right there waiting for him. Looking back to his truck he feels a slight catharsis at the sight of innumerable undead being easily plowed under. He can't yet tell who is driving, and he surely hopes that whoever it is not only sees him but is coming to save him. Gripping the shotgun tightly in both hands he watches as the truck swerves up the street, mowing through the walking dead with ease.

Come on, come on, come on…

The truck accelerates, veers right—toward the gas station—and zombie bodies go flying. As one tumbles up and over the hood, slamming against the windshield and flying over the light bar, Bill can't help but cringe. But he doesn't care about a little body damage at this point, not if it means getting off the roof, getting away from Redfield, and getting away from zombies.

The truck rapidly slows to a stop mere feet from the side of the building, crushing and pinning some walking corpses between brick and bumper. Bill shields his eyes from the glare of the light bar with one hand, peering down into the cab of the truck. There, he is beyond surprised to see his best friend, Jim, sitting behind the wheel and wearing a stupid grin.

"Jim?" he calls.

Jim rolls the driver side window down a crack and calls back, "Need a ride?"

Bill nods, mouth quirking into a smile of relief. "Back it up to the building," he says.

Jim puts the truck into reverse and backs it into the street. Making a three-point turn—and taking out a dozen zombies in the process—he then backs it as close to the building as he can get it.

Bill watches—almost happily—as Screamer, among others, is crushed to the wall and his stomach is impossibly and grotesquely squeezed out through his mouth. A split-second later he feels his gorge and thinks he might just lose it right over the side of the building. As he retches, Jim double-taps the horn; regaining himself, he steps right up to the ledge, looking down into the truck bed.

To his surprise, the zombie from earlier—the one who went flying over the truck's hood and roof—is lying there, twisted and broken from the waist down. She looks up at him, snarling, hands clawing at the air, desperately wanting to reach him. Reluctantly Bill shoulders the shotgun, taking aim at the dead woman's head. Fingering the trigger, he hesitates a moment.

"Bill?" Jim calls from the cab.

"Yeah," Bill calls back, "just a sec."

He squeezes the trigger; the shotgun kicks and reports instantaneously. The zombie's head explodes, splattering the back glass of the truck as well as most of the bed-liner nearby with gore. With that, he hops down from the ledge, into the truck bed, and, moving past the twice-dead body, hunkers down next to the cab. He smacks the back glass twice. "Go!"

Jim does as his friend instructs, putting the truck in drive and turning the wheel hard to the right as he accelerates.

In the back of the truck, Bill sways; he holds tight as desperately clinging zombies fall away a few at a time, left behind as they quickly shrink into the distance. Jim takes a right, and again Bill must hold tight to the truck bed where it meets the cab, his other hand holding just as firmly to the shotgun. And as they turn the corner, there is still a veritable sea of zombies lining the street. They pelt the front end of the truck as it pushes through the horde, and Bill is glad for the larger after-market wheels and tires he put on, as the added height keeps him well out of the things' full reach.

As the truck reaches the end of the street, past the zombies, Jim instinctively slows it to a stop at the corner. Bill takes the opportunity to quickly hop out of bed and goes to the passenger-side door. He tries the handle, and it is locked. He raps on the window with his knuckles; Jim is already fingering the auto-unlock switch. Bill pulls the door open and hastily jumps in. As they start into motion once more, he can see the zombies coming up fast in his mirror.

"Buddy, I owe you, big time."

Jim offers a glance; shrugs.

"No problem."

"How'd you make it?" Bill asks, staring out the windshield and into the night—vision lost beyond the reach of the light.

"The Sheriff," Jim offers. "She let a bunch of us hole up at her place."

"So that was you," Bill says with a chuckle.

"Yeah," says Jim.

"So where are they now?"

Jim shakes his head, offering Bill a sidelong glance. "They didn't…" he trails off.

"Oh," Bill says quietly.

The two are quiet for several moments on the short journey it takes to reach the edge of town. As they reach the REDFIELD CITY LIMIT sign, Jim slows to a stop. He looks at Bill.

"So," he says, "where to?"

Bill looks at him, shrugs, and says, "Anywhere but here."

Jim nods and starts to put the truck back into drive when Bill adds, "But I'm driving."

***

Bill crests a rise in the road and slows the truck to a stop. Down below is the small coastal town of Port Romero. The city limit/welcome sign they passed showed the population at around two thousand, but from the dark and deserted appearance of the town, it looks as if it was recently thinned down to about zero. Bill shuts off the low beams, then the engine, and sits looking down at the small, dark town.

"What do you think?" he says, not looking at Jim as he speaks.

Jim yawns. "Your call, buddy," he says with a shrug. "How many shells you down to?"

Bill looks down at the seat next to him, picks up a bandolier. He runs it through his fingers, sees that only half of the ammo loops hold shells.

"The twelve-gauge is full, and there are another dozen shells here." He sighs, bringing one hand up to rub the back of his aching neck. "I guess we need to go down—if only to look for supplies and ammunition."

"Yeah," Jim agrees, though not really wanting to contend with zombies in the dark. It had, in fact, become one of the rules of thumb that daytime zombies were much easier to see—and evade. They'd tried to tell this to some of the other survivors they'd met along the way—though those were few and far between—but usually, they wouldn't listen. For some reason, most of the people they'd met seemed to think that the cover of darkness would work in their favor.

At first, it meant absolutely nothing, and more often than not the zombies would attack so swiftly, and so violently, that if you did see them racing from the shadows, it was when they were already upon you—and therefore too late to stand much chance of escape. Both Jim and Bill had seen it—more than once. The worst was when a man—some wannabe soldier of fortune—insisted on keeping his family—a wife and daughter—right by his side while he ran into a small convenience store to loot any remaining supplies he could find. Bill had offered that either he or Jim could hang back and watch out for them while the other two went in for the supplies. But the man had instantly had the wrong idea about the strangers. Understandable, yes, but his mistrust ultimately ended up getting his family killed, devoured by the living dead right in front of him.

He'd then blamed Bill and Jim, saying that if they hadn't shown up, it never would've happened. Jim had been content to let the man lay blame wherever he wanted—or needed—if it would get him through. But Bill threw the man's own mistrust right back in his face, pointing out the truth of what had transpired and blaming the man for dragging them into town with him when it was obvious that they were both terrified. Bill had done his best to allay any fear the man had, even falsely claiming that he and Jim were "partners," but it hadn't worked. And the only reason Bill and Jim had gone into that particular town with the family was because of the wife and daughter. Bill had seen their fear and wanted to help out, if only for their sake.

When the man had pointed his AR at Bill and threatened to kill him, Jim hadn't hesitated in returning the favor, pointing both barrels of a sawn-off double-barrel shotgun that he'd picked up in a corner bar two towns over from Redfield at the man and aiming them right at his head. When the man had swung the narrow barrel of his rifle in Jim's direction, Bill had raised his shotgun and fired once, blowing nearly a dozen small holes into the man's chest. He'd flown backward several feet, and had only twitched a time or two before going totally still. By that time more zombies had made their way in from the outskirts of town, and Bill and Jim had had to leave without gaining much—except an AR, which was now mounted behind the seat of the truck along with Bill's shotgun.

Now, sitting in the darkened cab of the truck and looking down on Port Romero, Bill hands Jim the bandolier and tells him he can take first watch. Jim agrees, checks the sawed-off to see that it is loaded, and then settles into the passenger seat. While Bill tries to relax enough to nod off, Jim stares out the window, down to the town below and beyond, to the rhythmic ocean waves in the distance, sparkling with half-moonlight. He doesn't expect any seaweed-laden zombies to come up from the beach but does his level best to stay awake and keep watch all the same. It was how they'd managed to stay alive so far, after all—watching each other's backs.

It isn't long before Bill is softly snoring, and Jim feels his eyelids growing weighty with exhaustion. He watches as the waves in the distance slowly roll in and then back out—in and out; in and out; in and out.

In no time Jim too has succumbed and sits leaning against the passenger-side door, face mashed against the window and snoring softly as he catches up on much-needed slumber.

***

"Jim, wake up.

"Jim—wake the hell up!"

Jim stirs sits up to find Bill shaking his shoulder. Immediately he realizes that he fell asleep while on watch. "Shit," he groans sullenly.

"Look, man," Bill says.

"What?"

"Look, man."

"What, man; what is it?"

"Look," he says once more, "out there."

Jim blinks, eyes still itchy from sleep, and sees that Bill is pointing out the windshield. With a yawn, he looks to see what at, blinks, rubs at his eyes with the heels of his hands, and sees exactly what.

The sun has just begun to rise somewhere behind them, so it isn't exactly dark, but it isn't light yet either. And to the west, above the small port town, is a thin streak of smoke, attached like a tail to a burning point of light in the sky.

"Is that a… flare?" Jim asks, with a croak.

Bill nods. "A flare," he says thickly. "There's someone down there, Jim."

"Shit," says Jim. "Where do you think they're holed up?"

Bill shakes his head. "I don't know. But it's light out." He looks at Jim, "Time to get to work."

***

Bill lets the truck coast into town, not really needing to give it any gas since the road in is pretty much downhill all the way. Immediately, by the low light of dawn, they see

248

that there are no zombies to greet them. Lightly applying the brakes, Bill comes to a full stop. Both men scan the area, looking for any signs of life—or un-life—while the truck idles.

"Well," Jim says, "either it didn't get this far…"

"Or everyone here is already dead, or worse." Bill finishes.

He gives the truck a little gas and begins to creep along. On either side of the street are small businesses; a burger joint, a souvenir shop, a bait shop, et cetera. There are no signs of life within or around any of them so far as Bill can tell. When he comes to a cross-street, he again slows to a full stop. He looks both ways; still no signs of anyone or anything.

Jim too looks first one way then the other, then asks, "Which way?"

Bill leans forward to peek up through the windshield and can still see part of the fading, remnant trail belonging to the signal flare. "Wherever that was sent up from," he says.

Again he accelerates, getting the truck into motion and moving along at about two miles per hour. After about a block, as they get nearer the beach, Bill realizes something.

"You hear that?"

Jim looks at Bill, listens, and then shakes his head slightly.

"I don't hear anything."

Bill nods. "Exactly," he says. "No seagulls."

Indeed, they can hear the sound of the surf and nothing else.

"Let's just keep going," Jim says. "Someone had to send that flare up."

"Yeah," Bill says, "but why?"

Taking a right, Bill gives the truck a little more gas. After passing a small post office and a couple of beachside homes, he comes to another cross street, this one leading toward the town's city hall one way, and down to the boardwalk in the other.

"What do you say, wanna pop in on the Mayor?" Jim asks with a sly smirk.

"I was thinking more of a day at the beach," Bill says, turning onto the street that leads that way.

***

They come to the place where the street dead-ends, giving way to a boardwalk and then a beach. Bill puts the truck in park and shuts the engine off. Jim watches him quietly as he takes the twelve-gauge from the two-gun mount fixed to the back glass. He then cautiously opens the door and steps down out of it, shotgun in hand. With a low sigh Jim sets the sawed-off down in the center seat and takes the AR from the mount, and then he too opens his door—quietly—and exits the vehicle. He slings the AR over his shoulder and grips it at the ready as he rounds the front end of the truck.

"Split up or stay together?" he asks Bill.

They move quietly toward the sandy boardwalk and Bill has a quick glance in either direction.

"Split up," he says. "But be careful."

Jim starts to take leave and Bill adds, "Like you said; someone sent that flare up—and likely for us to see."

"Maybe they just need help," Jim says.

"Maybe," Bill offers back. "And maybe it's a trap."

With a nod Jim goes on, walking northward up the boardwalk, toward what looks like some kind of amusement area with carnival-style games and small shops.

Bill starts moving south, the sound of sand scraping on wood under his booted feet the only accompaniment to the sound of the not-so-distant surf. Soon he is off the boardwalk and into a narrow alley, and as he walks, he focuses on every shadowed nook and cranny, not wanting to be blindsided by either skulking zombie or ill-intending foes of the living variety, both of which he's dealt with since the start.

***

There had been a desolate stretch of road outside of Grimes, Arizona, and some of the surviving locals had put up a roadblock comprised of junk cars and loosely mortared together bricks. When Bill had stopped the truck, they had appeared—several men and a few women, all armed. Bill had instantly put the truck in reverse, and as soon as he'd given it gas, the people had raised their guns. One of them had called out for Bill to stop, firing a warning shot from his rifle, but there was no way. He'd backed up a good fifty feet before turning the wheel hard and spinning the truck around. Immediately they'd heard the gunfire, as well as the sound of bullets peppering the back of the truck. One had even come through the back window and lodged in the dashboard. Bill had driven at high speed for several miles before he was sure that no one had followed. He'd then had to backtrack another forty or so miles before finding an alternate route that completely avoided Grimes.

After that they'd moved up through Nevada, skirting the California/Nevada border for a few hundred miles. Just before crossing over to the West Coast they stopped in a very small, mostly desert town with a former population of—according to the sign they'd passed—ABOUT 245, called Three Oxen.

There they hadn't had the misfortune of running into post-apocalyptic "road-pirates," but they'd begun to notice something about the couple hundred or so zombies that roamed the half-dozen streets that made up Three Oxen.

No longer were the things fast-moving and vicious; not as they had been initially, anyhow. They still managed to tear apart anything they could get their bony, decaying hands on with all the ferocity of any starving wild animal. But they had gotten noticeably slower; moving like people walking with plaster casts on both legs, where once they seemed as lithe and limber as athletes. And they seemed to be less and less capable of scenting, hearing, or outright spotting their prey. They'd gotten easier to sneak up on, and therefore easier to kill—though it was still best from a distance.

When Bill had stopped outside the small gas station in Three Oxen they'd seen the zombies coming in plenty of time to react.

Bill had started the gas pumping and locked it so it would fill on its own. He and Jim then, using themselves as bait, had led the rickety zombies away, toward a small building marked with a sign reading GENERAL STORE. There they were stopped briefly by the locked door but soon remedied the situation with a nearby stone the size of a baseball. Jim had thrown it, sending it easily through the glass door, and had quickly cleared away all the jagged edges with the barrel of his shotgun. The two had then ducked inside—not opening the door but climbing through the newly-made portal—and began to gather what few supplies they could carry before the zombies had started trickling in.

The smallish opening in the door had made a nice bottleneck, and Bill and Jim had taken turns braining the zombies with things they'd found nearby: a shiny new shovel for Jim at first, and a heavy table leg for Bill, broken off from a nearby display table. And when Jim had snapped the head off the shovel while dispatching one of the walking corpses, he'd gone to using the remainder of the handle as a stave, stabbing at the zombies with the pointed end, and puncturing more than a few desiccated eye-sockets. When the bodies started to pile up, preventing any more zombies from coming in through the store's front door, the two had found the back way out (relieved to find there was one) and sneaked quietly away from the horde that remained at the front of the building.

The entire remainder of the undead populace of Three Oxen were gathered there, one great mass of walking death. It was easy enough for the two men to half-sprint quietly over to the truck, pull the gas nozzle from the truck, replace the gas cap, and get in. The zombies heard when it started up, but were in no shape to even begin to reach it before the truck rolled out of town in a cloud of dust.

***

Now Bill comes to a low gate looking onto a small patio. Across from the gate is the sliding glass door to a small apartment, standing open about two inches. He considers calling out—quietly—but decides against it; no need to tempt fate. Instead, he reaches down over the top of the gate, quietly works the latch that keeps it shut, and cautiously lets himself into the patio area. Shouldering the shotgun, he moves toward the door. Inside is nothing but darkness, and still there is no sound except the surf. Inching closer, he uses the barrel of the shotgun to try and work the door open a bit further—at least enough to peek in.

It sticks at first; there's no telling how long it has been that way. Then, with just a bit of force, it gives, sliding open another couple inches. Almost instantly there is a fetid stench that seems to wash over Bill. He takes a step back, covering his nose and mouth with one hand. Coughing, he rethinks whether or not he wants to put his head inside.

***

Jim walks the boardwalk listening to the sound of sand scuffing under his feet. He carries the AR shouldered loosely—as he's seen others do, though he has no actual training or personal skill with the weapon—and searches from place to place with a wary eye. The shops and attractions seem to be long-deserted, and most look as if they had been abandoned all at once. All have been well-looted. Food has been left out to rot, games seemingly dropped in mid-play. There are various ball and ring games; a booth with dozens of mini fishbowls, all of which now contain nothing more than tiny dried-out fish corpses.

I wonder if they came back, Jim thinks.

He reaches a snack booth and sees that there is still a meager selection of chips on a rack. With a gay chuckle, he glances around, sees no lingering threat, then hops over the booth's counter and lets the AR hang at his side as he grabs a snack-size bag, tears it open, and starts munching.

***

Bill takes a few deep, cleansing breaths before shouldering the shotgun once more and moving toward the sliding door. As he nears, the scent hits him again, though not quite so bad. It's still too dark inside to see anything, so he cautiously lets the shotgun's barrel lead the way. When he reaches the door, he peers in, into shadow, and tries not to gag. There is no one in sight, but the stench of something that's been dead awhile is strong in the stale air. He listens, half-expecting to hear the shambling gait of the walking dead at any moment. When he still hears nothing but the surf down by the beach, he forces himself to push the door open enough to squeeze through, using an elbow to slide the stubborn portal along with its runner. Once he's sure there's enough of a space to leave in a hurry if need be, he enters.

It takes several moments for his eyes to start to adjust to the dimness, though it's only little lighter outside yet. Reluctantly, he lowers the shotgun, fetching his pocket flashlight. He clicks it on and takes in what is around him, seeing then just what it is that causes the horrendous stench of death to permeate the apartment. Against the wall farthest from the sliding door is a couch, and on it sits what seems to have once been a woman and two young children. The mother sits between the children, one arm wrapped around the shoulders of either. In a reclining chair that sits just off to one side of the couch, angled to face both the door and television that sits against the near wall, sits the presumed father. And gripped loosely in his right hand is a compact revolver, the kind lots of guys buy strictly for "home defense" purposes. Bill takes a few tentative steps, getting close enough to see now that there is a bullet-hole at the temple of each member of the family—including the father. He turns away. He isn't sure how long they've been sitting, but the skin of each has had time to start to decay pretty severely, and there are maggots, not only at the head wound of each person but at the various splits and lesions in the skin of each body.

It takes only a moment for Bill to forget the possibility of searching the place for anything useful and quickly leave, stopping only long enough to shut the sliding door, desperate to get as far away from the smell as soon as possible. He barely reaches the low gate when he doubles over it and heaves. Having not eaten for several hours, he doesn't expel much—a small favor.

Afterward, he retches, but nothing more comes up.

"Shit…" he says thickly.

***

Jim crumples the small, lunchbox-size bag and tosses it to the ground. It lands next to two more as he takes a fourth down from the rack.

"Ah," he says, "Sour cream."

As he tears into the top-end of the small bag he hears a familiar kind of groaning drone coming from around the corner of a nearby ski-ball stand. It is accompanied by the smell of rot.

"Oh, shit," he says, dropping the bag to the ground only partially opened.

***

Bill hears the shot and looks to the north. He picks up the pace, going from a walk to a jog back up the alley.

As he reaches the place where he and Jim parted he glances about. Jim isn't at the truck when Bill passes, so he keeps going—north—up the boardwalk. Passing various shops and amusements, he still finds no sign. Shifting gears once more, he breaks into a run, and soon, as he nears the far end of the boardwalk, he notices a change.

All at once he realizes that the surf is no longer the only sound, and underneath that steady rhythm is another more familiar sound. Another sudden change is the slight scent of death that rides the light, salty breeze coming off the ocean's surface. It's nowhere near as bad as the stench in the apartment, but it's the smell he knows all too well nonetheless.

Suddenly the booths and games give way to a pier, and there Bill sees the source of the moans, the scent of rot, and decayed flesh.

Gathered at the pier—but being kept off it by a school bus being used as a blockade—are countless zombies. None yet seem to be aware of Bill's presence; they are too busy trying to find or force their way past the bus and onto the long pier. Instantly Bill thinks he knows exactly what—or who—they are after.

"Jim!" he calls out thoughtlessly, moving around the throng of undead, giving them a wide berth. There is no answer. He tries to get far enough around the zombies to see out onto the pier, but the combination of them and the school bus obstruct his view.

"Jim!" he calls again, the slightest quaver in his voice. By now the zombies have taken notice of him, and those nearest him have started to shift their attention.

There are far too many to start shooting; he'd be out of ammunition in seconds. Looking around, he sees a lifeguard tower out on the beach—a good fifty-yard dash or better. With no better options immediately available—and simply going back to the truck and leaving without Jim entirely out of the question—he makes for the beach, quickly descending a rickety, weatherworn flight of wooden steps down to the sand. As he goes, he sees that the zombies are not only packed at the front of the pier but also beneath it, desperately seeking access to whomever or whatever is barricaded there. Then he catches a glimpse of who they're after and stops.

Upon the pier, mostly hidden from view but still peeking over the side of the guardrail, is a young girl.

"Hey!" he calls, casting a brief glance behind him to the zombies that now stumble-step their way down the rickety steps after him. He returns his gaze to where the girl was, but she isn't there. What the fuck, he thinks. Then the dry shriek of a zombie coming up behind him spurs him into motion once more. He reaches the lifeguard station and quickly climbs the steps, throws open the door—surprised to find it open—and gets inside. Realizing the latch on the door is broken, and it won't stay shut on its own he drops to his knees, pressing himself fast against it and trying to stay out of sight. Huffing he looks around the small station, stunned to see two pale blue eyes, staring right at him from only a couple feet away.

"Jim!" he nearly shouts.

"Shush!" Jim says, putting a finger to his lips in a gesture of silence, then adds in a hiss, "You'll lead them right to us!"

"You're alive!" Bill hisses back. "Why didn't you come out when I called? Didn't you—"

"Shush!"

"I heard a shot, man. Didn't you hear me calling for you?" Bill asks in a whisper.

Jim nods. "I took a shot at one and missed. And I didn't answer 'cause I didn't wanna get their attention after I slipped past 'em," he says, rolling his eyes.

"Sorry," Bill offers with a shrug. He quickly looks around. "They weren't far behind me," he says. "Find something to barricade this door. When they get here and pile up, we can go out one of the windows."

Jim nods, duck-walking over to where a folding chair sits tucked into a corner. "Yeah, we got to get up to that pier—there're people up there. I couldn't get past the zombies on the bus, so I ran down here."

"I saw a little girl," Bill says.

"I saw a woman," Jim says, "and two boys—teenagers. The zombies were already at the barricade, but I saw the woman; she had the flare-gun."

He goes to his knees and walks toward Bill and the door, one hand dragging the chair along behind him. The legs scrape across the floor noisily, and both men cringe. Jim freezes. They listen, and almost instantly there is an audible increase in the dry, monstrous groans that approach the guard station.

"Shit!" Jim swears. He gets to his feet, as does Bill, and braces the chair against the door, lodging the back of it up underneath the door's handle.

"Think it'll hold?" he asks.

"Hope so," Bill says. "At least long enough for us to get out of here, and up onto that pier."

Jim nods his agreement, watching as the zombies begin to round the guard station and ascend the steps to the door.

"It's still gonna be hairy," Bill says.

"No shit," Jim retorts.

"I say we smash out that corner window, hop out and run like hell."

"Smartest thing you said all day," Jim says, forcing a chuckle.

"Watch your eyes!" Bill says, turning his head to shield his own as he smashes the butt of his shotgun through the window. It's plenty noisy and doesn't help any in diverting the zombies' attention, but most of it falls down to the sand in just a few large shards. Bill quickly clears away the remaining glass around the edges and climbs out, straddling the window's frame and then dropping down to the ground below, his boots crunching on the glass as he lands. He moves away, making a place for Jim to follow, and quickly glances around, getting eyes on the zombies.

Jim follows Bill's lead, first straddling the window's frame, then dropping down to the glass and sand below. When he lands, however, the largest piece of glass has already been shattered further, and he is unable to avoid the jagged, six-inch shard that tears through his jeans and raggedly into his right calf.

"Fuck!" he swears, cringing as he falls onto his side. He brings the injured leg up toward his chest, straining to reach the shard and remove it.

"Shit!" Bill hisses. He rushes over to his friend, going to one knee long enough to help him up. "Come on, man. We got to go. Deal with it later."

Jim groans in agony as he gets to a mostly standing position, unable to put any amount of weight on the injured leg. Bill hooks an arm around him, and together they manage to three-leg their way past the clumsily reaching zombies and over to the rickety steps.

"All right, one at a time, man," Bill says.

Holding loosely to the weathered handrail, Jim hops his way up the steps, the AR dangling behind him from its single-point sling. Bill follows closely behind, and as he feels a hand clasping at his shoulder, hears a high voice cry out from the direction of the pier. He turns, eyes going ever so briefly to the same little girl he saw earlier, now standing just on the other side of the school bus's hood and looking down at him, to the zombie that somehow managed to slip up close enough to get one bony, desiccated hand on Bill's jacket. He cries out in surprise and shrugs away, immediately bringing the barrel of the pump-action up under the zombie's chin and taking its head off in a veritable cloud of dust and decay with a single shot. When he looks back over to where the girl was, she is again gone. Perplexed, Bill hurries up the steps, once more going to assist Jim.

***

Bill and Jim reach the sandy boardwalk to find that there are still a good many zombies trying their best—and getting nowhere—to breach the school bus barricade's boundary. The bulk of the throng of undead is concentrated at the rear-end of the bus, as it was parked at an angle—obviously backed in—and looks as though there may be a way to push past it where it meets the pier's guardrail. Some, however, are already coming their way,

262

and Bill knows that they'll never be able to just waltz right past them with Jim's lame leg, and there are still too many to take out. He looks around, searching for any possible means of even temporary safety, maybe just somewhere that he could stash Jim until he can draw the zombies away, but there seems to be nothing close by.

Then a distantly-familiar sound pulls both men's attention back over to the school bus. They watch as the door creaks open; first to about halfway, and then the rest. A quick glance back to the zombies, and then Bill sees that it's the little girl.

"Hurry!" she urges, beckoning to them with one hand still on the door-opening lever. Jim half-hops his way toward the portal while Bill covers the zombies, and once Jim is inside the bus, Bill follows, strafing the zombies before quickly climbing in. He doesn't wait for the girl to shut the door; instead, he leans over and does it himself. Almost instantly he hears undead hands beating at the metal and glass that separates them from the outside world.

Jim is sitting in the first seat on the bus's passenger side, and Bill plops down just across the aisle with a short sigh. Momentarily he leans forward, intent on thanking the mystery-child, but he is cut off by the sound of a pistol hammer cocking, followed by a woman's frantic voice coming from right over his shoulder.

"Don't move! Cara, come over here! Get away from the men, honey!"

Bill freezes, wondering if he wouldn't have been better off making a run for the truck. He's all too aware of the flare-gun that is being aimed right at him.

"I don't know who you guys are, but you can't stay here."

Cara moves past Bill, and he sees a look almost like guilt on her sweet face.

"Look, we don't want any trouble," Bill says. "If you want we'll just stay on the bus. But we're not going back out there. Not yet."

"You're not staying—"

"Look, lady, I can't even walk!" Jim barks.

"They can help us," Cara says, tugging at the sleeve of the woman's wool sweater.

"They could also—" She stops; Bill can imagine what she's imagining.

"Listen," he says, swallowing dryly, "just let us hang in here a bit—then we'll be off. I just need to fix up my friend's leg." He ventures to turn his head enough to look the woman in the eye. His voice catches at first, caught off guard by how young and attractive she is. He pushes the thought aside. "He's hurt pretty bad."

The woman seems to glance down, quickly studying the large shard of glass that juts from the steadily growing patch of red in Jim's pant leg. Bill watches her a moment longer.

"Fine," she says, "but if either of you tries anything… you'll deal with this." She gives the flare-gun a light flourish before cautiously lowering it. Pulling Cara along with her, she backs toward the bus's rear exit. Bill watches her just a moment longer before a groan from Jim pulls his attention away.

Going to one knee, Bill tries to examine the glass, but he can't tell how deep it is. Since Jim isn't bleeding all over the place, he figures it isn't too deep, or at least that it hasn't severed an artery. Gingerly he takes hold of Jim's leg, starting to turn it, but Jim winces, and he stops.

"What do you want me to do?" he says.

Jim shakes his head. "I don't know, man. It hurts like a son of a bitch."

Bill considers whether he should pull the glass out first or try to rip the pant leg open first. Taking his jacket off and laying it across the seat behind him he shifts down to both knees. Then the slightest shift of the bus snaps his attention toward the rear exit once more.

The woman has reappeared, still pointedly toting the flare gun, but now also bringing along something else in the opposite hand. As she moves cautiously toward them, Bill sees that it is a first aid box. She stops just two seats away and sets it down, not taking her eyes from Bill.

"If you're gonna do it, you may as well do it right," she says. She starts to leave but stops when Bill speaks up.

"Thanks," he says, reaching over and grabbing the small plastic box. He seems to study her.

"What?" she asks defensively.

"I just…" he trails off, looking down at the box as he opens it, and briefly digs through the meager supplies.

She again starts to leave.

"Don't know who I'm thanking," Bill finishes. He takes the small pair of surgical-style scissors from the box and proceeds to carefully cut away the lower half of Jim's pant leg, leaving only a small patch that surrounds the spear of glass. He sets the half-soaked swatch aside and leans in again to get a better look at the wound and the shard. He still has no clue how deep it is, but the bleeding seems to have slowed if not stopped. Setting the scissors down, he takes out a sterilizing wipe and tears it open.

"Angel."

Bill stops halfway reaching for the shard and looks up at the woman. He can't help the tired puff of laughter that escapes his lips. Immediately he sees a look of vexation flit across her pretty face.

"Seriously?" he asks.

"Yeah—seriously," she says, then turning and hurriedly walking away.

Bill sighs, not having meant insult, but finding it most ironic that such a "sight for sore eyes" was earnestly named Angel.

He gingerly removes the shard of glass from Jim's leg. It's buried about two inches into the flesh, and Jim lets out a short, tight string of expletives as Bill smoothly pulls it free, bringing the remaining patch of blood-soaked denim with it. He then goes about wiping it down with the sterilizing pad.

"Son of a bitch, that stings!" Jim says through gritted teeth.

Bill quietly wraps what small amount of gauze there is in the kit around Jim's skinny leg. His friend looks studiously down at his suddenly too-quiet friend.

"I know what you're thinking, Bill," Jim says with a stifled groan.

"What do you mean?" asks Bill.

"I've seen that look in your eye before. The way you looked at her? I've seen it."

"Shut up, Jim," Bill says flatly.

"You had that same look the night you met Ronnie."

Bill stops just shy of adding the surgical tape to hold the gauze in place.

"Shut up, Jim," he says a bit more forcefully. He applies the tape and rises to sit on the bus seat, elbows resting on knees and head hanging.

"She reminds you of Ronnie, and the girl reminds you of Jess."

Bill doesn't deny but doesn't admit either that Angel did remind him of Veronica, and Cara made his heart skip, summoning thoughts of his daughter Jessica.

Jim says nothing else about it, unable to imagine what his friend is thinking—or feeling. It had been hard enough for him to see what had happened to weekend warrior's family, but now this?

"Thanks," he finally says, gesturing down to his newly bandaged leg.

Bill nods but says nothing.

***

A while passes, and Bill has neither seen nor heard any sign of Angel or the children—only one of which he's seen. He stares down at the plastic first aid box in the seat beside him and tries not to think about his family. He ventures a glance out the bus's dingy window, and there is still no sign of anyone on the long, deserted pier. With a shallow sigh, he stands, picking up the white box, and starts toward the back of the bus.

"I thought we were staying on the bus," Jim says dryly.

Bill stops, looking down at the kit.

"Why'd she signal if she didn't want help?" He glances up at Jim, who shrugs. "I get they're afraid, but… they can't wanna stay here."

Again Jim shrugs, not bothering with trying to stop his friend again.

Bill walks toward the back end of the bus, hearing the calls of the zombies just outside the tube of metal. Momentarily, he is almost grateful that his wife and daughter hadn't been around for all the shit he'd been through, all the shit they would've been through—were they lucky enough to survive.

Standing at the rear exit of the school bus he hesitates, not wanting Angel to think him a liar—and that much more untrustworthy. Then he rationalizes: she needs her first-aid kit back. Carefully he hops down, noting just how close a couple of zombie straining hands come to clasping his bared lower arm from under the back door of the bus.

Stepping out of their reach, he peers through the space left between vehicle and pier. They can't squeeze through, and countless sandbags placed all around the bus keep them from getting under and onto the pier, but he can't imagine that even this place would be safe forever. Turning, he starts out onto the pier.

Along either side sit numerous benches, and in between every other two is a garbage receptacle—each one marked with a PR. About halfway along the pier is a small shack offering BAIT and ROD RENTALS. Walking along and smelling the salt air Bill gets lost in more fleeting memories of the past. He'd worked extra hours and saved for six months because neither Ronnie nor Jess had ever seen the beach, and wanted to go that summer after Jess's first year of school. They'd all gotten sunburns, and the souvenir photo that hung above the TV in the trailer had shown what looked like three giant, smiling, humanoid lobsters.

Click!

Bill is stopped by the sound of the flaregun's hammer cocking back, yet again.

"I thought we had an agreement," Angel says.

Bill takes a deep, calming breath.

"I just wanted to return your first aid kit," he says.

"Set it down," she says. "I'll get it once you're back on the bus."

Bill lets out a short, quiet sigh, starts to lean down, to do as she said, then stops. He turns to face her.

"Why did you signal us?" he asks, unable to hide his indignation.

At first Angel looks angry, tensing up at his words; then she seems to relax a little, lowering the gun to "half-mast."

"I didn't," she says. "Cara did."

Bill just stares for a moment and then chuckles.

"She thought you guys—or whoever was in the truck— could rescue us."

Again Bill stays quiet, looking down at the first-aid kit in his hand.

"I guess all kids her age are like that."

He leans down, sets the box at his feet.

"My daughter was. She always saw the good."

Angel lowers the gun, not sure what to say. She doesn't flinch as Bill walks past her—mere inches away. She looks down at the box, steps forward and leans down to pick it up.

"We'll rest tonight—in the bus. Tomorrow—when we leave… you're welcome to join us."

***

Bill can't sleep on the bus. The seat wasn't meant to accommodate slumber, and between Jim's light, labored snoring and the ever-present din of the zombies, he knows that rest of any kind is an utterly futile endeavor. And despite the light breeze that comes off the ocean the air inside the bus has become both stifling and scented with dry blood. With a quiet groan, he sits up, looking over at his restlessly sleeping friend. He grabs his jacket, though doesn't expect he'll need it, and walks softly toward the back of the bus.

As he eases down, he is especially careful to keep out of the zombies' reach, practically hugging the doorframe of the bus's rear exit. Once his boots touch down firmly on the boardwalk, he moves swiftly away from the bus and walks, as quietly as possible, toward the end of the pier.

The salty breeze is refreshing, and the freshness of it even better, though it takes a minute for the smell of dried blood to fade from Bill's nostrils. As expected, there's no sign of either Angel or the children. He assumes now that they've been taking refuge in the small shop. As he passes it, he wonders briefly if he and Jim should consider staying a while longer. After all, it would be nice to rest for more than just a night. And with a little effort, they could probably wipe out the dead that surrounds them.

But he'd already said they would leave, and something inside him made him want to keep his word—if only for her sake. Still, he could at least offer.

As he reaches the end of the pier he stops, lays his jacket across the top of the guardrail and moves to lean against it.

Looking down into the blue-black water, he wonders if there are still fish, living fish; and if so, if they too have to swim for their lives from the undead. A puff of breath something like laughter escapes him.

"Hey," a feminine voice says softly.

Shit…

"Sorry," Bill says, guiltily turning around to face Angel. "I know I was supposed to stay on the bus. It was just so hot and cramped that—"

"It's okay," she says, and to his surprise actually offers something akin to a smile. He nods, offers his own. Then she moves toward the bench nearest the end of the pier and looks his way, motioning to it. Wordlessly he accepts the invitation, grabbing his jacket and then joining her. For a moment they sit quietly, and Bill is ultra-aware of Angel's close proximity. His pulse quickens, and he is about to excuse himself, to get up and go back to the bus when she surprises him yet again.

"So… you had a family?"

Bill's throat tightens.

"Were they," she pauses, "I mean—was it when this all started?"

Bill swallows dryly.

"No," he manages.

Angel waits and then realizes that it isn't something he wants to talk about.

"I'm sorry, I shouldn't—"

"It's okay," he says. "It was about a year before it started. My wife was playing with our little girl while I was working on my truck. I had my head buried under the hood, listening to—" he stops, the words catching in his throat, and takes a deep, shaky breath, "listening to Jess giggle. Her mom was playing with her, chasing her around outside our trailer."

Angel sees that Bill's hands are clutched tightly between his knees, and instinctively places a hand on his shoulder in a gesture of comfort. He seems to notice but makes no move to recoil or shrug her away.

"Then I hear a revving engine and squealing brakes...

"And then Ronnie screams..."

Angel bites back a shuddering sigh and feels the warmth of tears rimming her eyes.

"It was the town drunk," Bill says quietly. "He was an old war vet who fell into a bottle after a dishonorable discharge and never came back out."

Angel finally removes her hand from Bill's shoulder, bringing it up to wipe a single, thick tear from her cheek.

"His lawyer claimed post-traumatic stress—which was probably true—and got him manslaughter.

"Two counts.

"After that, I fell into a bottle. Got into some trouble, too, a lot of fights at the local bar." He chuckles thickly. "When this all started I was locked up in jail. If I hadn't been, I'd probably be…" he trails off, gesturing toward the school bus, and presumably, the zombies beyond.

"I'm sorry," offers Angel. Bill only nods, wiping his own hot tears away with the back of one hand. Again the two stay quiet for several moments, and again Bill considers returning to the bus, wondering if he's in for another nightmare—like so many he'd had before.

"Will there be room?" asks Angel.

At first, Bill isn't sure what the hell she's talking about, then realizes that she can only be referring to his truck. He's grateful that she let the subject of his past drop.

"It'll be cramped," he says. "But we can make it work. Do you only have the three kids?"

"Yeah," she says. "And they're not mine, by the way." She actually chuckles softly at that. Bill looks at her in the moonlight and briefly remembers Jim's words, then pushes them aside.

"So how—" Bill starts.

"I was a TA. And the day everything started, the school—a lot of the schools—just started loading buses and sending students home.

"This was the last stop on Fred's—the bus driver's—route. Port Romero doesn't have a school, so a few kids from here go to school in Everett, where I'm from. Normally I wouldn't come along for the ride, but there was just so much panic."

A gust of cool ocean air washes over the pier and Angel shivers. Before he can think about what he's doing Bill has draped his jacket over her shoulders. He feels like an idiot as she looks at him, wearing a thin, almost knowing smirk.

"Thanks," she says.

Bill grunts in response.

"Anyway, we got stuck here. And Fred managed to block off the pier before he—" she stops, looking down at her hands. "I don't even know where he got the sandbags. But, if not for him…"

Bill waits for a beat, watching her in the dim moonlight, and then realizes she's basically finished.

"We'll have to lure them away to get you all to the truck," he says thoughtfully.

"The boys, they—" she starts.

"You mean the kids?" Bill asks, tone verging on shock. Angel nods.

"Jack and Pete, they've done it before." She looks down, a bit guiltily. "That's kind of how we've managed to survive this long," she chuckles, but Bill can sense it is forced. "Snack runs, and competing with those things for… for seagulls." She nearly cringes.

That explains that, Bill thinks.

"They're smart. And they're quick," she says, her face now marked by optimism. "They can lure those things away; I can get Cara and help you get your friend to the truck."

Bill cracks a half-hearted smile and actually considers that it can work. He nods and suddenly feels how tired he is.

"Okay, then," he says simply. Angel smiles, and Bill feels a guiltily-familiar pang. He stands, stretches, and starts toward the bus.

"Sorry about before," Angel says. Bill turns, and she is standing. "I mean about the gun to your head, and… all that."

He smirks. "It's okay."

"It's just… we've met some bad people since we've been here. Men who—" she stops, looks down, and Bill feels a surge of emotion, a sudden overprotective anger, making a pit in his stomach. "Well, you can imagine," she finishes.

Bill takes a breath to steady his suddenly kick-started pulse. "What happened?" he asks.

Angel looks him in the eye, no hint of any definable emotion evident. "They were passed out, full of looted booze and tired from shoving the boys around and…" She stops, looks down again. "At least they left Cara alone."

Bill swallows thickly and his jaw tightens.

"One of them had a big hunting knife. I got it from him," she says. "And now they're out there," she gestures toward the land-end of the pier, "with the rest of those things."

***

By the time the sun is fully above the eastern horizon the morning has begun to heat up, despite the breeze coming off the water. Bill had sat—sleepless—on the bus for an indeterminate amount of time after talking with

Angel. He'd listened quietly to the zombies outside the bus, vainly scratching at the metal body, ever-desperate to get at the fresh meat therein. Over and over in his head, he'd accounted for the remaining ammo that he and Jim had between them. And he didn't know how many extra rounds—if any—Angel had for the flare gun. Finally, though, by the time the horizon was just starting to lighten up, he had dozed.

Now, after being too soon awakened by the restless slumber of his friend, he sits up. Feeling more exhausted than ever, he looks over at Jim. Quietly he moves to kneel down in the aisle, doing his best to examine the wounded leg. Immediately he is hit with a distinct smell of rot and cringes away. From where he is he can see that the bleeding must've never fully stopped; either that or it started up again during the night, because at least half of the meager dressing is now soaked through and stained with partially dried blood.

With a quiet, tired sigh he pushes himself back up to his seat.

✳✳✳

"Bill, this is Jack and his brother Pete," says Angel.

Bill offers a nod to either boy; each looks to be in their mid-teens, both tall and lanky. He can see at least partly how they managed not to get snagged by the zombies yet—especially with the things slowing down as time goes on and decay takes its toll.

"And of course you already met Cara."

Bill looks down at the girl—no more than eight—and offers a thin, friendly smile. She smiles back sweetly, and he has to choke back his emotions.

"How many times have you done this?" he asks the boy called Pete.

"Don't know; we didn't keep count."

"We just went whenever we needed food or water, clean clothes from one of the shops." offers Jack.

Bill nods.

"Okay. Get whatever you need," he says to Angel. "We'll take it to the bus, and when these two," he gestures toward the boys, "do whatever it is they do, we'll make a break for the truck." He once again regards the boys.

"Whatever you've done before—whatever got you back in one piece, do exactly the same thing. Don't take any chances. We only need enough time to get your stuff and my friend to the truck. And then we're out of here."

"That's right," says Angel, "nothing new, nothing fancy. Just lure them away and then circle back around."

Both boys nod their understanding and agreement. Bill turns once more to Angel.

"How much do you have to get?"

She shakes her head. "Not much. The kids have their backpacks, and I have a bag. A few things the boys scavenged. Not a lot."

"Okay," Bill nods. "Just get whatever you need that you can carry quickly." He starts to walk away, then stops and turns back to her.

"The bus—is there gas in the tank?"

She shakes her head. "The men who came before siphoned it. But after I... well... there's about half of a can full in there."

She points toward the shop, and he nods. He then looks at the flare gun, tucked into her waistband.

"Do you have any more shells for that?"

Angel takes the gun from her waistband and holds it up studiously.

"Just one," she offers.

"Okay," Bill says. "Bring that too."

With that, he leaves her and returns to the bus to find Jim sitting down on the bus's steps, peering out through the glass at the desiccated zombie faces that are pressed up against it, rotted teeth gnashing weakly.

"Hey, man, we're almost ready to get out of here."

Jim doesn't turn to acknowledge him but speaks in a lethargic tone.

"You think it hurts to be dead, Bill?"

Bill stares down at his friend, considers the question in earnest for a brief moment.

"I don't know, man. Just be ready, okay?" He starts to walk away, but Jim stops him, suddenly clutching at his pant leg with an iron grip. He looks up from the steps like a man literally at death's door.

"I think we both know this is the end of the line for me, buddy."

"You're gonna be—"

"I'm gonna be dead," he says placidly.

Bill wants to argue but knows he won't win; he knows his friend is right.

Jim slips the AR sling over his head and holds the rifle up to Bill.

"I won't need it much longer."

Bill takes it wordlessly and continues staring down at his friend. Jim just sits there and goes back to staring out the bus's door window, at the wretched zombie faces, like a man looking into a mirror-image of his future self. Bill slips the sling over his head and shoulder and walks away.

***

Just as Angel had said, each child totes a backpack. Cara wears hers as if she were going back to school, while Pete and Jack set their bags down among the sandbags. Each boy also carries a golf club, one a wood and the other an iron. Angel herself carries a small gym bag, slung over one shoulder. She holds the aforementioned gas can in one hand and Bill's jacket in the other. She sets the can down and offers the jacket back to him with a smile. He takes it, and she then pulls the flare gun from her waistband, offering it as well.

"You sure you don't wanna hang onto it?" he asks.

She shakes her head. "I'd probably set something on fire."

At that Cara giggles, and Bill feels a shudder run up his spine. More than anything he wants to get them—all of them—to some kind of safety. He takes the flare gun, breaks it open to see the one and only round is loaded, and then slips it down into his pocket. An arm at a time he slips his jacket on, then picks up the gas can, giving it a shake.

The liquid inside sloshes, but it doesn't feel as though there's very much of it.

"You really need the jacket?" Pete asks. "It's getting warm."

"This thing's stopped more than a few bites," says Bill.

"Okay, Angel, can you get Cara and the bags while I cover you with the shotgun?"

Angel nods, taking Cara by the hand.

"Whatever you do, don't let go, sweetie," Bill says to Cara. "Angel's gonna take care of you."

Cara nods and Bill turns his attention to the boys.

"Get ready," he says. They both nod and Bill jogs quickly over to the bus. He sets the gas can just inside the open back portal, and then hops up in after.

Jim now sits in the driver seat of the bus, looking more wretched than ever. Bill brings the gas can and sets it on the top step where he can grab it on the way out.

"You good, Jim?" he asks.

Jim looks up at him tiredly.

"I'm getting you out of here, man," Bill says, placing one hand on his friend's feverishly warm forearm, giving it a firm squeeze.

"What's that in your pocket?" Jim says in a croak, eyes going down to the flare gun. Bill glances down absently, and answers, "Flare gun."

"Why don't you let me hold onto it—just in case," says Jim.

Bill studies him for just a moment, then pulls the gun from his waistband, as well as the single shell from his pocket, and hands over both. Jim forces a thin, half-formed smile and nods his thanks.

"Long as I'm still useful," he quips.

Bill nods, offering another friendly arm-squeeze.

***

"Okay, whenever you guys are ready," Bill says.

He, along with Angel and Cara, sits nestled against the sandbags while Jack and Pete make ready to climb over the hood of the bus and lead the zombies away.

Jack goes first, using the hubcap of the tire as a foothold to push off of and get up onto the hood. Once he's up, his brother hands up the golf clubs. Pete follows suit and climbs up the tire and onto the hood like a smaller child navigating a jungle gym. Once he's up as well, Jack hands one club—the wood—back to him.

"Ready?" asks Jack.

"Born ready," Pete answers, and Bill has to stifle a chuckle. For a split second, he is reminded of Jim and himself.

"Be careful, boys," Angel says.

Both nod, and then Jack disappears from sight. It's obvious by the change in the sound of urgency coming from the zombies that they have taken notice of the teenage walking buffet. Bill leans out away from the sandbags, looking up toward the hood, and just sees Pete disappear from sight as well. As he listens, he hears Jack shouting instructions to his brother—which way to go; which zombies to watch out for. There is the occasional heavy thwack or metallic clunk, and he can tell that they are fighting—using the golf clubs against the heads of the undead—and can't help but wonder if they're taking unnecessary risks. He considers just going out and joining them—or at least covering them—but a single glance over at Angel and Cara and he can't bring himself to leave their sides. He sees that Cara wears a look of worry and places a comforting hand on her shoulder.

"Hey, Bill?" Jim calls from inside the bus.

Shit… what now? Bill thinks.

"Wait here," he says. Both Angel and Cara nod quietly. Staying at a crouch Bill moves to the back end of the bus. He stops at the corner and cautiously peeks around. For the first time, he sees no sign of the things right there waiting to try and snatch at him. Pleased that the plan seems to be working, he hops up into the bus, but as he jogs toward Jim, he realizes just why his friend is calling to him.

"Shit," Bill swears.

"It's not working," Jim says weakly. "Some of 'em followed the kids, but…"

Bill leans over the partition in front of the first passenger side seat and sees that there are still at least a dozen or so zombies that seem to be more interested in getting to Jim and himself, content to stay put and claw vainly at the bus door rather than try to chase down the two youths.

"I'll have to lead these away," Bill says.

Jim watches as his best friend moves hastily toward the back end of the bus, then his eyes shift down to the flare gun in his pale, sweaty, nearly-lifeless hand, and then once more over to the gas can that sits less than two feet away.

Bill hops down from the bus and hurries over to where Angel and Cara still sit huddled against the sandbags. Grabbing his shotgun, he takes a knee.

"Okay," he says, "the plan only half worked. Some of them are still right outside the bus, so I'll have to lead them away."

"No!" Cara whines, worry once again marking her pretty, rose-cheeked face.

"It's okay, sweetie. Bill knows what he's doing; he's gonna be fine." As Angel says the last, she looks at him, and he isn't sure if she believes what she's saying. Still, he nods and holds the shotgun out to her. She first just looks at it, and starts to shake her head, but she looks into his eyes and understands that he isn't sure, either. She takes it and holds it awkwardly.

"The truck's back the way we came, south down the boardwalk, keys in the ignition."

Just in case.

Angel nods, and he stands, following the boys' lead and moving to the front end of the bus. Putting the toe of one boot on the hubcap and using both hands to pull himself up on the hood's cool metal, he makes it with ease. There, he kneels, finding his balance on the slant and holding to the metal frame of the passenger side mirror in order to lean and peer around and down to the zombies at the door. From the corner of his eye, he catches movement within the vehicle. At first, he can't make out what Jim is doing, as the windshield has collected dust. He wipes crudely at it with one hand; and then his heart rises into his throat, dread and panic filling his belly.

"Jim," he cries, "what the fuck are you doing!?"

Jim ignores his friend, moving as fast as he's able on only one good leg. The pain in his injured limb is still present, though mostly it has gone to needles and pins. He manages to stay upright despite the lack of feeling. Doing his best with what little gasoline he has, he douses the floor and seats of the bus, hobbling from the front to the back.

Bill hops down from the hood of the bus and lands badly, twisting his left ankle and crying out as he goes briefly to the ground. He's right back up though, and half-sprinting to the back of the bus when he hears the rear door being closed.

"Jim?" he calls.

Jim sees Bill disappear briefly, but then is keenly aware of his head bobbing past the bottoms of the windows as he himself hurries—as quickly as possible—back to the driver seat. Holding to the back of it, he leans over and works the lever to open the front door. As it opens, the zombies that were pressed right against it fall forward into the bus, onto the steps.

"Come and get it, motherfuckers," he says in a low, exhausted taunt.

Bill gets to the rear of the bus and takes hold of the door handle, twisting, and pulling it open. As he laboriously climbs up into the aisle, he sees Jim coming his way—fast—using the seatbacks on either side to help himself along.

"What the hell do you think you're doing, ma—"

Jim doesn't slow as he reaches Bill. Instead, he body-checks his best friend, sending him right back out the way he came in. Bill falls roughly against the pier's guardrail, barely catching himself as his ankle tries to buckle beneath his weight.

"Sorry, buddy," Jim offers with a wince.

Bill tries to stand and has to favor his left leg.

"Jim…"

Jim forces a pained smile, with tears rimming his eyes.

"Bill…"

As Jim pulls the door shut for the second time, Bill notices that he now shakily grips the flare gun loosely in his other hand.

"Goddammit, Jim!"

He forces himself forward this time, practically throwing his body against the back door of the bus. Gripping the handle in both hands he tries to twist and pull, but there is limited give.

Inside the bus Jim holds as firmly as he can to the rear door's handle, using all of his weight, and every last ounce of strength which remains to him to keep the portal closed.

"Get out of here, Bill!" he yells, then adds hoarsely, "Clock's ticking."

Bill beats against the door with one hand as he tugs with the other until from around the side of the bus he hears Angel call out his name. Reluctantly he lets up on the door handle, sidesteps, and leans against the corner of the bus to peer around toward her and Cara.

"The boys are coming!" she says frantically. Bill takes a step back gingerly, looks up at the rear door and then punches it, growling in anger.

Jim watches the top of Bill's head as he moves along the side of the bus, back toward the woman and the little girl, toward his new family. An honest smile quirks his trembling lips before his eyes go blearily back to the zombies. A number of them have now made it up the steps, and are hastily shuffling up the aisle toward him, so much in a hurry that they stumble, fall, and practically have to climb over one another.

Bill first helps Angel up onto the hood, boosting her as she pulls herself up before handing up the boys' backpacks. He then lifts Cara up, shifting all of his and her weight to his right side. Angel meets him halfway, helping to pull the girl up. Last, he hands up the shotgun, which Angel also takes, and then once more climbs up onto the hood of the bus himself, careful of his ankle. It's a cramped space, and Bill only dares venture a fleeting glance through the bus's windshield, seeing no sign of Jim through the dirty glass, only the rough shapes of a dozen zombies. At the sound of a high-pitched whistle, he turns to see both boys, still alive and well, coming toward the bus at a jog.

"I told you they didn't all follow us," says Pete.

"Whatever!" Jack shoots back. "Let's just get the hell out of here!"

"Hey—catch," Bill says, tossing first one bag and then the other down to either boy.

Angel helps herself down, and this time Bill hands Cara down to her.

Jim leans weakly against the back door of the bus, barely able to stay upright. He smirks grimly as the zombies get almost within arms' reach of him. The flare gun hangs limply at his side. He fingers the trigger, hesitating only a moment before quickly squeezing it.

Bill is about to hand down the shotgun when he hears a puff-bang sound from inside the bus. Angel, Cara, and both boys stagger away from the bus in a panic.

"Oh, shit!" says Jack.

"Fire!" Cara shouts, pointing at the sudden flames dance and roar within.

"Shit," Bill swears, sliding down over the passenger side of the hood, being sure to land on his good leg.

Suddenly there is another cry from Cara, and Bill's eyes shoot first to her, and then to the thing she is pointing at.

He rights himself and shoulders the shotgun, taking aim at a flaming zombie as it stumbles down from the bus steps. It takes two steps before he has the sight set on its burning skull. He pulls the trigger, and half the zombie's head explodes, spattering against the doorframe and leaving it briefly aflame. The rest of the flame-engulfed carcass falls to the ground motionless, continuing to burn black smoke into the blue, mid-morning sky.

There seem to be no more coming back out of the bus, though in the distance—about fifty yards to the north— coming the same way that Jack and Pete had come, are the rest of the zombies; added to that are the ones that were previously occupied beneath the pier, now laboriously making their way up the beach and toward the burning beacon.

"Time to go," says Bill. "Everybody follow me."

***

The way back to the truck is clear, and even with Bill's twisted ankle, there is no chance of the shambling zombies catching up to them. Still, he keeps the shotgun loosely shouldered and at the ready.

When the vehicle comes into view the doors still sit ajar, just as he and Jim had left them, in case a hasty getaway had been necessary. Going to the driver's side, Bill quickly checks through the window to make sure there are no nasty, undead surprises. There are none.

"Everybody in," he says, leaning into the cab and replacing the shotgun on the rear-window mount. While the boys bicker over how all will fit into the truck, Bill looks back toward the beach, toward the black column of smoke that has begun to paint the sky above Port Romero in shadow.

"Come on," he says, slipping the rifle sling over his head and leaning into the truck once more. "Pete, Jack, you two hop in back for now. We'll figure it out later." He opens the small window in the center of the truck's back glass before returning the AR to the mount as well.

"Bill, no—" Angel starts.

"It's okay," he says, "I'll drive slow, and I'll stop as soon as we're out of town." He climbs into the driver's seat, and seeing Jim's sawed-off lying in the center, pulls it close, tucking it next to his leg. Already Jack and Pete are following his instructions; Cara, too, is making a place for herself, climbing into the cab and seating herself next to Bill. "The road in was totally desolate, Angel. We just need to get out of here."

With a brief glance toward the boys—and getting a reassuring thumbs-up from Pete—she quickly gets into the passenger seat and buckles in. While Bill does the same Angel buckles Cara in as well.

"Hang on, guys," Bill says. Both boys nod.

"We're ready," offers Jack, slapping the side of the truck bed.

Bill turns the key in the ignition, and it whines. He tries again, and the same thing happens.

"Bill?" Cara says a bit nervously.

"It's okay, sweetie," he says, first glancing down at her and then up at Angel. "It just takes a couple of tries sometimes."

He hopes he's right, hopes his rig hasn't finally reached the end of its road as well.

Over the distant sounds of fire, breeze and surf, the sound of groaning zombies slowly but steadily approaching comes into earshot.

Come on, motherfucker, start.

With the third turn of the key, the engine comes to life. Bill sighs and puts it in reverse. He gives it gas and turns the wheel to the left until he has the truck turned nearly one hundred eighty degrees, then puts it into drive and retraces the path that he took coming into town the morning before.

***

The truck crests the hill overlooking Port Romero for the second time, and Bill eases to a brief stop. Looking in the rearview mirror from so high, all he can see is ocean and horizon, though he doubts he'll soon forget what was lost there.

"Bill?" Angel says softly, reaching over and gently placing her hand atop his on the steering wheel.

"Last looks," he says. She gives him a squeeze and then takes her hand away.

Bill gives the truck some gas and they're on their way.

He looks over at Angel, and then down at Cara, and thinks, or gained.

7 ORDER OF THE SECOND DEATH BY DARREN TODD

While I was camping with my brother, the world ended and we never even knew. Not till we came out of the woods a week after we'd entered, only to find Garrett's car all tore up. Battery gone, gas gone. The trunk empty even of the fabric lining. Still, we figured we'd been robbed, even way out in Hanging Rock, a half hour from pretty much anything in southwest Virginia.

"You got your phone?" Garrett asked me, the first thing he'd said in ten minutes. He'd gone quiet, always did when he was super angry. That habit used to creep me out when we were kids, 'cause it meant he'd turned off our twin-senses and gone rogue on me, but I had to respect it now.

I dug into my cargo pants and turned on my cell. I'd done this only twice during our annual camping trip, once because I'd lost my flashlight and the other time to reference an ebook. At the site, I hadn't expected a signal and hadn't wanted one. Now, though, I waited patiently to latch onto some cell tower. Even 2G would be enough to call Triple-A.

"I got nothing, bro," I said after waiting a couple minutes. "Did we have service on the way in?"

He shrugged. Not sure why I even asked, just my sisterly compulsion to get him talking. When it came to phones, his twenty-five years looked more like fifty-five. He still had a flip-phone and had logged about ten minutes a month on it since cell technology began. In person, he'd talk your ear off, especially about film, and he'd pepper clients with emails so long you'd swear he'd slapped in a novel excerpt, but if you could keep him on the phone for more than a minute, you deserved a medal.

He held up his thumb and forefinger an inch apart. "I came that close to leaving the new recorder. Didn't want to get it dirty. Would've been long gone."

This was mostly talk. He'd picked up his latest toy not two days before the trip and would sooner have left his sleeping bag as leave behind a piece of tech. He'd been my sound guy for going on five films, and we'd finally landed enough investors to replace his DAT with a digital recorder at about a tenth the weight.

I dug around in the console. "I don't know about that," I said. "Whoever it was left about a hundred bucks worth of memory cards but drank the melted ice from my McDonald's soda. That or they poured it out, and it dried by now. Just seems weird."

"We could ask this jack-off," he said, his mood lightening some.

I poked my head out of the car to follow his pointed finger. Well behind us on the road was a guy walking our way. Only, it looked more like a drunken stumble, like he was falling forward as much as walking.

"Come to see if we have any white lightning to share," I said, adopting a hick accent I knew Garrett would appreciate.

"It's not even ten yet."

"It's five'o clock somewhere," I said. From my pack, I pulled the camcorder, the 3-CCD model I'd also just gotten, care of our recent investors. Just as Garrett had spent the week playing around with his new audio recorder, I had learned the in and outs of my new camera. Sure, most of our footage from the last week came from our two new GoPros, but nothing beats a clean camcorder image, especially with this baby's specs. My old camera had landed on eBay, not a day after the DHL guy delivered this one.

"So here we have a rare, native species of Virginian," I narrated, whispering so only Garrett could hear. The guy was still a good football field away, but the moxy I showed with a camera faltered when it came to sound; that was Garrett's job.

"He's gonna see you," Garrett said, but I could tell by his tone he thought it was funny.

"I've got about two minutes of battery left, and this is what I spend it on." I turned off the camera. "How far away is that bar on Thompson Memorial?"

Garrett's shoulders slumped. "We gotta walk that far?"

"You want to ask that asshole for a lift? Maybe he's got a phone we can use."

"Fine."

***

We rucked up, my pack feeling about twice as heavy as on the hike back, probably because I had figured on not wearing it again until the following year. The day was mild, and the trees filtered most of the sunlight, but still, the smell of sweat permeated the fabric of my pullover.

I closed my eyes as we walked the lonely road, imagining the exquisite feel of a proper, hot shower back at our apartment. Garrett would deal with the cops and the insurance company for a few hours, no doubt. I loved my twin brother to pieces, but by the time we'd covered another two miles, I had decided on an epic bath, complete with bubbles and music, maybe candles, and leave him to deal with the car details.

"He's still back there," Garrett said, his voice forcing my eyelids open.

I squinted into the sporadic flicker as the sun danced behind the tall trees. "Who?"

"The dude," he said and pointed back over his shoulder.

Sure enough, the stumbling drunk was extending his walk of shame, and no way could we write off his following us as coincidence.

"What's his deal?" I asked. "You got your hatchet?"

"Jesus, Shy, you want me to go all Dexter on the guy just for walking behind us? He could be headed to the same place. We haven't passed a car in twenty minutes, so what if he's hoofing it, too?"

"Yeah, but why? I've been that wasted maybe three times in my life, and I damn sure didn't cap it with a nice, four-mile trek down the road." I stared at the guy, who had lost a step or two behind us, but not many, maybe a couple hundred yards back.

Garrett shrugged. "We are headed to a bar. Makes sense he's going the same way. That or he's in the same boat we are, and I kinda doubt it."

"Whatever. When we get to the bar, just stay alert, all right? We may be a half-hour from Roanoke, but we're a million miles from civilization, if you get my drift … I'm really sorry about the car," I said.

"I know. You're gonna be even sorrier when you realize what was in the back seat." He made a teeth-clenched frown in mock horror.

After a few seconds of my brain's gears grinding, I shouted a hearty string of swear words into the cool air. "My tampons? Who does that?"

He shook his head. "The box was all torn up. Whoever took 'em must have been desperate. Probably needed them worse than you."

"Great, now I get to buy some at the shadiest gas station on the planet. I'll bet their bathroom is super clean, too."

Garrett pointed at the road ahead. "Well, we're gonna find out. There's the bar. The gas station's another quarter mile at most. You wanna run ahead while I make the call?"

Such was Garrett's trademark squeamishness over all things simultaneously feminine and sibling. Despite us sharing the same space since Mom's womb, he had a strict "nope!" policy regarding my feminine hygiene.

I sighed. "Yeah, I guess. Can you have them pick us up at the station? I have zero desire to sit in a bar for an hour waiting for them."

"Gas station parking lot sounds better?"

I'd spent a respectable number of hours lingering at bars, but this one held no appeal. It was a tinderbox: all unrefined, dark wood slapped together, though I'm sure it could weather worse than the tract home Garrett and I shared in Roanoke. The double doors were propped open, but no music came from inside. No light, either. A couple of cars littered the parking lot, but either the patrons were the most inconsiderate people ever, or they weren't parked so much as abandoned.

As we drew closer, I saw the vehicles were in no better shape than Garrett's Honda: all stripped and left with little more than the frames and the glass, and most of that shone white with deep spider-webbing as if victim to an epic hail storm.

"Umm… so that's ominous," I said.

"Stay out here," Garrett said and headed for the double doors.

"Screw that, dude. I'm coming with you."

We walked up a double-sided, cement staircase, Garrett on one side and me the other. We'd no sooner come level with the entrance when the smell hit me like I'd walked right into a glass door, but one made of the acrid, almost charred-plastic stench that could only mean one thing.

"Something died," I said through my fingers.

Garrett gagged. He turned and leaned over the railing with his mouth open like a fish, though he managed to keep down our oatmeal breakfast.

"There's a guy in there," I said. "Behind the bar. And someone else at the back." I waved my free hand at the entrance, unwilling to venture any closer for fear of gagging as well. "Hey in there. You guys okay?"

The guy behind the bar could only have been the bartender. He turned at the sound of my voice, revealing an aproned lower half complete with a hand towel, but the trademark white shirt was soiled like he'd thrown up down the front of it. Considering the fetid air, who could blame him if he had?

"You work here? You okay?"

The guy put out his hands and stumbled toward us, opening his mouth to reveal blackened teeth. He growled high and long, the sound alerting the other guy in the back, near the bathroom.

The other was skinny to the bartender's paunchy heft, but tall, too. Even with his shoulders all hunched, he easily had six inches on my brother. The tall guy never put up his hands, but he shuffled toward us all the same, his growl much lower, more like a moan.

"Garrett, something's wrong," I said. I grabbed him and yanked him upright.

"I gotta sit down," he said.

He slumped under my grip, but I shook him hard. "Snap out of it, dude. We've got to move,"

Garrett coughed. "What are you talking about?"

When I turned back to the open double doors, the bartender and his lanky friend had moved into the light of day. I couldn't help it: trite girl move or not, I screamed. I'd never worked an emergency room, but both of them looked like prime candidates. The viscera down the bartender's front wasn't puke, but blood and the tall guy was missing half his face. For all I knew, it was lining the bartender's shirt. And yet, neither seemed to want help but kept stumbling toward us. At least I redeemed myself when, a second later, I broke the damsel in distress paralysis and yanked Garrett toward the steps.

"What's your deal?" he said to them. "Back the fuck up, assholes." He put up his fists, but all I imagined were the diseases he'd get popping one of these psychos in the face.

"Forget them. Come on." This was right about where my heroine, straight-thinking streak ended, and I ran directly into the stumbling drunk who'd followed us for miles. Only, he wasn't drunk, and that stumble had proven more than adequate to pen us in. He was clad in low-hanging jeans faded to oblivion and a flannel torn at one elbow. Not much hung below the shredded, wet fabric but a few cords of flesh and what could only loosely be described as a hand beneath that. If, that was, people carried around their hands like a kid who's too lazy to rewind his yo-yo. The appendage had long ago stopped receiving any orders from the guy's nervous system and now looked waxy, fake even. But the iron stench of whatever carnage used to be his arm hung thick in the air, so I knew it was real.

The guy reached for me with his good arm, and I instantly forgot every self-defense class I'd taken in college. All I could do was watch that hand come in, grab me, and then shove me to the concrete. Garrett fared little better. He all but tripped over me and the one-armed stumbler trying to get away from the other two. Even when he began whaling on the one-armed guy on top of me, he might as well have been Rocky working a side of beef, as little effect as it was having. In the meantime, the bartender and the tall man had tumbled down the stairs and were just feet away from joining their buddy.

"For Charles," came a yell, somewhere beyond the mass of flesh bearing down on me. First Garrett was grabbed by what I thought was a giant robot arm and flung backward. Before I could piece together what was happening, the stumbling guy—his bared teeth not a foot from my face— had a head one moment and then nothing the next, just a neck from which a geyser of smelly blood flew mercifully past my face and over my shoulder.

All I could do was scream… again. Even minus a head, the body crushed down on me. I shoved it to the side and scuttled out into the parking lot and away from the two crazies from the bar.

On my feet at last, I saw that no robot had grabbed Garrett, but a knight in full armor. The gauntlet that had pulled him from the psycho attacking me still clung to my brother's shirt and pulled him along, away from the entrance. Two more knights, one in lighter chainmail and another in armor that looked like he'd pulled it off the side of a tank, spread out to deal with the bartender and the tall one.

Here most people would have run or even cried, but my muscle memory sent a different signal, one hardwired into me since I got a Hi-8 camcorder for my eighth birthday. I reached for the camera. No preamble, no babbling, not even fear, strictly speaking. I only knew that whatever was happening deserved recording. My fingers shook, my legs wobbled like I'd run five miles, but I took a knee and started rolling.

"Longshanks is mine," called the tank. Through the thick armor, his voice sounded filtered, like it came over a radio, but I heard it all right. He carried a weapon I'd only ever seen in the movies: a stick as big around as a Red Bull can with a fat chain that ended in a spiked ball. The chain jangled, and I thought—psycho or not—I pitied whatever was on the other end of that thing when it got to swinging.

And swing it did, the first arc bringing down the tall one like he was stuffed with straw. The guy never called out, didn't even grunt. He just crumpled, folded in on himself. The tank made a wide circle and brought the ball down on the tall man's head.

The bartender charged the other knight, not a smidge of fear inspired by his friend being brained. He splayed his bloody fingers and let out that high growl. The chainmail knight moved faster than the tank. He had a small ax in his left hand but dropped it in favor of the spear in his right. Not a spear exactly, but long, deadly, with a spike on the end that shined in the pale sun a moment before he drove it through the bartender's eye. I mean right through his eye like he'd meant no other target.

"For Sinistra," the knight yelled and pulled the spear free.

I filmed it all, and I turned to see Garrett had acted just as well on instinct, his digital recorder capturing the sounds even as the sword-bearing knight still clung to him.

And then my battery died.

***

As if Garrett had been holding it together for me to film and for him to record that single, insane moment, he threw

301

up immediately after the display on my camera went black. The knight who'd pulled him from the fray jumped back, lithe for a man in who-knows-how-many pounds of armor.

"Are you all right?" the knight asked him.

The tank pulled up his visor, revealing the scowling face of a man sporting a goatee, his forehead beaded with sweat. "Well, that's a waste," he said and then turned back to his victim.

The knight with the sword likewise presented himself, and the face on the other side of the visor looked a good bit kinder, apologetic almost, and easy on the eyes. "Are you sick or is it just the stress?" he asked Garrett. The man looked at me. "Has he been bitten, or is it nerves?"

I stammered. "Bit— bitten? I don't understand. No one bit him. They came out of the bar and started after us. It wasn't our fault, and—"

The man's incredulous look—hooked, single eyebrow and squinted eyes—stopped me mid-sentence. "You don't know? What's happening, I mean."

"I just watched three knights kill guys who looked about a minute this side of death. I don't think I even know the year, let alone what's happening." I hugged the camera to my chest and had to sit. Everything was shaking. A part of me wanted to get back behind the camera, but what was the point without juice?

The knight leaned down to my level, clanking. He doffed his helmet and sat on it. "Where have you been?"

"We were camping. All last week."

Garrett recovered and came to join us.

"Well," the knight said, "I won't mince words. There's been a zombie apocalypse."

I looked at Garret, and we both broke out laughing at the same time. It started with a normal I'm-in-on-the-joke laugh but blossomed into a full-on belly laugh. It felt good, actually. The stress left me, even as my core cramped and I fought for air.

The knight and his partners formed a semi-circle. They looked on, neither offended nor joining in the laughter. Eventually, we stopped, and I stared again at the good-looking knight. His face held the same concerned, serious expression as before. My laughter turned into confusion, then concern, then my own brand of incredulity.

"You're not serious," I said.

"They can't be," Garrett said, wrapping up his own laughing fit.

"I am Sir Gregory Boucher," the tank said. "I like to think I live up to my namesake. The butcher, that's where it came from. You saw a sliver of it just now. Only that wasn't enough to save my father. One of those freaks got a bite of his ankle." He pointed at the sword knight. "Philip here was good enough to lend me his sword. I cut off his leg below the knee. The man who raised me. Who worked nights at a stockyard that smelled worse these stale fucks for years so he could see me off to school, pick me up after. Taught me our history, taught me to fight. That was the man I swung a sword at, cut him up while he was screaming for me to stop. And it still didn't catch it in time."

He walked forward, close enough for me to smell the sweat on him, not body odor, but the smell of exertion, like passing by someone at a gym who'd worked out in the clothes they'd worn all day. "So tell me, mon Cherie. Do you think I'm serious?"

He leaned in even closer, staring me down. I could feel Garrett bristling beside me.

"Take it easy, Greg," the spear guy said. He tapped the Butcher on the back of his plate mail with his spear. "We've all lost someone. They don't know. You heard 'em. They weren't even here."

"You guys are for real," I said. But then the absurdity of the situation fell upon me. Their armor, the fight I'd witnessed. I'd never seen a damned fist-fight, let alone see three people die. For all I knew, the entire thing was staged—some elaborate prank.

As if reading my mind, Garrett said, "This is some role-playing thing, right? What do they call it? Lark."

"The term you're looking for is LARP," Philip said. "But no, this is no role-playing game. We're medieval re-enactors. Our gear isn't made of foam or plastic. It's all real, made just the way they made it a thousand years ago."

"But the fight, the zombie thing," I said. "That's part of your… re-enactment, right?"

The Butcher huffed and turned away. Philip kept that warm expression in place, only now it looked pitying. "I'm afraid not, ma'am."

"Shiloh," I said. "Shiloh Easter. And this is my brother, Garrett."

"Shiloh," Philip said. "I'm afraid this is as real as it gets."

The wind shifted, and the stench of the zombies and whatever carnage waited in the bar came over me. I teetered inches from losing my breakfast like Garrett had done. "I need to get out of here."

"We all do," said the spearman.

"And who are you?" I asked.

"Percy Meyer. We're headed to a safe place. A… castle, if you will. You should come along. Both of you."

"To a castle in southwest Virginia," I said, tone betraying my incredulity.

"If you will."

I palmed my camera, hand snug in the nylon strap. I loved the feeling. Love the weight of the thing, the power of it to capture whatever you aimed it at, no matter if whatever it stared at agreed or opposed. What I'd just filmed already would raise every eyebrow from every filmmaker I knew. Forget the news, this was bigger than some thirty-second story on a 24/7 news station. This was my chance to capture something else, something meaningful.

I tucked the camera back into my pack and adjusted my straps. "I need to make a stop first."

***

"For the record, this is a shit idea," Boucher said. He'd affixed the ball and chain thing to his back somehow. Some DIY magnet setup it looked like, which kept the handle in place. Not exactly period, but it seemed pretty sweet to me.

"There's a cluster of hotels on the way, almost as the crow flies. Maybe an hour off track at most." This from Percy. Though the spear must have weighed a good bit, he kept it propped over his shoulder and flipped through the folding map with his free hand, the small ax at his waist.

"Shouldn't be any zombies at a hotel," Boucher drawled. "Why not hit up the stadium while we're at it? Or a nice apartment complex."

"It's not a horrible idea," Philip said. "They'll have processed food, I imagine—stuff that'll keep. If it's power we're after, they're bound to have a genny and extra fuel. And think about it: who on earth would stay at a hotel just off the interstate? The infection spread fast, sure, but there's likely to be only a handful of stragglers. Nothing like in the shelters."

He turned to Garrett and me as we walked, his long sword over his shoulder like Percy. "You wouldn't believe how fast the shit hit the fan. All we've done to create a safe, abundant society...." He scoffed. "That's was all gone in days. Every store, bare. Every house, either abandoned or nailed up. You'd think the whole world was on the brink of collapse and the zombies were just the icing. You'd never guess that people were shopping at Wal-Mart and washing their cars and watching movies in the theater a week ago. Never."

"That's rural Virginia for ya," Percy said. "Salemites were probably happy it all went down. Validates their own parochial paranoia."

"Mister Downtown Roanoke," the Butcher said, mocking him. "Please tell us how civilized and orderly the infection spread on Campbell Avenue. I'm sure they're sipping tea at Mill Mountain as we speak, all well in hand."

"Clam it," Philip told them. "You heard the news; it's everywhere. I'd guess that whether you're in upper Manhattan or BFE Nebraska, the result is about the same."

"Which is what?" I asked. The breath had left me, not just from the walking or the backpack, which felt three times heavier than before. I just couldn't take much more of… whatever this was. It was too much. Half a day ago, I'd been indulging in the rare smoke while Garrett made us bacon over the fire on our last morning. I needed my goddamn camera.

"You'll see," Boucher said. He smiled, but his face radiated a coldness despite the perpetual sweat on his brow. "You think the bar was something? Wait till we get to your hotel. Philip was being nice when he said 'handful'."

"How nice?" Garrett asked.

Boucher only laughed, leaning his head back.

***

Like everything along Virginia's rolling hills, the hotels obeyed the topography, set down inside a small bowl and at odd angles. The interstate, packed with cars, sat behind a dense tree line above the bowl. An occasional moan cascaded down to where we set up just outside the Locus Inn. The air had grown warmer, but still cool enough to carry such noise fairly far, so I didn't worry about it.

Percy affixed a mirror to the deadly point of his spear and surveyed the area from a prone position. We all lay beside him, catching what glimpses we could in the glass.

"It's bulky, but that spear comes in handy," Garrett said.

Percy whipped his head around at that. "It's a lance, Mr. Easter. Big difference."

"Oh," Garrett said. "Sorry. I thought lances were for, y'know, guys on horses."

The other knights looked at each other, then over at Percy.

"I am heavy cavalry, Mr. Easter. I've just… lost my mount."

"Is that who Sinistra is?" I asked. "You called out the name when—"

"Yes," Percy said, cutting me off. "Sinistra was my mount. He fell in battle two days ago."

"I'm sorry," I said, and Percy nodded curtly.

"What's it mean, Sinistra?"

Percy smiled and grumbled a small chuckle, though absent any mirth. "He was a destria. The same war horse you would have found during the war. Destria comes from Latin for 'right.' When we were training together, Sinistra always went his own way. If I pulled him right, he was just as apt to go left to spite me. So I named him Sinistra. Latin for 'left'."

"It's a beautiful name," I said.

He pulled down the mirror and nodded to the other two. He made a few indecipherable hand gestures that smacked more of modern soldiers than medieval knights.

"What war?" Garrett asked.

The knights took to their feet, the plates clanking lightly.

"The Hundred Years War, of course."

"Did you think we worked for Medieval Times Dinner Theatre?" the Butcher said. "This armor is Milanese. Hand-crafted. It cost more than her fancy camera. The barbed flail is titanium with a depleted uranium core. Anachronism be damned, this thing could brain a bull with a single blow." He pulled down his visor, cutting off any response.

"We're re-enactors," Philip said, features soft. His tone blended earnestness and patience. I had a feeling he'd explained this a thousand times.

"For the medieval period," I said. "Yeah, I get it."

"For the Battle of Agincourt," Philip said. "This was our big one. Our annual re-enactment. The first biters came stumbling onto the battlefield, not two minutes after the whistle blew to get underway. Fortunate, really."

We eased down a small slope into the Locus Inn parking lot. Of the three cars in the lot, two held bodies, but they weren't moving.

"'Cause you had the armor on?" I said.

Philip made a see-saw gesture with one giant, gloved hand. "That, sure. But do you know much about Agincourt?"

"I know Joan of Arc fought in the Hundred Years War at some point, and that it didn't last a hundred years but slightly longer. That exhausts my college world history requirement."

Philip smiled, and it lit up the oval of his face in the helmet. It was the sort of smile that would have gotten my attention in a bar a week ago. Now, I didn't know what it meant.

"The French were defeated at Agincourt because the field was sodden with mud. Knights in seventy pounds of armor don't do so well when they have to wade through the knee-deep mud before battle. They reached the English exhausted and disheartened, so they were captured or killed with relative ease."

"Okay," I said.

"We're the French," he said. "They watered down the field, even got in there with hoes and tilled the soil. If the zombies had come just hours later, we'd have been too tired to stand, let alone fight."

"But you weren't tired. So what happened?"

Just then a moan sounded from near the entrance of the inn. One zombie became three, and then I spotted five more coming from around the corner or even getting up from the road where I thought they'd been just more dead bodies.

"You're about the find out, mon Cheri," called the Butcher. The voice came out crisp and held a note of bass and reverb. He must have installed a voice emitter inside his visor. The effect was chilling, which was no doubt his intention.

Philip shoved an armored finger toward an empty car, the doors hanging open. "Inside. Now!"

Garrett needed no prompting, but grabbed at me and yanked me toward the car. In seconds, we huddled inside, the doors locked. We'd seen them take apart the three guys back at Hanging Rock. Surely a few more would be okay.

No sooner had I considered this than a pool of undead spilled from the main entrance into the parking lot. Some wore hotel gear—maids and porters and kitchen staff. Why the hell had they stayed? Plenty of others wore military-grade riot gear. Wouldn't have figured them for undead if not for them stumbling all over one another. Some moved faster than others, but all held a desperate, horrible longing to get at us—at them.

My insides went instantly cold and tight. Tears welled in my eyes for what was about to happen. This was it, my breaking point. When they were through with the knights, they'd find us or just wait us out. What did they care? This was the end of the Easter Twins, I had no doubt.

The zombies spilled into a long line, trying to get around each other for the first crack at the knights. In effect, they formed a twenty-foot wide wall of flesh, rolling toward them. The knights backed up, whether meaning to or not, almost against our car. They stood only feet away, poised but doomed.

They let out their cries: "For Henry," "For France," "For Sinistra." That was when things got interesting.

Philip coiled himself like a snake preparing to strike, when he unwound, the long blade soared through a handful of zombies. The things never flinched, never wavered or cared. So Philip picked his spots as they drew closer: coil, strike, coil, strike. I could almost hear the wind whistling off that blade, could feel the power of the tremendous grunt he made, even without the Butcher's voice emitter.

All the while, Percy went to work jabbing his lance over and over, hitting their exposed, dauntless, milky eyes more often than not, yanking it free a fraction of a second later. He was a piston and not a man only minutes from death. Surely, despite their bravery and precision, still, death would come for them. There were too many. I thought this even as the fallen formed a wall, tripping up the others. I thought it when the dozens more spilled around the sides, forming a semi-circle and encasing the knights. I certainly thought it when Philip ran out of steam and had to fall back, leaning against our car as heavy and heedless as a slumping bull who'd run his race and now only awaited death.

And then the Butcher came to life. Through the voice-emitter boomed the terrible growl I would have thought echoed from the dead if I hadn't known better. The—what had he called it?—barbed flail swung as true and inexorable and arching as the sun itself. The heads of the zombies didn't seem to slow its grisly work, as the thing collapsed skull after skull.

Still, they came, spilling over their corpse wall and surrounding Boucher. They were all over him, ants on an anteater, too many for even this slayer of the dead to withstand. But what could they do? His armor was too thick. They bit, they tore, the clawed, but the dead might as well have gone at him with fingernails as ineffective as their teeth were on that metal. The lot of which he'd said cost more than my…. My camera! I acted on instinct, yanking the camera free from my pack, fumbling with the controls, unseating the spent battery and reseating it over and over.

"What are you doing?" Garrett hissed, as if—amid the carnage—the zombies had any hope of hearing us.

"I've got to film this. It's too… too important. I can't——"

"The batteries are all shot, Shy."

"Then give me your GoPro." I dug into his gear, fingers seeking the small cube.

"That's spent, too. I told you that. We don't have anything."

I looked up just as Boucher erupted from the dozen bodies on top and all over him. They fell at his feet, and Percy stuck them, holding the lance like a giant stabbing knife. Seemingly given his second wind, Philip rose from the car and rejoined his comrades, his swipes timed and lethal.

"My phone," I said and wrenched it free from my pants like it was on fire. I burst from the car, hit record, and entered my filming trance.

"What the hell are you doing?" the Butcher called, voice rough and angry.

I offered no answer, had none really. Philip turned around and spotted me and began my way.

"No," I yelled. "I'm fine. Get back to work."

The view from behind the phone lacked the filtered reality I enjoyed when using the 3-CCD camera, but it proved enough to keep my heart racing but steady—to keep my hands from shaking and ruining the shot. The grunt of the door opening telegraphed what I already counted on: Garrett, recorder capturing every audible nuance of this pandemonium, fell in beside me.

"Knew you couldn't resist," I said.

He put a finger to his lips and pointed at the still-coming horde. I got the message.

The fight continued for another five minutes. The wall of bodies grew, forcing the dumb latecomers to spend several seconds finding a way over or around their fallen ilk to get at us. This gave more than enough time for the knights to prepare. By the end, they were all heaving for breath, taking a knee at intervals, slapping one another and insisting this next one was theirs. Even before the last dead had fallen, they were laughing—laughing—and I even caught Boucher showing off for my makeshift camera, flourishing and adding several swings, building to the deathblow.

When the last of the zombies lay still, an intense tremor ran through me. Every sensation I'd stoppered during the battle now spilled out, compounded by an instant, tremendous weariness in my muscles. Even with the stench of the dead, their blackish, tainted blood flecked on my face, my clothes, my hands, I could only sit on the pavement, slumped forward like a toddler overtaken with an immediate need for slumber.

"You okay?" Garrett asked. His labored breathing told me he wasn't up for running a marathon, either.

"This," I managed, before pulling in a breath just to push words from my lungs. "This is so our new jam."

✳✳✳

314

As if a cosmic joke, our new knight friends knew as much about electricity as historical knights did. That is, virtually nothing.

"I'm an accountant," Boucher growled. "I could balance the books for an electric company, but past that, you got the wrong guy."

We'd settled into the penthouse, based more on the single entrance, they said, than the posh layout of the room. So after an impossible, if protracted, twenty-story climb, the knights spent the next half hour doffing their armor and inspecting one another like field medics over a wounded soldier.

Outside of his armor, Boucher was big but not huge. Percy was on the skinny side, and—sure enough—Philip was fairly gorgeous, even if the room had filled with the lingering scent of carnage: a mixture of iron and soured milk.

"How about the rest of you?" I asked. "Anyone ever fired up a generator, at least?"

"Retail manager," Percy said, an arm over his eyes, lying over the white couch with his legs dangling over one side. "I can give you thirty percent off without breaking a sweat but couldn't tell the maintenance guys where the generator was even located."

I looked at Philip.

"Come on," he said. I was sitting in a wicker chair, and he held out a hand for me to take.

"Me? I'm… I'm a cameraman. What the hell can I do?"

Philip left the hand mid-air, but his face broke into a smile. "You want power. You have to work for it. If I wanted pancakes right now, I wouldn't expect Boucher to run to the Waffle House."

"Waffle House doesn't do pancakes," Boucher said. "I used to ask for them just to piss 'em off, though."

"Well, they don't even do waffles anymore," Percy said. "But I get Phil's point, Miss. I wouldn't want to take those stairs again, either, but we are kinda here for you."

I shook my head. "No, I get it. Sorry." I took his hand, and he lifted my cement-laden body off the chair. "You coming, bro?"

Garrett looked up from the bed. He'd only taken off his shoes before plopping down, the dirt and blood on him already painting the sheets. "I'm the sound guy. My stuff's still got a charge. Your damn cameras are the battery hogs."

Philip shrugged and led the way back down.

***

We'd secured the doors in case any zombies from the other hotels came to investigate. Still, a fear crept over me as we got closer to the ground floor. I'd yet to encounter a zombie I'd known as a human, and maybe that was for the best. I never saw them as anything but monsters. The downside was, the farther I got from the rest of the crew, especially Garrett, the more I felt alone and helpless.

Philip must have felt at least some of that, perhaps as much because he no longer had his armor as being away from the other two. He lacked the confidence he'd shown

316

while armored. Sure, he still had his sword, but now it looked comically large. His underclothes looked more like pajamas than anything, compounding the more vulnerable effect.

Still, once we'd come back to the lobby, he kept his cool and used a map behind the concierge desk to locate the generator room.

"So, what, you're familiar with this kinda stuff?" I asked him.

"No," he said. "Not at all, actually. I… I'm a musician. That's my… day job, I guess."

"You don't sound so sure about that."

"Few musicians are."

"What do you play?"

"Percussion."

"Oh, you're a drummer."

He jerked his head around to look at me. "Not like you're thinking. Percussionist. Drums, sure, but other stuff. I'm not in a rock band."

We reached the generator room. I figured we'd have to search out keys or push buttons at the desk, but the door was propped open with a toolbox. Philip pulled a flashlight from the top shelf and surveyed the room.

"I getcha. We've got a percussion guy we worked with on scores. For the docs we've worked on before. Maybe you could take his place." I laughed, but an image of the guy we'd used for the score on our last two projects appeared in my head. A second later, he morphed into a zombie and bared his teeth. I pushed the image away and shuddered.

"You honestly think there'll be a market for the film after this?"

We eased deeper into the room, the light dancing along the walls and around corners.

"This won't last," I said.

"You're a week behind schedule, Shiloh," he said, and despite his admonishing tone, I liked the way my name sounded coming from him. "No offense, but I don't know you're qualified to say that."

"I saw what you guys did out there. Three of you."

"We got lucky."

"No, there wasn't a smidge of luck as far as I could see, and I think the footage will say the same."

He sighed and stopped moving for a moment. He turned and pointed the flashlight at my chest, I guessed to keep from blinding me. Chivalrous even in anger. "If we were anything but lucky, this wouldn't have happened at all. You understand? If humankind were meant to endure this, we would have. You've been in the woods, and good for you. But you don't know how fast things fell apart. You don't want to know."

Exhaustion sapped any words. All I could say, after several seconds of silence, was: "There's the genny."

***

Between a drummer and a cameraman, we had the genny running in ten minutes, which beat out my best expectations. From a panel of power boxes on the wall, we threw the ones labeled elevators and penthouse and left the rest of them tripped. Neither of us could guess how long the diesel would hold out, but why push it?

We rode the elevator up to the penthouse, every cell in my body saying a silent thanks for avoiding another trek up the stairs. The sound of music and celebration penetrated the doors before they opened. We entered the penthouse to find three pajama-wearing men dancing on the beds drinking booze from airplane bottles. Music poured from a Bose stereo where Garrett had jacked in his phone.

Philip sighed but grinned at the odd scene. "Save me the Crown Royal," he said.

I joined them, kicking off my shoes. Already the room was filling with the sweaty smell of us, and my eyes kept cutting to the Jacuzzi tub just visible past the cracked bathroom door. But Garrett put a tiny bottle of Bacardi in my hands, tapped it with this own, and we danced to a Taylor Swift song I never even knew Garrett had on his playlist.

***

The broad, bay windows showed black outside by the time I finished my bath and joined the others. I'd let them shower first, both so they wouldn't continue to stink up the place, and so I could enjoy a long bath without harassment.

"'Bout time, Shy," Garrett said. "You fall asleep?"

I worked the incredibly soft towel over my hair. "I could have. Everything charged up yet?"

He stood from the lazy circle the guys had formed around a poker pot made up of minibar snacks: pretzels and nuts and mints. "Yeah, the first set. I put on the spares, so they should be charged soon." He dug into his pack. "Oh, and I found you these in the linen closet." He tossed me a box of Tampons, beaming with pride.

The others looked at me and then promptly returned to their game.

"Now you care about that?" I said, the words hot with my embarrassment. I shoved the box into my pack. "Might not matter anyway, since we're somehow on this subject. I don't think Aunt Flow is making any visits today."

"You're not pregnant, are you?" Garrett asked me, genuine shock on his face.

"No," I barked.

"'Cause there was that guy you brought home from Flannery O'Connor's like a month ago—"

"Shut up," I said and cut my eyes over to Philip without meaning to.

"It's the stress," Percy said. "I did a tour in the Navy. The stress of basic training often stalls menses. Some girls even skipped a month. The guys just couldn't… Well. Couldn't go number two." He dipped his head in sudden embarrassment.

"This is all very fascinating, but can we return to getting shitfaced?" Boucher said.

"Not too much. Got a long walk tomorrow," Philip said.

"Thanks, Dad. I'll be sure to drink responsibly and get a ride home." Boucher threw down his cards. "I got nothing. I'm gonna dip down into some other rooms and raid their minibars. Won't be long."

"Take the flashlight," Philip said. "And a weapon."

"Sure thing, Pops."

"So you're the leader?" I asked Philip.

He shrugged. "We're all noblemen. In the re-enactment, I mean. If anything, Percy's the highest ranking. But we're not… doing that now."

"Yeah, I know," I said. "I wasn't saying it was weird or anything."

Percy laughed, and Garrett joined him. "You just kinda did, Shy."

"I know what it looks like," Philip said. "We all do. Seems like dress up or a role-playing thing. But it's really as much about history and camaraderie as anything else. It's our lineage."

I picked up a chip from the pot and ate it, suddenly aware of how hungry I was. "How do you mean?"

"We're all descendants of men who fought in that battle. I mean, as near as we can track that history. Hard to know for certain, but the surname says a lot. The genealogy is more for bragging rights. We're pretty inclusive. Nowadays there's plenty of women in armor as well."

"And authentic," I said. "Somehow I doubt the Comic-Con LARP crowd has weapons that can decapitate zombies."

He laughed. "We have plenty of respect for our LARPer cousins, actually, but yes, staying period gets pretty intense."

"And expensive," Percy said. "Damn good thing I got no other hobbies 'cause I don't think I could afford another one."

"Pretty big return on investment now, though," Garrett said.

Percy put up a fist and bumped it with Garrett's.

"So the castle is period?" I asked. "Where we're headed. I've never heard of it before. I'm assuming it's not, like, historic, but a private home. Built to be a modern-day castle. Something like that? I read about those in a magazine once. The guy who wrote *Fight Club* did a story on them."

The knights shifted a bit, something that would have made a clanking sound if they still wore their gear. Silence spooled out before us, and my worry grew with each elongated second.

"Right?"

Philip shrugged. "Not period, per se. But it's safe. High walls, running water, excellent vantage points for archers. Even has a moat."

He turned his gaze to Percy, who coughed and said, "That's right. It's safe, most of all. It'll be just the place for us."

"Phones?" Garrett asked.

I knew my twin brother so well, I could hear the subtext in his tone as if he'd said the words out loud. He was asking about Mom and Dad. I'd barely allowed myself to think about them. That was the thing about them being, like, three thousand miles away in California: I didn't think of them all that often anymore. Sad, but true. If they still lived in town, we'd have gone straight to them and probably died on the journey.

"No phones," Percy said. "And not because of the place. There's just not enough power pushing them anymore. Even if you restore power locally, it's not enough to have it on one end and not in-between. And hardly anyone even has landlines anymore anyway. Most of it's Internet-based or cell technology."

"So what about, like, sat phones?" I asked.

He shrugged. "Probably. But the guy on the other end has to have a sat phone, too. Some people had satellite Internet, as well, but—again—good luck Skyping with someone who doesn't have power or isn't also using satellite Internet."

"It went down like a glass-jawed boxer," Philip said, then sipped from his Crown Royal. "All of it."

The stairwell door banged open, and Boucher tumbled in a moment later, arms laden with thick plastic baggies. A few spilled from his arms, and I grabbed one. In giant type along the mud-brown front I saw: "Meal, Ready-to-Eat."

"No way," I said.

He dropped the rest of them in the middle of our poker circle. "I raise you a week's food."

"Where in the hell?" Percy said.

"Musta been a prepper of sorts. The kind what holes up in a damn hotel come Armageddon. Idiot."

"So where is he?" Garrett said.

I slapped his knee. "Or she."

"It doesn't have much of a face left, so take your pick on the gender. Had a shit-ton of food but rode the bullet train outta town. Or the buckshot train, more accurately, but that doesn't sound as cool."

"Did you grab the shotgun?" Garrett asked.

The knights stopped rifling through the MREs and looked at him.

"What?" he asked.

Boucher sat, ripped open an MRE like it was made of paper, and dug into a pound cake before speaking. "We came across a National Guard garrison out by Thaxton. You remember?" He turned to the other knights, who nodded but said nothing. "An infantry company. Small, certainly, but secure. Weaponized, armored. You know what we found there?"

"Not sanctuary, I guess," Garrett said, head hung.

"It was a noble attempt," Boucher said. "But futile. No, we found zombies in well-ironed uniforms and polished boots. Nothing more."

"You don't polish ACU boots," Percy said. They're suede, so you just—"

Boucher held up a finger and Percy stopped talking. "So let's be clear, Garrett. Guns have failed us. We're going to take back this world—if we even can take it back—with shield and spear and blade. What began as a tribute to our fallen ancestors has become…. Are you filming this?" Boucher looked at me, finger still pointed skyward.

I'd assembled my camera and engaged it automatically like a soldier would a stripped weapon. "I… was. Sorry."

Boucher laughed, and the others joined him. "Go right ahead. Need me to start again?"

"If you would."

***

We set out the following morning, my pack lighter despite the MREs. I'd ditched all my film books, my notes on our latest project, and a container of camp fuel. Modernity would furnish us with enough gas and diesel for a while, I figured. No engines burned that stuff anyway.

Garrett and I got to work, setting up shots, filming b-roll, and capturing the knights when they dispatched the occasional stray zombie. Our trek lay mostly along the grassy, rolling hills, where you couldn't see a half-mile ahead of you, but you could damn sure see around you well enough to spot any biters.

I'd woken to find the knights polishing their armor, their faces stern and their brows crinkled in concentration. Now they shone in the morning sun. I imagined their weapons had received the same treatment: as ready to dispatch another horde as the day they were forged.

We stopped for lunch at a park, as much for the three-sixty view as for the picnic tables. From my tablet, I edited footage, whittling it down to as small as possible. Philip slid behind me and watched me work. It felt good to show off. Garrett and I enjoyed a full-on escort to a castle, of all things, so I welcomed the swell of pride as my fingers flew over the screen.

"You're fast at that," Philip said.

"Yeah. I've only got so much storage, and this new camera is a pig, so I'll have to keep it tight."

"What's OSD?" he asked, pointing to the title of a project file.

I hadn't even thought about it, really. Just picked what first came to mind and made it my naming convention. Our camping trip was SGTT—Shiloh, Garrett Training Trip. The inspiration for the knight footage had come just before sleep in one of those flashes I half expected to disappear by morning, but it hadn't.

"The Order of the Second Death," I said and turned to find his face less than a foot from mine. "That's you guys. Before, you re-enacted how your ancestors died, and now—"

"I get it," he said, smiling. "And now we're sending these things to their second death. I like it."

"It's a favor, y'know?" I told him. "Not one of them would have wanted to stay like this, as one of those things."

He nodded. "I think you're right. I hope so. We don't really have room for conjecture, not when they're trying to kill us, but still, I'm glad to hear you say that." He leaned closer, perhaps reading some clue in my face, and we kissed.

The sound was minuscule, but you'd have thought were broadcasting it because we looked up to find everyone else staring at us. Only Garrett averted his eyes at being discovered. He knew better than to gawk.

"All right, let's move it," Philip said, though his tone lacked any agency.

***

The closer we got, the more I sensed an odd tonal shift. I thought at first it was because Philip had kissed me, as if the others saw that as—I don't know—against the knight's code or something. But whenever I caught Philip's gaze or shot more footage of him, he brightened and seemed only pleased to have us around.

The knights marched on with the lingering, constant energy they somehow managed in all that armor, but they swapped furtive glances and studied the ground in front of them instead of the landscape. I kept filming, sure, but—as a cameraman—I knew I wouldn't use any of this footage. Viewers would sense the same lack of spark I could see in them. What had happened in the last few hours?

Finally, I couldn't take any more of it. The knights walked in a triangle, and Philip was on the back right, a good thirty feet from Percy up front with Garrett.

"Everything all right?" I asked.

Philip smiled—simpered, really—and nodded.

"Y'see, I paid way too much in film school to hone this weird power. I can sense when something's up. When my subjects are… stiffening. Happens sometimes. That's when you quit filming and figure out what's changed."

Even in the armor, I could see Philip's shoulders slump. "I've not been completely honest with you, Shiloh. The castle—"

"We got company," Garrett yelled and pointed beyond the hill he and Percy had crested.

Percy said something to him. He buried his lance in the earth and waved his gloved hands in front of him, gesticulating to himself, to what lay over the hill, and back to himself.

I knew Garrett, sometimes better than he knew himself, surely better than he knew me, and I watched as a weight settled on him. Or maybe it was just his spirit leaving him. Whatever it was, by the time he pivoted on Percy—slinging a hand behind him as if waving off the cavalryman—and trotted up to me, a lump had formed in my throat and a boulder in my stomach.

"What is it, bro?"

"It's not a castle, Shy. It's a fucking water park. It's… it's nothing. It's a park. For kids."

Philip's gauntlet reached out to the crook of my elbow, but I shook it off. I ran to the crest of the hill, and the features came into view: water slide, scaffolding, lazy river encasing the lot of it.

A few dozen people milled about the interior; archers manned the tops of the slides, where—just a week ago— bored teenagers reminded a thousand kids a day not to go down head first. Around the perimeter, armored knights walked the high fences, as somber as the guards of Buckingham Palace.

All of the comforts I'd allowed myself over the last two days fell away like plates of my own, invisible armor, which I had proudly worn in the knights' company. The gravity of this new world fell on my shoulders, and I collapsed to one knee under its weight. My eyes teared, sending the grass at my feet into swirls of watery green.

I felt a hard hand on my shoulder and spun to find Philip standing over me.

"It's more than you think," he said, but he couldn't meet my gaze. "Just think about—"

I discovered the strength to take my feet and to shove him hard in the chest. He staggered, despite the armor. He made no move to defend himself as I slapped at his face. My hands banged against his helm, finding only meaningless purchase on the flesh beneath and sending stabs of pain up my arms.

"I believed in you," I growled over and over.

Finally, he grabbed my hands and pinned them between us. "What did you think it was?" he said. "You thought we'd come upon a king's keep manned by a thousand men? Walls thick as trees?" He spun me around and wrapped his arms around me from behind. He pointed to what a kiddish sign at the entrance dubbed "Splash Kingdom." "Every person in this place is just like us: knights all. Every one has carved their way here through the dead."

"It's a water park," I sobbed. "How can you—"

"Clean water," Percy joined in. "The filters run on diesel. They're industrial grade. High vantage points, dry goods, fences that kept out the freeloaders do a damn fine job of keeping out the dead, too."

I slumped in Philip's arms, my energy sapped, my will alongside it.

Garrett bent down to my level. "You believe this shit, Shy?" he whispered. "Not quite what we had in mind, huh?" He turned back to the park, shook his head, then shrugged. "These guys aren't knights. No one's anointed them. They don't own land or have coffers full of gold. They bought their stuff with minimum wage." He took my face in his hands. "But you've seen 'em in action. We both have. Do they seem like knights to you?"

Tears continued to flow, but I nodded.

"So could this just as well be a castle?" He moved to open my view of the park, filled with men and women as dedicated to their code, I knew, as the Order of the Second Death had been these last couple of days.

And then I saw it: high walls and grand parapets. Banners popping in the wind, order amid chaos. A dozen people as sharp as Percy, as dauntless and mighty as the Butcher, as noble and staid as my Philip.

"They're only missing one thing," Garrett said.

"What?" I said, the weight of this newly rotten world lifting slightly.

"Bards," he said and held out my camera. "Now let's get to work."

8 YAKUZA DEAD BY T. S. ALAN

DEDICATION: For Isamu

And for the members of the Hachioji Police Department at the Hachioji Station North Exit Police Box, without whose inspiration this story would not have been imagined.

I. Tokyo Ninkyo

"Rumors of an ARS counteragent are lies spread by detractors, including political opponents, who wish to undermine the government's authority and robust measures at keeping the nation contagion free," Prime Minister Toyoizumi countered, having been accused by news reporters that he and his administration were hoarding an antiviral drug for the plague, which had been acquired from a trade deal with the United States' military. "The government assures its people that though there is no cure or counter-response for ARS at this time, we are still safe and infection free and will remain so as long as citizens respect and obey the government's rule."

Isamu Kudo turned off the television and immediately put the remote down and addressed the senior clan members that were gathered around the table. "The Prime Minister must think us all stupid. No counteragent, infection free? — All lies. We have a cure."

Advisor Jun Okabe was quick to respond to his boss's statement, correcting him not only for incorrectly saying "cure," for there was none, and for the fact that they had lost the counteragent that could combat the virus. "Correction, Boss. We had a supposed antiretroviral."

Isamu responded tersely to his subordinate's clarifications, "Do you think me an idiot? I am aware of the situation. Why do think I called this meeting?"

Okabe immediately arose from his chair, bowing and apologizing for his impoliteness, "Moushiwakearimasen! It was not my intention—"

"Sit down, Okabe and quit groveling," Isamu instructed, and then turned to Senior Advisor Kuniyoshi Otsumi. "Otsumi. The laboratory has been completed and we are ready to start production? Is that correct?"

"Hai," he responded, confirming.

"Then I shall retrieve what is ours tonight," Isamu informed the five senior members at the table.

As one of the clan's inner circle and the senior advisor, it was Otsumi's obligation to point out that his boss's proposed action was highly inappropriate and risky, and not being in the best interest of the clan or that of the clan leader's health and welfare.

"With all due respect, you are being rash. You have many seniors that you could send, all who are willing and competent for the task."

First Lieutenant Akira Kimura stood quickly and bowed respectfully, eager to offer his service for the job that needed to be done.

"It would be an honor," he said to his clan leader, "if you allowed me to lead our men against the Tohno Clan. I will not fail you. I will retrieve what was stolen."

"I have no doubt in your success. But I trusted Tohno like he was blood, and he betrayed my trust by stealing from the family."

Otsumi again advised against his leader's decision. "There is no need to risk your life."

However, Isamu was steadfast in his resolve. "Tohno's breaking rank and forming his own family has not only cut into our profits, but by stealing the antiretroviral he has condemned our family to death. This has made me look weak and unfit to lead."

"No one thinks you are weak," Advisor Okabe stated. "Any disgrace falls on Tohno and the brothers who followed him."

Isamu knew his newest advisor was trying to be tactful, but his statement was not true, and his attempt at placating him was irritating.

"If you wish to kiss ass," he replied, "then perhaps you should wait for me to drop my pants before doing so. I hear the talk. I have lost face with the family, and I must regain their respect and trust by dealing with the traitor myself. And it needs to be tonight."

This time Okabe decided not to rise and apologize. He didn't want to be admonished again.

"With all due respect. I feel Tohno's bragging and your bruised ego are clouding your judgment. An attack on his headquarters is too risky," Senior Advisor Otsumi stated, again showing his objection to his boss's need to lead an attack against rival Gaku Tohno.

However, Chief Shigeru Yamada did not agree with Otsumi's advice, especially knowing the urgency of the situation.

"No. I agree with the boss. We cannot wait. The government secretly sends those they believe to be infected to Hachijojima. If the virus has reached Japan, how long will it be before it reaches us? The opportunity to destroy Tohno Clan and punish those who betrayed the family is tonight. Brother Hazaki has informed me that all Tohno heads have been called to Nakayasu this evening for a meeting. Hazaki has gone to great risk getting us this information. We must act upon it."

Isamu was glad he had the support of his senior executive and that of his first lieutenant. As clan leader he had the right to reject his counsel's advice, but it was important that all his senior staff be given the opportunity to voice any concerns before rendering a decision. Isamu looked down the table to Kenichiro Saito, who had been silent, the entire meeting.

"Saito," Isamu addressed his assistant chief.

"Hai," Saito quickly responded.

"You have been silent since you arrived. Do you not have an opinion on this matter?"

Kenichiro Saito stood to address the group. He voice reflected disgust and contempt as he spoke about those who had defected. "It is no secret how I feel about those brothers, who I recruited and who snuck away like chinpira under cover of darkness to join former Assistant Chief

Tohno. Their treachery and disloyalty are unforgiveable and dishonor us all."

The assistant chief felt the most displeasure and betrayal over one former member in particular, and that was Advisor Ryota Sakurai. Sakurai had been Saito's mentor and the person who had instilled in him the proper meaning of honor and loyalty, only to betray everything that he stood for by deserting the clan.

However, Saito was not the only one with a personal vendetta against a former clan member. Akira Kimura also had an issue with one of his former clan subordinates, and that was with Second Lieutenant Murakami. Kimura had recommended Murakami for second lieutenant when he was promoted to first lieutenant. Kimura was eager to make him pay for the dishonor. Pleased with what Saito had imparted, Isamu announced, "Then there is no reason why we should not go tonight."

***

At first the news of a highly infectious disease that had begun to spread around the globe, killing the infected and then causing them to rise from the dead and devour the living, seemed preposterous. Zombies only existed in the movies and in stories. However, when the World Health Organization announced that a coronavirus identified by a number of laboratories was the causative agent, the Japanese government realized it was no piece of fiction. No world health agency could confirm where the first case occurred, only that it spread faster than the bubonic plague had through Europe during the early modern period. It was being called acute reanimation syndrome (ARS).

There had been a rumor that the U.S. Army Medical Research Institute of Infectious Diseases at Fort Detrick, MD, had found a counteragent shortly after the U.S. administration fell, and that Japan's government had been contacted by the remaining military forces, offering the antiretroviral in exchange for a cargo ship full of rice. The deal could not be confirmed, and was continuously refuted by top government officials as being unfounded and preposterous. Even though the rice exchange sounded like an odd deal and most likely false, Isamu Kudo decided to see if the rumors—at least in regard to the counteragent—had any validity.

Using his connections in the Japanese Self Defense Force (JSDF), he confirmed that a counteragent had supposedly been discovered. He also learned that Japan had acquired a large batch of the serum through a secret trade for 326 long tons of rice with the U.S. military at Raven Rock. However, because of Japan's isolation and lack of internal resources, the alleged serum could not be replicated in large amounts and had only been dispensed to key government officials and mid- to high-level JSDF personnel. However, the most disturbing bit of news Isamu uncovered was that Japan may not be infection free, and that Hachijojima Island, located in the Philippine Sea, was being used as an isolation ward for those who were suspected of being ill with the virus, though it could not be confirmed if anyone sequestered to the island had turned into a zombie.

Before the fracture, Kudo Clan was one of the largest yakuza organizations in the Kanto Region and had great influence and resources. When Isamu's clan could not buy favor with key members of the local government or the JSDF, they resorted to blackmail, extortion and violence when necessary. It was smart business to have assets within certain government agencies and the military, and this time it paid off with great reward. It had been a high ranking government official named Masahito Tada that they extorted to acquire the antiretroviral. However, Tada could not confirm the antiretroviral worked. According to what Tada knew, no top echelon government administrator had contracted ARS. That bit of information, however, didn't matter to Isamu. He believed if the government was secretly hording the serum, then the counteragent must be effective.

The clan's former assistant chief had stolen what was to be the clan's salvation if the plague made it to the mainland. It was imperative that it be recovered and those responsible for stealing it severely punished.

***

While Isamu discussed his plans for retribution from his headquarters located inside Nin Jin House, across the river his nemesis Gaku Tohno was in a meeting with his own top executives in the penthouse of the Nakayasu Hotel, discussing profits and plans at striking Kudo Clan territory.

The large penthouse suite rivaled that of the fourth floor of Nin Jin House, both in size and décor. The suite had three large bedrooms, one transformed into a conference room, two full baths, and a large kitchen/dining room, along with a spacious central living area.

Gathered around the long conference table were Tohno's advisors and executives, several having been recruited from his former clan. Closest to Gaku and opposite one another were Advisor Kakusaburo Kitagawa and Senior Advisor Ryota Sakurai, both looking very serious. Further down, and also opposite one another, were Headquarters Chief Eiichi Yazawa and Assistant Chief Haruki Murakami. Finally there was First Lieutenant Masaharu Fukuda who sat across from Accountant Yasuo Hazaki, who was nearly done giving his financial report.

"It is with great pleasure that I report that our family has earned an 11.3 percent profit for the first quarter, which under these trying times is much greater than expected."

The serious looks on Kitagawa and Sakurai's faces became pleased expressions, conservatively smiling at the good news.

"I project that profits," Hazaki continued, "will be tripled next quarter as word spreads of the unique entertainment experience Nakayasu offers its clientele, not only in our prostitution service but also in the food and alcohol businesses. We owe our prosperity to the boss. His vision and business savvy is the reason behind this success."

All the members gave their clan leader head bows in recognition of his great leadership.

"That concludes my report," Hizaki said, taking his seat.

"Thank you, Hazaki for that report," Chief Yazawa told him, "but before we adjourn, the boss has an announcement."

"As you know," Gaku reminded them, "the intention behind auctioning off one bottle of the ARS serum was to use the money to fund the resources needed for our own replicative laboratory. However, Kudo Clan's completion of their laboratory has left us with an opportunity to not only ensure the survival of our members, but also turn a quicker profit. Isamu's weakened state has left him with fewer members, which he spreads thinly throughout his territory. Tomorrow night we shall seize his facility and produce the counteragent ourselves. Brother Murakami will explain the plan."

***

It was nearly midnight when Isamu went to his eight-year-old daughter Nozomi's bedroom to bid her a good night and to let her know he was going out on family business. Nozomi was fully aware of what family business meant and who her father was. She was proud of her father, for while other normal families suffered because of the reduced resources caused by Japan's isolation from the rest of the world, her yakuza family fared much better in attaining items that were controlled by the government, which was just about everything Japan produced.

Isamu pulled the sheets up, tucking Nozomi in, and then handed his daughter her most prized possession—a

Walt Disney Thumper plush toy. She squeezed it tightly as two AH-64D Apache Longbow attack helicopters passed outside, high overhead.

"Will you see mommy tonight?" she asked.

Isamu tried to be vague. "Perhaps," he told her, though he knew he would most likely see her.

"Will you tell her I miss her?"

"That woman is dead to us. Let that go," he told her, tempering his true feelings for his daughter's sake. "Brother Yamada will check on you later. Be good. You don't want the Namahage to come for you." Isamu attempted a scary face and clenched his hands like they were claws. "Namakemono wa ine ga. Nakuko wa ine ga."

They were words from a centuries-old story from Isamu's hometown in Akita Prefecture in northern Honshu that he often told her, that the ogres in the mountains—the Namahage—would come down and steal away misbehaving and lazy children and eat them. "No lazy people. No crying children."

Nozomi laughed and told him, "Daddy you're funny. It's only a story."

The two hugged and Isamu tucked his daughter back under the covers.

Ever since Isamu's wife left them, he kept his daughter at the clan's headquarters. Though Nin Jin House was not the ideal place to raise a child, he knew that every clan member would lay down his life if need be to protect her. Tonight he would entrust his daughter not only to his headquarters chief, but also someone who had never protected her before, and that was Yuji Osawa, who reported, as instructed, to Boss Kudo outside his daughter's bedroom.

"Osawa. Saito has informed me that you are his most trusted bodyguard."

Bowing, Osawa replied, "Assistant Chief Saito honors me."

"Therefore, I am leaving you in charge of headquarters security and the most important person in my life."

Osawa bowed again and swore, "I will not fail you."

"I known you won't. Pick eight of your most competent brothers. That is all I can spare."

II. Kudo no Gyakushu

Saito, Kimura, and nine other men exited the building and went to their motorcycles, but none of them moved to straddle or start them. At precisely midnight, Isamu exited Nin Jin House with Enforcer Toshiyuki Matsumoto following. Isamu mounted his Triumph T100 Steve McQueen Edition motorcycle.

With a very concerned look, Matsumoto questioned, as he bowed slightly, "Shitsureisimasu. Isn't the car safer?"

Isamu looked at him for a moment as he zipped up his One Star Perfecto leather jacket, and replied in a joking but sarcastic manner, "Oh, yes, you're right. Until you reminded me just now, I was going to ride against traffic in the wrong lane at high speeds. But now I have reconsidered. I won't ride in the wrong lane."

"Oyurushikudasai," he apologetically responded, bowing low. "I meant—"

"Matsumoto. I have seen you fearless in the face of the enemy, but you tremble like a woman every time we ride. Go with Brother Saito; he has a helmet you can wear. Saito!"

"Hai!" Saito responded.

"Brother Matsumoto will ride with you tonight. For Brother Matsumoto's sake, keep it under sixty and don't ride against traffic."

"Hai!" Saito affirmed.

The clan leader grinned and told his enforcer, "And Matsumoto. Don't be afraid to hold onto Brother Saito. I wouldn't want you to fall off."

Saito handed Matsumoto his extra helmet, telling him, "Do not worry so, Matsumoto-san. It takes time to be an expert rider."

Matsumoto scoffed, and replied, "Then perhaps I should drive."

Isamu started his motorcycle, followed by the rest of the clan. Kimura signaled to the men to move out, the boss taking the lead.

***

Sergeant Shogo Hamada stood next to his patrol car at the center of the bridge. He and his three patrolmen were in charge of securing the main Asakawa River crossing of the northern end of the city. This had been the seventeen-year veteran Hamada's decision; there were not enough police to secure both ends of the bridge. The Hachioji Police Department, like all of Japan's police forces, was stretched thin on personnel ever since the government invoked martial law and placed a mandatory nighttime curfew on the country. The JSDF had taken charge of securing all transit hubs, ports, airports, and patrolling the coastlines, but it was up to local law enforcement to enforce the curfew ordinance in their own cities

From Nin Jin House, the clan rode their motorcycles north to the Akatsuki-bashi crossing of the Asakawa River and right into a waiting Sergeant Hamada. Isamu and his crew slowed down as Sergeant Hamada waved his LED light baton in warning.

As a gesture of respect, Shogo stepped around the barricades to meet the clan leader. But before he could bow, Assistant Chief Kenichiro Saito was dismounted and challenging him with several armed men, who had spread out behind him as support.

"Bakayarou!" Saito insulted the sergeant, and then began to berate him. "This is Isamu Kudo, head of the Kudo Clan. How dare—"

Sergeant Hamada tried not to express any feeling of intimidation, even though he was greatly outmanned. He also ignored Saito's ranting and looked directly at the boss. "I know who you are, Boss Kudo," he interrupted, addressing the clan leader, trying to take control of the situation. "But you will need to return to Nin Jin House, or it will be my duty to arrest all of you for violating national curfew."

"Impudent bastard," Saito stated in an irate tone, as he angrily pointed an index finger at the police sergeant. "How dare you challenge Boss Kudo? You are nobody," he stated, sweeping the threatening finger at all the patrolman. "Move now or—"

Not dissuaded, Hamada moved past the man and closer to his boss. "I respectfully request you turn back now, and I will forget that you are violating curfew," Hamada said to Isamu, ignoring Assistant Chief Saito's threatening gesture. "If you refuse, then—"

"What!" Enforcer Toshiyuki Matsumoto interrupted, rising from Saito's motorcycle to challenge the officer.

The boss gestured for Matsumoto to back down and got off of from his motorcycle to personally address Sergeant Hamada's edict.

Hamada's men drew closer to their commander in support, though they had no weapons to defend themselves if the confrontation turned violent. First Lieutenant Akira Kimura and Assistant Chief Saito drew their pistols as a warning to Hamada and his men, but the police sergeant stood his ground as Isamu approached him.

"Are you going to arrest me?" Isamu calmly asked, as he grabbed the sergeant by the front of his shirt.

Sergeant Hamada had had prior confrontations with yakuza members before, none of which had ever been violent in nature, but when the clan leader grabbed him, he took it as a sign of aggression and immediately attempted to raise his light baton for defense. Before he could get it chest high, Boss Kudo slapped him hard alongside the face. It was something Isamu quickly regretted.

"Idiot," Isamu told him as he stopped the faltering sergeant from collapsing, and then helped him stand up, straightened the man's disheveled uniform, and then calmly stated, "I respect your integrity, but I have business at the Nakayasu."

It was rare that any true yakuza would harm any police officer. The relationship between the two organizations was one of mutual respect. The higher rank on either side garnered you more respect from the other's side. It was an ideology that had been a long-standing tradition throughout modern Japanese history.

Boss Kudo stepped back, and then gave Hamada a slight bow, letting the officer know that he was sorry for the disrespect he had shown him.

However, Isamu's anger had not been assuaged, in spite of the apology. As he turned from Hamada, he looked at the sergeant's three dumbfounded men and insulted them. "Useless. I beat up your boss and you do nothing. Not one honorable man amongst you—only Hamada. You should be ashamed."

Isamu picked up one of the nearby lightweight plastic A-Frame traffic barricades and threw it at them. Hamada's men scrambled out of the way.

"Bakadomoga," he insulted them again, and then signaled for his men to move out.

Sergeant Hamada quickly waved his light baton at his men, signaling for them to clear the way. He let Isamu and his subordinates pass without further challenge.

***

At the same time Kudo Clan was being challenged by Hachioji Police Sergeant Hamada, the manager of the Ryotei Nakayasu, the restaurant inside the Nakayasu Hotel, was confronting the pale and perspiring Jiro Sato on why he was sitting on a crate in a corner of the kitchen near the service elevator, instead of taking a food order to a very important client.

"Sato, why are you sitting there?" the manager demanded to know. "You know Mr. Tada is to get his sushi platter at 12:30. Now get going!"

Sato looked up at the man with indifference and told him, "Get someone else to do it. That crazy old man attacked me earlier. He bit me!"

The manager balked at the accusation. "That's ridiculous. Mr. Tada is one of our best customers. Now go deliver his food."

"Ridiculous?" Sato exclaimed, rebuking his boss's implication that he was lying. Sato pulled back his shirt sleeve and revealed his bandaged arm. "Does this look like I am being ridiculous?" he asked, as he stripped back the dressing to reveal a deep bite wound that was bruised and festering. "I haven't felt good ever since."

Disgusted, his boss stated, "That looks nasty. Did you see a doctor about that?"

"Doctor? Don't be stupid. If I go to a doctor, they'll send me to Hachijojima."

"Then get off your ass and take Mr. Tada his food."

"I told you, get someone else."

"Do what I tell you or I will have Mr. Souta throw you out," he warned Jiro.

"You can't do that. I'll be arrested for violating curfew."

The restaurant manager kicked the crate, warning him, "Don't make me tell you again."

Sato reluctantly rose, commenting, "Unbelievable."

***

Approaching the first crossing over the Asakawaobashi Bridge, the group saw a distant line of headlights approaching. They sped up and made a left onto Hiyodoriyama Road, and then a quick right, stopping on Owada Road.

First Lieutenant Kimura hung back, stopping around the corner of the turnoff to observe the approaching convoy as the rest of the clan pulled farther up the street and turned off their engines. It was a dozen defense force vehicles in a hurry. The vehicles crossed through the intersection without slowing.

"A convoy," Kimura reported, pulling up. "In a hurry. Didn't even look our way," he told his boss.

"Good," Isamu replied to the news. "Then we continue."

***

Kenji Souta and Jinichi Nitta, both in their early thirties and sharply dressed, stood in front of the guest services counter with swords in their hands, waiting for Madame Fumiko Ikeda to get off the telephone.

After a moment, the Madame hung up the telephone, and then addressed Souta.

"I need you to send someone up to Mr. Tada's room. No one is answering and several customers have reported a woman screaming from inside the room. The old man might have hurt one of my girls."

Standing by the elevator were two low-level subordinates, denoted by their off-the-rack suits that signified their lower station.

Souta turned to the two, and called to them. "Kase, Sakata."

The two men hurried to the counter.

"Yes, Big Brother," Kase respectfully replied, almost in unison with Sakata's same words.

"Go to room 417," Souta told them. "One of the girls may have been roughed up. Make sure everything is okay. But remember," he added as a reminder, "Mr. Tada is a government official, so show him respect."

They urgently hurried to the elevator. Kase pushed the call button and the doors immediately opened to reveal a female operator inside.

"Fourth floor, please, Ms. Otomo," Kase requested, as he and Sakata stepped inside the car.

***

At the top of the hill was Migita Hospital. As he passed the building, Isamu smiled at the thought that some members of Tohno clan might shortly be in need of their emergency room. Turning left onto Akatsukicho Street, they could see the green neon sign atop the ten-story Nakayasu Hotel in the distance. Travelling halfway down the street, they pulled into the Echo Mansion Apartment complex. If they travelled any further by motorcycle, the sound of their approach would give them away.

"Kimura. You know the plan. Just make sure you buy us enough time."

Kimura bowed slightly to his boss, responding, "Hai! It will be done."

Staying close to the walls along the right side of the poorly lit street, they made the half-mile trek to the Hotel Nakayasu undetected. There was no formal parking lot attached to the hotel grounds, for the building was situated in a dense area of two-story houses. The parking lot was across the street and the pathway that led to the main entry of the hotel was accented by a dense wooded garden on both sides. Two Tohno Clan sentries stood near the entry door twenty feet from the street. They did not venture much further from under the large eave entry for it would constitute being out after curfew, and their boss could not afford to have his men arrested or a heavy fine imposed on his business if they were deemed to be breaking the law.

***

Boss Kudo was a shrewd businessman. Though the curfew had severely impacted the profits of the clan's prostitution business because few patrons were willing to take the risk of possible imprisonment for carnal pleasures after dark, Isamu had devised a way to circumvent it and bolster his business. He had opened the Nin Jin House; a four-floor building that included a bar/restaurant in the basement, two levels of private rooms, and their headquarters on the top floor.

Their customers did not have to worry about curfew, for they could spend the evening being "entertained," as well as enjoying food and liquor all night long. Business had been so profitable that they were planning on expanding by opening two larger facilities, which would raise much-needed capital to support the biomedical facility they had just taken over. He had set his headquarters chief and senior advisor to the task of acquiring the Nakayasu, but Tohno and Sakurai had betrayed him, acquired the hotel on their own, stolen the antiretroviral, and convinced nearly a dozen clan members to follow them to form the basis of Tohno Clan. Adding insult to injury, Gaku utilized the business plan Isamu had devised for the hotel's unique services, providing pleasure to clients of every taste and imaginable fetish and by offering a unique menu to satisfy almost everyone's palette in the hotel's large restaurant, which was to be called Isami House.

However, tonight Isamu was going to set everything right and prove to the clan that he was still capable of running the organization by retrieving the stolen ARS counteragent and punishing everyone who had betrayed the clan.

***

Approaching the hotel, the Clan broke into two groups. Boss Kudo led a group of eight men in between two houses, while Saito, Kimura and two subordinates stayed behind. After a moment, the two underlings moved away, strutting down the street to the hotel's entry walk.

Saito had chosen these two to lead the frontal attack not only because no one from Tohno's crew would recognize them, but also because he knew both were capable of drawing the guards away from the entry with little difficulty. Satoichi Kurosawa and Hiroki Matsui had moved up the ranks from low-level foot soldiers to junior leaders quickly by proving themselves not only with brawn but also guile. They vowed to Saito they would lure the guards away from the door so Saito and Kimura could climb over the garden wall from the side street and come up behind their enemy.

Kurosawa and Matsui knew there could be no failure, but they were confident they could get the job done with little difficulty. They had a plan.

As they approached, Matsui, with a wooden baseball bat in hand, shouted, "Oy! We want to join up. Let us see your boss."

The two sentries, both in their early twenties and both dressed in off-the-rack suits, stepped away from the door and to the edge of the high overhang.

"Hey. What are you two doing here?" one sentry, named Takeo, asked. He held a lighted cigarette "Leave now."

"Are you deaf?" Kurosawa asked, as he held a sheathed katana sword over his shoulder. "We're here to join up."

"You two punks need to leave now, or we'll show you what we do to idiots like you!" Takeo warned, throwing the cigarette down and grinding it out on the landing.

"Idiots?" Matsui stated, with a tone that reflected not offense but amusement at the attempted insult. "I can't believe your boss lets two peons guard the entry. He must not be very smart."

"Impudent bastard!" Naoki, the shorter of the two guards, exclaimed, taking offense. He moved forward, but Takeo stopped him.

"We heard Tohno Clan was important and tough," Matsui taunted, "but you tremble like two chinpira. Useless."

The insult of cheap punks that Matsui had called the two Tohno sentries was all they would tolerate. Takeo stepped from under the entry eave and a few feet onto the pathway with Naoki following behind.

"What?" Takeo asked, in a tone that dared the insult be repeated.

Kurosawa replied, "Deaf... and stupid."

The final goad drew the two sentries up the path, giving First Lieutenant Kimura and Assistant Chief Kenichiro Saito the opportunity to climb over the garden wall undetected. As the two Tohno members were about to meet Kurosawa and Matsui's challenge, a rustling in the shrubbery behind them drew Naoki's attention. As Naoki turned to investigate, Saito slashed his sword down across his chest, and then thrust it through his abdomen. Saito twisted the sword before he pulled it free.

At the same time, Takeo saw Kimura coming toward him and panicked. As he turned to flee, a bone-crushing whack from a baseball bat hit the side of his skull. As Takeo fell to his knees, Kurosawa thrust his sword through the man's torso, then withdrew it. Takeo slumped face first to the sidewalk.

"Useless," Matsui stated, as he and Kurosawa stood smiling, looking down at their bloodied enemy.

While the skirmish was taking place in the front of the building, Boss Kudo led his attack on the hotel using the exterior kitchen entry at the rear of the building. There had been only one sentry posted, who was too preoccupied with smoking a cigarette to notice Kudo Clan's approach.

With a wakizashi in hand, Enforcer Toshiyuki Matsumoto grabbed the inattentive sentry from behind. Covering the man's mouth with one hand, he drove the blade into the base of the skull with his other. The sentry's eyes widened with a look of pain and bewilderment as he momentarily twitched.

Matsumoto twisted the blade, and then released the man. He grinned with perverse pleasure as he looked down at the corpse, and then pulled out a wiping cloth.

Isamu and his men approached, Isamu signaling for them to enter. He tapped Matsumoto on the shoulder, a gesture that not only told his enforcer he had done a good job, but also that it was time to move. Matsumoto finished cleaning his wakizashi and followed his boss through the door.

As soon as the kitchen staff saw Isamu and his men enter, they moved immediately out of his way, and as the clan members headed toward the door that would lead them into the dining room, the kitchen staff fled out the back door.

It was well after 1:00 am, and the dining area had been closed for the day's business for some time. The only person in the space was the restaurant manager, who was taking orders for room delivery. When the man saw Isamu, he respectfully bowed, keeping his eyes low. Isamu did not know the man, but gave him a smirk as he passed. The manager quickly departed, heading towards the kitchen, nearly running into Matsumoto who was on his cell phone sending a text message, and was not aware of the man's flight.

***

In the courtyard Matsui and Kurosawa were nearly done dragging the two dead Tohno Clan sentries from the pathway and into the garden when Kimura's cell phone beeped. It was a message from Matsumoto, letting him know they had made it inside the building.

***

Souta and Nitta were still at the guest services counter with Madame Ikeda.

"What is taking those two idiots so long?" Nitta questioned aloud. "They should have called in by now."

When the automatic doors of the restaurant parted, neither Souta nor Nitta bothered to turn around from the counter to see who was exiting. Like all Tohno Clan members they believed that no rival family would dare make a raid on their headquarters, and there was no threat in regard to a rival entering undetected, especially after curfew, so only an employee would have been exiting from Ryotei Nakaysu. However, when Madam Ikeda's expression turned from neutral to fearfully surprised, the two immediately turned to where she was looking, but they were too late.

Moving swiftly from the dining room into the lobby towards the reception area, seven of Isamu's men brought Nitta and Souta down before they could draw their weapons to defend themselves. As Saito and his three men came from the opposite direction, Kimura saw Ikeda drop behind the counter. He immediately went to the cowering woman and dragged her before his boss's feet.

Madame Ikeda begged and bowed for forgiveness, for she had once been one of the clan's top-earning whores.

"You pig. Betraying whore," Isamu berated her. "I took you off the street. Trained you. Made you our Madame. Put you in charge. This is how you repay me?"

"Forgive me, Boss Kudo. Please forgive me."

Outraged, Isamu informed her, "Your betrayal is unpardonable. Your treachery deserves something special. But you are not worthy for me to punish. Matsumoto!" Isamu addressed his enforcer, who was purposely cruel and sadistic when he was called upon to kill.

"Yes."

"Punish her," he instructed, vindictiveness in his voice.

The Madame screamed as Matsumoto grabbed her by the hair, lifted her up, and without hesitation drove his wakizashi into her stomach. Matsumoto looked into her eyes as he sadistically smiled, and then kissed her lips as he twisted the blade and disemboweled her.

While his boss was getting his revenge, Assistant Chief Saito stepped to the elevator and pushed the call button. When the elevator door opened, the female operator gasped with surprise, "Annta!"

Seeing her, Isamu exclaimed, "Natsuko!"

Miss Otomo bowed before him. "Forgive me, annta."

"How dare you call me that?"

"Please, I beg of you. Take me back."

"Stupid pig," he said. "Did you truly believe Tohno would give you more than what you had? Ignorant hick. Look how far you have fallen."

Natsuko's insult and betrayal was far greater than the brothel Madame. He had given her a hostess job when no other business would, mainly because she had a thick Yamagata accent. However, Natsuko desired more than just a lowly position. She knew that her country upbringing and below-average intellect would not get her what she most desired—money and power. She had only two assets she could use to get what she wanted, her well-proportioned figure and her feminine guile. She had seen an opportunity in advancing her station. She had seduced Isamu and become pregnant.

He knew that he had been tricked, but this is not why he wanted to kill her. Her insult and betrayal had been that she had become Gaku's mistress and left with him when he broke from the clan, leaving Nozomi motherless.

Isamu had not murdered anyone since his street gang days, before he went legitimate and formed the Kudo Clan, and as a yakuza boss he no longer had to soil his hands with such lowly business, which was the job of his men. But this was not business; it was personal.

Miss Otomo groveled, bowing again. "Please do not kill me. I will do anything. Please forgive me."

It would have given him great satisfaction to watch her die slowly, but for Nozomi's sake he would spare her life.

Your words are hollow," he told her. "But for our daughter's sake, I will spare your pathetic life."

Holding the elevator door, First Lieutenant Kimura stepped partially out of the elevator car and addressed his boss.

"Boss. Forgive the interruption. But the floor is locked."

Saito grabbed Otomo by her hair and raised her head.

"Where is the key?" Isamu asked.

Feigning ignorance, she replied, "What key?"

Immediately Saito kicked her in the ribs for the disrespect. She groaned and cried in pain.

"Stupid pig. Should I have Matsumoto kill you after all?" Isamu asked.

Otomo was well aware of Enforcer Matsumoto's brutal ways when killing. She raised her right hand, revealing a wrist key chain with a singular key. Saito grabbed it from her.

Saito directed underlings Haruto and Yuuta to dispose of the bodies, and remain on guard in the lobby. He followed his clan leader and the other men into the elevator.

Isamu looked at Otomo with disgust, as Kimura pushed an elevator floor button.

"May your life be long with suffering for what you have done," he imparted as the elevator door closed.

***

Standing on guard in the hallway of the penthouse level, Yoshio and Nobu stood opposite and adjacent to the elevator.

Yoshio was transfixed on the lighted floor numbers above the door. The number was at three and ascending.

"All we ever do is guard the elevator. It's boring," Yoshio complained. "We should be in celebrating with the others."

Nobu warned, "Careful what you say. If Yazawa hears you complaining, he'll demote you and make you a doorman like Takeo and Naoki."

"Yeah, but at least they get to be outside. This is stupid work."

A chime announced the elevator's arrival.

"Nani?" Nobu said aloud, confused.

Nobu and Yoshio drew their swords. The door opened but the car was empty.

"Empty. What is going on?" Nobu questioned, and then pulled a radio from his waistband. "Souta. Souta," he called into it. "What is going on? Why did the elevator come up with no one on it?"

He waited for a response, but none came.

Yoshio told him, "He's probably talking to Madame Ikeda again."

***

Haruto and Yuuta carried the body of Souta behind the guest services counter, and tossed his corpse atop Madame Ikeda. Over a radio came the voice of someone calling for one of the dispatched Tohno members.

"Souta. Answer me. What is going on down there?" the man's voice asked.

"That's the second time. You should answer that, Yuuta," Haruto directed.

"Souta. Answer now or I will let Chief Yazawa know you are fucking off again," the voice demanded.

Yuuta removed Souta's radio and tersely responded. "What?"

In the penthouse hallway, Nobu responded, "Souta. Why did elevator come up without Miss Otomo?"

Yuuta smiled at Haruto, and then responded to the radio caller's question.

"Shut up and mind your own business."

***

Nobu was confused by the rude reply. Souta could act like a jerk on occasion, but was never rude to his fellow equals.

"What?" he called back to who he believed to be Souta, just as the elevator chimed again.

As the elevator door opened, Isamu's men burst forth, surprising Nobu and Yoshio. As they did, the rumble of a group of low-flying helicopters from outside shook the hallway.

III. Akatsukicho Outlaws

Boss Tohno's arrogance was only exceeded by his self-centeredness. High in the penthouse suite, surrounded by his most trusted men, he believed he was untouchable. No one would dare challenge his power and no one was reckless enough to try attack him at his headquarters.

Gaku did not even fear reprisals from his former boss, even though he had recruited many of whom he believed were some of his former clan's best men and whores, and the most prized possession that could potentially make him millions of yen. Kudo Clan was too weak now to challenge him, and the sooner that he could replicate the antiretroviral, the sooner he would be able to sell it on the black market. This would make his clan wealthy and give him the financial ability to recruit more men, and then wipe out his former clan and take over their territory.

He never thought of himself as over-confident and therefore never considered that Isamu was capable or desperate enough to seek revenge. Isamu had lost face, as well as significant clan profits. However, it was Isamu's protégé's theft that was the driving force behind the daring raid.

Inside the penthouse, the heavy rumble of a group of low flying helicopters from outside shook the suite, nearly drowning out the celebration that was in full swing. No one at the party seemed to notice the noise or vibration, with the exception of First Lieutenant Masaharu Fukuda. He moved immediately out to the balcony to investigate. On approach he saw a group of AH-64D Apache Longbow attack helicopters escorting four Boeing CH-47 Chinooks.

The sight of helicopters was nothing new; they were on constant patrol twenty-four hours a day, and frequently passed over the building heading to their base. However, he had never seen such a large contingent of aircraft heading to Air Defense Command at Yokota Air Base in such a hurry. It concerned him.

Stepping partly through the doorway, he addressed his superior with his concern.

"Shitsureishimasu. Excuse me, Brother Murakami... I think you should come and see this."

Assistant Chief Haruki Murakami was seated on a sofa with a half-naked girl on each side of him, enjoying the company of the very attentive females. He looked at Fukuda who was gesturing to him from the balcony doorway.

Slightly annoyed, he responded, "What is it now, Fukuda? Can't you see I'm busy?"

"There are a lot of helicopters. They're heading towards Fussa."

Murakami became more annoyed; everyone knew why the helicopters made their flight path through the neighborhood.

"Don't be so stupid. Helicopters always fly towards Fussa. That's where Air Defense Command is."

Fukuda knew this, but there was something different tonight. With urgency in his voice he responded, "This is different. I've never seen so many."

Reluctantly, Murakami rose. "Don't you two move," he told the girls, "I'll be right back."

In the night sky Fukuda pointed to the distant flashing of aviation lights. "Do you see?"

Murakami responded, "All I see are specks of flashing lights."

"But I know what I saw. There was—"

From behind and out of sight came another rumble of distant approaching helicopters. This time Gaku and his bodyguard Kenji Shimizu, a handsome man with the exception of a jagged scar on his face, stepped away from a conversation with Chief Yazawa, having heard the helicopters' approach. They moved towards the balcony to investigate.

"That's the second group, Boss, in as many minutes," Fukuda said. Tohno and Shimizu stepped out just as the choppers came into view.

***

At the entry door Kimura, Kurosawa, Matsui and eight underlings were poised to enter, when they too heard the approach of another group of helicopters.

"Wait," Saito stated, as his first lieutenant reached for the doorknob. "Let the chopper noise cover our attack."

When the hallway shook, they burst in, catching everyone off guard.

A melee of clashing swords, swinging baseball bats and slicing knives ensued. All six topless strippers screamed and dashed for the door as blood splattered and intestines unraveled and fell out of gaping abdominal wounds.

Isamu and Matsumoto entered as the half-naked girls ran out, nearly colliding with them.

In the hall Norito Yamamoto and Ryota Hamasaki were on guard, in case any Tohno Clan member entered the floor from the elevator. When the topless girls ran from the room, Yamamoto stepped away from the wall and watched as they ran to the elevator, unaware that there was one more exiting the penthouse. A large-breasted girl ran directly into him, knocking him off balance.

"Looking for another party?" he asked her, as she dashed to join her companions. "Don't be like that." He watched as one girl frantically and repeatedly pushed the call button, and then he shouted to the group, "Come back later. Kudo Clan will show you a better time."

When the girls rushed into the car, Yamamoto turned to his partner and asked, "Did you see the breasts on that one?" He cupped his hands and motioned them back and forth at chest height. "They were huge."

"I'd eat her all night long," Hamasaki crassly commented.

"Eat her? What a waste of time."

Hamasaki snickered and then commented, "No wonder you don't have a girlfriend."

***

Inside the elevator car the panic-stricken, large-breasted girl pushed the fourth floor button. An older small-breasted girl pushed her aside, and nastily remarked, "Stupid bitch. Your brains are in your tits," and then depressed the lobby button.

***

The fight between Kudo and Tohno Clans was over in less than two minutes. In the aftermath, two Kudo Clan underlings were dead, but eight Tohno Clan members, including Kitagawa, were also dead, and six Tohno juniors along with Yazawa and Sakurai had surrendered. The defeated knelt before Kimura.

***

The elevator door opened to the fourth floor, revealing a man dressed in pajamas, standing before them. His head was down and he lightly swayed to and fro. He made no attempt to get on.

"Stupid!" The small-breasted girl snapped at him. "Wake up! Elevator is here."

Mr. Tada looked up, revealing a sickly face, dead eyes, and blood running down his chin and neck. He lunged at the small-breasted woman, driving her from the doorway to the back of the car.

***

Kurosawa and Matsui returned from searching the other rooms and shook their heads "no" at Saito.

Saito knew there was only one place they could be and that was the balcony.

"Boss Tohno," Saito called out. "We know you are here. Come out now and surrender."

The assistant chief gestured to Kurosawa and Matsui to check the balcony. As he did, Murakami and Fukuda charged out with pistols firing, striking three Kudo clan members dead. Matsumoto immediately pulled Isamu out of harm's way as Saito and Kimura returned fire. When the shooting was over, Fukuda was dead and Murakami had been shot through the shoulder.

Matsui and Kurosawa dragged the Tohno assistant chief to the others and placed him next to Sakurai.

"Fukuda is dead, Boss Tohno!" Saito loudly announced. He looked down at the bleeding Tohno senior. "Murakami. Well, he's bleeding all over his nice suit. Maybe I should have him put out of his misery."

With that pronouncement, Kimura stepped to Murakami and placed a pistol to his head.

***

Inside the hotel's entry Haruto stood behind Yuuta who was shaking the main door.

"Okay. All secure," Yuuta confirmed, making sure for the second time within twenty minutes that the door was still locked.

From behind them came a girl's scream. They turned and saw a topless large-breasted girl in a mini skirt running toward them.

Pushing between them, the girl hysterically shouted, "Zombies! Zombies!"

Haruto and Yuuta looked at the girl, and then looked at each other.

"Zombies? What do you mean, zombies?" Haruto asked her, incredulously.

The girl was too terrorized to even hear the question. She shook the door screaming, "Let me out! Let me out!"

"Not so fast," Haruto told her, needing explanation to her odd pronouncement. "What do you mean, zombies?"

The panicked girl fumbled at the door lock.

"Let me out, I said!"

Yuuta grabbed her, and told her, "No. Not until you tell us what you are talking about."

"A zombie. It got on at the fourth floor and ate everyone. Now let me out!"

Yuuta shook her.

"Bakajane! Zombies don't wait for elevators." He threw her against the door as Haruto unlocked and opened it.

The girl didn't hesitate; she bolted to the pathway and out of sight.

Haruto scoffed as he locked the door. "Zombies on the elevator. All tits and no brains."

***

"Boss Tohno. Should I have your dog put down?" Saito called out to the balcony.

Saito moved in front of Murakami and smiled knowingly.

Though Gaku took the threat on his assistant chief's life seriously, he also knew Saito would not pull the trigger himself nor would any other senior. A high-ranking clan member would never kill a leading clan rival; it just wasn't done. They would, however, order a junior member to carry out the assassination.

Gaku struggled between deciding on surrendering or making a Butch and Sundance style exit like Fukuda and Murakami had. But his indecisiveness was about to force his hand. From inside the suite a single shot rang out.

"Those bastards," Gaku stated, bitterness in his tone.

Shimizu pulled out his two pistols.

"I will avenge him for you." he stated, ready to sacrifice himself for the clan's honor.

"You have no honor, Gaku. You sacrifice your men needlessly," a voice called out from inside the suite.

Gaku recognized the voice. It belonged to his former friend and boss. "Isamu. I didn't think he had the balls," he commented to Shimizu.

"Give me permission to kill him," Shimizu requested, cocking the hammers of his pistols.

"No, Shimizu," Gaku said. "I will not sacrifice anyone else. We must surrender."

With hands raised, Shimizu stepped into the room first; however, Tohno hesitated. Multiple flashes of light emanating from the Fussa area caught his attention. Rumbles immediately followed the flashes. Gaku Tohno knew something was seriously wrong at the air force base, but the matter of facing his old boss was at hand. He stepped off the balcony and into the suite. As Gaku looked to his kneeling clan members he saw that it was Sakurai who had been killed not Murakami. A momentary sense of relief came to his face, but then it turned to anger when he saw Saito with a cocky grin on his face as he stood above Sakurai's lifeless body. Gaku took it as an insult, believing Saito was letting him know he took great pleasure in having ordered his employee's execution, not realizing it had been Saito who had pulled the trigger as an act of reprisal for the betrayal he felt over Sakurai's hollow words of integrity and loyalty having joined Tohno Clan. However, the perceived cocky grin was not over Sakurai at all; it was a smug smile of satisfaction at knowing that the former assistant chief was going to pay dearly for his treachery. Gaku gave Saito a look of disdain as Matsui and Kurosawa disarmed him and Shimizu, and forced both of them to kneel before Isamu. Gaku's contempt turned quickly to one of his own men when he saw his accountant standing in the background.

"Hizaki-san, you traitor!" Gaku shouted at the man.

Isamu laughed at the outburst. "Traitor? That's like the eye booger laughing at the nose snot. Hizaki has always been loyal to Kudo Clan. He is honorable."

Gaku snapped back, "You know nothing of honor."

***

Norito Yamamoto stood transfixed by the dead Nobu and Yoshio, who lay near the elevator unceremoniously, having been tossed aside like the dead, useless corpses that they were. However, Yamamoto was not staring at the dead bodies out of some erotic attraction; he was observing them with such intensity because he thought he had seen one move. As he watched keenly, he saw Nobu twitch for the second time and became alarmed.

"Hey, I think one of them is still alive," Yamamoto told his partner Ryota Hamasaki, as he moved a few paces down the hall.

"Do you see him breathing?" Hamasaki asked.

"No," Yamamoto replied.

Hamasaki warned, "Then get back over here before Boss Saito sees you have left your post."

Yamamoto ignored Hamasaki's advice and moved to Nobu.

"But I saw this one moving."

Don't be stupid," Hamasaki told him. "They're dead."

***

"Just because you keep your business on the other side of the river, did you think I would not come for what is mine? You are an arrogant little punk. I gave you everything. You were blood to me, and this is how you repay my generosity? You've betrayed all your brothers and their families because of your disloyalty and greed."

Gaku repudiated Isamu's admonishment.

"You gave me nothing. I earned it. Who protected you when we were kids? Killed for you as we worked our way up the ranks? I did. And what did I get for my loyalty? To be your lap dog. I should have been boss."

"Always too impatient," Isamu told him. "Always thinking with your fists and not your brains. I would have nominated you when I was ready to step down."

A few distant rumbles, like the sound of an approaching storm, came from the open balcony doorway.

"Rain," Isamu commented, hearing the faint thunder. "What a shame. But then again a good cleansing rain will help wash away the scum."

"I don't think that is rain. I think its rockets."

Isamu ridiculed, "Rockets? Don't be stupid."

Gaku replied, "I'm telling you, that's the sound of rockets, not thunder. Go look for yourself."

"You first," Isamu told his nemesis, gesturing to him with his pistol.

***

The junior yakuza member was not convinced that the slain Tohno member was truly dead. He knelt down to check Nobu's body.

"I'm telling you," Yamamoto stated with certainty, "this one moved."

Hamasaki responded, "Then just stick him in the head with your katana, and get back over here before you get us in trouble."

As Yamamoto drew his sword from its scabbard, Nobu's eyes popped open, startling him.

"Shit!" Yamamoto exclaimed. "He is alive."

Nobu grabbed onto Yamamoto's leg and bit into him. Yamamoto cried out, and then leapt up and repeatedly stabbed Nobu in the torso in an attempt to get the Tohno junior to release his grip. But Nobu was unaffected by the multiple piercings and pulled Yamamoto down, biting into his face. The young yakuza let out a wail as he tried to shake Nobu loose.

Down the hall Hamasaki stood paralyzed with a terrified look on his face as he watched his partner being eaten, and then saw Yoshio rise and join in at tearing chunks of Yamamoto's flesh from his body and devouring it.

Norito Yamamoto flailed and screamed as the meat was ripped from his torso. Hamasaki wanted to help, but all he could do was clasp his hand to his mouth in an attempt to prevent himself from vomiting. Yoshio turned from his chewing and glared at Hamasaki.

***

Looking toward the east, all they could see were distant flashes of white emanating from the clouds, followed by low rumbles.

"The sound of Hellfire air-to-surface missiles in Fussa," Gaku said.

"Don't be stupid. Why would they bomb their own base?"

This could not be the sound and sights of missiles; even at such a long distance they would have made a more powerful noise, Isamu thought. Besides, if the infection had extended from the islands of the North, then certainly it would have not reached Tokyo Prefecture without word of its spread onto the mainland. And why would the government bomb their own base? No, Gaku was wrong, of this Isamu was certain.

***

Ryota Hamasaki had been horrified at the sight of the cannibalism. But what panicked him more than seeing his associate being eaten alive was that he was about to fall to the same fate if he didn't immediately take action. He stepped through the penthouse entry and announced, "Zombies! Zombies! Zombies eating Brother Yamamoto!"

The Kudo Clan members in the room looked at their comrade in disbelief.

Kimura turned and demanded, "What's all the shouting about?"

Hearing the commotion, Isamu, Matsumoto and Tohno stepped off the balcony and back into the room.

Without apologizing, Hamasaki began, "Zombies are eatin—"

Yoshio seized and pulled him back into the hall before he could finish, and then bit into his face. Hamasaki let out an ear-piercing cry of pain-filled terror.

At the entryway came the other undead Tohno hall guard, Nobu. A large gash ran from one shoulder to the opposite hip. From the gaping wound large intestines dangled, nearly touching the floor. His dead eyes momentarily surveyed the room. Nobu charged in, seizing a Kudo Clan underling.

Those struck down in the first melee began to rise, going for the closest victims they could find.

***

As the chaos in the penthouse suite was happening, Haruto and Yuuta returned to the reception area, Yuuta walking towards the elevator.

"Yuuta. Don't be stupid," Haruto told him. "There are no zombies."

But Yuuta didn't listen. Not that he believed zombies were in Hachioji, but something had frightened the girl enough to make her hysterical and want out of the hotel. Even if it was only what she may have suffered from witnessing their raid on the penthouse suit, he would be remiss in his duty if he did not at least look in the elevator car.

"We need to make sure," he said to Haruto.

The door opened to an elevator full of blood and dead topless strippers. Squatting on the floor was Mr. Tada.

Yuuta was shocked. He pointed at the man and yelled, "Zombie!"—not realizing that his loud voice would draw its attention.

Mr. Tada turned around. Blood ran from his mouth as he chewed. He looked at Yuuta and rose.

"A zombie! Do something!" Yuuta told Haruto.

***

Isamu surveyed the carnage, and then stepped to one of the dead zombies and kicked it in the head.

"Useless government. They can't even keep us safe. We suffer because of the quarantine and the virus still comes," he said angrily, kicking the zombie again. "I hate zombies."

A loud rumble of helicopters from outside passed overhead, heading west.

A noise came from the doorway. It was Yoshio. Isamu turned with his pistol in hand as zombie Yoshio lunged towards him. He pulled the trigger. The shot impacted Yoshio's face and exploded his skull, sending brain matter scattering.

Zombie Yoshio fell at the clan leader's feet. Isamu looked down at the young man, shaking his head with displeasure, and then turned his attention to Tohno.

Pointing at his former assistant, Isamu said, "This is your fault."

"My fault?" Gaku asked.

"Yes," Isamu told him, and then cocked the trigger on his pistol and pointed it at the man's face. "If you hadn't betrayed me, then my men would still be alive."

"They're dead because of ARS," Gaku corrected him.

"No. It is because of your betrayal. We could all be at Nin Jin House drinking. But because of your theft, Clan Kudo had to come here." Isamu turned to his assistant chief, ordering, "Put bullets in the heads of all the dead. I don't want any more zombies."

As Saito, assisted by Kimura, began to shoot, Tohno Clan Senior Advisor Kakusabaru Kitagawa rose behind Isamu.

"Boss!" Hizaki warned, and then jumped at zombie Kitagawa, knocking it to the ground. Kitagawa bit into Hizaki's hand as he attempted to keep it at bay.

In a single motion Enforcer Matsumoto swung his wakizashi across the back of zombie Kitagawa's neck, lopping off its head; the torso collapsed onto Hizaki.

Isamu looked down at the decapitated head, its eyes rolling up at him, gnashing its teeth.

"Stupid Tohno zombie. Not so tough now," Isamu told the head, and then kicked it across the room.

The clan leader saw the bleeding hand of his accountant. He gestured to Akira Kimura, and then reached down to the man to help him stand, and as he did he said, "I promise to take care of your family." Akira shot Yasuo Hizaki in the head. The bookkeeper collapsed with a blank look on his face.

"You see what I had to do? — Kill my men," Isamu announced, directing his hostilities at the Tohno leader. "I want the serum, now!" he demanded.

Isamu aimed his pistol at Gaku, and as he did, a thunderous timpani of helicopters swept low over the building, followed by a series of nearby explosions. A loud, shrill squeal, like that of an oversized firework's rocket whistling on ascension, passed over the building and was followed by a loud explosion in the parking area. Another rocket whistle followed near street level and struck the lower part of the building. A third came seconds apart from the last whistle and struck the upper part of the building.

The intense, violent blast shook the structure and knocked everyone in the suite to the floor. Gaku, his bodyguard Shimizu, Chief Yazawa, and one underling took advantage of the event and bolted for the door. As Murakami got his footing, he grabbed someone's dropped pistol and ran, too.

Kudo Clan First Lieutenant Kimura saw his nemesis scramble by, and as Murakami passed, Kimura snatched up his dislodged pistol and fired from the floor; the bullet struck the casement as the Tohno lieutenant made it through the archway.

"Get them," Saito yelled at his men, as he began to rise.

As Matsumoto ushered his boss out the door, Saito, Kurosawa and Matsui followed. Kimura sat up, holstered his pistol, and then picked up his sword. As he began to rise, the shrill whistle of a rocket bore down on the suite. The room exploded. The shockwave from the blast launched Kimura through the doorway and into the hall, slamming him against the far wall. He landed near dead Hamasaki.

Saito had not seen his first lieutenant blown into the hallway, but had turned in time to see him flop to the floor. He rushed to his aid. "Are you okay?" he asked.

"I'm fine," Kimura assured him, trying to catch his breath. "Don't let Tohno get away because of me."

Saito moved several feet down the hall but turned back.

He waved him off. "Boss, please. Go. I'll follow."

Kimura staggered to his feet, and then stepped to the penthouse doorway and looked in. The bright light of a hovering Apache helicopter swept across the destroyed room revealing that his two underlings and the remainder of Tohno Clan were dead.

***

Some of the ceiling in the lobby had collapsed, but it hadn't dissuaded Mr. Tada from pursuing the two Kudo underlings. A dirtied and dazed Yuuta and Haruto staggered towards the entry door.

"Hurry up. The zombie is coming," Yuuta warned, as Haruto fumbled to get the lock open.

Haruto jiggled the door, hoping it would free the mechanism. "I think it's jammed," he told Yuuta with slight panic in his voice.

As Mr. Tada stepped within a dozen feet, Yuuta threw his baseball bat at him. It struck Tada's chest but the pajama-clad zombie did not falter.

IV. Battles Without Honor and Humanity

Gaku and his men had run to the closest set of emergency stairs. They had made it down two flights of steps when they discovered the rest of the route, at least several floors below them, no longer existed. The four men ran back up one level and exited onto the eighth floor as Isamu and his remaining men entered the stairwell exit on the floor above. Hearing the door close one level below them, Saito signaled to Kurosawa and Matsui to hurry.

"Eighth floor," he told them. "Hurry."

The four Tohno Clan members had run for the stairwell on the opposite side of the hallway in hopes of evading the pursuing Kudo Clan. When Isamu and his men entered onto the floor, Tohno Clan was not in sight. The distinct sound of gunshots echoed from around the junction of the distant hallway.

From around the corner Gaku and his men ran towards them with urgency. Waving his arms feverishly in the air, he shouted, "Zombies! Zombies!"

Isamu stepped out in front of his clan members, pointed his pistol at Gaku, and pulled the trigger.

***

Outside the building, Yuuta and Haruto pushed hard against the door to keep Mr. Tada at bay, who scraped and banged at the door trying to get out.

An Apache Longbow helicopter hovered nearby, sweeping its large light along the street area across from the parking lot. A 30 mm chain gun rattled, alarming Haruto.

"Yuuta, do something before the helicopter sees us."

"It's your turn," Yuuta told him, not interested at making another attempt at dispatching Mr. Tada.

"To do what?" Haruto questioned.

"I don't know. But we can't stay out here. We'll get blown up."

"Better blown up then being eaten," Haruto said.

The helicopter's light swept across the front of the eave, and then moved away.

"Don't be a pussy," Yuuta told him. "Stab it with your katana."

"I don't want to open the door. I don't want to be eaten."

Yuuta smacked him. "Just do it," he insisted.

"We should take our chances out here."

Yuuta turned around and pushed his back against the door. A shocked and frightened look came to his face, as he gazed out to the pathway. He aggressively tapped Yuuta on his biceps.

"Brother. Stop hitting me," Haruto told him. "I'm not going to open the door."

He hit him again.

"Brother. Zombie. Zombie!" Yuuta said frantically.

Haruto turned and saw zombified Naoki with a gaping chest wound moving down the walk toward them.

"I don't want to die," Haruto said. "Now what?"

Yuuta pointed at the zombie and told him, "Kill it. Kill it!"

Haruto acquiesced and fearfully moved forward, but then faltered in his advance, stepping backwards.

Yuuta urged, "Brother, hurry. The old geezer is strong. I can't hold the door much longer."

Haruto drew a deep breath and then expelled it in the form of a war cry. As he did he charged with the blade up and outward, ramming it into Naoki's mouth and out the back of his neck. But Naoki kept advancing, attempting to grab onto Haruto as he held the katana. The blade inched further out the back of Naoki's neck as he drew closer.

Haruto pleaded, "Brother, help me."

Yuuta let go of the door and ran to Haruto's aid, allowing Mr. Tada to push the door open. He grabbed zombie Naoki by the back of his suit jacket, pulling him, but the jacket tore free. Yuuta saw the pajama-man zombie almost upon Haruto.

"The old geezer is coming," Yuuta warned. "Run brother, run!"

Haruto turned to see Mr. Tada reaching out. He spun out of the man's reach just in time, but left the sword still lodged in Naoki's mouth. Yuuta took Naoki's jacket and tentatively tossed it at the old man. It haphazardly landed atop Tada's head. The two Kudo brothers bolted for the door.

Yuuta locked the door behind them as zombie Naoki and Tada stepped under the eave.

Relieved, Haruto commented, "I think we are going to need more weapons."

***

For a moment Isamu thought about shooting Gaku in the legs and letting the pursuing undead rip the flesh from his worthless body, but he thought better of it. If there were to be any chance of saving his daughter and those he swore to protect, he needed to know where Gaku hid the antiretroviral. It was a matter of honor and obligation.

The warning shot struck a nearby wall, halting Tohno and his men.

"If you let me die, you'll never get the serum," Gaku warned.

Isamu cocked the hammer back again. He wanted Gaku to know that the drug was not the only reason he had come to Nakayasu. As the zombies came around the corner, Haruki Murakami shot at the advancing pack, but after one pull of the trigger; the weapon was empty. Murakami threw the pistol at the oncoming undead, as he joined the rest of his clansman.

Isamu smiled wryly and then lowered the weapon.

***

Yuuta and Haruto were behind the guest services counter, picking up the swords of Souta and Nitta, when Yuuta made a perplexing discovery.

"Haruto. What happened to the other one?"

"What?" Haruto questioned, not having noticed the missing corpse. He looked down at the bodies. Souta was missing. His face lighted with alarm. "Shit."

Yuuta and Haruto looked around the small lobby, but the Tohno Clan member was not in sight.

"Maybe he left," Yuuta said.

"Don't be stupid," Haruto told him. "He couldn't have passed us unnoticed. He pointed toward the restaurant. "Only one way."

***

Scrambling for the exit door, Gaku Tohno, his headquarters chief Eiichi Yazawa, bodyguard Kenji Shimizu and underling Yoshiki Inoue made it to the stairs and headed back to the penthouse level under guard. Haruki Murakami was not as lucky. Haggard and clutching his bullet wound, he was slow and having difficulty standing. As he drew near the exit Murakami stumbled.

In the doorway Kimura watched as the man regained his footing, but he did nothing to assist the faltering Tohno member as the zombies were nearly upon him.

Murakami was feet away from the egress when a zombie grabbed onto his suit jacket, nearly dragging him down. "Help me," he pleaded, seeing Kimura watching.

Akira Kimura gave him a self-satisfied grin, stepped back, and then shut the door.

With a fear-stricken look, Murakami appeared at the small window of the door Kimura was securely holding.

He pounded wildly on the exit, as several zombies grabbed onto him.

"Kimura!" he shouted, hoping his Kudo rival would show mercy. But there was to be none.

"Traitor!" Akira said to him from behind the window, grinning as he watched his former associate be pulled away and devoured.

"Bastard!" was the last word Murakami said before his twisted right hand fell out of view.

Akira had gotten the revenge he had wanted, and it was much sweeter knowing Murakami would suffer far more being eaten alive than having been executed by katana.

***

The automatic doors of the restaurant parted, and Yuuta and Haruto cautiously stepped backwards through the archway with zombie Souta following. Haruto looked over his shoulder as they moved in reverse towards guest services. From behind the counter he saw zombified Ikeda and Nitta rise.

"We're trapped."

Yuuta responded, "Time to join our brothers."

Zombies Nitta, Souta and Ikeda, with her entrails dragging on the floor, followed Yuuta and Haruto to the only escape route that remained—the elevator. Retreating, Haruto stuck Ikeda in the throat with his sword as Yuuta fumbled for the call button behind him.

***

Tohno Clan stood guarded by Kudo Clan at the elevator door waiting for the car that Assistant Chief Saito had called. Saito looked up to the overhead floor indicator light, but it remained at lobby level.

"Where's Murakami?" Gaku asked.

"Dining with friends," Kimura told him.

"You bastard!" he exclaimed, outraged.

As he moved in anger toward the man he knew had killed his first lieutenant, Matsumoto punched him in the side, knocking the breath out of him.

"In a hurry to join him at the All-You-Can-Eat buffet?" Isamu asked his former friend.

Saito impatiently pushed the elevator call button several more times. The light still indicated the lobby.

"What are those two clowns doing downstairs, holding the elevator?" Isamu asked. Then he pushed the call button as his assistant chief got out his cell phone.

***

When the elevator door opened, Yuuta retreated backward, keeping his focus on Haruto and the three zombies, and then pushed the penthouse floor button, never noticing what was behind him.

"Hurry!" Yuuta urged his companion.

Haruto turned just in time to see several zombified bare-chested girls inside the elevator car grab Yuuta from behind.

"Yuuta!" Haruto shouted in a warning that came too late. As the zombies dragged him down, Yuuta's cell phone began to ring.

***

"Shitsureishimasu, Boss. But there is no answer." Saito spoke, and then looked up at the indicator light, which still remained at lobby level.

"Useless idiots," his boss said, and then asked Tohno, "Where's the service elevator?"

"Down the hall," Tohno informed him, and then continued, "but the stairs on the other side will be the fast way down."

"Don't be stupid. I'm not walking down all those stairs with zombies everywhere." He waved the pistol at him, and then ordered, "Move!"

Approaching the service elevator, Saito arrived first and pushed the call button. When the door opened, a zombified Jiro Sato stepped out and seized him, biting off his nose.

Matsumoto grabbed Sato and drove his wakizashi through the side of his head, and then twisted the blade. Saito's nose plopped out of the restaurant employee's mouth.

Isamu shook his head in disbelief. "You fear motorcycles but not zombies. I don't understand you, Matsumoto."

Saito held a handkerchief to his bleeding face while repeatedly stomping on Jiro Sato's head, abrasively reprimanding the dead youth.

"Son-of-a-bitch! You got my new suit bloody."

Kudo and Tohno Clans watched the bleeding Saito as he stomped until Sato's head caved in and brain matter oozed out, not once having cried out in pain from the attack.

Saito noticed them staring.

"What?" he asked, wondering what the big deal was with making sure the zombie was truly dead.

"You're bit," Kimura said.

Saito was well aware of his dismembered appendage and reached down and picked up his nose and pistol.

"I know," he acknowledged, as he held his detached nose. "Do you think I can sew it back on?"

Akira raised his pistol and took aim at his friend and superior.

"Boss. I am sorry," he apologized for what he was about to do. "But we can't take a chance of you becoming a zombie."

Saito looked down to the pistol in his own hand and then back up to Kimura. First Lieutenant Kimura cocked the pistol hammer.

Saito looked to him, and asked his clan brother for a favor.

"Kimura. Sew my nose back on for my burial."

The assistant chief dropped his nose and then quickly raised his pistol and shot himself in the temple. Brain matter and blood splattered onto the wall.

"I don't want a zombie getting me. Give me a gun," Gaku demanded, looking at his former boss.

"Do you think I am stupid?" Isamu inquired.

"And if I die? Then how will you get your revenge?"

"Revenge is not the only reason I am here," he reminded him.

"Then once you have the vials, how are you going to escape? By motorcycle? I have a car in the lot."

"Maybe I brought my car."

Boss Tohno knew this to be untrue. "Not likely. You're wearing that stupid Brando jacket. You look like a cheap punk."

"Cheap punk? You. You look like a third-class salary man in that suit," he returned, which was one of the lowest slurs one could give someone of Gaku's standing.

However, Gaku was not interested in exchanging verbal jabs with his rival. He was more interested in finding a way out of his current situation, and he knew he would have to use Isamu to accomplish that feat.

"You'll never get out of here alive if we don't work together."

"I'd rather kill you and take the keys."

"The zombies will eat you before you figure out which car it is," Tohno told him.

"Do you think I don't know how to use a locator device?"

Gaku scoffed. "Huh. And attract the zombies. And you still won't have what you came for. Now give me a gun."

Isamu paused, rethinking his position and realized he needed to keep his adversary alive until the serum was in his possession.

"Okay," he said. "I'll kill you later… Kurosawa."

"Yes, Boss," the junior responded.

"Give Boss Tohno your katana and take Brother Saito's pistol," he instructed his employee.

"Yes, Boss."

"What about me?" Yazawa asked, having been silent for so long.

Isamu looked at the Tohno chief and conveyed, "You won't need one. You and the rest are zombie bait."

Isamu pushed the elevator's call button and the door re-opened. Kimura pushed Yazawa into the car first; the rest of Tohno Clan followed.

Looking at the serving cart with the tray and lid, Isamu pulled off the cap to reveal a platter containing various sushi. He picked up a piece and smelled it.

"Did you fish this out of the Asakawa River?" he asked with disgust, as he dropped the fish back onto the plate. Isamu removed Gaku's pocket-handkerchief from his suit jacket and wiped his hands with it. When he was finished, he stuffed the soiled handkerchief back into Gaku's pocket.

What should have been a quick ride down ten floors was not to be. The elevator abruptly shuddered and slammed to a halt between the third and fourth floors. The door opened to reveal four feet of exit space above their heads.

"Stupid elevator," Isamu said, and then ordered Gaku to push the lobby button again, but the car did not respond. "You should be ashamed," he told his former associate. "This is the worst hotel I've ever been in. Where is your pride?"

Isamu ordered Tohno Clan member Kenji Shimizu to look out the opening, but Gaku's bodyguard refused to do it.

"You're not my boss," Shimizu reminded him.

"Is that so?" he replied to the remark. "Should I have Matsumoto cut you open and stuff your bleeding body through the gap? I'll know then if it is clear."

Drawing his wakizashi, Matsumoto gave Shimizu a wide grin.

Chief Yazawa ordered his underling, "Inoue. Go see if it is clear," but Isamu was not going to have his authority undermined.

"Scarface goes or you die," he told the Tohno chief, aiming his pistol at him.

Shimizu acquiesced and Inoue held the serving cart while his superior climbed atop of it.

Looking out the gap, he checked both ways to see if the corridor was empty, but he also observed that a section of the building and floor had been destroyed.

"It's clear, Boss," he stated, and then withdrew his head from the space and turned around. "But there's—"

As Shimizu moved to get off the cart, two pairs of hands thrust through the opening and grabbed onto his jacket collar, pulling him back.

Inoue and Yazawa gripped Shimizu's legs as he struggled to unbutton his jacket, but the hands now had him around his neck and started to pull him out.

Gaku grabbed hold as Shimizu began to scream in horrific pain. Shimizu's head ripped from his body, and his torso flopped back onto the cart. For a moment the headless carcass spurted blood from its neck stump.

Zombified Kase and Sakata peered in. They attempted to crawl through the breech when pistol shots from Isamu, Kimura and Kurosawa rang out. Dripping blood and brain matter, the two former Tohno henchmen dangled into the car with their skulls blown apart.

Pointing to Inoue, Isamu stated, "You. Peon. Go up and see if there are any more."

"Send one of your own men," Yazawa told him, tired of being zombie bait.

The statement had not been a request, so Isamu made a clearer declaration. He shot Inoue in the head; the peon's brains and blood splattered onto Yazawa.

"Now you go," he instructed Yazawa.

"You're insane!" Tohno exclaimed.

"I'm a father trying to save his child," Isamu snapped back.

***

A few feet from the elevator there was a gaping hole in the outer wall and a huge section of floor missing, making one direction impassable.

Matsui helped Tohno out of the car. As he was pulled clear, he saw his chief on his knees with Isamu's lieutenant aiming a pistol at his head.

"I'm done with the games," Isamu informed his former associate. "Tell me where the vials are or I will kill this peon."

Gaku snapped, "Show him some respect. He is my chief."

Kimura cocked the pistol's hammer.

"Then tell me where the vials are or I will kill this chief peon."

"Boss. Don't tell him," Eiichi Yazawa said, and then offered up his life. "It will be an honor to die for you."

Isamu laughed. "Finally, one Tohno member with honor. Kill him."

Kimura pressed the pistol against Yazawa's head, showing the Tohno leader there would be no mercy.

However, Gaku knew Isamu could be bargained with. He believed there was one thing the Kudo Clan leader wanted more than exacting revenge. That was the antiretroviral.

"No, wait! I'll tell you. But your word. Your word if I do, you won't kill him."

"You value your chief peon that much? Then you have my word."

"Or Kimura!" Tohno added, just to make sure his statement of intent was clear.

"Deal," Isamu agreed.

Isamu motioned for Kimura to back away. The first lieutenant did as instructed, but kept the pistol aimed at

Yazawa, ready to fulfill his boss's order if the Tohno boss did not give up the information.

"Tell me before I change my mind," Isamu warned.

Gaku said, "The only place where it is cool and dry. The wine cellar."

Isamu gestured with his pistol, and then said, "Now show me."

Kimura lowered his weapon. His part in the strategy was complete, but the scheme had not come to complete fruition. As Yazawa came to a full stand, Matsumoto drove his wakizashi through Eiichi's neck and forced him over the edge of the building.

"You fucking prick!" Gaku exploded with outrage at the treachery. "Where is your honor? Does your word mean nothing?"

With anger, Isamu told him, "You have no right to question my honor."

"I'm not questioning your honor. I'm refuting it exists."

"I don't give a damn about what you think. You put profit before family. Yourself above the welfare of the clan," he reminded his former associate, and then venomously added, "My daughter's life is in peril. For that I take everything you value."

"You think I'll stand here and take this from you, motherfucker!"

Raising his sword, Tohno charged at him, but Matsumoto struck it from his hand with his wakizashi and then punched the Tohno boss in the face, knocking him to the ground.

Isamu stepped on the blade as Gaku tried to reach for it.

"Motherfucker?" Isamu questioned. "You should have stopped at fucking prick. Always thinking with your fists instead of your brains. You've outlived your purpose."

Defiantly Gaku responded, "Go ahead—kill me. But it will take you hours to find where I hid it. Do you think Nozomi has that long?"

Isamu hit him in the face with his pistol, nearly knocking him out.

"Bring him," he ordered.

Kimura motioned for Matsui and Kurosawa to pick the dazed man up. Matsumoto reached down for Tohno's discarded sword. He handed the weapon to his boss.

Passing the open door to room 417, they walked around the corner and into a hall awash with zombies feeding on corpses. For a moment everyone remained frozen and silent, and then cautiously retreated. Their presence went undetected by the undead.

Near the corner, Matsumoto stood by the edge keeping watch, while the others stood a few feet away whispering.

"What are you waiting for?" Gaku asked in a low voice. "The stairs are at the other end. Just shoot them."

"What do you think, we have endless bullets?" Isamu replied in a soft voice. "Use your brain for once. Kimura."

"Hai," the first lieutenant responded, presenting himself.

Isamu whispered into his ear.

"Understood. Saito, Matsui."

"Yes, Boss," Matsui answered.

Kimura pulled them aside and out of earshot of the Tohno boss.

"What are you planning?" Tohno questioned Isamu.

"A diversion."

"For what?"

Kurosawa and Matsui moved down the corridor checking doors. Tohno watched, perplexed at why Isamu's men were checking rooms.

"Do you remember when we were fifteen and I lured those three bullies into the dead end alley so you could come up behind them?" Isamu asked Gaku.

"Of course," he replied. "I stabbed all three of those little pricks in their asses. They were too embarrassed to come back to school for a month."

"And they never bothered us again."

"So what does—" Gaku began to ask, but was interrupted by Isamu's returning juniors.

Kurosawa bowed slightly before giving his report.

"Boss. It is all set."

Isamu smiled and then said, "Kurosawa, Matsui, Kimura. Go. Matsumoto. Make sure Tohno here gets the zombies' attention, and then join us."

Matsumoto pressed his wakizashi into Tohno's back. Gaku now understood what Isamu had planned for him. He objected.

"Oh, hell no!" his voice no longer in a cautionary low tone.

Isamu smirked as he departed, telling Gaku, "This time you're the bait. Lead them back to the elevator."

Matsumoto prodded him with the wakizashi, pushing him forward and around the corner.

Matsumoto shouted, "Hey zombies! Look what I brought you! Nice fresh meat!" The undead looked toward the noise. "That's right. Come and get him!" he encouraged the undead that were now focused on them.

Matsumoto kicked Tohno in the side of the knee, forcing him to the ground, and then he ran, leaving the Tohno leader behind.

Gaku struggled to rise as the nearly dozen zombies moved towards him. He limped around the corner.

There was no sign of his adversaries. He struggled to walk, hobbling, using the wall to help support himself. The zombies were close behind.

He came to room 417. The door was closed, but he knew that was where his enemies had taken refuge. He pounded on it as he watched the zombies getting closer.

"You bastards!" he condemned those behind the entry who refused him help. He had no choice but to continue on down the hall and to the service elevator.

Gaku stopped at the edge of the large section of missing floor. He looked across to the other side and then into the gaping hole. He knew, even if his knee had not been injured, that only a person of great agility and strength could jump across the abyss safely, even if they had enough room for a good running start, which now was ever shortening with the undead nearly upon him.

"Bastards," he whispered to himself, and then turned around to face his undead adversaries. They were just yards from him. He knelt down and shouted at the top of his voice, "You bastards!" The yell resonated down the hallway. He closed his eyes, not in cowardice at the face of certain death, but at accepting his fate.

Behind the darkness of closed eyelids, the sound of shuffling and thudding filled his ears, and then everything went quiet. He opened his eyes. There was a pair of female legs in front of him. He looked up and saw a knife blade protruding from the woman's eye. The blade retracted.

Matsumoto forced the zombie over the edge of the missing floor. Wiping his wakizashi, he looked at Tohno with a wide grin of satisfaction.

"You can get up now," Isamu told him as he approached.

With a displeased look he responded, "Fucking bastard."

"You're welcome. Now we go."

V. Beware the Fury of a Patient Man

Zombies Souta, Nitta and Ikeda tussled with several half-naked living dead girls within the open elevator car for Haruto's corpse. The three pulled and tugged on Haruto's legs, until they tore free from his body. The elevator doors closed with Haruto's torso and the girls inside.

***

Finally reaching the basement, Matsui grabbed the door handle and pulled, but the door would not open.

"Shitsureishimasu, Boss," he apologized for his inability to open the entry. "It's locked."

"Open it," Isamu instructed Gaku.

"I don't have a key."

"What kind of bullshit is that?" Isamu asked.

"Do you think I carry around every key for the building?" Gaku asked.

"Kurosawa."

"Yes, Boss."

"Shoot the window," Isamu instructed.

"Yes, Boss."

Kurosawa shot, but the bullet only made a crack, and the slug fell to the floor.

"Heavy tempered safety glass," Tohno informed them.

Kurosawa shot again. The second bullet made a hole and cracked the glass even more, but the window did not shatter. He aimed the pistol again and pulled the trigger, but the gun clicked.

"Forgive me, Boss. I am out of bullets."

"Idiot," Tohno remarked. "Now you know why I didn't ask you to join me." Gaku turned to Matsui. "Give me your bat."

Matsui ignored him.

"Idiot," he told the Kudo junior. "Give me the bat."

"Hey," Isamu snapped, "who you calling an idiot, stupid?"

"Just give me the bat," Gaku demanded.

Isamu gestured to Matsui, giving him permission to relinquish his weapon to their enemy. Gaku took the bat and whacked the glass. It fell away.

"Satisfied?" Gaku asked, and then snidely remarked, "Old school still works."

Isamu gestured with his pistol.

"What?" Gaku responded to the motion.

"The bat. Give it back," Isamu told him.

Displeased, Tohno handed the bat back to Matsui, as Kurosawa reached through the window frame and unlocked the door.

***

Kudo underling turned zombie Ryota Hamasaki walked aimlessly by the elevator of the penthouse hallway. The elevator chime drew his attention. The door opened and revealed several topless strippers gorging themselves on flesh. He was immediately drawn to the smell of the meat.

Moving to feed on Yuuta, the small-breasted girl rose, giving a low guttural groan, and pushed the interloper into the elevator call button panel. Hamasaki's back pushed against the board, lighting a few buttons.

***

The basement was large and filled with many wine racks, mainly containing bottles of sake. Isamu was impressed at his rival's ability to acquire such a large and varied collection, which now belonged to him as spoils of conquest.

Under the majority of the racks sat traditional sake tubs. Tohno pulled one out with a cherry blossom label design.

"This is it," he told Isamu.

"You put it in sake?"

Gaku replied, "Do you think I'm stupid? It's empty."

Isamu gestured for Gaku to move back, and then gestured to Matsumoto. With his wakizashi he cut off the rope bindings that helped to keep the small drum sealed, and pulled away the wrapping and carefully broke open the lid. Isamu reached in and found what had been stolen. He withdrew a clear sealed bag containing two small bottles and several syringes.

Holding up the bag, Isamu questioned Gaku's ethics. "You would sell this on the black market? You are pathetic and dishonorable—worse than a chinpira."

Isamu reached into his leather jacket and retrieved his cell phone.

"Hello. Hello... Yamada. Yamada. Stupid voice mail."

No one saw the sommelier come from behind the large wine rack until it was too late. The zombified wine steward grabbed Kurosawa from behind and bit into the side of his neck, ripping a chunk of flesh away.

Bleeding heavily, Kurosawa pulled away and attempted to hold back the crimson flow as he screamed for help. Matsumoto ran his wakizashi through the sommelier's head as the junior collapsed.

Kneeling on the floor, pale and still clutching his neck, Shuichi Kurosawa knew he was doomed. He beseeched his leader to end his life.

"Boss. Please. Don't let me become a zombie. Honor me. Take my life."

Yakuza custom obligated Isamu to fulfill the man's last request. He drew his pistol, and told the dying man, "You die with honor."

Kurosawa's head blew apart, creating a large spatter of blood and brains on the floor.

***

The dining room was a shambles. Part of the ceiling had collapsed and light fixtures lay broken on the floor, while others were hanging precariously from the ceiling, flickering. From the kitchen the remainder of Kudo Clan and former associate Tohno made their way toward the entry.

Natsuko Otomo limped toward them, barely able to walk, her flesh riddled with bite wounds.

As Isamu moved toward his former lover, he raised the katana Matsumoto had handed him earlier.

"Only death will cure a fool," he told her, as they drew near each other.

He was about to cut her down, but hesitated. He looked at her for a moment, reconsidering, and then lowered the weapon.

"You don't deserve pity."

The group moved from her path and to the exit.

As the restaurant's automatic doors opened, Madame Ikeda shuffled toward the group, her intestines tangled around her legs.

"We should have cut off your head," Isamu remarked. As he passed, he sliced the top of her head off. The skullcap spun like a Frisbee to the ground.

As they moved quickly past the guest services counter, they saw Nitta and Souta feeding. The two former Tohno Clan members took notice of the group's flight. Two zombies would not be difficult to dispatch, but then the elevator door opened, revealing three topless strippers and Hamasaki, who also noticed the fleeing fresh meat. The small-breasted girl dropped the arm she carried in the hallway as and joined zombies Souta and Nitta in their pursuit of a better meal.

Observing the discarded arm, Hamasaki discontinued his pursuit and took up the partially eaten appendage and bit into it, tearing at the remaining flesh.

The group hurried to the door. Matsui pushed on it, but it was locked. He quickly released the mechanism and pushed the door again, but it was jammed.

"It's jammed," he announced, putting a shoulder to it to force it open.

"Boss, your katana," Matsumoto requested. "I'll hold them off."

Isamu handed him the sword, and with wakizashi in one hand and katana in the other, Matsumoto moved toward the encroaching zombie pack.

Matsui and Kimura pushed on the door as Tohno walked away, heading to aid Matsumoto.

"Where are you going?" Isamu demanded. Tohno did not answer.

As Tohno approached the Kudo enforcer, Matsumoto decapitated Souta.

"I'll help. Give me the katana," Tohno told the man.

Without thought, Matsumoto handed Tohno a blade.

At the entry, Kimura and Matsui had finally smashed the door open. Isamu turned to Matsumoto and Tohno and shouted, "Let's go!"

Tohno ran his sword through the chest of one of the partially nude girls, and shouted back, "Coming!"

Matsumoto had noticed his enemy's ineptness at killing the undead. "In the head, like this," he illustrated, driving his wakizashi into Nitta's eye socket.

***

From the path, Matsui moved cautiously to the low-lit, bullet-destroyed street that was punctuated with corpses. He checked both directions, but only saw a few undead moving in the distance.

He crossed to the partially destroyed parking lot.

***

Matsumoto unwittingly had handed Tohno the katana without believing that the clan leader would be that dimwitted to challenge him with it, but he had underestimated Tohno's treachery. Gaku drove his sword through the enforcer's leg and Matsumoto collapsed.

"That's for Yazawa," he told him, in a tone that reflected retribution. "And for making me zombie bait."

As he departed, he let Matsumoto know, "Now it's your turn."

Three topless strippers descended on Toshiyuki Matsumoto.

***

Hiroki Matsui stood on the path near the building's eave. He gestured to his superiors, giving them notice it was safe to advance, just as Tohno stepped out of the entryway.

"Hurry. Only a few zombies down the street," he urged the men.

From out of the shrubbery stepped Naoki, the katana still lodged in his mouth. Matsui saw his approach and took his baseball bat and swung an upper cut, which forced the sword to pitch up and slice Naoki's head in two.

He turned back to the entry and gestured again. As he motioned, Mr. Tada came out of the shrubbery and grabbed him, forcing him to the ground.

Kimura rushed to his aid, but Mr. Tada had already ripped out Matsui's throat. Hiroki Matsui twitched with a glassy look of fear in his eyes and gasped for air, as Mr. Tada continued to feed on him.

First lieutenant Kimura shot Tada in the head, splattering chunks of brain and a mist of blood into the air. Mr. Tada collapsed atop Matsui. Akira Kimura looked at the junior. Blood and air bubbled out of his gaping throat wound. Akira put him out of his pain.

Under the eave, Gaku stepped forward and was about to step onto the path when Isamu grabbed his arm.

"Where's Matsumoto?" he asked.

Indifferently, Gaku informed him, "Dead. Some strippers got him."

"Bullshit! Not even a dozen dead strippers could kill him."

"Then go check for yourself," Gaku told Isamu. "He sacrificed himself so I could escape."

Gaku pulled away and headed up the path.

Isamu paused when he came to Masahito Tada and Hiroki Matsui. He looked at the mutilated government official, and remarked, "Cosmic irony or karmic justice? Either, or the gods are just." He then put his sights to his fallen man, Matsui. The junior's baseball bat lay near him. Isamu smiled.

At the path's edge that bordered the street, Kimura checked both directions to make sure there were no zombies to contend with before crossing to the parking lot. The breaking dawn revealed that the immediate area was devoid of the living dead. The group quickly crossed to the other side.

The parking lot had been struck by several rockets, which destroyed not only the lot's paving but also some of its contents.

"You still have a car?" Isamu questioned.

Gaku pointed with his katana to an area that contained no destruction, and then pointed a key fob at a black Lexus LS Sport Vertex. The lights flashed and the vehicle alarm beeped twice. At that the moment, Isamu exacted his revenge.

As the last beep of the car alarmed signaled the vehicle's location, Isamu swung Matsui's baseball bat into the clan leader's ribs, fracturing them and painfully forcing the air from his lungs. As Gaku faltered, Isamu swung again, this time in the back of the man's left knee, sending him crashing to the ground.

Gaku tried to scream out from the immense pain, but he could barely take a breath. He moaned and gasped for air, not even able to look at his assailant.

"This is my revenge," Isamu announced, looking down at the incapacitated clan leader and pointed the bat at him. Isamu raised the bat and came down with it like a man trying to ring the bell on a carnival strongman game. The impact broke Gaku's leg.

"Jigô-jitoku," he told the traitor, and tossed the bat down next to him. "Now you are zombie food."

Twenty zombies moved towards the car, having been attracted by the sedan's locator signal. Kimura picked up the dropped keys.

***

The arm Hamasaki fed on was now stripped to the bone. He dropped it and walked towards the entry. He passed a pile of dead topless zombie strippers, never noticing the semi-fresh meat under it.

VI. Revenge Proves Its Own Executioner

It was a necessity to quickly get back to Nin Jin House and to his daughter Nozomi. Chief Yamada would never ignore a call from his boss, unless something dreadful had happened.

Akira drove, taking an alternate and more direct route back to the city and to headquarters. Remarkably, along the short trip back, they had only seen a few living dead wandering around. As they neared their destination they saw the surrounding neighborhood had been partially leveled by JSDF rockets, and the area now seemed to be abandoned.

As they pulled the car in front of their headquarters, morning had arrived, and there was no sign of the guards who were always stationed outside their establishment.

"Something is wrong," Akira stated with trepidation. "There are no guards."

Isamu wasn't as concerned about the guards as he was about what else was missing. "There are no people," he observed. "No bodies, no zombies. Not even a squawking crow."

"Maybe everyone was evacuated."

"They don't evacuate crows," his boss told him.

Isamu moved cautiously towards the entry, holding the antiretroviral in one hand and his pistol in the other. Kimura followed.

Entering the building, the two checked the reception area and parlor, but the floor was devoid of anyone living or undead. They continued up one flight to the first hotel room level.

"Check the rooms," Isamu told him. "But be careful. I'm going to find Nozomi."

"Boss, I have a bad feeling. We should stay together."

"I feel it, too. But I need to find Nozomi. Now go," Isamu ordered him.

"Hai," the first lieutenant replied, bowing slightly and then headed down the hall.

Isamu headed to the fourth floor.

The clan leader phoned his chief again, but it went to voice mail. He moved quickly to Nozomi's bedroom, but she was gone. The Thumper plush toy lay atop the disheveled bed.

Akira Kimura did not find anyone in any room, neither dead nor living, which concerned him. Not because the rooms had been emptied, but because of what had been left behind. He couldn't believe that even in a state of panic, so many clients would have left their personal belongings behind. He headed up to headquarters level.

***

Isamu stood in his office near a large open safe with his back to the partly open door. He had changed out of his soiled clothes and into a tailored suit. A noise came from the parlor. He turned, grabbed his pistol from the nearby desk, and aimed it at the door. From the other side rose a voice.

"Boss? Boss!"

It was his first lieutenant.

"In here, Kimura."

"Boss," he said again, as he pushed the door open and stepped in. "There's no one here. Maybe they went to the safe house."

"No." Isamu picked up the Thumper plush toy from atop the desk and held it out. "This was from her mother. Nozomi would never have left it. Yamada knows this. He would have made sure she had it."

"Perhaps there was no time. They are probably at the safe house," Kimura said. "We will take it to her."

"Take some ammo from the safe. Then we'll get some food and sake and head to the mountain house. But you should change first. Your clothes are bloody," Isamu told his lieutenant.

Stepping out the door, the clan leader, with Thumper in hand, and his subordinate descended the stairs and headed to the basement where the bar/restaurant was located.

Looking into the pitch-black establishment, Kimura told his boss, "I'll get the lights," and then stepped through the archway and to the nearby light switch, but there was no power. "Breakers must be out," he said, as he stepped into the light of the stairway. "I can go look."

"Do you have a flashlight?" Isamu asked his lieutenant.

"No, but I can use my cell phone."

"Maybe we should forget it. It's too dark."

"I know where they are," Akira said. "In the kitchen. Besides we need supplies. It's a long journey to the mountain house."

"Okay, but be careful," Isamu warned.

Akira disappeared into the darkness, as Isamu stood by the entry straining to hear. After a moment came a muffled thud, like something hitting the floor.

"Kimura. Kimura," Isamu called out, concerned for his subordinate's welfare.

"Moushiwakearimasen," Akira called back. "I'm okay. Just a chair."

The light from a cell phone screen illuminated Kimura's face. He touched the screen and activated his flashlight app, turning on the phone's camera flash. Akira pointed the light outward, using it to guide himself to the kitchen doors.

***

In the archway of the entry, Isamu dialed his cell phone.

***

In the kitchen Akira's cell phone light illuminated the breaker box. He engaged the handle. The kitchen lights came on.

***

At the doorway, Isamu put his cell phone to his ear. From the stairs he could see the restaurant was lit. "Very good, Kimura!" he shouted out, congratulating his lieutenant.

***

From the other side of the kitchen doors, Kimura heard a ringing cell phone. He stepped through the doors into the restaurant.

***

From inside the restaurant, Isamu, too, heard the ringing of the cell phone. He stepped through the archway and into the room.

***

As Kimura stepped through the swinging doors, he was confronted with a pack of zombies. In the front of the group were Chief Yamada and Senior Advisor Otsumi. Yamada's cell phone was ringing.

On the other side of the room, Isamu saw the group but for a moment did not realize that they were no longer living.

"Kimura! They're here!" Isamu's shout turned some of the pack around. He realized his men were undead. "Kimura! Zombies!" he warned.

"Run!" Akira yelled, grabbing for his pistol as Shigeru Yamada and Kuniyoshi Otsumi set upon him.

Isamu saw his seniors drag Kimura down, and then he saw the remainder of the pack, led by bodyguard Yuji Osawa, coming for him. In his haste to retreat, he dropped Thumper. Reaching the top of the stairs, he heard two shots from inside the restaurant. Isamu turned back, but there was nothing to be done. The zombies were now climbing the stairs.

Fleeing from the building, Isamu headed to the Lexus. Opening the door he saw the keys were not in the ignition, nor were they above the driver side visor or in the storage compartment between the two seats—they were with Akira. Isamu knew he could not go back into Nin Jin house to retrieve them. However, he knew of another vehicle that he could use to make his escape—his own.

Isamu knew that the keys would be where he always stashed them—in the storage compartment between the front seats—and that with its keyless-go ignition system all he had to do was to input a security code and push a button to start the vehicle. He also knew that his black Mercedes S65 AMG sedan would be where it was always parked, on the side street with its doors unlocked. No one, not even the lowest thief, would even consider stealing a yakuza boss's car.

As he neared his vehicle, he saw that a heavy coating of dust had settled on it. He shook his head with disbelief and dissatisfaction. No yakuza boss would ever be seen in a vehicle that wasn't freshly washed and polished to a high-gloss shine. It would be disgraceful and show that he had no class if he was seen in a car in such a state. With disgust, Isamu opened the door and stepped in behind the wheel. He knew there was nothing that could be done under the circumstances, but that didn't make his embarrassment any less.

As he shut the door, a hand thrust in between the front seats from the back, and grabbed onto his arm, pulling it back.

Startled, Isamu cried out, "Shit!" It was a word that he seldom used.

A head popped out between the seats and bit into him. Isamu violently and repeatedly punched the familiar face, until the zombie let go. Isamu stumbled from the car, nearly falling to the street. He pulled his pistol from his waistband and looked back to the sedan. From between the front seats he saw the young boy who he had hired to keep his car properly clean. The lad was just thirteen years of age and not much older than Isamu had been when he had had the honor of earning money by keeping a yakuza boss's car tidy and presentable.

The undead boy crawled between the bucket seats, out the passenger door, and onto the street.

"Tomio. You couldn't clean my car before you became a zombie?" Isamu asked the boy, knowing full well Tomio did not understand. "This is unforgivable. Kono Bakagakiga."

The boy rose and moved toward him.

Isamu aimed his pistol and pulled the trigger. The bullet tore through the youngster's throat and ricocheted off the edge of the vehicle's roof.

"I hate zombies," Isamu angrily screamed, upset over the car damage, as he moved forward with raised pistol. "Go to hell!" he told zombie Tomio, and then pulled the trigger again. The bullet exploded the lad's skull.

Sitting in his sedan with the doors locked, he looked down at the vial of serum and syringe he held in his hand. He no longer had a choice. The antiretroviral his clansmen had died retrieving was no longer going to save those he promised to take care of. If he were to survive and find his daughter, he knew he would have to inject himself. His bitten hand trembled as he inserted the needle into the vial and extracted a whole syringe full of the liquid, and then took the hypodermic in his left and injected half its serum into the vein of his left arm. He paused for a moment and then tucked vial and hypodermic in an outer suit jacket pocket. After reloading his pistol, he set the box of ammunition on the passenger seat and drove away.

***

He turned from the side street onto the main road in front of Nin Jin House. He had not driven more than twenty-five feet past the building when he had to quickly brake. His daughter stood before him holding her Thumper and blocking his path.

"Nozomi, Nozomi," he called to her. As he exited the vehicle, he pulled the half-filled syringe from his pocket. The girl stood silent, her head bowed and her long hair hanging over her features. He grabbed his daughter and hugged her closely, but she did not respond to his embrace. "Nozomi!" he cried. "What is wrong?" He raised her chin and brushed the hair from her face. That is when he saw, but it was too late. Nozomi bit into his cheek and pulled a piece of flesh away. Isamu reeled back, landing on the roadway. His daughter lunged at him and he reacted, stabbing the syringe into her eye and depressing the plunger.

His eight-year-old daughter stood motionless for a moment, and then began to convulse. Flopping to the pavement, the child shook and contorted.

"Nozomi!" Isamu cried.

He scooped his daughter into his arms and held the tremulous child.

"Forgive me," Isamu begged of his daughter.

After a moment, the tremors stopped, and his daughter spoke. "Let me go," she demanded, in a raspy tone that indicated displeasure.

Isamu pushed her away, her voice frightening him. She had never spoken so harshly to anyone. But she was speaking, so he believed that the antiretroviral must have had an effect. But he was wrong. A look of shock and terror came over his face. He stumbled back in retreat as Nozomi rose up with a ghastly, evil look.

He turned toward the Mercedes, but those from the basement restaurant now surrounded it. The undead stood silent and nearly motionless, staring at him. He began to slowly step backwards, and as he turned, Nozomi's voice rose again.

"Bad daddy," she scolded, pointing a finger at him.

Nozomi plucked the syringe out of her left eye, and then tossed it to the ground. As Isamu moved around her in an attempt to flee up the street, zombies begin to emerge from every alleyway. Running towards the intersection, he saw a large horde suddenly appear, blocking his escape route.

Looking to the front of the pack he saw a uniformed man. It was Hachioji Police Sergeant Shogo Hamada and he looked very displeased. Isamu pointed his pistol at the sergeant and discharged five shots, but Shogo remained erect and still.

"Kono Zombie yarou!" Isamu shouted.

From behind him, his daughter repeated, "Namakemono wa ine ga. Nakuko wa ine ga"— No lazy people. No crying children.

Isamu turned around and saw his daughter pointing at him.

"Nozomi!" he cried out in dismay and anguish.

"Namakemono wa ine ga. Nakuko wa ine ga," Nozomi's refrain continued, as she still directed an accusing finger at him.

Isamu put the pistol to his head and pulled the trigger. The hammer clicked against the empty chamber as the zombies encircled him, Hamada in the fore.

VII. All Tits and No Brains

Isamu had not gone back to see if Matsumoto was alive; he had been preoccupied with plotting his revenge. As Isamu came down on Gaku's leg, shattering it, from under the three dead strippers in the Nakayasu lobby came grunts and groans. The pile of corpses began to move, first with a quiver of appendages and then with a rising of bodies.

Matsumoto pushed off the three girls he lay under and stood up. His face was pale with dark circles around his eyes. He was perspiring, and not been from the work of getting out from under the rank, smelling bodies.

"Stupid zombie bitches," he told the lifeless strippers, as he tucked in his shirt.

He straightened his tie and brushed off his suit jacket. He looked down at the bleeding gash across his leg. He knew what Gaku had done to him. He had been purposely infected from the katana that had been used on him. There was nothing he could do about it at the moment, but if he could make it back to Nin Jin House, he knew his boss would save him.

After wrapping his leg with his tie, he picked up his wakizashi and hobbled toward the open door.

As he stepped out from under the eave, a katana sword from behind thrust through his pectoralis minor. He looked at the protruding bloody blade as it withdrew.

On the other end of the weapon was the big-breasted, topless stripper, who earlier had nearly run into him as she fled the penthouse suite.

Her face lit up with fear when Matsumoto turned around, realizing she had stabbed a man and not a zombie.

"All tits and no brains," he told her and then slashed his wakizashi across her torso.

The girl collapsed. Her glossy and panicky eyes remained transfixed on Matsumoto, until she bled out.

Matsumoto dropped to his knees, his wakizashi falling next to him. He collapsed forward and onto the dead girl, his face coming to a rest on her breast.

Hamasaki appeared above them. He looked at Matsumoto and then at the girl. He dropped to his knees, put his head between the girl's spread legs, and ate into her crotch. Matsumoto lay in a semi-conscious state on the topless girl's fleshy breast like it was a plumped up pillow, his lips pursed against her nipple. He wasn't going to die nuzzled to the tit of some low-rental party girl, he told himself. If he was going to die with his face in tits, it was going to be in between the breasts of his favorite high-class prostitute.

He cautiously moved his hand along the walkway searching for the wakizashi he knew had dropped next to him. He grasped it and then plunged it into one of Hamasaki's eyes. Matsumoto hobbled away with his wakizashi in one hand and the dead girl's katana in the other, and headed toward the Echo Mansion apartments.

VIII. The Great Escape

"Nozomi!" Isamu cried again. "Please, forgive me?"

The loud rumble of a Triumph T100 motorcycle on a fast approach over powered Nozomi's repetitive, ominous words of warning. The horde parted as zombie heads flew into the air.

The Triumph slid to a stop in front of Isamu.

"Boss, time to go," Matsumoto told him, holding out a katana to him.

As they sped off together, Isamu sliced off Hamada's head in passing. The cranium bounced twice and then rolled to Nozomi's feet. She picked up Hamada's decapitated head and looked toward her father as his motorcycle turned a corner.

"Bad daddy," Nozomi scolded.

The Triumph had not traveled down the highway far before it began to wobble and slow. Matsumoto pulled onto the shoulder and parked. As he dismounted, he turned to his boss and said, "I'm sorry, Boss. I can't—" He collapsed before he could finish.

Isamu rushed to his comrade's aid. Matsumoto appeared to be dead, but he wasn't sure. He shook the man, trying to rouse him.

"Matsumoto! Matsumoto! I order you not to die," Isamu demanded. "Matsumoto, do you hear me?"

Isamu reached into his lower suit jacket pocket and retrieved the antiviral and a syringe. He held it before the lifeless Matsumoto.

"Matsumoto! I have the cure. I can save you."

Isamu hurriedly prepared a syringe, hoping it wasn't too late. As he was about to inject the serum into Matsumoto's neck, Matsumoto's eyes popped open. Isamu reeled back in shock. Matsumoto reached out and grabbed Isamu's suit jacket by the bottom right pocket, tearing it. Isamu never saw the vial and last unused syringe fall out. As his savior attempted to grab him again, he stabbed Matsumoto in the eye injecting the antiviral. Matsumoto collapsed. Momentarily, the clan enforcer violently shook and contorted and then went limp.

Isamu saw that they were no longer alone. Zombies were closing in. He mounted his motorcycle and bade farewell to his most trusted man.

"Matsumoto, you were always loyal and honorable. I'll never forget your sacrifice."

Isamu sped away, and a moment later Matsumoto awoke in a half-zombie state. He pulled the syringe from his eye and looked at it. As he threw it to the ground, he saw the vial and the unused syringe. He picked them up and then walked away, the nearby zombies following.

***

Nozomi held onto Matsumoto's hand with one hand, and Sergeant Hamada's blank faced, decapitated head by the hair in her other. She looked up to her protector.

"Matsumoto-san, arigato gozaimasu for my new friend," Nozomi said gratefully, and then looked to the cranium she held and asked it, "Sergeant Hamada, can we play?"

Hamada's eyes looked to Nozomi.

The sergeant's emotionless expression turned to glee, as he excitedly replied, "Yes. We could play cops and robbers. I could be the robber!"

Nozomi gave a wicked giggle and then looked back to Matsumoto.

"He's funny," she announced and then told her guardian, "I'm hungry."

Matsumoto looked down at her and replied, "So am I, Nozomi-chan. So we shall go."

The two departed hand in hand. A horde of zombies followed.

"Dammit, Swan. You said Brunswick was small and quiet." Briggs pulled her machete out of the zombie's skull, scanning in every direction. Six bodies now littered the sidewalk in front of the Potomac Street Grill.

Joshua Swan picked the map back up with his left hand from the middle of the street without resheathing his katana.

"The handle is loose on this machete and we are out of duct tape. I wish I had my ax back," she whispered, out of habit. Gail Briggs lowered her hood so she could see and hear better. They stood in front of the double doors of the Potomac Street Grill. "Get this door open. And be quiet about it this time."

"Do you have to nag and complain all the time?"

He smiled as he cleaned his blade on a zombie's hoodie and slid his sword into its sheath. He folded the map perfectly, and with speed that Briggs could never believe.

"I like complaining." She smiled. "I'm serious about the ax. We should find a hardware store." She cleaned her blade on another body, sheathed her machete, swung her AR15 to the front, and affixed a bayonet.

The double doors both had windows, unbroken. Swan cupped his eyes and looked inside.

"Looks empty, but be ready." He pulled out a crowbar and, as quietly as he could, he wedged the door open. He slipped in, followed by Briggs, who was shaking her head.

"I'm always ready, asswipe." She pulled the door closed behind her and was surprised that it latched.

"You have splatter on your face again," Swan said, knowing she hated that.

"Dammit," she said. "Clear the place first, clean up after."

The dining area was dusty but organized. The tables had silverware neatly rolled inside a paper napkin. With the ease of long practice, the two of them moved through the space. They checked behind the bar. Behind the counter was next. They could see into the kitchen through a large arch over a counter.

"Clear," Swan said quietly. He scanned continuously with his Glock 9mm. The suppressor was affixed.

"Clear," Briggs replied.

The bathroom doors were both propped open with Caution Wet Floor signs.

"Clear," she whispered.

Together they moved into the kitchen. One to the left and one to the right. Clear again. Neither of them reached for the walk-in fridge/freezer door handle.

Briggs and Swan had made that mistake in the past. Rotten food was the best result. Zombies were the worse result.

There was a closed door here next to the walk-in.

Swan placed his left hand on the knob and waited.

Briggs turned on a bright tactical light that was attached to her rifle. She was two paces back with the light fixed on the door.

At her nod, Swan opened the door, quietly, but fast. He knelt low in case she shot. Light came from the far end of the storeroom. It was a long, narrow room with metal storage shelves on either side. The shelves were mostly empty. Dishes were scattered and broken on the floor.

"Clear," he said, after looking both directions and even up. "Someone cleaned it out in a panic a long time ago."

Briggs turned and scanned the kitchen again before she lowered the rifle and turned off its light.

"I'll search in here. You take the kitchen." Swan said. "Don't forget. Hot sauce. I NEED hot sauce!"

Briggs slung her AR15 around to her back but left the bayonet attached. She systematically went through all the cabinets. She started piling her finds on the counter. There were large containers of salt, pepper, sugar and even two gallons of pancake syrup. She also found six pounds of Chock Full o'Nuts coffee, still sealed in the cans.

Going table to table, she collected eleven bottles of Brenda's Bootie Burner hot sauce. She hid them behind a gallon of pancake syrup, just in time. Swan came out of the back room with an old cardboard box that was closed, with a dozen rolls of toilet paper stacked on top. There was a box balanced on top that also fell when he set it all on the counter.

He tossed the box to her. It was full of individually wrapped handy wipes. She wrapped an arm around his neck and kissed him. It only smeared a little blood onto his nose. She had two packets open in a flash and was scrubbing her face, moaning with pleasure.

"I thought you'd like that." He moved the TP from the top of the box and flipped it open. There were about thirty cans of Spam inside.

"Oh, my god. I am suddenly so hungry!" she said, smiling wide.

Swan was looking over the rest of the salvage. He was pleased.

Then Briggs slid aside the gallon of syrup revealing the hot sauce. Swan began to smile as wide as she was.

"Cold Spam with hot sauce." He picked up one of the bottles. "Remember that night in Druid Ridge Cemetery just outside of Pikesville when you got hot sauce in your…"

That's when the screaming began.

***

It was outside and louder than seemed possible. A woman screaming. Between shrill cries, she was screaming something. Words.

"What the fuck did she just say?" Briggs said, her rifle shouldered as she moved to the window to the left of the door. She unlatched it and slid it open. The screaming got louder.

"…This is a recording." The screaming began again. She backed away from the window when she saw zombies in the street, moving toward the sound.

The screaming stopped, and the voice yelled like she was calling for help but actually was saying, "This is not real! I am drawing them to the roundhouse. I do not need help! This is a recording." And more screams.

About fifteen zombies shuffled by before the screaming stopped.

"I think those stairs beyond the bathrooms go to the house above. Let's see if there's a window with a view," Swan said.

They cleared two more levels quickly. It smelled musty, not like the rot of zombies, for once. The east window on the third floor had a view across Potomac Street to the rail yard. With binoculars, they could see that there were lights on by a huge warehouse. These included Christmas lights on the railing of a ramp that went to a single open door on the second level.

Briggs opened the window.

"You hear that?" She said. "It's music. The Doobie Brothers, I think."

"I hear a diesel generator. A big one. And something else," Swan said.

The last zombie went through the door, and it eventually slammed closed, and the light went out. After a few more minutes the sound of one machine then another was silenced.

The world was quiet again. The unnerving hush descended that forced them to whisper all the time.

"It will be dark in an hour. Might as well sleep here tonight," Briggs said.

"Let's give the place one more search and then pile supplies in the kitchen up here," Swan said.

Briggs nodded her head.

The linen closet had a supply of sheets. They covered the windows on the front door and stacked tables in front of the doors. It wouldn't keep anyone out, but it would make a racket if they pushed their way in. They pulled metal shelves across the back door outside the storeroom. The candles were collected from the tables before they barricaded the door at the top of the stairs.

They surveyed the place and came up with a way to exit in an emergency. "Nice of them to have real fire escapes," Swan whispered.

They even found ten gallons of vinegar that they could use to fill the flush tank a couple times on one of the toilets.

"Don't say it. Please." Briggs said, as she was closing the bathroom door.

"If it's yellow, let it mellow…" Swan couldn't stop himself.

When she got out of the bathroom, Swan didn't hear it flush. When she walked into the kitchen, she saw that Swan had a small gas grill there. He had pulled it in from the covered porch off the living room.

"Miss Briggs. I am declaring three days of R&R." Swan flung open three cabinet doors and then the pantry door. They were nearly full. Swan had found them while sweeping the house.. The supplies were way more than they could carry.

"I say we take a week. The hot water tank is the glass-lined type and has about seventy gallons of water," Briggs said.

***

They made grilled Spam steaks, with canned corn and canned peas. They ate at the dining room table by candlelight with real plates and silverware. If it weren't for the blankets that covered the windows at night and handy guns on the table, it would have felt normal.

They talked about lighting a fire in the fireplace, but the autumn was not cold enough to risk it. Briggs said, "We had this same conversation on the day I first met you. Remember that apartment above the funeral home in Baltimore?"

"Yes," Swan chuckled. "We almost killed each other."

"We stayed up all night whispering. And fell asleep together at daylight."

"Dumb asses," Briggs said. "How did we survive that first week?"

"We ran. We ran a lot." Swan was making light of it. They both knew the horrors of that first month held memories and topics they'd never revisit.

***

After dinner was cleaned up. Briggs and Swan felt safe enough and had a good bath. They had the extra water. They always called it a "bucket wash." They stood in the shower with a bucket of soapy water and a bucket of clean. They scrubbed each other with wash cloths and real soap that had not been available for weeks on the road.

They found clean underwear, socks, and t-shirts, as well as very fashionable, over-large tracksuits. They still wore their boots, always. They would never make that mistake again either. "Be ready to run" was a mantra that had served them well.

Their weapons were never far from reach. Their packs were packed with water, food and all the supplies they could carry easily, first thing. Ready to grab and run at any moment. Briggs found a leather jacket that fit well enough and would allow her to keep her AR15 on her single-point harness handy and out of the rain.

They would stay here and rest and eat the food they could not carry away. Briggs and Swan would put some of the weight back on that they had lost. They would repair their gear, mend their clothes, and try to sleep. They would rest and be quiet and read the books they found in the house.

They had learned from past mistakes. They were always ready to run, and they knew there would be a time to move again.

Two nights passed quietly. They even considered briefly sleeping together instead of taking watches. They stood their usual watches.

They still slept fully clothed.

They made love for the first time since the hot sauce incident in the cemetery long ago. They were clean, after all. And human.

"I heard something last night." Briggs said. "I wasn't sure. I didn't see anything until I went out on the balcony at first light, before dawn. They're gone."

"Who is gone?" Swan was puzzled. "The people in the warehouse?"

"The zombies we killed in the street. The bodies are gone…"

***

It was late afternoon of the third day when Swan walked into the living room where Briggs was reading *The Martian* by Andy Weir. She always read when she was trying to distract herself. Swan knew her well.

"Look what I found." He handed her a placemat from the restaurant. It had a cartoon depiction of Brunswick. Her eyes went directly to the exaggerated Potomac Street Grill.

Swan pointed to a different spot on the cartoon map. "Ace Hardware is about ten blocks from here. I need more duct tape. You still want an ax?" he asked.

"Are we talking about hitting the hardware when we head out to Harper's Ferry?" she asked. "It's in the opposite direction from the railroad tracks we plan on following."

"Want to hit the hardware running light and come straight back here?" Swan asked. "We've done it before. It's a risk, but if it's a goldmine at the hardware, we could carry more." He spread out the street map and compared it to the placemat.

Briggs' head came up when she heard it. "The diesel generator."

They both grabbed their binoculars and ran upstairs. When they got to the window, the large overhead door was already going up at the roundhouse. When it reached the top, a huge dump truck pulled out, and with a great gout of black smoke from the dual stacks, onto the road. The front had a V-shaped snow plow that was covered with stains.

The cab had four men inside, and four more clung to the sides, two on each side. All healthy, heavily muscled and well-armed. They all wore blue coveralls.

"That plow is smart," Swan said. "Shamblers in the street are no problem. They must be getting fuel from the trains in the rail yard. I have no idea how they are keeping the fuel from going bad."

"Why don't they ride in the back? It'd be way safer," Briggs said. She knew the macho types that rode on the running boards in towns full of zombies.

Violent gangs of men who preyed on the living. Especially women. They would lop heads off for sport.

"Holy shit," Swan said. "Look in the back."

It was bones. There were a couple hundred skulls visible. Complete skeletons were stripped clean of flesh, disassembled and piled in there.

"What the fuck," Briggs said. "They can't be… eating them?"

***

Two hours later they heard the big generator start again. Two minutes after that they saw the truck return. The back was now full of cut and split firewood. Swan's placemat

431

had a depiction of Wilson's Firewood. It had cartoon mountains of cut and split firewood.

The four men that had been riding the running boards on the way out sat on the leading edge of the dump bed with their feet on the roof of the truck. All four were laughing at something, even though they all had AR15s at ready.

The sun dipped behind the mountain to the west as the overhead door closed.

The screaming started again.

They could now tell that the screams, the voice, was coming from PA speakers mounted on the warehouse. The lights came on, and five minutes later the first zombies appeared. They followed the sound up the ramp and into the warehouse. The screaming stopped when the last of them started up the ramp. The lights went out, and just before the door slammed behind the last one, it was silhouetted by firelight from somewhere within.

"Briggs. You have that look," Swan said. "What are you thinking?"

"They seem to be harvesting those shamblers," Briggs said, as she lowered her binocs. "But why?"

"Look, I don't really care. It's safer to mind our own business. Stay quiet. Survive." It was a mantra that Swan had said a hundred times before.

"But what if they aren't assholes?" Briggs said.

"Do you remember what happened last time we tried?" Swan was mad now. "You almost got raped, and I... killed a real person. Yes, an asshole that asked for it. But I am talking about risk."

"Then we simply recon. We are better at it now." Briggs knew she would get her way. "We need information. Even if we never contact them."

Swan was shaking his head when he looked up into her eyes. "OK. But let's hit the hardware first."

She kissed him.

***

They were geared up at first light. It was a cold morning. It was their light recon armor. This meant denim jackets and jeans that had been reinforced at "bite points" with heavy duct tape. The arms, shoulders and body of the jackets were covered in duct tape that needed patching. They wore leather gloves but regretted not having more duct tape to close the seam between glove and sleeve. They carried guns and blades only. Each wore an empty backpack for any salvage goods to bring back.

They checked each other to make sure their gear was securely silenced and ready. Quietly, they slipped out the front door and closed it behind them.

They stepped to the center of the road and proceeded in a direct line toward the hardware. In the predawn light, nothing moved except them. Scanning side to side for anything unusual, Biggs pointed out a building they were passing about halfway to the hardware. It was a micro-brewery, but the entire front of the building was gone. The building had been gutted and any equipment that had been there was gone.

"Someone was really thirsty…" Swan whispered.

Briggs just shook her head and kept moving.

They reached the hardware, and all remained still. The glass was all broken in on the front of the store. It had been professionally looted. No axes, no tools at all remained.

"Dammit," Briggs cursed quietly.

Swan clicked his tongue and pointed with his chin at Klein's Antiques across the street. All the glass was intact.

The sun was not up yet. They moved across the street and flanked the door. The door had been kicked in, but someone had secured it closed again to the iron railing with a bungee cord.

"Why are there no shamblers in this town?" Briggs asked, before they opened it.

"Quit your complaining. Maybe we got lucky for once."

He unhooked and let the door swing in. It bumped into a single zombie standing directly beyond.

With practiced ease, Briggs stabbed with the bayonet, in and out, like a snake, of the old woman's eye. The corpse fell back into the room. They slipped inside and quietly closed the door.

Swan positioned the cadaver to hold the door closed as they activated the tactical lights on their weapons.

An old man was moving toward them down a long aisle, and Swan advanced as Briggs covered his back. His sword stabbed in and out and the zombie fell with a crash as it knocked over a lamp and a vase.

They froze as the sound echoed.

There was nothing after two minutes. They moved without a word.

The store was small but crowded with antiques. They cleared all three aisles and a small office before they began their search.

They met back at the counter, where Swan was smiling as the sun peeked in the window.

Briggs placed a massive meat cleaver on the counter and an old, long, dull bayonet from World War II. "No swords, dammit."

"Look in that umbrella stand to your right," he said.

It was full of canes, golf clubs, and a single cavalry sword. She lifted it out and slid it from its black leather sheath.

She smiled wide. "It's still sharp."

"I also found this under the counter." He placed a very short, sawed-off, double barrel shotgun on the counter and an old box with 23 shells still in it.

"Oh my, Mrs. Klein." She looked at the old woman propped up to hold the door closed. "Don't you know short shotguns are illegal in Maryland?"

***

The return to the house was uneventful. Briggs spent the afternoon making a sash that held the saber securely at her hip. Swan fashioned a similar one for the sawed-off shotgun.

"With only two shots before reloading that thing isn't worth much," Briggs said.

"I know. But I can save those two for us," Swan said, looking away. "At least we can be sure."

"I hate it when you talk that way," she said.

"What if West Virginia is a bust?" Swan said. "The cabin sounded like a great idea when we started. I'm not so sure now. When we left, I thought all we had to do is last longer than they did. They are rotting."

"We didn't know that everyone had it then," Briggs said quietly.

"It will never be over," Swan said.

"There are no happy endings," Briggs said. "Because nothing ends."

Swan looked up at that. And smiled.

"I read it somewhere," she said and kissed him.

***

They moved out before dawn the next day.

The plan was to climb the structure on the side that was clearly not in use and move across the roof to the high windows. From there they would be able to see inside.

When they reached the windows, they were so filthy they could not see anything. They didn't open either, so they moved along until they found a single pane of glass that was missing. Swan looked in.

It was a giant warehouse-size space that had been designed for performing maintenance on trains. There were only two train cars in there, in a space that could have held forty. There was a propane tanker and a water tanker. He could also see six massive trailers with Costco on the side and a mountain of canned goods. Several years' worth of food. That explained why the pantry at the house had not been looted.

Swan also counted twelve Winnebagos and three other Airstream camper trailers. That was just what he could see from this angle.

A man with wet hair was busying himself in the large area set up as a camp kitchen. He poured kibble into a trough-shaped bin as two German shepherds and a Basset hound lumbered up. The Basset was more interested in a pat on the head and an ear scratch than food.

Swan strained to follow him as he carried two steaming cups of coffee to an area set up with three large sofas. An elderly man was in a wheelchair talking to a woman in a green bathrobe and her hair in a towel. She kissed the old man on the cheek and then the one that had brought her coffee before going to one of the Airstreams.

"Have a look," Swan said to Briggs.

While she was looking through the window, Swan noticed that the area between the roundhouse and the river had been cleared and secured with tall chain link fences and shipping containers all the way to the river.

There were goats.

All the grass looked mowed. He was smiling and shaking his head when he saw them.

There were twenty or more shamblers in the water, moving slowly through the shallow muddy bottom.

"Briggs," he said, louder than he intended, "we have to warn them."

Briggs followed his line of sight.

"Dammit. They'll get the goats."

Then they heard the voice behind them.

"Freeze, if you want to live." It was a woman's voice, calm, confident and serious. They froze.

"Turn around slowly and keep your hands where we can see 'em," she said.

Swan noticed the word "we."

They turned slowly to see a woman squatting on her heels with a handgun trained on them. She wore military camo with a tactical vest that was full of magazines, flashlights and even a walkie-talkie—the professional kind. Her hair was dark and cropped super short, inexpertly but practical.

"Look, we'll explain later, but there are shamblers coming out of the river. You have to warn them," Briggs said.

"And that right there is why you are not dead and in the vats already." She stood smoothly. Into a radio, she said, "I have the two live ones on the roof. Hold your fire, Mike."

Swan looked around, just moving his eyes.

"We have an overwatch post in the crane cab," she said, but didn't lower her gun. "Briggs and Swan. Yes, I know your names. You can call me Laura. So, what's your story?"

"You're not worried about the zombies coming out of the river?" Briggs asked.

"We have been here a long time. Since the beginning. Jeff is on river watch now. If you look close, the fences will bottleneck them all between those shipping containers. Jeff will spear them from above." Laura looked out to the water. "We get fewer and fewer each month. We're down to running one vat."

"Vat? Look, we are not here to hurt anyone." Briggs said.

"I know." Laura holstered her gun. "You ain't got that look on ya." She lifted her radio. "Mike, relax. I'm taking our guests to see Brain."

"Brain?" Swan asked.

"It's a joke." She snickered. "His name is actually Bryan, but we call him Brain, like in that movie *Escape from New York*. Because he showed us how to make the gas. Diesel, actually. Bio-diesel. Don't call it gas, for god's sake, not in front of Brain."

With that, Laura turned her back on them and began walking toward the access door.

"You're crazy. You know that, right?" Briggs said, "You didn't disarm us or search us or even know if there are others with us."

Without turning around, she said, "We've been watching you for days." She stopped and turned back to Briggs. "You are the crazy ones." To Swan she said, "You know she falls asleep on watch every night?"

"I do NOT!" Briggs protested.

"And you should draw the damn curtains on the second floor when you get frisky. I'm never going to hear the end of it from Mike!" She went down the stairs, knowing Briggs was blushing. "I know the walkers can't see in from the street on the second level, but damn."

The stairs led to a catwalk in the rafters that wound around the entire enormous space of the roundhouse. At the opposite end, they could see three men and a woman, in blue coveralls, tending a fire below a giant vat.

The vat was full of dark liquid, and in it they could see bodies moving.

"Sorry about the smell up here," Laura said absently, as they began to descend to the warehouse floor. "We keep the operation at that end. Excellent ventilation."

Briggs looked at Swan and made their private sign for WTF?

By the time they crossed over to the living spaces, the old man was parked at the end of a large conference table. There were four guards stationed around the area in tactical vests with new-looking SCAR military rifles.

"Briggs, Swan," Laura said, "this is Brain. He's driving this bus."

"Oh, stop that." He held out his hand. "I'm Bryan Mitchell. These kids let me think I'm in charge around here. They do all the work. All I do is read books."

"He used to be the librarian for Brunswick. He retired the week before all this started. He's the one that showed us how to make biodiesel out of them," Laura said. "Two birds one stone kinda deal."

"I was wondering how you had a truck that still ran," Swan said. "All the fuel went bad last spring."

Everyone's radios clicked. "Help. Me."

Over the radio, Mike said urgently, "Jeff fell off the roof of the shipping container. No clear shot from overwatch."

Laura ran for the door. "You four stay here and guard the children."

Running after Laura, Briggs said, "You have children here?"

They crashed out the door, out of the warehouse toward the pen made of shipping containers. A seven-foot-tall wall had been erected between shipping containers. There was a ladder leaning there that was tied to another on the other side. Laura was up and over the wall without missing a beat.

Briggs and Swan were right behind her.

Jeff was dragging himself towards them as Laura stopped to help him. Briggs and Swan passed them and set upon the hoard of muddy shamblers with practiced ease.

Katana and saber danced as Briggs laughed out loud. The space was perfect for the two of them to have enough room. Their blades never stopped moving, creating a swirling area around them. Hands seemed to fall off as if by magic, followed by heads. The battle line advanced as Briggs and Swan ran out of targets and moved seamlessly ahead.

Briggs chanced a glance back to see Jeff was halfway up the ladder, hands helping from above. Laura stared in awe at their dance. Briggs stopped laughing as the task became less fun and more like work.

The last two heads flew off in synchronized arcs.

"Your estimate was low. I counted fifty-five," Swan said conversationally, only slightly out of breath.

They both held their hand up to Laura as she approached. "Stop," Swan and Briggs said in unison. "Gotta clean up."

Swan stabbed a severed head that was still snapping its jaw.

"I really like the new saber, sweetie," Briggs said, with exaggerated casualness. "Balance is way better than the machete."

"Sweetie again, is it?" he said. "Don't embarrass me in front of the neighbors."

They finished off the last of the zombies and helped carry Jeff back to the warehouse.

Two of the men guarding Brain were named John, and both happened to be EMTs. One of the Winnebagos had been set up as a clinic. Jeff had dislocated his knee and broken three fingers on his right hand. When Swan and Briggs stepped out of the RV, there were about thirty people assembled. They silently parted as Briggs, Swan and the two Johns carried Jeff to the sofa right next to Brain.

When they returned, fresh coffee was handed all around. There were even six children there now.

All were silent.

Solemnly, Brain spoke to them. "You are invited to join us. You must be weary to come so far and to have become so skilled." Brain had a tone of sadness. "We'll help you tow an Airstream over from RV World if you decide to stay. But there is one thing you must do first. If you want to join us."

They both nodded without even looking at each other.

"First. The Door," Brain said flatly.

***

The big diesel generator started. Lights came on above them. In bright yellow spray paint was written, "THE DOOR."

The recorded screaming over the loudspeaker began. Together, Swan and Briggs realized it was Laura's voice.

They opened the door. A rope was tied to the crash bar so they could close it remotely. Zombies were already coming that way.

Swan and Briggs moved along a walkway just inside where it wound around to the edge just above the empty vat on the level below. A rail and a 4x4 crossed the edge to a makeshift catwalk made of scaffolding on the far side.

There was a light directly above them. The vat below was darkness. They were the bait.

When the first zombie shambled in the door, they waved their arms and called out, "Hey, over here."

They came to them, at them, with hunger in their clouded eyes, horrible wounds in their flesh. They were moths to the flame.

As each one fell into the vat, reaching for them, Briggs and Swan said, "Thank you. We're sorry this happened to you." Swan was crying as they fell. One was a little girl.

There were only six by the time Briggs closed the door by pulling the rope. Swan used a spear and brought the second death to the little girl and then to all but two, as requested. The strongest, largest men floated in the vat of rainwater, constantly moving.

***

They joined the others at the sofas. It was movie night. It always was after The Door. Microwaves had been working while the generator was on, making a ton of popcorn. Battery banks recharged. Tonight was *The Big Lebowski.* It would be projected on the king-sized sheet they hung as a screen.

"Biodiesel, eh?"

"But why leave two, you know, undead?"

Laura smiled as she helped Jeff get comfortable before the movie. "Making biodiesel, you have to stir it in the early stages, as you boil it down. They are good agitators."

"That's kinda creepy," Swan said.

"Want to know what's creepy?" Laura asked, as she reclined under Jeff's arm.

"What?" Briggs and Swan said in unison.

"Watching the two of you dancing through those walkers," she said.

Jeff chimed in. "You were both smiling the whole time."

"Yep. Kinda creepy," Laura said. "But in a good way…"

ABOUT THE AUTHORS

If you would like to contact one of the authors, please email us at info@tannhauserpress.com.

Quarantine, © 2017 by Vincent L. Scarsella

Church of the Walking Dead, © 2017 by Chris Louie

The Skeleton People, © 2017 by Matthieu Cartron

The Jilted Loser, © 2017 by A. P. Sessler

Swords and Cups, © 2017 by Edward Charlonis

The Dead Walk, © 2017 by J. L. Smith

The Order of the Second Death, © 2018 by Darren Todd

Yakuza Dead, © 2018 by T. S. Alan

The Door, © 2018 by Martin Wilsey

ACKNOWLEDGMENTS

I'd like to thank Donna Royston for all the heavy lifting with the editing chores associated with this project. As always, I'd like to thank The Hourlings writers group for their support and encouragement as well as their participation in these anthologies.

I want to thank my excellent wife, Brenda Reiner, for continuing to be generally awesome.

Mostly, I want to thank my childhood friend, Ray Clark. We were friends when they were still a real thing. In the real world. We would plan sleepovers based on the Creature Feature TV schedule in TV guide, to be watched on my black and white TV. Zombies were chief on the priority list then. Followed closely by Godzilla and Hammer Films.

Ray Clark, my childhood friend, died in the mid-1980s.

It's almost 40 years later, and I still have not visited his grave. When we were kids, he swore he'd reach up through the dirt and grab my ankle if I ever stood on his grave.

Maybe I'll have the courage soon… maybe.